Beautiful BASTARD

An ambitious intern.
A perfectionist executive.
And a whole lot of name calling.

"Filled with plenty of hot sex and sizzling tension . . ."

—**RT Book Reviews**

". . . deliciously steamy . . ."

—**EW.com**

"A devilishly depraved cross between a hardcore porn and a very special episode of *The Office*. . . . For us fetish-friendly fiends to feast on!!"

—**PerezHilton.com**

"The perfect blend of sex, sass and heart, *Beautiful Bastard* is a steamy battle of wills that will get your blood pumping!"

—**S. C. Stephens,** *New York Times* **bestselling author of** *Thoughtless*

"*Beautiful Bastard* has heart, heat, and a healthy dose of snark. Romance readers who love a smart plot are in for an amazingly sexy treat!"

—**Myra McEntire, author of** *Hourglass*

"*Beautiful Bastard* is the perfect mix of passionate romance and naughty eroticism. I couldn't, and didn't, put it down until I'd read every last word."

—**Elena Raines**, *Twilightish*

Beautiful STRANGER

A charming British playboy.
A girl determined to finally live.
And a secret liaison revealed in all too vivid color.

"Hot . . . if you like your hookups early and plentiful . . ."

—**EW.com**

"I loved *Beautiful Bastard*, truly. I wasn't sure how Christina Lauren planned on topping Bennett. . . . They did it. Max is walking hotness."

—**Bookalicious**

"The thing that I love the most about Christina Lauren and the duo's *Beautiful* books is that there is always humor in them. As well as hot steamy moments and some of the sweetest I love you's."

—**BooksSheReads.com**

"When I say *Beautiful Stranger* is hot, I mean *Beautiful Stranger* is HOOOOOOOOOOOOOTTTTTTT!!! This book has some of the steamiest, sexiest, panty-dropping scenes and dialogue of any book I've ever read."

—*Live Love Laugh & Read*

BOOKS BY CHRISTINA LAUREN

Beautiful Bastard
Beautiful Stranger
Beautiful Bitch
Beautiful Bombshell
Beautiful Player
Beautiful Beginning

Beautiful PLAYER

CHRISTINA LAUREN

G

GALLERY BOOKS

NEW YORK • LONDON • TORONTO • SYDNEY • NEW DELHI

Gallery Books
A Division of Simon & Schuster, Inc.
1230 Avenue of the Americas
New York, NY 10020

First Gallery Books trade paperback edition October 2013

GALLERY BOOKS and colophon are registered trademarks of Simon & Schuster, Inc.

For information about special discounts for bulk purchases, please contact Simon & Schuster Special Sales at 1-866-506-1949 or business@simonandschuster.com.

The Simon & Schuster Speakers Bureau can bring authors to your live event. For more information or to book an event contact the Simon & Schuster Speakers Bureau at 1-866-248-3049 or visit our website at www.simonspeakers.com.

Manufactured in the United States of America

10 9 8 7 6 5

Library of Congress Cataloging-in-Publication Data

Lauren, Christina.
  Beautiful Player / Christina Lauren. — First Gallery Books trade paperback edition.
    pages   cm
I. Title.
  PS3612.A9442273B467   2013
  813'.6—dc23   2013030584

ISBN 978-1-4767-5140-5
ISBN 978-1-4767-5141-2 (ebook)

Beautiful
PLAYER

Prologue

We were in the ugliest apartment in all of Manhattan, and it wasn't just that my brain was especially programmed away from art appreciation: objectively these paintings were *all* hideous. A hairy leg growing from a flower stem. A mouth with spaghetti pouring out. Beside me, my oldest brother and my father hummed thoughtfully, nodding as if they understood what they were seeing. I was the one who kept us moving forward; it seemed to be the unspoken protocol that party guests should make the circuit, admire the art, and only *then* feel free to enjoy the appetizers being carried on trays around the room.

But at the very end, above the massive fireplace and between two garish candelabras, was a painting of a double helix—the structure of the DNA molecule—and printed across the entire canvas was a quote by Tim Burton: *We all know interspecies romance is weird.*

Thrilled, I laughed, turning to Jensen and Dad. "Okay. *That* one is good."

Jensen sighed. "You *would* like that."

1

I glanced to the painting and back to my brother. "Why? Because it's the only thing in this entire place that makes any sense?"

He looked at Dad and something passed between them, some permission granted from father to son. "We need to talk to you about your relationship to your job."

It took a minute before his words, his tone, and his determined expression triggered my understanding. "Jensen," I said. "Are we really going to have this conversation *here*?"

"Yes, here." His green eyes narrowed. "It's the first time I've seen you out of the lab in the past two days when you weren't sleeping or scarfing down a meal."

I'd often noted how it seemed the most prominent personality traits of my parents—vigilance, charm, caution, impulse, and drive—had been divided cleanly and without contamination among their five offspring.

Vigilance and *Drive* were headed into battle in the middle of a Manhattan soiree.

"We're at a party, Jens. We're supposed to be talking about how wonderful the art is," I countered, waving vaguely to the walls of the opulently furnished living room. "And how scandalous the . . . something . . . is." I had no idea what the latest gossip was, and this little white flag of ignorance just proved my brother's point.

I watched as Jensen tamped down the urge to roll his eyes.

Dad handed me an appetizer that looked something like a snail on a cracker and I discreetly slid it onto a cocktail napkin as a caterer passed. My new dress itched and

I wished I'd taken the time to ask around the lab about these Spanx things I had on. From this first experience with them, I decided they were created by Satan, or a man who was too thin for skinny jeans.

"You're not just smart," Jensen was telling me. "You're fun. You're social. You're a pretty girl."

"Woman," I corrected in a mumble.

He leaned closer, keeping our conversation hidden from passing partygoers. Heaven forbid one of New York's high society should hear him giving me a lecture on how to be more socially slutty. "So I don't understand why we've been visiting you here for three days and the only people we've hung out with are *my* friends."

I smiled at my oldest brother, and let my gratitude for his overprotective hypervigilance wash over me before the slower, heated flush of irritation rose along my skin; it was like touching a hot iron, the sharp reflex followed by the prolonged, throbbing burn. "I'm almost done with school, Jens. There's plenty of time for life after this."

"*This* is life," he said, eyes wide and urgent. "*Right now.* When I was your age I was barely hanging on to my GPA, just hoping I would wake up on Monday and not be hungover."

Dad stood silently beside him, ignoring that last remark but nodding at the general gist that I was a loser with no friends. I gave him a look that was meant to communicate, *I get* this *coming from the workaholic scientist who spent more time in the lab than he did in his own house?* But he remained impassive, wearing the same expression he had when a compound he expected to be soluble ended up a goopy suspension in a vial: confused, maybe a little offended on principle.

Dad had given me *drive,* but he always assumed Mom had given me even a little *charm,* too. Maybe because I was female, or maybe because he thought each generation should improve upon the actions of the one before, I was meant to do the whole career-life balance better than he had. The day Dad turned fifty, he'd pulled me into his office and said, simply, "The people are as important as the science. Learn from my mistakes." And then he'd straightened some papers on his desk and stared at his hands until I got bored enough to get up and go back into the lab.

Clearly, I hadn't succeeded.

"I know I'm overbearing," Jensen whispered.

"A bit," I agreed.

"And I know I meddle."

I gave him a knowing look, whispering, "You're my own personal Athena Poliás."

"Except I'm not Greek and I have a penis."

"I try to forget about that."

Jensen sighed and, finally, Dad seemed to get that this was meant to be a two-man job. They'd both come down to visit me, and although it had seemed a strange combination for a random visit in February, I hadn't given it much thought until now. Dad put his arm around me, squeezing. His arms were long and thin, but he'd always had the viselike grip of a man much stronger than he looked. "Ziggs, you're a good kid."

I smiled at Dad's version of an elaborate pep talk. "Thanks."

Jensen added, "You know we love you."

"I love you, too. Mostly."

"But . . . consider this an intervention. You're addicted to work. You're addicted to whatever fast track you think you need your career to follow. Maybe I always take over and micromanage your life—"

"Maybe?" I cut in. "You dictated everything from when Mom and Dad took the training wheels off my bike to when my curfew could be extended past sunset. And you didn't even live at home anymore, Jens. I was *sixteen*."

He stilled me with a look. "I swear I'm not going to tell you what to do just . . ." He trailed off, looking around as if someone nearby might be holding up a sign prompting the end of his sentence. Asking Jensen to keep from micromanaging was like asking anyone else to stop breathing for ten short minutes. "Just call someone."

" 'Someone'? Jensen, your point is that I have no friends. It's not *exactly* true, but who do you imagine I should call to initiate this whole get-out-and-live thing? Another grad student who's just as buried in research as I am? We're in biomedical engineering. It's not exactly a thriving mass of socialites."

He closed his eyes, staring up at the ceiling before something seemed to occur to him. His eyebrows rose when he looked back to me, hope filling his eyes with an irresistible brotherly tenderness. "What about Will?"

I snatched the untouched champagne flute from Dad's hand and downed it.

⌐━━━━━⌐

I didn't need Jensen to repeat himself. Will Sumner was Jensen's college best friend, Dad's former intern, and the object of every one of my teenage fantasies. Whereas I had always been the friendly, nerdy kid sister, Will was the bad-boy genius with the crooked smile, pierced ears, and blue eyes that seemed to hypnotize every girl he met.

When I was twelve, Will was nineteen, and he came home with Jensen for a few days around Christmas. He was dirty, and—even then—delicious, jamming on his bass in the garage with Jensen and playfully flirting away the holidays with my older sister, Liv. When I was sixteen, he was a fresh college graduate and lived with us over the summer while he worked for my father. He exuded such raw, sexual charisma that I gave my virginity to a fumbling, forgettable boy in my class, trying to relieve the ache I felt just being near Will.

I was pretty sure my sister had at least *kissed* him— and Will was too old for me anyway—but behind closed doors, and in the secret space of my own heart, I could admit that Will Sumner was the first boy I'd ever wanted to kiss, and the first boy who eventually drove me to slip my hand under the sheets, thinking of him in the darkness of my own room.

Of his devilish playful smile and the hair that continually fell over his right eye.

Of his smooth, muscled forearms and tan skin.

Of his long fingers, and even the little scar on his chin.

When the boys my age all sounded the same, Will's voice was deep, and quiet. His eyes were patient and knowing. His hands weren't ever restless and fidgety; they were usually resting deep in his pockets. He licked his lips when he looked at girls, and he made quiet, confident comments about breasts and legs and tongues.

I blinked, looking up at Jensen. I wasn't sixteen anymore. I was twenty-four, and Will was thirty-one. I'd seen him four years before at Jensen's ill-fated wedding, and his quiet, charismatic smile had only grown more intense, more maddening. I'd watched, fascinated, as Will slipped away into a coatroom with two of my sister-in-law's bridesmaids.

"Call him," Jensen urged now, pulling me from my memories. "He has a good balance of work and life. He's local, he's a *good guy*. Just . . . get out some, okay? He'll take care of you."

I tried to quell the hum vibrating all along my skin when my oldest brother said this. I wasn't sure *how* I wanted Will to take care of me: Did I want him to just be my brother's friend, helping me find more balance? Or did I want to get a grown-up look at the object of my filthiest fantasies?

"Hanna," Dad pressed. "Did you hear your brother?"

A waiter passed with a tray of full champagne flutes and I swapped out the empty one for a full, bubbly glass.

"I heard him. I'll call Will."

Chapter One

One ring. Two.

I stopped pacing long enough to pull back the curtain and peek out the window, frowning up at the sky. It was still dark out, but I reasoned it was bluer than black and starting to smudge pink and purple along the horizon. Technically: morning.

It was three days after Jensen's lecture and, fittingly, my third attempt to call Will. But even though I had no idea what I would say—what my brother even *expected* me to say—the more I thought about it, the more I realized Jens had been right: I was almost always at the lab, and when I wasn't, I was home sleeping or eating. Choosing to live alone in my parents' Manhattan apartment instead of somewhere closer to my peers in Brooklyn and Queens didn't exactly help my social options. The contents of my refrigerator consisted of the odd vegetable, questionable takeout, and frozen dinners. My entire life to this point had revolved around finishing school and launching into the perfect research career. It was sobering to realize how little I had outside of that.

Apparently my family had noticed, and for some reason, Jensen seemed to think the solution to saving me from impending spinsterdom was Will.

I was less confident. Much less.

Our shared history was admittedly scant, and it was entirely possible he wouldn't remember me very well. I was the kid sister, scenery, a backdrop to his many adventures with Jensen and his brief fling with my sister. And now I was calling him to—*what*? Take me out? Play some board games? Teach me how to . . .

I couldn't even finish that thought.

I debated hanging up. I debated climbing back into bed and telling my brother he could kiss my ass and find a new improvement project. But halfway through the fourth ring, and with the phone clenched so tightly in my hand I'd probably still feel it tomorrow, Will picked up.

"Hello?" His voice was exactly how I remembered, thick and rich, but even deeper. "Hello?" he asked again.

"Will?"

He inhaled sharply and I heard a smile curl through his voice when he said my nickname: "Ziggy?"

I laughed; of course he'd remember me that way. Only my family called me that anymore. No one really knew what the name *meant*—it was a lot of power to give then-two-year-old Eric, nicknaming the new baby sister—but it had stuck. "Yeah. It's *Ziggy*. How did you—?"

"I heard from Jensen yesterday," he explained. "He

told me all about his visit and the verbal ass-kicking he gave you. He mentioned you might call."

"Well, here I am," I said lamely.

There was a groan and the whispering rustle of sheets. I absolutely did not try to imagine what degree of naked was on the other end of the line. But the butterflies in my stomach flew into my throat when I registered he sounded tired because *he'd been asleep*. Okay, so maybe it wasn't technically morning *yet*. . . .

I chanced another look outside. "I didn't wake you, did I?" I hadn't even looked at my clock, and now I was afraid to.

"It's fine. My alarm was about to go off in"—he paused, yawning—"an hour."

I bit back a groan of mortification. "Sorry. I was a little . . . anxious."

"No, no, it's fine. I can't believe I forgot you lived in the city now. Hear you've been holed up over at P and S, pipetting in a safety hood for the past three years."

My stomach flipped slightly at the way his deep voice grew husky with his playful scolding. "You sound like you're on Jensen's side."

His tone softened. "He's just worried about you. As your big brother, it's his favorite job."

"So I've heard." I returned to pacing the length of the room, needing to do something to contain this nervous energy. "I should have called sooner . . ."

"So should I." He shifted, and seemed to sit up. I heard him groan again as he stretched and closed my eyes

11

at the sound. It sounded exactly, precisely, and distractingly like *sex*.

Breathe through your nose, Hanna. Stay calm.

"Do you want to do something today?" I blurted. So much for calm.

He hesitated and I could have smacked myself for not considering that he'd already have plans. Like work. And after work, maybe a date with a girlfriend. Or a wife. Suddenly I was straining to hear every sound that pushed through the crackling silence.

After an eternity, he asked, "What did you have in mind?"

Loaded question. "Dinner?"

Will paused for several painful beats. "I have a thing. A late meeting. What about tomorrow?"

"Lab. I already scheduled an eighteen-hour time point with these cells that are really slow-growing and I will legitimately stab myself with a sharp tool if I mess this up and have to start over."

"Eighteen hours? That's a long day, Ziggs."

"I know."

He hummed before asking, "What time do you need to go in this morning?"

"Later," I said, glancing at the clock with a wince. It was only *six*. "Maybe around nine or ten."

"Do you want to join me at the park for a run?"

"You run?" I asked. "On purpose?"

"Yes," he said, outright laughing now. "Not the I'm-being-chased running, but the I'm-exercising running."

I squeezed my eyes closed, feeling the familiar itch to follow this through, like a challenge, a damn assignment. Stupid Jensen. "When?"

"About thirty minutes?"

I glanced out the window again. It was barely light out. There was snow on the ground. *Change*, I reminded myself. And with that, I closed my eyes and said, "Text me directions. I'll meet you there."

It was cold. Ass-freezing cold would be a more accurate description.

I reread Will's text telling me to meet him near the Engineers Gate at Fifth and Ninetieth in Central Park and paced back and forth, trying to stay warm. The morning air burned my face and seeped through the fabric of my pants. I wished I'd brought a hat. I wish I'd remembered it was February in New York and only crazy people went to the park in February in New York. I couldn't feel my fingers and I was legitimately worried the cold air combined with the windchill might cause my ears to fall off.

There were only a handful of people nearby: overachieving fitness types and a young couple huddled together on a bench beneath a giant spindly tree, each clasping to-go cups of something that looked warm, and delicious. A flock of gray birds pecked at the ground, and the sun was just making an appearance over the skyscrapers in the distance.

I'd hovered on the edge between socially appropriate and rambling geek most of my life, so of course I'd felt out of my element before: when I got that research award in front of thousands of parents and students at MIT, almost anytime I went shopping for myself, and, most memorably, when Ethan Kingman wanted me to go down on him in the eleventh grade and I had absolutely no idea how I was supposed to do so and breathe at the same time. And now, watching the sky brighten with each passing minute, I would have gratefully escaped to any one of those memories to get out of doing this.

It wasn't that I didn't want to go running . . . actually, yes, that was a lot of it. I *didn't* want to go running. I wasn't even sure I knew how to run for sport. But I wasn't dreading seeing Will. I was just *nervous*. I remembered the way he'd been—there was always something slow and hypnotic about his attention. Something about him that exuded sex. I'd never had to interact with him one-on-one before, and I worried that I simply lacked the composure to handle it.

My brother had given me a task—go live your life more fully—knowing that if there was one way to ensure I'd tackle something, it was to make me think I was failing. And while I was pretty sure it hadn't been Jensen's intent that I spend time with Will to learn how to date and to, lets face it, get *laid*, I needed to get inside Will's head, learn from the master and be more like him in those ways. I just had to pretend I was a secret agent on an undercover assignment: get in and out and escape unharmed.

Unlike my sister.

After seventeen-year-old Liv had made out with a pierced, bass-playing nineteen-year-old Will over Christmas, I'd learned a *lot* about what it looks like when a teenage girl gets hung up on the bad boy. Will Sumner was the definition of that boy.

They all wanted my sister, but Liv had never talked about anyone the way she talked about Will.

"Zig!"

My head snapped up and toward the sound of my name, and I did a double take as the man in question walked toward me. He was taller than I remembered, and had the type of body that was long and lean, a torso that went on forever and limbs that should have made him clumsy but somehow didn't. There'd always been *something* about him, something magnetic and irresistible that was unrelated to classically symmetrical good looks, but my memory of Will from even four years ago paled in comparison to the man in front of me now.

His smile was still the same: slightly crooked and always lingering, lending a constant sense of mischief to his face. As he approached, he glanced in the direction of a siren and I caught the angle of his stubbly jaw, the length of smooth, tan neck that disappeared beneath the collar of his microfleece.

When he got to me, his smile widened. "Morning," he said. "Thought it was you. I remember you used to pace like that when you were nervous about school or something. Drove your mom nuts."

15

And without thinking, I stepped forward, wrapped my arms around his neck, and hugged him tight. I couldn't remember ever being this close to Will before. He was warm and solid; I closed my eyes when I felt him press his face to the top of my head.

His deep voice seemed to vibrate through me: "It's so good to see you."

Secret Agent Hanna.

Reluctantly, I took a step back, inhaling the way the fresh air mixed with the clean scent of his soap. "It's good to see you, too."

Bright blue eyes looked down at me from beneath a black beanie, his dark hair tucked haphazardly beneath it. He stepped closer and placed something on my head. "Figured you'd need this."

I reached up, feeling the thick wool cap. Wow, that was disarmingly charming. "Thanks. Maybe I'll get to keep my ears after all."

He grinned, stepping back as he looked me up and down. "You look . . . different, Ziggs."

I laughed. "No one but my family has called me that in for*ever*."

His smile fell and he searched my face for a moment as if, were he lucky enough, my given name would be tattooed there. He'd only ever called me Ziggy, just like my siblings—Jensen, of course, but also Liv and Niels and Eric. Until I left home, I'd *always* just been Ziggy. "Well, what do your friends call you?"

"Hanna," I said quietly.

He continued to stare. He stared at my neck, at my lips, and then took time to inspect my eyes. The energy between us was palpable . . . but, no. I had to be completely misreading the situation. This was precisely the danger of Will Sumner.

"So," I started, raising my eyebrows. "Running."

Will blinked, seemed to realize where we were. "Right."

He nodded, reaching up to pull his hat down farther over his ears. He looked so different than I remembered—clean-cut and successful—but if I looked close enough, I could still see the faint marks where his earrings used to be.

"First," he said, and I quickly pulled my attention back to his face. "I want you to watch out for black ice. They do a good job of keeping the trails clear but if you're not paying attention you can really hurt yourself."

"Okay."

He pointed to the path winding around the frozen water. "This is the lower loop. It surrounds the reservoir and should be perfect because it only has a few inclines."

"And you run this every day?"

Will's eyes twinkled as he shook his head. "Not this one. This is only a mile and a half. Since you're just starting out we'll walk the first and last bit, running the mile in the middle."

"Why don't we just run your usual route?" I asked, not liking the idea of him slowing down or changing his routine for me.

"Because it's six miles."

"I can totally do that," I said. Six miles didn't seem like that many. It was just under thirty-two thousand feet. If I took big strides, that was only maybe sixteen thousand steps . . . I felt my mouth turn down at the corners as I fully considered this.

He patted my shoulder with exaggerated patience. "Of course you can. But let's see how you do today and we'll talk."

And then? He winked.

⸻

So apparently I wasn't much of a runner.

"You do this every day?" I panted. I could feel a trickle of sweat run from my temple down my neck and didn't even have the strength to reach up and wipe it away.

He nodded, looking like he was just out enjoying a brisk morning walk. I felt like I was going to die.

"How much farther?"

He looked over at me, wearing a smug—and delicious—grin. "Half a mile."

Oh God.

I straightened and lifted my chin. I could do this. I was young and in . . . reasonably good shape. I stood almost all day, ran from room to room in the lab, and always took the stairs when I went home. I could totally do this.

"Good . . ." I said. My lungs seemed to have filled

with cement and I could only take tiny, gasping breaths. "Feels great."

"Not cold anymore?"

"Nope." I could practically *hear* the blood pumping through my veins, the force of my heartbeat inside my chest. Our feet pounded on the trail and, no, I definitely wasn't cold anymore.

"Other than being busy all the time," he asked, breath not even the slightest bit labored, "do you like the work you're doing?"

"Love it," I gasped. "I love working with Liemacki."

We spoke for a while about my project, the other people in my lab. He knew my graduate advisor from his reputation in the vaccine field, and I was impressed to see that Will kept up with the literature even in a field he said didn't always perform the best in the venture capital world. But he was curious about more than my job; he wanted to know about my *life*, asked about it point-blank.

"My life is the lab," I said, glancing at him to gauge his level of judgment. He barely blinked. There were a few graduate students, and an army of post-docs cranking out papers. "They're all great," I explained, swallowing before taking in a huge gulp of air. "But I get along best with two that are both married with kids, so we aren't exactly going to go hit the pool tables after work."

"I don't think the pool tables are still open after you're done with work anyway," he teased. "Isn't that why I'm here? Big-brothering—getting you out of your routine kind of thing?"

"Right," I said laughing. "And although I was pretty annoyed when Jensen flat-out told me I needed to get a life, he's not exactly *wrong*." I paused, running a few more steps. "I've just been so focused on work for so long, and getting over the next hurdle, and then the next one, I haven't really stopped to enjoy any of it."

"Yeah," he agreed quietly. "That's not good."

I tried to ignore the pressure of his gaze, and kept my eyes pinned on the trail in front of us. "Do you ever feel like the people who mean the most aren't the people you *see* the most?" When he didn't respond, I added, "Lately I just feel like I'm not putting my heart where it matters."

From my peripheral vision I saw him glance away, nodding. It took forever for him to reply, but when he did, he said, "Yeah, I get that."

A moment later, I looked over at the sound of Will laughing. It was deep, and the sound vibrated through my skin and into my bones.

"What are you *doing*?" he asked.

I followed his gaze to where my arms were crossed over my chest. I winced inwardly before admitting, "My boobs hurt. How do guys do this?"

"Well, for one, we don't have . . ." He waved vaguely to my chest region.

"But, what about the other stuff? Like, do you run in boxers?" *Holy hell, what is wrong with me? Problem number one: no verbal filter.*

He looked over at me again, confused, and almost tripped on a fallen branch. "What?"

"Boxers?" I repeated, making the word into three full syllables. "Or do you have things that keep your man parts from—"

He interrupted me with a loud barking laugh that echoed off the trees in the frigid air. "Yeah, no boxers," he said. "There'd be too much stuff moving around down there." He winked and then looked forward at the trail, wearing a flirty half-grin.

"You have extra parts?" I teased.

Will threw me an amused look. "If you must know, I wear running shorts. Form-fitted to keep the boys safe."

"Guess girls are just lucky *that* way. No stuff down there to just"—I waved my arms around wildly—"flop all over the place. We're compact down below."

We reached a flat part of the trail, and slowed to a walk. Will laughed quietly next to me. "I've noticed."

"You *are* the expert."

He threw me a skeptical look. "What?"

For a split second my brain attempted to hold back what I was about to say, but it was too late. I'd never been particularly good at censoring my thoughts—a fact my family was more than happy to point out whenever the chance arose—but here it felt like my brain was stealing this rare opportunity to let it all out with the legendary Will, as if I may not get another chance. "The . . . *pussy* expert," I whispered, all but mouthing the P-word.

21

His eyes widened, his steps faltering a bit.

I stopped, bending to catch my breath. "You said so yourself."

"When would I ever have said I was the 'pussy expert'?"

"Don't you remember telling us that? You said Jensen was good with the saying. You were good with the doing. And then you wiggled your eyebrows."

"That is *horrifying*. How in the world do you remember all this?"

I straightened. "I was twelve. You were a nineteen-year-old hot friend of my brother who joked about sex in our house. You were practically a mythical creature."

"Why don't I remember any of this?"

I shrugged, looking past him at the now-crowded trail. "Probably for the same reason."

"I don't remember you being this funny, either. Or this"—he took a moment to covertly look me up and down—"grown-up."

I smiled. "I wasn't."

He reached behind him, pulling his sweatshirt up and over his head. For a brief moment, his shirt underneath was pulled up with it, and a long stretch of his torso was exposed. I experienced a full-body clench at the sight of his flat stomach and the dark hair that trailed from his navel down into his shorts. His running pants hung low enough for me to see the carved lines of his hips, the enticing suggestion of man parts, and man legs and . . . holy crap Will Sumner's body was unreal.

When he tugged the hem of his shirt back down, he broke my trance and I looked up to take in the rest of him, arms now bare below the short sleeves of his shirt. He scratched his neck, oblivious to the way my eyes moved over his forearm. I had a lot of memories of Will from the summer he'd lived with us while working for Dad: sitting on the couch with him and Jensen while we watched a movie, passing him in the hallway at night wearing nothing more than a towel around his hips, inhaling dinner at the kitchen table after a long day at the lab. But only from the evil influence of dark magic could I have forgotten about the tattoos. Seeing them now, I could remember a bluebird near his shoulder, a mountain and the roots of a tree wrapped up in vines on his bicep.

But some of these were new. Swirls of ink formed a double helix down the center of one forearm, the etching of a phonograph peeked out from beneath his sleeve on the other. Will had grown quiet and I looked up to find him smirking at me.

"Sorry," I mumbled, smiling sheepishly. "You have new ones."

His tongue darted out to lick his lips, and we turned to start walking again. "Don't be sorry. I wouldn't have them if I didn't want people to look."

"And it's not weird? With the business job and every-thing?"

Shrugging, he murmured, "Long sleeves, suit jack-ets. Most people don't know they're there." The problem with what he said was it didn't make me think about the *most people* who remained ignorant to his tattoos. It made me wonder about the ones who knew each and every line of ink on his skin.

The Danger of Will Sumner, I reminded myself. *Everything he says sounds filthy, and now you're thinking of him naked. Again.*

I blinked away, searching for a new topic. "So what about *your* life?"

He eyed me, wary. "What do you want to know?"

"Do you like your job?"

"Most days."

I acknowledged this with a smile. "Do you get to see your family often? Your mom and sisters are in Washington, right?" I remembered that Will had two much older sisters who both lived close to their mother.

"Oregon," he corrected. "And yes, a couple of times a year."

"Are you dating anyone?" I blurted.

He furrowed his brows as if he hadn't quite understood what I'd asked. After a moment he answered, "No."

His adorably confused reaction helped me forget how inappropriate my question had been. "Did you have to really think about it?"

"No, smart-ass. And no, there is no one I would introduce to you by saying, 'Hey Ziggy, this is so-and-so, my *girlfriend.*'"

I hummed, studying him. "What a very specific evasion."

He pulled his hat from his head, running his fingers

through his hair. It was damp with sweat and stuck up in a million directions.

"No one woman has caught your eye?"

"A few have." He turned his eyes on me, refusing to shrink from my interrogation. I remembered this about Will; he never felt the need to explain himself, but he didn't shy away from questions, either.

Clearly he was the same Will he'd always been: often with women, and never with just one. I blinked down, looking at his chest as it widened and retracted with his slowly-steadying breaths, at his muscular shoulders leading to a smooth, tan neck. His lips parted slightly and his tongue peeked out to wet them again. Will's jaw was carved and covered in dark stubble. I had a sudden and overwhelming urge to feel it on my thighs.

My eyes dropped to his toned arms, the large hands relaxed at his sides—*holy shit what those fingers probably knew how to do*—his flat stomach, and the front of his running pants that told me Will Sumner had plenty going on below the belt. Good sweet baby Jesus, I wanted to bang the smirk off this man.

Silence ticked between us and awareness trickled in. I wasn't living behind a damn two-way mirror and I'd never had a poker face. Will could probably read every single thought I'd just had.

His eyes darkened in understanding, and he took one step closer, looking me over from head to foot as if inspecting an animal caught in a trap. A gorgeous, deadly smile tugged at his mouth. "What's the verdict?"

I swallowed thickly, closing my fists around sweaty hands, saying only, "Will?"

He blinked, and then blinked again, stepping back and seeming to remember himself. I could practically see the realizations tick through his mind: *this is Jensen's baby sister . . . she's seven years younger than I am . . . I made out with Liv . . . this kid is a dork . . . stop thinking with your dick.*

He winced slightly, saying, "Right, sorry," under his breath.

I relaxed, amused by the reaction. Unlike me, Will had an infamous poker face . . . but not *here*, and apparently not with me. That understanding sent a jolt of confidence through my chest: he might be nearly irresistible and the most naturally sensual man on the planet, but Hanna Bergstrom could handle Will Sumner.

"So," I said. "Not ready to settle down, then?"

"Definitely not." His smile pulled up one corner of his mouth and he looked *completely* destructive. My heart and lady bits would not survive a night with this man.

Good thing that's not even an option, vagina. Stand down.

We'd circled back around to the beginning of the trail, and Will leaned against a tree. "So why are you diving into the world of the living *now*?" He tilted his head as he turned the conversation back to me. "I know Jensen and your dad want you to have a more active social life, but come on. You're a pretty girl, Ziggs. It can't be that you haven't had offers."

I bit my lip for a second, amused that *of course* Will

would assume that, for me, this was about getting laid. The truth was . . . he wasn't entirely wrong. And there was no judgment in his expression, no weird distance around such a personal topic.

"It's not that I haven't dated. It's that I haven't dated *well,*" I said, remembering my most recent, completely bland encounter. "I know it might be hard to tell behind all this smooth charm but I'm not very good in those kinds of situations. Jensen's told me stories. You managed to get through your doctorate with top honors and what sounds like a whole lot of fun. Here I am, in a lab with people who seem to consider social awkwardness a field of study. Not really that many jumping in the boat, if you know what I mean."

"You're young, Ziggs. Why are you worrying about this now?"

"I'm not *worried* about it, but I'm twenty-four. I have functioning body parts and my mind tends to go to interesting places. I just want to . . . explore. You weren't thinking about these things when you were my age?"

He shrugged. "I wasn't stressing over it."

"Of course you weren't. You'd lift an eyebrow and panties would hit the floor."

Will licked his lips, reaching to scratch the back of his neck. "You're a trip."

"I'm a *scientist,* Will. If I'm going to do this I need to learn how men think, get inside their head." I took a deep breath, watched him carefully before saying, "Teach me. You told my brother you'd help me, so do that."

"Pretty sure he didn't mean *Hey, show my kid sister the city, make sure she isn't paying too much for rent, and, by the way, help her get laid.*" His dark brows pulled together as something seemed to occur to him. "Are you asking me to set you up with a friend?"

"No. *God.*" I wasn't sure whether I wanted to laugh or crawl into a hole and hide for the rest of *forever.* Despite his DEFCON 5 degree of hotness, what I needed was for him to help me bang the smirk off *other* men. Maybe then I'd be properly degeeked and socialized. "I want your help to learn . . ." I shrugged and scratched my hair beneath the hat. "*How* to date. Teach me the rules."

He blinked away, looking torn. "The 'rules'? I don't . . ." He shivered, letting his words fall away as he reached up to scratch his jaw. "I'm not sure I am qualified to help you meet guys."

"You went to Yale."

"Yeah, and? That was years ago, Ziggs. I don't think they offered this in the course catalog."

"And you were in a band," I continued, ignoring that last part.

Finally, amusement lit up his eyes. "What's your point?"

"My point is that I went to MIT and played *D&D* and *Magic*—"

"Hello, I was a fucking *D&D* pro, Ziggs."

"My point," I said, ignoring him, "is that Yale-attending, lacrosse-playing former bass players might have ideas about how to improve the dating pool options of bespectacled, nerdtastic geeks."

"Are you fucking with me right now?"

Instead of answering, I crossed my arms over my chest and waited patiently. It was the same stance I'd adopted back when I was supposed to be rotating through several labs to help decide what type of research I wanted. But I didn't want to do lab rotations for my entire first year of graduate school; I wanted to get started on my research with Liemacki, immediately. I'd stood outside his office after explaining why his work was perfectly positioned to move away from viral vaccine research into parasitology, and what I thought I could work on for my thesis. I'd been prepared to stand like that for hours, but after only five minutes he'd relented and, as the chair of the department, made an exception for me.

Will looked off into the distance. I wasn't sure if he was considering what I was saying, or deciding whether he should just start running and leave me wheezing in his snow-dust.

Finally, he sighed. "Okay, well, rule one of having a broader social life is never call anyone except a cab before the sun is up."

"Yeah. Sorry about that."

He studied me, eventually motioning to my outfit. "We'll run. We'll go out and do stuff." He winced, waving vaguely at my body. "I don't really think you need to do anything but . . . fuck, I don't know. You're wearing your brother's baggy sweatshirt. Correct me if I'm wrong, but I have a feeling that's pretty standard attire, even when you're not jogging." He shrugged. "Though it is kind of cute."

"I am not dressing like a hoochie."

"You don't have to dress like a *hoochie*." He straightened, messing up his hair before tucking it beneath his beanie again. "*God.* You're a ballbuster. Do you know Chloe and Sara?"

I shook my head. "Are those some girls you're . . . *not dating*?"

"Oh, hell no," he said with a laugh. "They're the women who have my best friends by the balls. I think they'd be good for you to meet. Swear to God you'll all probably be best friends at the end of the night."

CHAPTER TWO

"So wait," Max said, pulling out his chair to sit down. "Is this Jensen's sister you shagged?"

"No, that's the other sister, Liv." I sat across from the Brit and ignored both the amused grin on his face as well as the uncomfortable twist in my stomach. "And I didn't shag her. We just hooked up a little. The youngest sister is Ziggy. She was only a kid that first time I went home with Jensen for Christmas."

"I still can't believe he took you home for Christmas and you made out with his sister in the backyard. I'd kick your ass." He reconsidered, scratching his chin. "Ah fuck that. I wouldn't have given a shit."

I looked at Max, felt a small grin pull at my mouth. "Liv wasn't there when I came back a few years later for the summer. I behaved myself the second time around."

All around us, glasses clinked and conversation carried on in a quiet murmur. Tuesday lunch at Le Bernardin had become a routine for our group in the past six months. Max and I were usually the last ones to the table, but apparently the others had been held up in a meeting.

"I suspect you want an award for that," Max said, studying his menu before closing it with a snap. Truthfully, I'm not sure why he even bothered to open it in the first place. He always got the caviar for his first course, and the monkfish for the main course. I'd recently surmised that Max kept all of his spontaneity for his life with Sara; with food and work, he was a quiet creature of habit.

"You just forget what *you* were like before Sara," I said. "Stop acting like you lived in a monastery."

He acknowledged this with a wink and his big, easy smile. "So tell me about this little sis."

"She's the youngest of the five Bergstrom kids, and in grad school here at Columbia. Ziggy's always been this ridiculous brain. Finished undergrad in three years, and now works in the Liemacki lab? The one who does the vaccine work?"

Max shook his head and shrugged as if to say, *The fuck are you talking about?*

I continued, "It's a very high-profile operation over at the med school. Anyway, last weekend in Vegas when you were off chasing your pussy to the blackjack tables, Jensen texted to let me know he was coming to visit her. I guess he gave her a *Come-to-Jesus* about not living among the test tubes and beakers for the rest of her life."

The waiter came by to fill our water glasses, and we explained that we were waiting on a few more people to join the table.

Max looked back to me. "So you have plans to see her again, yeah?"

"Yeah. I'm sure we'll go out and do something this weekend. I think we'll run together again."

I didn't miss the way his eyes widened. "Letting someone in your private little running headspace? That seems like it would be more intimate than sex to you, William."

I waved him off. "Whatever."

"So it was fun then? Catching up with the little sis and all?"

It *had* been fun. It hadn't been wild, or even anything all that special—we'd gone for a run, of all things. But I still felt a little shaken by how unexpected *she* had been. I'd gone in thinking there had to be a reason for her isolation, other than her long work hours. I'd expected she would be awkward, or hideous, or the poster child for inappropriate social behavior.

But she'd been none of those things, and she definitely didn't seem anything like someone's "little sister." She was naïve and a bit unfiltered at times, but really she was simply hardworking and had found herself trapped in a set of habits she didn't enjoy anymore. I could relate.

I'd first met the Bergstroms over Christmas, my sophomore year in college. I hadn't been able to afford to fly home that year, and Jensen's mother had such a fit at the idea of me staying alone in the dorms that she drove down from Boston two days before Christmas to pick me up and bring me home for the holidays. The family was as loving and loud as one would expect with five kids spaced almost exactly two years apart.

True to form for that stage in my life, I'd thanked them by secretly fooling around with their oldest daughter in the shed out back.

A few years later I'd interned for Johan, and lived at the Bergstrom house. Most of the other kids had moved out or stayed near college for the summer, so it was just me and Jensen, and the youngest daughter, Ziggy. Theirs had come to feel like a second home to me. Still, even though I'd lived near her for three months, and had seen her a few years ago at Jensen's wedding, when she'd called yesterday, it had been hard to even remember her face.

But when I saw her at the park, more memories than I realized I'd had came flooding in. Ziggy at twelve, her freckled nose hidden behind books. She'd offer only the occasional shy smile across the dinner table, but otherwise avoided contact with me. I'd been nineteen and nearly oblivious anyway. And I remembered Ziggy at sixteen, all legs and elbows, her tangled hair cascading down her back. She spent her afternoons wearing cutoff shorts and tank tops, reading on a blanket in the backyard while I worked with her father. I'd checked her out, like I'd checked out every female at the time, as if I were scanning and cataloging body parts. The girl was curvy, but quiet, and obviously naïve enough about the art of flirting to earn my scornful disinterest. At the time, my life had been full of curiosity and kink, younger and older women who were willing to try anything once.

But this afternoon, it felt as though a bomb had gone off in my head. Seeing her face was—strangely—like being home again, but also like meeting a beautiful girl for the first time. She didn't look anything like Liv or Jensen, who were towheaded and gangly, almost carbon copies of one another. Ziggy looked like her father, for better or worse. She had the paradoxical combination of her father's long limbs and her mother's curves. She inherited Johan's gray eyes, light brown hair, and freckles, but her mother's wide-open smile.

I'd hesitated when she stepped forward, wrapped her arms around my neck, and squeezed. It was a comfortable hug, bordering on intimate. Other than Chloe and Sara, I didn't have a lot of females in my life who were strictly *friends*. When I hugged a woman like that—close and pressing—there was generally some sexual element. Ziggy had always been the kid sister, but there in my arms it fully registered that she wasn't a kid anymore. She was a twenty-something woman with her warm hands on my neck and her body flush to mine. She smelled like shampoo and coffee. She smelled like a *woman,* and beneath the bulk of her sweatshirt and pathetically thin jacket, I could feel the shape of her breasts press against my chest. When she stepped back and looked me over, I'd immediately *liked* her: she hadn't dressed up, hadn't put on makeup or expensive workout gear. She wore her brother's Yale sweatshirt, black pants that were too short, and shoes that definitely looked like they'd seen better days. She wasn't trying to impress me; she just wanted to *see* me.

She's so sheltered, man, Jensen had said when he'd called a little over a week ago. *I feel like I let her down by not anticipating she had Dad's work-obsession genes. We're going down to visit her. I don't even know what to do.*

I blinked back into awareness when Sara and Bennett approached the table. Max stood to greet them, and I looked away as he leaned over to kiss Sara just beneath her ear, whispering, "You look beautiful, Petal."

"Are we waiting on Chloe?" I asked once everyone was seated.

Bennett spoke from behind his menu. "She's in Boston until Friday."

"Well, thank fuck," Max said. "Because I'm starving and that woman takes forever to decide what she wants."

Bennett laughed quietly, sliding his menu back on the table.

I was relieved, too, not because I was hungry but because I was fine occasionally having a break from the role of fifth wheel. My four coupled-up friends were two steps away from Smug and had *long* ago skipped past Overly-Invested-in-Will's-Dating-Life. They were convinced that I was two breaths away from having my heart ripped out by the woman of my dreams and were eager for the show.

And, only increasing this obsession, upon returning from Vegas last week, I'd made the mistake of casually mention-ing that I was feeling detached from my two regular lovers, Kitty and Kristy. Both women were happy to meet regularly for no-strings fucking and didn't seem to mind the existence of the other—or the occasional new fling I might have—but lately I felt like I was just going through the motions:

Undress,

touch,

fuck,

orgasm,

(maybe some pillow talk),

a kiss good night,

and then I was gone, or they were.

Had it all become too easy? Or was I finally getting tired of just sex—sex?!

And why the fuck was I thinking about all of this again, *now*? I sat up, scrubbed my face with my hands. Nothing in my life had changed in a day. I'd had a nice morning with Ziggy, that's it. That was *it*. The fact that she was disarm-ingly genuine and funny and surprisingly pretty shouldn't have thrown me so dramatically.

"So what were we discussing?" Bennett asked, thanking the waiter when he slid a gimlet on the table in front of him.

"We were discussing Will's reunion with an old friend this morning," Max said, and then added in a stage whisper, "a *lady* friend."

Sara laughed. "Will saw a woman this morning? Why is this news?"

Bennett held up his hand. "Wait, isn't tonight Kitty? And you had another date this morning?" He sipped his gimlet, eyeing me.

In fact, Kitty was the exact reason I'd suggested to Hanna that we meet up this morning instead of tonight: *Kitty* was my late meeting. But the more I thought about it, the idea of spending my usual Tuesday with her seemed less and less appealing.

I groaned, and both Max and Sara burst out laughing. "Is it weird that we all know Will's Weekly Hookup Calendar?" Sara asked.

Max looked over at me, eyes smiling. "You're thinking of canceling plans with Kitty, aren't you? Think you're going to pay for that one?"

"Probably," I admitted. Kitty and I dated a few years back, and it ended amiably when it came out that she wanted more than I did. But when we met up again in a bar a few months ago, she said this time she just wanted to have fun. Of course I'd been game. She was gorgeous, and willing to do almost anything I wanted. She insisted our just-sex arrangement was fine, fine, fine. The thing was, I think we both knew she was lying: every time I had to ask for a rain check, she would become insecure and needy the next time we were together.

Kristy was almost the complete opposite. She was more contained, had a fetish for being gagged that I didn't share, but wasn't against indulging, and rarely stayed beyond the moment of our shared release.

"If you're interested in this new girl, you should probably end it with Kitty," Sara said.

"You guys," I protested, digging into my salad. "There isn't a thing with Ziggy. We went *running*."

"So why are we still talking about it?" Bennett asked with a laugh.

I nodded. "Exactly."

But I knew we were talking about it because I was tense, and when I was tense I wore it like a neon sign. My brows pulled together, my eyes got darker, and my words came out clipped. I turned into an asshole.

And Max *loved* it.

"Oh, we're talking about it," the Brit said, "because it's getting William riled up, and that's my favorite fucking thing. It's also very bloody interesting how pensive he's being today after a morning with this little sis. Will doesn't usually look like he's thinking so hard it hurts."

"She's Jensen's youngest sister," I explained to Sara and Bennett.

"He snogged the older sister when they were teens," Max added helpfully, overplaying his accent for dramatic effect.

"You are such a shit-stirrer," I said, laughing. Liv was a short blip; I could barely remember much about what had happened other than some heated kissing and then my easy evasion when I'd returned to New Haven. Compared to some of my relationships at the time, what happened with Liv barely registered on the sex meter.

Our entrées came and we ate in silence for a little bit. My mind started to wander. Partway through our run, I'd given up and just outright stared at Ziggy. I stared at her cheeks, at her lips, at the soft hair that had fallen free from her messy bun and lay straight against the soft skin of her neck. I'd always been open about my appreciation for women, but I wasn't attracted to every woman I saw. So what was it about this one? She was pretty but definitely not the prettiest girl I'd ever seen. She was seven years younger than I was, green as an apple, and barely came up from her work to breathe. What could she possibly offer me that I couldn't find somewhere else?

She'd looked over and caught me; the energy between us was palpable, and confusing as fuck. And when she smiled, it lit up her whole face. She looked as open as a screen door in the summer, and despite the temperature, some-thing warmed in my veins. It was an old, yet familiar hunger. A desire I hadn't felt in forever, where my blood filled with adrenaline and I wanted to be the only one to discover a par-ticular girl's secrets. Ziggy's skin looked sweet; her lips were full and soft, her neck looked like it had never been marked with teeth or suction. The beast in me wanted to look more closely at her hands, at her mouth, at her breasts.

I looked up when I felt Max watching me, chewing thoughtfully.

He lifted his fork, pointed it at my chest. "All it takes is one night with the right girl. I'm not talking about sex, either. One night could change you, young m—"

"Oh, stop," I groaned. "You're such a fucking asshole right now."

Bennett straightened, joining in. "It's about finding the woman who gets you thinking. *She'll* be the one who'll change your mind about everything."

I held up my hands. "It's a nice thought, you guys. But Ziggy really isn't my type."

"What's your type? Walks? Has a pussy?" Max asked.

I laughed. "I guess she just feels young?"

The guys hummed and nodded in understanding, but I could feel Sara watching me. "Out with it," I said to her.

"Well, I'm just thinking you haven't found anyone who makes you *want* to delve deeper. You're choosing a certain type of woman, a type you know will fit into your structure, your rules, your limits. Aren't you bored yet? You're saying this sister—"

"Ziggy," Max offered.

"Right," she said. "You're saying Ziggy isn't your type, but last week you said you were feeling detached from the women who happily screw you without strings attached." She forked a bite of her lunch and shrugged as she started to lift it to her mouth. "Maybe you should reevaluate *your type.*"

"Illogical. I can be losing interest in my lovers and it doesn't have to mean that I need to overhaul the whole system." I continued to poke at my food. "Though actually, I do have a favor to ask."

Sara swallowed, nodding. "Of course."

"I was hoping maybe you and Chloe could take her out? She doesn't have any real girlfriends here and you guys—"

"Of course," she said again quickly. "I can't wait to meet her."

I glanced at Max from the corner of my eye, unsurprised to see him biting his lip and looking like the cat that had caught the canary. But Sara must have picked up a thing or two from Chloe and had him by the balls beneath the table, because, for once, he was uncharacteristically quiet.

Do you ever feel like the people who mean the most aren't the people you see the most? Lately I just feel like I'm not putting my heart where it matters.

Her voice and wide, honest eyes when she'd said this had made me feel full and hollow all at once, like the ache was so heavy I couldn't tell if it was pain or pleasure.

Ziggy wanted me to show her how to get out and date, how to meet people she wanted to get to know . . . and the reality was I wasn't even doing that myself. I might not be the one sitting in my apartment alone, but that didn't mean I was happy.

Excusing myself to the men's room, I pulled my phone from my pocket and typed a text to the mobile number she'd given me.

> Project Ziggy still on your mind? If so, I'm in. Running tomorrow, plans this weekend. Don't be late.

I stared at the phone for a few seconds but when she didn't reply right away I returned to my lunch, my friends.

But later, when I left the restaurant, I noticed there was a single message now and I laughed, remembering that Ziggy mentioned an old flip phone she barely ever used.

> Aw3esome!Icantfindthespacekey=butIwillcall you.

———

Between Ziggy's, Chloe's, and Sara's crazy schedules, the three of them couldn't get together until the weekend. But thank God they finally made it work, because watching Ziggy run every morning with her arms crossed across her chest was actually staring to make *my* boobs hurt.

That Saturday afternoon, Max was sitting at a table at Blue Smoke when I arrived, panting from my six-mile run and famished. As always seemed to happen with this group, a plan was formed without any of my help, so I woke to a text from Chloe that I was supposed to have Ziggy meet them for breakfast and shopping, meaning I'd be running by myself for the first time in days.

It was fine. *Good*, even. And even though my run felt silent, and strangely dull, Ziggy needed to get out and get some *things*. She needed running shoes. She needed running clothes. She could even stand to get some regular clothes if she was serious about dating, because most guys were shallow dicks and relied on the shorthand of first impressions. Ziggy wasn't very strong in this department, but part of me didn't want to push too much on her. I liked looking at well-dressed women, but oddly enough, with Ziggy, what was most intriguing was that she wasn't really concerned with any of that. I figured we should probably stick with what was already working for her.

Without even looking up, Max moved the stack of newspaper pages from my chair and waved to the waitress to come take my order.

"Water," I said, using the paper napkin to wipe my brow. "And maybe just some peanuts for now. In a little bit I'll have some lunch."

Max took in my clothes and went back to his paper, handing me the Business section of the *Times*.

"Weren't you out with the girls earlier?" he asked.

I thanked the waitress when she put my drink down in front of me, and took a big gulp. "I dropped Ziggs off this morning. I wasn't sure she would be able to navigate her way around anything past the Columbia campus."

"Such a loving mother hen, you."

"Oh, in that case I should lovingly let you know that Sara accidentally texted a picture of her ass to Bennett." There was virtually nothing I loved more than giving Max shit about his and Sara's kinky photo obsession.

He looked at me over the top of his paper and his face relaxed when he saw that I was kidding. "Tosser," he mumbled.

I flipped through the Business section for a few minutes before turning my attention to Science and Technology. Behind his wall of newspaper, Max's phone rang. "Hey, Chlo." He paused, putting the paper down on the table. "No, 's just me and Will here getting a bite. Maybe Ben's on a run?" He nodded and then handed the phone to me.

I took the call, surprised. "Hey . . . everything okay?"

"Hanna is adorable," Chloe said. "She hasn't bought new clothes since college. I swear we aren't treating her like a doll, but she's the cutest thing I've ever seen. Why didn't you bring her around sooner?"

I felt my stomach tighten. Chloe hadn't been at the lunch where we discussed Ziggy. "You know she's not a girlfriend, right?"

"I know, you're just banging, whatever, Will—"

I started to interrupt but she continued on.

"—just wanted to let you know we're all good. She looks like she would get lost in this Macy's if we didn't keep track of her."

"That's exactly what I said."

"Okay, that's all I got. Was just calling to see if Max knew where Bennett was. More shopping."

"Hey wait," I said before I really considered what I was about to ask. I closed my eyes and remembered jogging with Ziggy the past few days. She was relatively slim but damn, there was a lot up front.

"Hmm?"

"If you're shopping, make sure Ziggs gets some . . ." I glanced up at Max, confirming he was absorbed in his newspaper before I whispered, "Make sure she gets some bras. Like, for jogging? But maybe also . . . just . . . regular ones, too. Okay?"

I felt rather than heard the silence on the other end of the line. It was leaden, and pressed down on my chest as the awkwardness grew. And grew. When I chanced a look up, Max was staring at me, wearing an enormous shit-eating grin.

"You are so lucky I'm not Bennett right now," Chloe said, finally. "The amount of crap I would give you is on the planetary scale."

"Don't worry, Max is here and I can tell he's enjoying this enough for the both of them."

She laughed. "We're on it. Bras to support the supple breasts of your nongirlfriend. God, you're a pig."

"Thanks."

She hung up and I handed the phone back to Max, avoiding his eyes.

"Oh, *Victoria*," he said, giddy. "Do you have a *Secret*? Do you have a fondness for helping women find well-fitting ladywear?"

"Fuck off," I said through a laugh. His expression was as if Leeds United had just won the fucking World Cup. "She's been joining me on my morning run, and she wears these . . . whatever. They're not sports bras. And her bras do that . . ." I gestured to my chest. "That weird four-boob thing up front? I just figured if they were out shopping already . . ."

Max leaned his chin on his fist and smiled at me. "Christ you're precious, William."

"You know how I feel about breasts. It's no joking matter." And, I didn't add, Ziggy was stacked like a pinup girl.

"Indeed not," he agreed, lifting his paper again. "I just like how you're pretending you wouldn't cream your panties for a girl with four tits."

About half an hour later, the door behind Max opened and I looked up as a tangle of shiny hair and shopping bags careened toward our table. Max and I stood, helping Ziggy unload her loot on one of the chairs.

She wore a pale blue sweater, dark fitted jeans, and green flats. She wasn't dressed like she was coming off a runway, but she looked comfortable, stylish. Her hair was . . . different. I narrowed my eyes, studying it as she slipped her messenger bag from her shoulder. She'd cut it, or maybe it was that she just had it down instead of confined to her trademark messy bun. It fell past her shoulders, thick, and straight and smooth. But despite the changes in her clothes and hair, she, fortunately, still looked like *Ziggy*: a tiny bit of makeup, bright smile, sun-kissed freckles.

She reached her hand out for Max's, smiling. "I'm Hanna. You must be Max."

Grasping her hand, he said, "Nice to meet you. I trust you had a good morning with the two crazy women?"

"I did." She turned to me, wrapped her arms around my neck, and I tried not to groan when she squeezed. I both loved and hated her hugs. They were tight, almost smothering, but disarmingly warm. When she let go, she collapsed into a chair. "That Chloe likes her lingerie, though. I think we spent an hour in that section alone."

"Let me find my surprised face," I murmured, discreetly checking out Ziggy's chest as I sat back down. The girls looked fantastic: full and high. Just perfectly in place. She must have purchased some lingerie herself.

"On that note . . ." Max stood, slipping his wallet into his back pocket. "I think it's time for me to find the Petal and see how successful *her* shopping ventures were. Nice to meet you, Hanna." He patted my shoulder, winking at her. "Have a nice lunch."

Ziggy waved to Max, and then turned to me, eyes wide. "Wow. He's . . . *hot*. I met Bennett earlier, too. You guys are like the Hot Men's Club of Manhattan."

"I don't think that's a thing. And anyway, do you really think we'd let Max in?" I said, grinning. "You look great, by the way." Her head shot to me, eyes surprised, and I quickly added, "I'm glad you didn't let them cover you up with makeup. I would miss your freckles."

"You would miss my *freckles*?" she asked in a whisper and I winced inwardly at how forward I sounded. "What man says that? Are you trying to make me have an orgasm right now?"

Whoa. I no longer felt like *I'd* been too forward. I worked very hard to not look at her chest again when she said that. I was still getting used to the way she seemed to let out every thought she had. Glancing down at her shopping bags, I softly redirected, "I . . . uh, it looks like you bought plenty of running shoes."

Bending, she rummaged through a few things and I blinked up to the ceiling, ignoring the view of her full cleavage. "I think I got *everything*," she said. "I've never shopped like that. Liv is probably going to pop some champagne when she hears." When I finally looked back down, her eyes were scanning my face, my neck, my chest as if she were just now seeing me. "Did you go for a run this morning?"

"And a bike ride."

"You're so *disciplined*." She leaned forward with her hands on her chin and batted her lashes at me. "It does really nice things for your muscles."

Laughing, I told her, "It calms me. Keeps me from . . ." I searched for words, feeling my neck heat. "From being stupid."

"That isn't what you were originally going to say," she said, sitting up. "It keeps you from what? Like getting into bar fights? Release of tension and man angst?"

I decided to test her a little. I had no idea where the urge came from, but she was a confusing mix of inexperienced and wild. She made me feel reckless, and a little drunk. "It keeps me from wanting to fuck all the time."

She barely skipped a beat. "Why would you want to run instead of fuck?" She tilted her head, considering me for a beat. "Besides, exercise increases testosterone and blood flow. I think, if anything, you're having better sex *because* you exercise."

Talking about this with her felt dangerous. It was tempting to look at her a little too long, and Ziggy didn't shrink under my inspection. She would look right back at me.

"I have no idea why I told you that," I admitted.

"*Will*. I'm neither a virgin nor a woman trying to get into your pants. We can discuss sex."

"Hmmm, I'm not sure that's such a good idea." I lifted my juice to my lips, taking a sip while I watched her drink some of her water, her eyes locked on mine. She wasn't trying to get into my pants? Not even a little?

The air between us seemed to hum quietly. I wanted to reach forward, run my finger over her lower lip. Instead, I put my juice down and curled my hands into fists.

"I'm just saying," she said, "there's no need to sugarcoat with me. I like that you're not a guy who talks around things."

"Are *you* always this open with people?" I asked.

She shook her head. "I think this might be you-specific. I say a lot of things, really, but I especially feel stupid around you, and I can't seem to shut up."

"I don't want you to shut up."

"You've always been so obviously sexual and open about it. You're this hot, player guy who doesn't apologize for enjoying women. I mean, if I noticed that about you when I was twelve, it was *obvious*. Sex is natural. It's what our bodies *do*. I like that you are who you are."

I didn't respond, didn't know what to say. She liked the thing about me that every other woman wanted to tame, but I wasn't sure I liked that this was her primary impression of who I was.

"Chloe said you asked them to take me bra shopping."

I looked up to catch her eyes as they flickered away from my mouth.

Her smirk curled into a playful smile. "How thoughtful, Will. So nice of you to think about my boobs."

I bent to take a bite of my sandwich, murmuring, "We don't need to discuss that conversation. Max already gave me an appropriate amount of shit."

"You're a mysterious man, Player Will." She lifted the menu, skimming the choices before putting it back down. "But, fine. I'll change the subject. What should we talk about?"

I swallowed, watching her. I couldn't imagine this wild

young thing with the intense and poised combination of Chloe and Sara. "Whatever you ladies talked about today," I suggested.

"Well, Sara and I had a fun conversation about what it feels like to be almost revirginized after not having sex for so long."

I almost choked, coughing loudly. "Wow. That's . . . I don't even know what that is."

She watched me, amused. "Seriously though. I'm sure it's not like that for guys. But for girls, after a while, you're like . . . does the virginity grow back? Is it like moss over a cave?"

"That is a disgusting image."

Ignoring me, she sat up straighter, excited now. "Actually this is perfect. You're a scientist so you'll totally appreciate this theory I recently developed."

I pressed back farther into my chair. "You just ended with a moss over a cave analogy. Honestly, I'm a little scared."

"Don't be. So, you know how a girl's virginity is considered kind of sacred?"

I laughed. "Yes, I've heard of this concept."

She scratched her head, her freckled nose wrinkling a little. "My theory is this: Cavemen are making a comeback. Everyone wants to read about the guy who ties the girl up, or gets all violently jealous if—God forbid—she wears something sexy outside the bedroom. Women supposedly like that, right? Well, I think the new fad is going to be revirginization. They'll want their man to feel like he's their first. And can you imagine how women will do this?"

I watched her eyes grow increasingly excited as she waited for me to attempt an answer. Something about her sincerity, her earnest consideration of this topic tightened an invisible band beneath my ribs. "Um, with lies? Women always assume we can read braille with our cocks. What's that about? I honestly probably wouldn't know a girl was a virgin unless she—"

"With surgery first, probably. Let's call it 'hymen restoration.'"

Dropping my food, I groaned. "Jesus Christ, Ziggs. I'm eating brisket. Can you just hold off on the hymen talk for like—"

"And then"—she drummed her hands on the table, building suspense—"everyone is waiting to see what stem cells can do for us. But spinal cord injury, Parkinson's . . . I don't think that's where they'll start. You know what I think the big splash will be?"

"Edge of my seat," I deadpanned.

"I bet it will be a restoration of the maidenhead."

I coughed again, loudly. "Dear God. 'Maidenhead'?"

"You said no 'hymen,' so—but am I right?"

Before I could answer and tell her the theory was actually pretty good, she barreled on. "Stupid amounts of money are spent on this kind of thing. Viagra for boners. Four hundred different shapes of fake boobs. Which filler feels the most natural? It's a man's world, Will. Women won't stop to think that you're putting *actively growing cells* in their *vagina*. Next year, one of your nongirlfriends will get her hymen regenerated, and she'll give her new virginity to you, Will."

She leaned down, put her lips around her straw, and sucked, her gray eyes locked on mine. And with that lingering, playful look, I felt my cock harden slightly. Releasing the straw, she whispered, "To *you*. And will you appreciate what a gift that is? What a sacrifice?"

Her eyes danced and then she tilted her head back and burst out laughing. Holy fuck, I liked this girl. I liked her a lot.

Leaning forward on my elbows, I cleared my throat. "Ziggy, listen up because this is important. I'm about to impart some wisdom."

She sat up, her eyes narrowing conspiratorially.

"Rule one we've already covered: don't ever call someone before the sun is up."

Her lips twitched into a guilty little smile. "Right. Got that one."

"And rule two," I said, shaking my head slowly. "Don't ever discuss hymen regeneration over lunch. Or . . . like, ever."

She dissolved into giggles and then moved out of the way when the waitress brought her food. "Don't be so quick to mock it. That's a billion-dollar idea, moneyman. If that comes across your desk soon, you'll thank me for the heads-up."

She dug into her salad, taking an enormous bite, and I tried not to study her. She wasn't like any of the girls I knew. She was pretty—actually, she was beautiful—but she wasn't poised or contained. She was silly, and confident, and so much her own person it almost made the rest of the world seem monochromatic. I had no idea if she even took herself seriously, but she certainly didn't expect me to.

"What's your favorite book?" I asked, the question bubbling up out of nowhere.

She sucked her bottom lip into her mouth and I blinked down to my sandwich, picking at the tiny pieces of crispy meat at the edges.

"This is going to sound cliché."

"I sincerely doubt that, but hit me."

She leaned forward, and whispered, *"A Brief History of Time."*

"Hawking?"

"Of course," she said, almost offended.

"That's not cliché. Cliché would be if you said *Wuthering Heights* or *Little Women.*"

"Because I'm a woman? If I asked *you,* and you said Hawking, would you be cliché?"

I considered this. I imagined saying that book was my favorite, and getting a few *Dude, of course's* from my grad school friends. "Probably."

"So that's bull, for it to be cliché for you and not me just because I have a vagina. But anyway," she said, shrugging and popping a small bite of lettuce into her mouth, "I read it when I was twelve, and—"

"Twelve?"

"Yeah, and it just blew me away. Not so much what he said—because I don't think I understood everything then—but more that he thought that way. That there were people out there who spent their lives trying to figure these things out. It opened up a whole world for me." Suddenly she closed her eyes, taking a deep breath, and smiled a little guiltily when she opened them again. "I'm talking your ear off."

"Yes, but lately you're *always* talking my ear off."

With a little wink, she leaned forward to whisper, "But maybe you kind of love it?"

Unbidden, my mind flooded with the fantasy of her neck arched, her mouth open in a hoarse plea while I licked a line from the hollow of her throat to her jaw. I imagined her nails digging into my shoulders, the sharp sting of pain . . . and blinked, standing and pushing my chair back so quickly that it hit the chair behind me. I apologized to the man seated there, apologized to Ziggy, and practically sprinted to the restroom.

Locking the door behind me, I wheeled around on my reflection. "What the actual *fuck* was that, Sumner?" I bent to splash a handful of cold water over my face.

Bracing my hands on the sink, I met my own eyes in the mirror again. "It was just an image. It wasn't anything. She's a sweet kid. She's pretty. But, one: she's Jensen's sister. Two: she's Liv's sister, and you practically dry-humped Liv in a shed when she was seventeen. I think you cashed in your single Bergstrom-Sister-Hookup Card already. And three . . ." I bent my head, took a deep breath. "Three. You wear track pants around her way too often to be having sexual fantasies without her getting wise. Put a lid on it. Go home, call Kitty or Kristy, get some head, call it a day."

When I returned to the table, Ziggy had nearly polished off her salad and was watching people move down the sidewalk. She looked up when I sat down, concern etching her features. "Stomach troubles?"

"What? No. No, I . . . had to call someone."

Fuck. That sounded douchey. I winced, and then sighed. "I actually should probably go, Ziggs. I've been here for a couple of hours, and was planning to get a few things done this afternoon."

Damnit. That sounded even douchier.

She pulled her wallet from her purse and put down a few fives. "Of course. God, I have a ton to do, too. Thanks so much for letting me meet you here. And thanks so much for hooking me up with Chloe and Sara." With one more smile she stood, hitched her bag over her shoulder, collected her shopping bags, and walked to the door.

Her sandy hair shone and fell most of the way down her back. Her spine was straight, her gait steady. Her ass looked fucking amazing in the jeans she wore.

Holy fuck, Will. You are so goddamn screwed.

Chapter Three

This running thing really wasn't getting any easier.

"This running thing will get easier," Will insisted, looking down at where I sat, slumped over in a whiny pile on the ground. "Have some patience."

I pulled a few blades of brown grass from the frost, mumbling to myself exactly what Will could do with his patience. It was early, the sky was still dull and gray and not even the birds seemed willing to venture out into the cold. We'd run together almost every morning for the past week and a half, and I was sore in places I didn't even know I owned.

"And stop being a brat," he added.

Looking up at him, eyes narrowed, I asked, "What did you say?"

"I said get your ass up here."

I stood, lagging behind a few steps before jogging to catch up. He glanced over at me, assessing. "Still stiff?"

I shrugged. "A little."

"As stiff as you were on Friday?"

I considered this, rolling my shoulders and stretching my arms over my head. "Not really."

"And does your chest still feel like—how did you put it—like someone doused your lungs in gasoline and lit them on fire?"

I glared at him. "No."

"See? And next week it'll get easier. And the week after that you'll crave running the way I bet you sometimes crave chocolate."

I opened my mouth to lie but he quieted me with a knowing look.

"This week we'll call and get you with someone who'll keep you on track and before you know it—"

"What do you mean 'we'll get me with someone'?" We moved into a jog and I lengthened my stride to match his.

He gave me a brief glance. "Someone to run with you. Like a trainer."

The bare trees seemed enough to insulate us because, though I could see the tops of buildings and the skyline in the distance, the sounds of the city felt miles away. Our feet pounded over fallen leaves and bits of loose gravel in the path, and it narrowed just enough that I had to adjust my steps. My shoulder brushed against his and I was close enough to smell him, the scent of soap and mint and a hint of coffee clinging to his skin.

"I'm confused, why can't I just run with you?"

Will laughed, drawing an arc with his hand as if the

answer were suspended in the air around us. "This isn't really running for me, Ziggs."

"Well, of course not; we're barely *jogging*."

"No, I mean I'm supposed to be training."

I looked at our feet and up at his face, my eyes full of meaning. "And this isn't training?"

He laughed again. "I'm doing the Ashland Sprint this spring. It'll take more than a mile-and-a-half run a few days a week to get me ready."

"What's the Ashland Sprint?" I asked.

"A triathlon just outside Boston."

"Oh." The rhythm of our steps echoed in my head and I felt my limbs warm, could almost feel the blood pumping through my body. It wasn't entirely unpleasant. "So I'll just do that with you."

He looked down at me, eyes narrowed and a smile pulling at the corners of his mouth. "Do you even know what a triathlon is?"

"Of course I do. It's the swim, run, shoot a bear thing."

"Good guess," he deadpanned.

"Okay, so enlighten me, Player. Exactly how long is this triathlon of manliness?"

"Depends. There's sprint distance, intermediate, long course, and ultra-distance. And no bears, dumbass. Swim, run, *bike*."

I shrugged, ignoring the steady burn in my calves as we reached an incline. "So which one are you doing?"

"Intermediate."

"Okay," I said. "That doesn't sound too bad."

"That means you swim about a mile, bike for twenty-five, and then run the last six."

The petals of my blooming confidence wilted a little. "Oh."

"And that's why I can't stay over here on the bunny trail with you."

"Hey!" I said, shoving him hard enough that he stumbled slightly.

He laughed, steadying himself before grinning over at me. "Has it always been this easy to get you worked up?"

I raised my brows and his eyes widened.

"Never mind," he groaned.

The sun finally broke through the gloom by the time we slowed to a walk. Will's cheeks were pink from the cold, the ends of his hair curling up from beneath his beanie. A hint of a beard covered his jaw and I found myself studying him, trying to reconcile the person in front of me with the guy I thought I remembered so well. He was such a *man* now. I bet he could shave twice a day and still have a five o'clock shadow. I looked up in time to catch him staring at my chest.

I ducked to catch his gaze but he ignored my attempt to redirect his attention. "I hate to ask the obvious, but what are you looking at?"

He tilted his head, studying me from a different angle. "Your boobs look different."

"Don't they look awesome?" I took one in each hand.

"As you know, Chloe and Sara helped me pick out new bras. Boobs have always been sort of a problem for me."

Will's eyes widened. "Boobs are never a problem for anyone. Ever."

"Says the man without a pair. Boobs are functional. That's it."

He looked at me with genuine fire in his eyes. "Fucking right they are. They get the job done."

I laughed, groaning. "They aren't functional for *you*, frat boy."

"Wanna bet?"

"See, the problem with boobs is if you have big ones, you can never look thin. You get these burns on your shoulders from bra straps, and your back hurts. And unless you're using them for their intended purpose, they're always in the way."

"In the way of *what*? My hands? My face? Don't you blaspheme in here." He looked up to the sky. "She didn't mean it, Lord. Promise."

Ignoring him, I said, "That's why I had a reduction when I was twenty-one," which is when his expression morphed into one of horror.

You'd have thought I told him I made an amazing stew from tiny babies and puppy tongues.

"Why on earth would you do that? That's like God giving you a beautiful gift and you kicking him in the nuts."

I laughed. "God? I thought you were agnostic, Professor."

"I am. But if I could motorboat perfect tits like yours I might be able to find Jesus."

I felt my blush warm my cheeks. "Because Jesus totally lives in my cleavage?"

"Not anymore he doesn't. Your boobs are now too small for him to be comfortable in there." He shook his head, and I couldn't stop laughing. "So selfish, Ziggs," he said, grinning so widely that I actually stumbled a little.

We both snapped around at the sound of a voice. "Will!"

I glanced from the perky redhead jogging toward us, to Will, and back again.

"Hey!" he said awkwardly, waving as she passed.

She turned to run backward, calling out to him, "Don't forget to call me. You owe me a Tuesday." She gave him a flirty little smile before continuing down the path.

I waited for an explanation but none came. Will's jaw was tight, his eyes no longer smiling as he focused on the trail ahead of us.

"She was pretty," I offered.

Will nodded.

"Was she a friend?"

"Yeah. That's Kitty. We . . . hang out."

Hang out. *Right.* I spent enough time on college campuses to know that ninety-five percent of the time the phrase *hanging out* was boy-code for *doing it.*

"So, not someone you would introduce as a girlfriend."

His eyes shot to mine. "No," he said, looking almost as if I'd offended him. "Definitely not a girlfriend."

We walked in silence for a few moments and I looked back over my shoulder, understanding dawning. She was a nongirlfriend. "Her boobs were . . . *wow*. She clearly knows Jesus."

Will completely cracked up and wrapped his arm around my shoulders. "Let's just say finding religion cost her a lot of money."

Later, when we were done, and Will was stretching on the ground next to me, reaching for his toes, I peeked over at him and said, "So I have this thing tonight." And then I winced.

Beneath his track pants I could see the pop of muscles in his thigh and so almost missed it when he repeated, "A thing?"

"Yeah. It's sort of a work . . . thing? Well, not really. Like, a social mixer, an interdepartmental thing. I never go to these, but in the spirit of not dying alone surrounded by feral cats, I figured I'd give it a go. It's Thursday night so I'm sure it's not going to be *that* wild."

He laughed, shaking his head as he switched his position.

"It's at Ding Dong Lounge." I paused, chewing my lip. "Seriously, is that a made-up name?"

"No, it's a place over on Columbus." Reaching up, he scratched his stubbly jaw, thinking. "Not far from my office actually. Max and I go there sometimes."

"Well, a bunch of my coworkers are going, and this

time when they asked if I was going I said I was, and now I realize that I totally have to at least pop in and see what it's about, and who knows, maybe it could be fun."

He peeked up at me through his thick lashes. "Did you even breathe during that entire sentence?"

"Will." I stared him down. "Will you *come* tonight?"

He snickered, shaking his head as he looked down, stretching.

It took me a beat to understand why he was laughing. "Ugh, *pervert*." I groaned, shoving his shoulder. "You know what I mean. Will you come with *me*?"

He looked up at the sound of me smacking my forehead.

"Oh my God, that's worse. Just text me if you're interested in coming." I winced, turning to walk down the trail toward my apartment building and basically wanting the trail to crack open and transport me to Narnia. "Forget it!"

"I like it when you ask me to come!" he called after me. "I can't wait to come tonight, Ziggy! Should I come around eight? Or do you want me to come around ten? Maybe I'll come both times?"

I flipped him the bird, and kept moving away down the trail. Thank God he couldn't see my smile.

CHAPTER FOUR

My legs burned from sitting at my computer all day, and be-yond that I had a wild itch to get to the Ding Dong Lounge—never thought I'd say that—pull up beside Ziggs at the bar and just . . . relax. It had been a long time since I'd had so much fun with a woman without getting naked.

Unfortunately for me, the more time I spent with Ziggy, the more I wanted it to morph into something that involved being naked. Which felt like a cop-out, like my brain and body wanted to fall back on the familiar comfort of sex over emotional depth. Ziggy pushed me, even if she didn't know it; she made me think about everything from why I did my job to why I kept sleeping with women I didn't love. It had been forever since I'd felt like I wanted to take over some-one's sexual history, completely overwrite it with my hands and dick and mouth. But with Ziggy, I couldn't tell if that was because sex would somehow be easier than the way she had my brain all twisted, or if it was because I wanted her to twist me in other ways entirely.

So I stayed away until around ten, wanting to push her to socialize and spend time with friends from her lab. When I arrived, I spotted her at the bar without too much trouble, and slid up next to her, bumping her shoulder with mine. "Hey, lady. Come here often?"

She beamed at me, eyes lit with happiness. "Hey, Player Will." After a pause pregnant with some strange, mutual inspection, she said, "Thanks for com . . . *showing up*."

Biting back a laugh, I asked, "Did you have dinner?"

She nodded. "We went to a seafood place down the street. I had mussels for the first time in years." When I made a face, she shoved me playfully. "You don't like mussels?"

"I hate shellfish."

She leaned closer, whispering, "Well, they were *delicious*."

"I'm sure they were. All floppy and chewy and tasting like dirty ocean water."

"I'm happy to see you," she said, abruptly changing the subject. But she didn't shrink away from the proclamation when I looked over at her. "Outside of running, you know."

"Well, I'm happy to be seen."

She looked at my eyes, my cheeks, my lips for a long moment before meeting my eyes again. "Your smoldering might eventually kill me, Will. And the best thing is I think you have no clue that you look at women this way."

I blinked. "My *what*?"

67

"What can I get for you?" the bartender asked, startling us both when he slapped two cardboard coasters down in front of us and leaned closer. It seemed like Ziggy's lab friends had left, and the Ding Dong was uncharacteristically quiet; usually the bartenders here took my drink order from halfway down the bar, while pouring someone else's beer.

"Guinness," I said, then added, "And a shot of Johnny Gold."

The bartender looked to Ziggs. "Something else for you?"

"Another iced tea, please."

His eyebrow rose and he smiled at her. "That all you want, sweetheart?"

Ziggy laughed, shrugging. "Anything stronger and I'll be asleep in fifteen minutes."

"I'm pretty sure there are plenty of strong things back here that could keep you up for hours."

What he said made me draw back, look over at Ziggy to assess her reaction. If she looked horrified, I might have to kick this guy's ass.

She laughed, oblivious and embarrassed for having been called out on being square in a bar, and spun her coaster in front of her. "You mean a coffee with Bailey's or some-thing?"

"No," he said, resting on his elbows right in front of her. "I had something else in mind."

"Just the iced tea," I cut in, feeling like my blood pres-

68

sure had gone up about seven thousand millimeters. With a smirk, he stood and left to get our drinks.

I could feel Ziggy watching me, and I grabbed a cocktail napkin in order to have something to studiously shred.

"What's with the stern tone, William?"

I blew out a breath. "Did he not see me sitting here with you? He was all over you. What a dick."

"Taking my drink order?" she asked, giving me a baffled stare. "What a *jerk*."

"Innuendo," I explained. "Surely you speak it."

"Surely you're kidding."

"'Something strong behind the bar that could keep you up for hours'?"

Her mouth formed a tiny O as she seemed to figure it out, and then she grinned. "Isn't that the point of our little project? To get some more innuendo in my life?"

The bartender returned and set our drinks in front of us, winking at Ziggy before walking away.

"I suppose," I grumbled, sipping my beer.

Beside me, I saw her sit up a little straighter and turn on her stool to face me. "Not to change the subject, but I watched some porn last night."

I coughed, putting my beer down on the rounded edge of the bar, then barely catching it before it spilled all over me. Even so, some of it slopped over the lip of the glass, and onto my lap. "Christ, Ziggs, you have *zero* filter." I grabbed a small pile of cocktail napkins and wiped my pants.

"Don't you watch porn?"

I stared at my shot of whiskey and downed it, before admitting, "Sure."

"So why is it weird that I did?"

"It's not weird that you watched it. It's weird that it's the start of a conversation. I just . . . I'm still getting used to this. Before Project Hot Chick, I just knew you as the dorky little sister. Now you're this . . . porn-watching woman who had a breast reduction and develops theories about hymen restoration. It's an adjustment."

That, and I find you almost irresistible, I thought.

She waved me off. "Anyway, I have a question."

I looked at her out of the corner of my eye. "Okay?"

"Do women really make those noises in bed?"

I stilled, grinning over at her. "*What* noises, Ziggy?"

She didn't seem to realize I was completely fucking with her, and she closed her eyes, and whispered, "Like, 'Oh, oh, Willll, I need your cock' and 'Harder, harder, oh God, fuck me, big daddy' . . . and so on." Her voice had gone soft, and breathy, and I was horrified to feel my dick lengthen. Again.

"Um, some do."

She burst into laughter. "It's ridiculous!"

I fought a smile, loving her natural confidence even on a topic I suspected she had little experience with. "Maybe they *do* need my cock. Wouldn't you like to want someone so much you *need* their cock?"

She took a long pull on her iced tea, considering this.

"Actually, yeah. I don't think I've ever wanted someone so much I would beg for it. A cookie? Yes. A cock? No."

"That would have to be one hell of a cookie."

"Oh, it was."

Laughing, I asked, "What movie was it?"

"Um." She looked up at the ceiling. Not blushing, not even a little embarrassed. "*Frisky Freshmen*? Something like that. A lot of college girls having sex with a lot of college guys. It was kind of fascinating, actually."

I fell quiet, losing my thoughts down a weird trail from college coeds, to Ziggy at work in the lab, to Jensen's hope that she would make new friends, to the bartender hitting on her right in front of me, to my still-lengthened cock.

"What are you thinking about?" she asked.

"Nothing, really."

She put her tea down, and turned on her stool to stare at me. "How is that possible? How can men say they're not thinking about anything?"

"I'm not thinking about anything of substance, how's that?" I clarified.

"We're talking about porn and you're not even thinking about sex?"

"Strangely, no," I said. "I'm thinking about how naïve and sweet you are. I'm wondering what I've agreed to do here, when I said I would help you figure out the whole dating world. I'm worried I'm going to make you into the most vulnerable bombshell in the history of the planet."

"You were thinking of *all* of that just now?"

I nodded.

"Wow. *That's* something of substance." Her voice had gone quiet, and soft. Kind of like her pretend porn voice, but with real words, and real emotion. But when I looked over at her, she was staring out the window. "I'm not naïve and sweet, though, Will. I know what you mean, but I've always been kind of obsessed with sex. Mostly the mechanics of it. Why different things work for different people. Why some people like sex one way, and others like it another. Is it anatomy? Is it psychology? Are our bodies really organized that differently? Things like that."

I had literally no idea how to respond to this, so I just drank. I'd never thought about these things, had instead preferred to just try anything and everything that a given woman wanted, but I found that I really liked that Ziggy pondered all of this.

"But lately, I'm kind of figuring out what *I* like," she admitted. "That's fun, but it's hard not having a way to figure it out firsthand. Hence, porn."

She took a long drink and then grinned over at me. Two weeks ago if Ziggy had said something like this to me, I would have been secondhand embarrassed for her to be so open in her inexperience. Now I found that I wanted to protect it, just a little.

"I can't believe I'm encouraging this conversation,

but . . . I worry porn might give you a false sense of what sex should be like."

"How so?"

"Because the sex you see in porn isn't very realistic."

Laughing, she asked, "You mean most men don't have a Pringle can in their pants?"

This time I didn't choke. "That's one difference, yes."

"I have had sex before, Will. Just not much variation. Porn is a good way to see what rings the old bell, if you know what I'm saying."

"You surprise me, Ziggy Bergstrom."

She didn't respond for several long beats. "That isn't my name, you know."

"I know. But it is what I call you."

"Will you always call me 'Ziggy'?"

"Probably. Does it bother you?"

She shrugged, swiveling on her stool to face me again. "A little maybe? I mean, it doesn't really fit me anymore. Only my family calls me that. Not, like, friends."

"I don't think you're a kid, if that's what you're worried about."

"No, that isn't what I'm worried about. Everyone grows up being a kid, and learns how to be a grown-up. I feel like I've always known how to be a grown-up, and am just learning how to be a kid. Maybe Ziggy was my grown-up name. Maybe I want to let loose a little."

I tweaked her ear, and she squealed, pulling away. "So you start to let loose by watching porn?"

"Exactly." She studied the side of my face. "Can I ask you some personal things?"

"You need my permission now?"

She giggled, shoving my shoulder. "I'm serious."

I slid my empty pint glass down the bar a little and turned to meet her eyes. "You can ask me anything you want if you buy me another beer."

She raised her hand, catching the bartender's attention immediately. Pointing, she said, "Another Guinness," before turning back to me. "Are you ready?"

I shrugged.

Leaning forward, she asked, "Guys really like the anal, don't they?"

I closed my eyes for a beat, holding in a laugh. "It's just called anal. Not *the* anal."

"Don't they?" she repeated.

Sighing, I rubbed my face. Did I even want to go there with her? "I guess? I mean, yeah."

"So you've done it?"

"Seriously, Ziggy?"

"And you don't think about how you're in—"

I held up a hand. "No."

"You don't even know what I was going to say!"

"I do. I know you, Ziggs. I know *exactly* what you were going to say."

She made a face, turning back to the television above the bar, where the Knicks were killing the Heat. "Guys can just turn off their brains. I don't even get that."

"Then you haven't had sex worth turning off your brain for."

"I think *you* turn your brain off even for mediocre sex."

Laughing, I admitted, "Probably. I mean, you had mussels for dinner. That's like . . . sinewy, chewy sea shit. But still, you could give me a blow job and I wouldn't be thinking about how you just swallowed mussels."

I detected a hint of a blush beneath her cheeks. "You'd be thinking about my awesome blow job skills."

I stared at her. "I . . . what?"

She started laughing, shaking her head at me. "See? You're already speechless and I haven't even done anything yet. Men are so easy."

"It's true. Guys would fuck every orifice they could."

"Every *fuckable* orifice."

Turning on my seat to face her, I asked, "What?"

"Well, not every orifice is fuckable. Like a nose. Or an ear."

"You obviously haven't heard 'The Man from Nantucket.'"

"No." She wrinkled her nose, and I glanced at her freckles. Tonight her lips seemed especially red, but I could tell she wasn't wearing makeup. They were just . . . flushed.

"*Everyone* has heard this. It's a dirty limerick."

"With me?" She pointed to her chest, and I struggled to not look down. "This doesn't increase the odds."

"'There once was a man from Nantucket. Whose dick was so long he could suck it. He said with a grin with some come on his chin, if my ear was a cunt I could fuck it.'"

She regarded me steadily. "That's . . . kind of gross."

I loved that *this* was her first reaction. "Which part? The come on his chin or the ear fucking?"

Ignoring that, she asked, "Would you suck your own dick if you could?"

I started to say there is no way in hell, but then reconsidered. If it was even possible, I probably would at least once, just out of curiosity. "I guess . . ."

"Would you swallow?"

"Jesus, Ziggs, you're really making me think here."

"You have to *think* about it?"

"I mean, I would sound like an asshole if I said there is no way I would swallow, but there is really no way I would swallow. We're talking about a hypothetical situation where I'm sucking my own dick, and I like it when *girls* swallow."

"Not every girl swallows, though."

My heart picked up, not only faster but harder, as if it were punching me from the inside. This conversation felt like it was careening quickly out of control. "Do *you*?"

Ignoring *that,* she asked, "But guys don't really like going down on girls, do they? I mean, if you're being totally honest."

"I like going down on some girls. Not everyone I'm with, and not for the reason you're thinking. It's intimate, and not every woman is totally relaxed about it, which makes it hard to have fun. I don't know, for me a blow job is like a hand job, but feels way better. But giving a girl head? I feel like that's a little farther into a relationship. It requires trust."

"I've never done either. They *both* seem pretty intimate to me."

I stopped, quietly thanked the bartender when he put the beer down in front of me, but had no idea how to restrain the weird victory surging in my blood. What was that even about? It wasn't like I was going to be her first head. It wasn't like I could go there with her. Besides, Ziggy was so up front about what she wanted . . . with a tightening of my gut I realized that if she wanted me that way, she probably would have already said it. She would have walked up to me, put her hand on my chest, and said, *"Would you fuck me?"*

"See?" she asked, leaning closer to grab my attention. "What are you thinking about *now*?"

Tilting my bottle to my lips, I said, "Nothing."

"If I was a violent woman, my palm would be smacking your cheek right now."

This made me laugh. "Fine. I was just thinking that it's a little . . . unusual for you to have had sex before but not given anyone oral sex, or been on the receiving end."

"I mean," she started, leaning back a little on her bar stool, "I guess I kind of gave this one guy a blow job, but I literally had no idea what I was doing, so I ended up just going back up to the face zone."

"Guys are pretty easy: you stroke up and down and we shoot."

"No, I mean . . . I get that. I just mean for *me*. How to do it and breathe, and not worry that I would bite him? Have you ever walked through a china section at a fancy store and you have that panicked moment where you're totally sure you're going to flail suddenly and break all of the Waterford crystal?"

I leaned over, laughing. This girl was fucking *unreal*. "So you're worried when you have a dick in your mouth you're just going to . . . bite?"

She started laughing, too, and then before I knew it we were doubled over at the prospect. But almost at the same time, we died down a little and I realized she was staring at my mouth.

"Some guys *like* teeth," I said quietly.

"'Some guys' . . . like you?"

Swallowing, I admitted, "Yeah. I like girls to be a little rough."

"Like, scratching and biting and stuff?"

"Yeah." A charged thrill ran through me just hearing her say those words. I swallowed heavily, wondering how long it would be before I'd be able to get the image of her *doing* those things out of my head. "How many guys have you been with?" I asked.

She took a sip of her iced tea before answering. "Five."

"You've never given head but you've had sex with *five guys*?" My stomach dropped into an abyss, and although I knew my irritation was wildly hypocritical, I couldn't rein it in. "Holy shit, Ziggs, *when*?"

She rolled her eyes, actually laughing at me. "I lost my virginity when I was sixteen. The summer you worked with my dad, actually." Covering my mouth with her hand when I started to protest, she added, "Don't even start on me, Will. I know you probably lost yours when you were thirteen."

I closed my mouth, sat up. She'd guessed right.

With a knowing smile, she continued. "And *please*. I'm sure you've had sex with hundreds of women. Five is not that many. I slept with a few guys over the next couple of years and then decided I was doing it wrong. It wasn't very interesting. I had one boyfriend in college for a little while but . . . I feel like I'm broken. Sex is kind of fun until the actual sex part. Then I'm like, 'Hmmm, wonder if I have enough cells plated to run the dose response curve with the tool compound tomorrow.'"

"That's pathetic."

"I know."

"Sex is *not* boring."

She studied me, and then shrugged. "I don't think it's *supposed* to be boring. I think it's boring because most guys my age have no idea what to do with the female body." She looked away, and I almost told her to come back. I was growing addicted to the buzz I felt when she was looking directly at me. "I'm not blaming them. That's some complicated stuff down there." She waved a hand over her lap. "It's just been so long since I met anyone who made me want to see what the big fuss is about." She looked at my lips before blinking away and studying the wall of draft beers on tap.

I blinked down to my beer in front of me, turned it in little circles on the coaster. Of course she was right, and so many women I knew had sex for reasons other than getting off. Kitty once told me she felt close to me after we fucked. She said it right as I'd begun mentally cataloging my fridge. I felt so much closer to Hanna right now than I'd ever felt to Kitty before, during, or after sex.

Something about her made me feel hungry, like I wanted to be as honest and calm about everything in my life as she was. I wanted to know Hanna, to hear her thoughts on *everything*.

I paused, my fresh beer partway to my lips, and registered that I'd thought of her as Hanna. It sort of felt like letting out a long-held breath.

Ziggy was Jensen's sister. *Ziggy* was the kid I never knew.

Hanna was this uninhibited, self-possessed woman in front of me who I was pretty sure was going to effectively wreck my world.

Chapter Five

I'd come to a decision: if I was going to monopolize Will's time and insist on training with him, then I would have to actually . . . you know . . . *train* for something.

I'd decided to get serious, to stop thinking of it as a game and start really treating it like an experiment. I started going to bed at a decent hour so I could get up and run with him and still get to the lab early enough for a full day of work at the bench. I expanded my running wardrobe to include some quality workout gear and an extra pair of shoes. I stopped thinking of Starbucks as a food group and cut back on the complaining. And with much flailing on my part and much reassurance on his—we signed up for a half marathon in mid-April. I was terrified.

But it turned out Will was right: it *did* get easier. Just a few weeks in and my lungs had stopped burning, my shins had stopped feeling like they were made of brittle sticks, and I no longer felt like vomiting by the time we reached the end of the trail. In fact, we'd actually been able to increase our distance and move to his normal trail along the outer loop. Will said if I could handle the six miles a day and get up to eight-mile runs twice a week, he wouldn't need to train additionally without me.

It wasn't just that it started to feel good. I'd started to *see* a difference, too. Thanks to genetics, I'd always been relatively thin, but never what you'd call *fit*. My stomach was a tad soft, my arms did that weird jiggle thing when I waved, and there was always this damn little pooch over the top of my jeans if I didn't keep that shit sucked in. But now . . . things were changing, and I wasn't the only one who noticed.

"So what's happening here?" Chloe asked, eyeing me from inside my closet. She pointed a finger at me and swept it around. "You look . . . different."

"Different?" I asked.

The point of Project Ziggy actually wasn't to spend as much time as possible with Will—even though he was quickly becoming my favorite person—but to help me find balance, to have a life outside the lab. In the past couple of weeks, Chloe and Sara had become an important part of the effort, dragging me out for dinner or coming over to just hang for a few hours at my apartment.

This particular Thursday evening they'd brought take-out and we'd somehow migrated into my room, where Chloe had taken it upon herself to go through my closet, deciding what could stay and what absolutely had to go.

"Different good," she clarified, and then turned

to Sara, who was stretched across my bed, thumbing through some sort of financial file for work. "Don't you think so?"

Sara looked up, eyes narrowing as she considered me. "Definitely good. Happy, maybe?"

Chloe was already nodding. "Was just going to say that. There's definitely some kind of glowy thing happening in your cheeks. And your ass looks *amazing* in those pants."

I looked at my reflection, checked out the front and turned to see the back. My ass did look pretty happy. My front wasn't too bad, either. "My pants are a little loose," I noted, checking the size, "And look, no muffin top!"

"Well, that's always a plus," Sara said with a laugh, shaking her head, then going back to her documents.

Chloe started putting things on hangers, shoving others into plastic bags. "You're toning up. What have you been doing?"

"Just running. And lots of stretching. Will is big on the stretching. He added sit-ups to our routine last week, and let me be clear on how much I hate those." I continued to study my reflection, adding, "I can't remember the last time I had a cookie, and that feels like a crime."

"Still training with Will, huh?" Chloe asked, and I couldn't miss the look that passed between her and Sara. The look that said I'd just dropped a giant nugget of awesome in their lap and they were going to talk it to death and then dissect it until I begged for mercy.

"Yeah, every morning."

"Will trains with you *every* morning?" Chloe asked. Another look exchanged.

I nodded, moved to pick up a few errant things lying around. "We meet at the park. Did you know he does triathlons? He's in great shape." I snapped my mouth shut, realizing it probably wasn't safe to be as obliviously unfiltered with Chloe as it was with Will. I knew her well enough at this point to know she didn't let very many things slide.

And indeed, she lifted a brow and reached up, pushing a thick wave of dark hair behind her shoulder. "So, about William."

I hummed, folding a pair of socks together.

"Do you see him outside of this daily running date?"

I could feel their attention like heated laser beams on the side of my face so I nodded, not looking over at either of them.

"He's very handsome," Chloe added.

Danger danger, my brain warned. "He is."

"Have you seen each other naked?"

My eyes shot to Chloe's. *"What?"*

"Chloe," Sara groaned.

"No," I insisted. "We're just friends."

Chloe snorted, moving to the closet with a handful of clothes draped over her arms. "Right."

"We run in the mornings, meet up for coffee sometimes. Maybe breakfast," I said, shrugging and ignoring the way my honesty meter seemed to flare into the red zone. Lately we'd been having breakfast together almost every morning, and talked at least one other time during the day. I'd even started to call him for advice on my experiments when Liemacki was traveling or just busy . . . or just because I valued his scientific opinion. "Just friends." I glanced at Sara. Her eyes were trained on her papers but she was smiling, shaking her head.

"Bullshit," Chloe all but sang. "Will Sumner doesn't have any women in his life that are *just* friends, outside of family and the two of us."

"This is true," Sara reluctantly agreed.

I didn't say anything, just turned and began searching through my drawers for a sweater. I could feel Chloe watching me, though, could feel the pressure of her gaze against the back of my head. I'd never had a lot of female friends—and I'd definitely never had one like Chloe Mills—but even I was smart enough to be a little afraid of her. I got the distinct impression that even *Bennett* was a little afraid of her.

I found the cardigan I'd been hunting for and slipped it over my favorite *Firefly* T-shirt, doing my best to keep my expression neutral and my head free of anything Will-related that ventured outside of the friend zone. Something told me these two would see through that in a second.

"How long have you guys known each other?" Sara asked. "He and Max go way back, but I've only known him since I moved to New York."

"Same here," Chloe added. "Spill, Bergstrom. He's too smug and we need some ammo."

I laughed, grateful for the semi-shift in topic. "What do you want to know?"

"Well, you knew him when he was in college. Was he a giant dork? Please say he was in the chess club or something," Chloe said, hopeful.

"Ha, *no*. I'm pretty sure he was the guy who turned eighteen and all of the moms wanted to bang." I frowned, considering. "Actually, I think I might have heard that exact story from Jensen. . . ."

"Max said something about him dating your sister?" Sara asked.

I chewed on my lip and shook my head. "They hooked up once over a holiday, but I think they just made out. He met my oldest brother, Jensen, on their first day of college, and then he lived with us and worked with my dad after graduation. I'm the youngest, so I didn't really hang around with them that much other than at meals."

"Stop evading," Chloe said, narrowing her eyes. "You have to know more."

I laughed. "Let's see, he's the youngest, too. He has two sisters who are way older than him, but I've never met them. I get the feeling he was sort of mothered a lot. I remember hearing him talk one time about how his parents are both physicians, and they divorced long before he was born. Years later, they met up at a medical conference, got drunk, and reconnected for one night . . ."

"And boom. Will," Sara guessed.

I nodded slowly. "Yeah. But his mom raised him. So,

his sisters are twelve and fourteen years older than he is. He was their little baby."

"Well, that would explain why he thinks women were put on this earth to cater to him," Chloe added, flopping on the bed next to Sara.

That didn't sit right with me, and I sat down, shaking my head. "I don't know if it's that. I think he just really, *really* likes women. And they seem to like him, too," I added. "He grew up surrounded by women so he knows how they think, what they want to hear."

"He definitely knows how to play the game," Sara said. "God, some of the stuff Max has told me."

I thought back to Jensen's wedding and watching Will slip off, otherwise unnoticed, with two women at once. I was pretty sure that wasn't the first or last time something like that had happened.

"Women have always loved him," I said. "I can remember overhearing some of my mom's friends talk about him when he worked for Dad. Jesus, the things they would have done to that boy."

"Cougars!" Chloe squealed, delighted. "I *love* it."

"God, every girl was in love with him." I pulled a pillow to my chest, remembering. "I had a few girlfriends in school—I was twelve the first time he came home with Jensen—and they would find all these crazy reasons to need to come over. One of them pretended like she had to return my sweater on Christmas Eve, and it was *her* sweater she gave me. I mean, picture Will now but as a nineteen-year-old guy, playful, clearly wise to the ways of the female body, and with that damn cheeky smile. He was in a band, had tattoos . . . he was walking sex. Then when he lived with us over the summer? He was twenty-four and I was sixteen. It was unbearable. It was like it offended him to wear a shirt in the house and he had to show off all that smooth, perfect man skin."

I broke out of my memory to see both of them grinning at me.

"What?"

"Those were some very lascivious descriptions, Hanna," Sara said.

Glancing over at her, I asked, "Did you just use the word *lascivious*?"

"She most certainly did," Chloe said. "And I agree. I feel like I just watched something dirty."

I groaned, getting up off the bed.

"So, clearly, teenage Hanna had a bit of a crush on Will," Sara said. "But, more importantly, what does twenty-four-year-old Hanna think of him now?"

I had to think on this for a beat, because to be honest, I thought about Will a lot, and in every possible way. I thought about his body and his dirty mouth and of course all the things he could do with them, but I also thought about his brain, and his heart. "I think he's surprisingly sweet, and he's absurdly smart. He's a total player but underneath that, a genuinely good guy."

"And you haven't thought about banging him at all?"

I stared at Chloe. "What?"

She stared right back at me. "*What* what? You're both

young and hot. There's a history there. I bet it'd be incredible."

Hundreds of images flashed through my mind in only a few seconds, and even though I thought about *banging* him more than I should probably even admit to myself, I forced the words out: "I am absolutely *not* having sex with Will."

Sara shrugged. "Not yet, maybe."

I turned to her. "Aren't you supposed to be the demure one?"

A laugh burst out of Chloe's mouth and she shook her head, giving Sara a playfully scolding look. "*Demure*. It's always the ones who *seem* sweet and innocent, trust me."

"Well, regardless," I said, "Will thinks of me as a little sister."

Chloe sat up, pinning me with a serious expression. "I can tell you that when a man meets a woman, he puts her in one of two categories: unequivocal friend, or possible banging candidate."

"Doesn't he have scheduled booty calls?" I asked, wrinkling my nose. I liked the idea of dating, but I got the impression that Will was more structured in his relationships than just a conversation about keeping things casual. To have regular nights scheduled the way he seemed to? I wasn't sure I could get behind that kind of boundary regarding something as fluid and shapeless as sex.

Sara nodded. "Lately, Kitty is Tuesday nights, Kristy is Saturday evening." She hummed thoughtfully and added,

"I don't think he's seeing Lara anymore, but I'm sure others make cameos here and there."

Chloe shot her a look and Sara stared back. I blinked away, letting them have their little showdown in private.

"I'm not suggesting she fall in love with him," Chloe said. "Just bang the hell out of him."

"I'm only making sure everyone knows the score," Sara answered, a challenge in her eyes.

"Well," I started, "it doesn't matter anyway. Given that he's my brother's best friend, I think we can pretty safely assume I am in unequivocal friend territory."

"Has he talked about your boobs?" Chloe asked.

I felt the heated blush crawl up my neck. Will talked about, stared at, and seemed to idolize my chest. "Um, yes."

Chloe smiled, smug. "I rest my case."

The next morning, I'm sure Will was convinced I was on some sort of mood-altering medication . . . or needed to be. I was distracted during our run and kept going over my conversation with Sara and Chloe in my mind. Not only was I thinking about how often Will looked at my boobs, gestured to my boobs, and *spoke* to my boobs, I was unfortunately thinking about Will with the other women I knew were in his life: what he did with them, how they felt when they were with him, and if they had as much fun with him as I did. Plus the fact that he was probably naked with women . . . a lot.

This, of course, led to me thinking about Will naked,

which did nothing to help my focus, or my ability to go in a straight line down the path in front of me.

I forced my thoughts away from the man running in easy silence beside me, and to the work I had waiting at the lab, the report I needed to finish, the exams I needed to help Liemacki grade.

But later, when Will leaned over me, stretching my right leg after I'd basically crumpled on the trail from a leg cramp, he stared at me so intently, his eyes moving slowly over my face, every thought I'd tried to banish came rushing back. My stomach twisted and a delicious heat spread from my chest and down to the neglected ache between my legs. I felt like I was melting into the cold ground.

"You okay?" he asked quietly.

I was only able to nod.

His brows drew together. "You're so quiet this morning."

"Just thinking," I murmured.

His sexy little smile appeared and I felt my heart trip and then begin to hammer in my chest. "Well, I hope you're not thinking about porn or blow jobs or how you want to experiment with sex, because if you think you're keeping that shit to yourself, you're in trouble. We have a rhythm now, Ziggs."

I took a particularly long shower after that run.

⁂

I'd never been a texter—in fact, before Will, my only texts had consisted of one-word responses to my family or coworkers.

Are you still coming? Yes.

Can you pick up a bottle of wine? Sure.

Are you bringing a date? Ignore.

Until a week ago—when I'd finally unwrapped the iPhone Niels had given me for Christmas—I still used a flip phone Jensen teased was the first cell phone ever made. Who had time to type a hundred messages when I could call and get it over with in less than a minute? It definitely didn't seem very efficient.

But with Will it was fun, and I had to admit, the new phone made it easier. He would text me random thoughts throughout the day, send me pictures of his face when I made a particularly bad joke or a photo of his lunch when the chicken breast he'd been served was shaped like a penis. So, after my . . . relaxing shower, when my phone buzzed in the other room, I wasn't surprised to see it was Will.

What I was surprised by however, was the question: What are you wearing?

I felt my brows pull together in confusion. It was random but by far not the weirdest thing he'd ever asked me. We were meeting for breakfast in a half hour and maybe he was worried I would show up looking, as he liked to say, like a graduate student hobo.

I looked down at the towel around my otherwise naked chest and typed, Black jeans, yellow top, blue sweater.

No, Ziggy. I mean *insert innuendo* WHAT ARE YOU WEARING.

Now I really was confused. I don't get it, I typed.

I'm sexting you.

I paused, looked down at the phone for a few more seconds before responding with What?

He typed so much faster than I did, and his response appeared almost immediately. It's not nearly as hot when I have to explain it. New rule: you need to be at least borderline competent in the art of sexting.

Understanding went off like a lightbulb in my head. Oh! And ha! "Sexting." Clever, Will.

While I appreciate your enthusiasm and the fact that you think I'm witty enough to have come up with that, he replied, I didn't invent the term. It's been around in popular culture for quite some time, you know. Now, answer the question.

I paced the room, thinking. *Okay. An assignment, I could do this.* I tried to think of all the sexy innuendo I'd ever heard in movies and of course, in the moment, could not think of a single thing. I thought back on every pickup line I'd heard my brother Eric use . . . and then shuddered, reconsidering.

I drew a total blank.

Well, actually I'm not dressed yet, I typed. I was standing here trying to decide if it's against the rules to go without underpants because I think my skirt shows all the lines but I hate wearing thongs.

I stared at the phone as the little dots indicated he was

replying. Shit that was pretty good kid. But don't say underpants. Or blouse. Never sexy.

Don't make fun of me. I don't know what to say. I feel like an idiot standing here naked texting you.

I waited.

A few moments passed before my phone lit up again. OK. So you've obviously gotten the hang of it. Now say something dirty.

Dirty?

I'm waiting.

Oh God. Did I have time to google something? No. I searched my mind and typed the first semi-dirty thing I could think of: Sometimes, when we're running and you're controlling your breathing and lost in the rhythm of it, I wonder what noises you make during sex.

So maybe that was a bit more than semi-dirty, and for what felt like an eternity, he didn't reply. *Oh God.* I put my phone down, convinced that Will was going to walk away and not reply ever again. He probably wanted something playful and not so . . . *honest.*

I walked into the bathroom, pulled a brush through my wet hair, and then piled it into a knot on top of my head. In the other room, I heard my phone buzz on the desk.

WHOA, was the first message.

The second message: Way to just . . . dive on in there. OK I'm gonna need a minute. Or five.

OMGIMSOSOEEY I typed, with stupid fumbling fingers and completely ready to climb into a hole and die. I
MEAN SORRY I CANTBELIEVEISAIDTHAT

You're kidding me, he replied. That was like
Christmas. Clearly I need to up my game. Hold
on, I might need to stretch first.

I rolled my eyes. Waiting.

Your tits looked great today.

That's all you got? I typed. Honestly, he'd said
more perverted things to my face. To my *boobs*. Did he
really think he was schooling me in being sexy right now?

Really? You're completely unimpressed?

Zzzzzzzzzz, I wrote back.

Can I SEE your tits next time?

Well. I felt a little warmth in my cheeks but there was
no way I was admitting that.

Yawn. I smiled like an idiot at my phone.

The little text bubble appeared in the window to show
that he'd started typing. I waited. And waited. Finally,
Can I touch them? Taste them?

I hitched my towel up higher over my breasts and
swallowed, shaking. My face wasn't the only thing that
was warm now. I replied, That was a little better.

Can I lick them and then fuck them?

I dropped my phone, and scrambled to pick it up.
Pretty good, I typed with shaking hands. I closed my
eyes, struggling to push away the image of Will's hips moving over my chest, his cock sliding over the skin between
my breasts.

I could almost feel his determination through the phone when he said, Let me know when you need a minute of ALONE time. Are you ready?

No. Absolutely not. Yes.

You were wearing this shirt the other day, the pink one. Your tits looked fucking phenomenal. Full and soft. I could see your nipples when the wind picked up. All I could think about was what you'd feel like in my hands, your nipples against my tongue. What my cock would look like against your skin and how it would feel to come all over your neck.

Holy shiiiit. Will? Can I just call you?

Why?

Because it's hard to type with one hand.

He didn't reply for a minute and I let myself imagine he'd dropped *his* phone this time. But then he replied: YES! Are you touching yourself??

I laughed, typing, Gotcha, and then threw my phone to the side and closed my eyes.

Because yes, I absolutely was.

Since at the end of our run I'd agreed to meet Will for breakfast at Sarabeth's, after I finished "thinking" about his texts, I hurried to dress and ran out the door. Despite the temperature and the snow starting to fall, I felt the heat of my blush all the way to Ninety-third, and wondered if it was possible to sit across from him and not have him figure out I'd just masturbated to his texts. Things felt like they were veering off course, and I tried to remember when it had happened. Was it the run earlier this morning when he'd hovered over my body, looking as if he were climbing on top of me? Or was it a couple of weeks back, at the bar when we'd started talking about porn and sex? Maybe it was even before that, the first day we went running together and he'd slipped a hat on my head, giving me a smile that made me feel like I'd just been fucked against a wall?

This was not going well. *Friends,* I reminded myself. *Secret agent assignment. Learn the ways of the Ninja, and escape unharmed.*

I kept my head down as I crunched through the thin layer of snow, cursing the March weather, as snowflakes tangled in my loose hair. A young couple was just leaving the restaurant, and I managed to slip in through the open door as they passed.

"Zig," I heard, and looked up to see Will smiling down at me from the loft seating area. I waved before I walked to the stairs, taking off my hat and scarf as I went.

"Fancy seeing you again," he said, standing as I neared the table.

I found myself becoming irrationally annoyed by his good manners, even more so by his still-damp hair and the way his sweater clung to his unending torso. He had a white shirt underneath and, with the sleeves pushed up his forearms, the lines of his tattoos peeked out from beneath the folded cuffs. Gorgeous *asshole.*

"Morning," I said back.

"A little grumpy? Maybe a little tense?"

Scowling, I said, "No."

He laughed as we each took a seat. "I ordered your food."

"What?"

"Your breakfast? The lemon pancakes with berries, right? And that flower juice thing?"

"Yeah," I answered, eyeing him from across the table. I picked up my napkin and unfolded it, laying it across my lap.

He bent to meet my eyes, looking a little anxious. "Did you want something else? I can get the waitress."

"No . . ." I took a deep breath, opened my mouth, and closed it again. It was such a small thing—the food I always ordered, the type of juice I liked, the fact that he'd known exactly how to stretch me this morning—but it felt big, important somehow. It made me feel a little bad that he'd been so sweet and I couldn't seem to keep my head out of his pants. "I just can't believe you remembered that."

He shrugged. "No big deal. It's breakfast, Zig-zag. I'm not donating a kidney here."

I forced away the unreasonably bitchy attitude that flared up at that. "Well, it was just really nice. You surprise me sometimes."

He looked somewhat taken aback. "How so?"

I sighed, deflating somewhat into my chair. "I just assumed you'd treat me more like a kid." As soon as I said this, it was clear he didn't like it. He sat back in his chair and let out a slow breath, so I continued on, rambling, "I know you're giving up your peace and quiet to let me run with you. I know you've canceled plans with your non-girlfriends and had to rearrange things to make time for me, and I just . . . I want you to know that I appreciate it. You're a really great friend, Will."

His brows drew together and he stared down at his ice water instead of looking at me. "Thanks. Just, you know, helping out Jensen's . . . baby sister."

"Right," I said, feeling my irritation flare up again. I wanted to take his water and dunk it over my own head. What was with the hot temper?

"Right," he repeated, blinking up to me and wearing a playful little smile that immediately defused my crazy and made my girl parts perk right back up. "At least that's the story we'll tell everyone."

CHAPTER SIX

Something had changed, some switch had flipped in the past few days, and there was a leaden weight between us now. It had started a few mornings ago, on our run when she was quiet and distracted and had fallen to her side when her leg cramped up. Afterwards at breakfast, she'd clearly been irritated, but that was easy to read: she was fighting something. She was annoyed in the same way I was, as if we should be able to wrestle against this magnet that seemed intent on pulling us to a different place.

A non-friend-zone place.

My phone buzzed on the coffee table and I jerked upright when Hanna's picture lit up the screen. I tried to ignore the warm hum of levity I felt simply because she was calling.

"Hey, Ziggs."

"Come to a party with me tonight," she said simply, completely bypassing any traditional greeting. The classic sign of a nervous Hanna. She paused, and then added more quietly, "Unless . . . shit, it's Saturday. Unless you have an otherwise-platonic regularly-scheduled-sex-partner over."

I ignored the elaborate implied second question and considered only the first, imagining a party in a conference room at the Columbia biology department, with two-liter bottles of soda, chips, and grocery store salsa.

"What kind of party?"

She paused on the other end of the line. "A housewarming party."

I smiled at the phone, growing suspicious. "What kind of *house*?"

On the other end of the line, she let out a groan of surrender. "Okay, fine. It's a grad student party. A guy in my department and his friends just moved into a new apartment. I'm sure it's a shithole. I want to go, but I want you to come with me."

Laughing, I asked, "So it's going to be a grad school *rager*? Will they have kegs and Fritos?"

"Dr. Sumner," she sighed. "Don't be a snob."

"I'm not being a snob," I said. "I'm being a man in his early thirties who finished grad school years ago and considers it a wild night when he goads Max into spending over a thousand dollars on a bottle of scotch."

"Just come with me. I promise you'll have an awesome time."

I sighed, staring at a half-empty bottle of beer on my coffee table. "Will I be the oldest person there?"

"Probably," she admitted. "But I know for a fact you'll also be the hottest."

I laughed at this, and then considered my night without this option. I'd canceled on Kristy, and I still wasn't really sure why.

That was a lie. I knew exactly why. I felt weird, like maybe I was being unfair to Hanna by being with other women when she seemed to be giving so much of herself to me. When I told Kristy I needed a rain check, I knew she heard something else in my voice. She didn't question why or try to reschedule, the way Kitty would have. I suspected I wouldn't be sleeping with that particular blonde again.

"Will?"

Sighing, I stood and walked over to where I'd left my shoes near the front door. "Okay, fine, I'll come. But wear a shirt that shows off your tits so I have something to entertain me if I get bored."

She let out a small, breathy laugh, managing to sound both girlish and seductive. "You have yourself a deal."

———

It was exactly what I'd expected: a serial renter to poverty-level graduate students, and an entirely familiar scene.

I was hit with a small wave of nostalgia as we stepped inside the cramped apartment.

The two couches were droopy futons, with stained, drab covers. The television was propped on a board balanced between two milk crates. The coffee table looked like it had seen better days, before having some very bad days, and *then* had been given to these guys to trash further. In the kitchen, a horde of bearded, hipster grad students huddled around a keg of Yuengling and there were assorted half-full bottles of cheap booze and mixers on the counter.

But from the look on Hanna's face you'd think we just stepped into heaven. Beside me, she bounced a little and then reached for my hand, squeezing it. "I'm so glad you came with me!"

"Seriously, have you actually ever been to a party before?" I asked.

"Once," she admitted, pulling me deeper into the mayhem. "In college. I drank four shots of Bacardi and barfed on some guy's shoes. I still have no idea how I got home."

The image made my stomach twist. I'd seen that girl— wide-eyed, trying out *wild*—at virtually every party I'd been to in college and grad school. I hated to think of *that girl* ever being Hanna. In my eyes she was always smarter than that, more self-aware.

She was still talking, and I leaned in to catch the rest of what she said. ". . . wild nights were mostly spent playing *Magic* in our dorm lounge and sipping ouzo. Well, everyone else would be drinking ouzo. I can barely smell it without wanting to puke." She looked back at me over her shoulder, clarifying, "My roommate was Greek."

Hanna introduced me to a group of people, mostly guys. There was a Dylan, a Hau, an Aaron, and what I think was an Anil. One of them handed Hanna a cocktail made with a trendy plum sake and fizzy soda water.

I knew Hanna wasn't much of a drinker, and my protective instincts kicked in. "Would you rather have something nonalcoholic?" I asked her, loud enough for the others to hear me. What dicks, just assuming she wanted booze.

They all waited for her to answer, but she sipped the drink and made a quiet cooing noise. "This is *good*. Holy crap!" Apparently she liked it. "Just make sure I only have the one," she whispered to me, sliding closer into my side. "Otherwise I can't be held responsible for my actions."

Well, fuck. With that one line she managed to derail my plans to be the good, big-brother figure for the evening.

Hanna drank her cocktail faster than I expected and her cheeks grew rosy, her smile lingered. She met my eyes and I could see her happiness there, lighting her up. *Christ, she's pretty,* I thought, wishing she and I were alone at my place watching a movie, and making a mental note to make that happen soon. I looked around the room and realized how many more people had joined the party. The kitchen was growing crowded. Another graduate student joined our little circle partway into a conversation about the craziest professors in the department and introduced herself to me, stepping between me and Dylan on my right. To my left, I could feel Hanna watching my reaction. I felt hyperconscious around her, seeing myself through her eyes. She was right when she said I noticed women, but while this other woman was pretty, she did nothing for me, especially not with Hanna so nearby. Did Hanna really think I made a habit of having sex with someone every single time I went anywhere?

I met her eyes and gave her a scolding look.

Hanna giggled, mouthing, "I know you."

"You really don't," I murmured. And fuck it, I let it all out: "There's still so much you could learn."

She stared up at me for several long, loaded beats. I could see her pulse in her neck, see the way her chest rose and fell with her quickened breathing. She looked down, put her hand on my bicep, and ran her fingertips over the tattoo of the phonograph I'd had done when my grandfather died.

In unison, we stepped away from the group, sharing a secret little smile. *Fuck, this girl makes me feel unhinged.*

"Tell me about this one," she whispered.

"I got that a year ago when my Pop died. He taught me how to play the bass. He listened to music every second he was awake, every day."

"Tell me about one I've never seen before," she said, attention moving to my lips.

I closed my eyes for a beat, thinking. "I have the word NO written just over my smallest rib on my left side."

Laughing, she stepped closer, close enough for me to smell the sweet plum drink on her breath. "Why?"

"I got it when I was drunk in grad school. I was on an antireligion kick and didn't like the idea that God made Eve out of Adam's rib."

Hanna threw her head back, laughing my favorite laugh, the one that came from her belly and took over her entire body.

"You're so fucking *pretty*," I murmured, without thinking, running my thumb over her cheek.

She jerked her head back upright, and, with a lingering glance to my mouth, pulled me out of the kitchen, a small, devilish smile on her face.

"Where are we going?" I asked, letting her lead me down a narrow hall lined with closed doors.

"Shh. I'll lose my nerve if I say it before we're there. Just come with me."

Little did she know I'd follow her down this hallway even if it caught fire. I'd come to this dirty bohemian party with her after all.

At a random closed door, Hanna stopped, knocked, and waited. She pressed her ear to the wood, smiled up at me, and when we heard nothing, turned the knob, letting out a cute, nervous squeak.

The room was dark, blessedly empty, and still relatively sterile from the recent move. A bed was freshly made in the middle of the room, and a dresser was pressed tight in a corner, but the far wall was still lined with boxes.

"Whose room is this?" I asked.

"I'm not sure." Reaching around, she flipped the lock at my back, and then stared up at me, smiling. "Hi."

"Hi, Hanna."

Her mouth dropped open and her beautiful eyes went wide. "You didn't call me Ziggy."

Smiling, I whispered, "I know."

"Say it again?" Her voice came out husky, as if she was asking me to *touch* her again, to *kiss* her again. And maybe when I'd called her Hanna it felt like a kiss. It certainly had to me. And part of me—a very large part of me—decided I didn't care anymore. I didn't care that I'd kissed her sister twelve years ago and her brother was one of my closest friends. I didn't care that Hanna was seven years younger than I was, and, in many ways, very innocent. I didn't care that I'd probably fuck it up, or that my past would bother her. We were alone, in a dark room, and every inch of my skin felt like it was buzzing with my need for her to touch me.

"Hanna," I said quietly. The two syllables filled my head, hijacked my pulse.

She smiled a secretive little smile and then looked at my mouth. Her tongue slipped out, wetting her bottom lip.

"What's going on, Mystique?" I whispered. "What are we doing in this very dark bedroom, exchanging flirty eyes?"

She held up her hands, her words coming out in a breathless tumble. "This room is Vegas. Okay? What happens here stays here. Or, rather, what's *said* here stays here."

I nodded, mesmerized by the soft curve of her bottom lip. "Okay . . . ?"

"If it's weird, or if I cross a friendship boundary that by some force of magic I haven't yet crossed, just tell me, and we'll leave, and it will be the same level of ridiculous it was before we walked in."

I whispered, "Okay," again, and watched as she took a deep, shaky breath. She was tipsy, and nervous. Anticipation pricked along the back of my neck, and down my spine.

"I'm so wound up around you," she said quietly.

"Just me?" I asked, smiling.

She shrugged. "I want you . . . to teach me things. Not just about how to be around guys but how to . . . be *with* a guy. I think about it all the time. And I know you're comfortable doing this stuff without being in a relationship, and . . ." She trailed off, looking up at me in the dark room. "We're friends, right?"

I knew with absolute certainty where this was going, and murmured, "Whatever it is, I'll do it."

"You don't know what I'm asking."

Laughing, I whispered, "So *ask*."

She stepped a little closer, put her hand on my chest, and I closed my eyes as her warm palm slid down to my stomach. I wondered for a beat if she could feel my heart hammering all the way down my torso. *I* felt my pulse everywhere, slamming through my chest and all along my skin.

"I watched another movie," she said. "A porny one."

"I see."

"Those movies are actually pretty bad." She said this quietly, as if she was worried she might be offending my male, porn-loving sensibilities.

With a quiet laugh, I agreed, "They are."

"The women are so over-the-top. Actually," she said, considering, "so are the guys for most of it."

"*Most* of it?" I asked.

"Not at the end," she said, her voice dropping to barely a decibel. "When the guy came? He pulled out of her and did it *on* her." Her fingers moved beneath my shirt, tickling over the line of hair that went from my navel and beneath the waist of my pants. She sucked in a breath, running her hand up higher and over my pectorals, exploring.

Fuck. I was so worked up I could barely keep my hands from reaching for her hips. But I wanted her to lead this conversation. She'd pulled me in here, started this. I wanted her to get it all out before she turned it over to me. And then I wouldn't hold back.

"That's pretty common in porn," I said. "The guys don't come inside the women."

She looked up at me. "I *liked* that part."

I felt myself grow rigid in my pants, and swallowed thickly. "Yeah?"

"I liked it because it felt *real*. I feel like I'm just figuring these things out. I haven't really tried before . . . or maybe I haven't wanted to explore it with the guys I've been with. But ever since I started hanging out with you, I can't stop thinking about these things. I want to figure out what I like."

"That's good." I winced in the dark room, wishing I hadn't answered so quickly, sounded so desperate. I wanted more than anything for her to ask me to carry her over to the bed and fuck her so loud the entire party knew where we'd gone and what she was getting.

"I don't really know what feels good to men. I know you say guys are easy, but they aren't. To *me*, they aren't." She took my hand, and with her eyes trained on my face, she brought it to her breast. Beneath my palm, she was exactly how I'd imagined a hundred fucking times. So full and soft, all lush curves and creamy skin. It was all I could do to keep from lifting her, and crushing her between my body and the wall.

"I want you to show me how," she said.

"What do you mean 'show you how'?"

She closed her eyes for a beat, swallowing. "I want to touch you, and make you come."

I took a deep breath and glanced over at the bed in the middle of the room. "Here?"

She followed the path my eyes had taken, and shook her head. "Not there. Not a bed yet. Just . . ." She hesitated and then very quietly asked, "Are you saying yes?"

"Um, of course I'm saying yes. I'm not sure I could say no to you even if I should."

She bit back a smile, slid my hand down to her hip.

"You want to give me a hand job? Is that what you're asking?" I bent my knees to look her in the eyes. I felt like an asshole being so blunt, and this whole conversation felt *completely* surreal, but I had to be clear what was actually happening before I let go of my tenuous self-

control and took it too far. "I'm just making sure I understand."

She swallowed again, suddenly shy, and nodded. "Yeah."

I stepped closer and when the light botanical smell of her
shampoo hit me, I grew aware of how amped up I was. I'd
never been nervous before, but right then I was terrified. I
didn't care so much about how good it was for me—it could
be awkward and fumbling, too slow or fast, too soft or too
hard—I knew I'd fall apart in her hands. I just wanted her to
keep feeling this open with me, every second. I wanted sex
to be *fun* for her.

"It's okay to touch me," I told her, trying to carefully balance my need to be gentle with my tendency to be demanding.

She reached for my belt, unfastening it, and I moved my
fingers from her hips, sliding up her waist to the top button
of her shirt. Her smile was giddy, and she tried to duck her
head to hide it but failed. I had no idea what I looked like, but
I imagined my eyes were wide, mouth parted, hands shaking
on her tiny buttons. Slipping her shirt from her shoulders, I
noticed the way she hesitated on my fly, fingers unsure, before she moved away to let her shirt fall to the floor.

She stood in front of me in a simple white cotton bra. I
reached behind her, meeting her eyes for permission before
I unclasped it and slid it from her arms.

I'd been unprepared for the sight of her naked chest,
and stood staring, dumbly.

"Just so you know," she whispered, "you don't have to do anything to me."

"Just so *you* know," I said, just as quietly, "keeping my hands to myself would be impossible right now."

"I want to pay attention. You might . . . distract me."

I groaned; she was killing me. "Such a good student," I said, leaning to kiss the juncture of her shoulder and neck. "But there's no way I can stand here and not look at these. You may have noticed I'm a bit obsessed with your chest."

Her skin was soft and smelled amazing. I opened my mouth, bit her gently, testing. She gasped and pressed into me, the *best* fucking reaction. My mind flooded with images of her nails digging into my back, my mouth open and pressing hard and hungrily into her breast as I rocked over her.

"Touch me, Hanna." I lifted the weight of her breast in my hand, pushed it higher, squeezing. *Holy fuck, she's edible.*

She'd moved her hands back to my fly, but they remained there, unmoving. "Show me how to do this?"

It was probably the hottest thing I'd ever heard a woman say. Maybe it was the tone of her voice, a little hoarse, a lot hungry. Maybe it was knowing how accomplished she was, and this one task felt so far out of her comfort zone but she'd asked *me* to help. Or maybe it was simply that I was wild for her, and showing Hanna how to pleasure me made me feel like I was telling the universe, *This one belongs to me.*

I moved her hands to the waist of my jeans, and together

we worked them and my boxers down my hips, freeing my cock between us.

I let her look at me while I lifted both hands to slide her hair behind her neck, leaning in to kiss her throat. "You taste so fucking good." I was so hard I felt my pulse hammering along my length. I needed relief from this tension. "Shit, Hanna, wrap your hand around me."

"*Show* me, Will," she pleaded, running both hands over my stomach and down, just barely touching where the tip of my cock strained, erect. We looked down the length of our bodies and swayed slightly in unison.

I took her warm hand, wrapped it around the middle of my shaft and slid it down and then back up, groaning a long, drawn-out *"Fuuuck."*

She moaned quietly—a tight, excited sound—and I almost broke. Instead, I squeezed my eyes shut, leaned down again to kiss a line up her neck, and guided her. It was so slow. I hadn't had a hand job in forever, and would take head or sex over a hand one hundred percent of the time, but this, right here, was perfect.

Her lips were so fucking close to mine. I could feel her breath, could taste her candy-sweet plum drink.

"Is it weird that I'm touching you here and we haven't even kissed yet?" she whispered.

I shook my head, looking down to where her fingers wrapped around me. I swallowed, could barely think. "There's no right or wrong here. No rules."

She lifted her eyes from where she'd been staring at my mouth. "You don't have to kiss me."

I gaped at her. I'd wanted to kiss her for weeks now. "Shit, Hanna, yes. I do."

Her tongue slipped out to wet her lips. "Okay."

I bent low, hovering so close, moving her hand up and down my length, and just taking her in. Her lips were a breath away from mine, her little sounds coming out whenever she reached the head of my cock and I let out a grunt. It felt too good to be just a hand job. And all of this was suddenly too intimate to be *just friends.*

I looked at her eyes, and then her mouth, before moving that last inch to kiss her.

She was so fucking sweet and warm, our first kiss was unreal: just a slide of my lips over hers, asking: *Let me do this. Let me do this and be gentle and careful with every part of you.* I kissed her a few times, full lips, careful kisses so she knew I'd take this as fucking slowly as she needed me to.

When I opened my mouth just enough to suck on her bottom lip, a thrill ran through me at the sound of her tight moan. *Christ,* I wanted to lift her up, fuck her mouth with my tongue, and take her against the wall, with the party raging outside and my eyes on her face, watching her process every single sensation.

When she pulled back, she studied my mouth, my eyes, my forehead. She studied *me;* I couldn't tell if it was a general fascination with what she was learning, or specific to this moment, to me. But nothing would have pulled me out of my trance. Not fireworks outside, or a fire in the hall. My need to someday be inside her—to completely possess her—spiked through me and planted beneath my ribs, pressing.

"You'll tell me if this is lame, right?" she asked, voice quiet.

I laughed, wheezing. "Oh, it's not lame. It's so fucking good, and it's just your hand."

Looking unsure, she asked, "Do . . . others not do this?"

I swallowed thickly, hating the mention of other women right now. Before, I'd almost wanted them to be a lingering presence, a reminder to all parties what was and wasn't happening in a moment like this. With Hanna, I wanted to wipe their shadows from the wall. "Shh."

"I mean, do you usually just have sex?"

"I like what we're doing. I don't want something else right now; will you just focus on the dick in your hand?"

She laughed, and I pulsed in her palm, loving the sound. "Fine," she whispered. "I just have to start with the basics."

"I like that you want to learn how to touch me."

"I like touching you," she murmured against my mouth. "I like that you're showing me."

We were moving faster together now; I showed her how hard to squeeze, letting her know it was okay to hold on tight and that I needed it to start getting faster and harder than she'd expected.

"Squeeze it," I whispered. "I like it pretty hard."

"It doesn't hurt?"

"No, it's fucking *killing* me."

"Let me try." She gently pushed my arm away with her free hand.

It freed me to cup her breasts, and I bent down to suck one nipple into my mouth, blowing lightly over the peak.

She moaned, her rhythm slowing for a moment before she sped up again. "Can I keep doing this until you finish?" she asked.

I laughed quietly into her skin. She had me practically vibrating, struggling to not lose it every time she slid her hand down and over the head of my cock. "I was kind of counting on that."

I sucked on her neck, closing my eyes and wondering if she'd let me mark her there, so I could see it tomorrow. So everyone could. All around me the world seemed to spin. Her hand felt good, of course, but the reality of *her* absolutely rocked me. The smell and taste of her smooth, firm skin, her sounds of pleasure simply from touching me. She was sexual and responsive and curious, and I wasn't sure I'd been this turned on in a long, long time.

The familiar tension built deep in my belly, and I began to rock forward in her grip. "Hanna. Oh, shit, just a little faster, okay?" The words felt so much more intimate this way: spoken into her skin, my breath ragged.

She faltered for only a second before responding, pulling

harder and faster, and I was close—embarrassingly soon—and I didn't give a single fuck. Her long, slim fingers wrapped tight around me and she let me suck on her bottom lip, her jaw, her neck. I knew she would taste good *everywhere*.

I wanted to show her how it felt to be fucked.

With that thought, of falling over her and into her, making her come with my body, I leaned into her, begged her to bite me, bite my neck my shoulder . . . *anything*. I didn't care how it sounded; somehow I knew that she wouldn't balk, or recoil from the reality of this admission.

Without hesitation, she leaned in, opened her mouth on my neck, and pressed her teeth sharply into me. My thoughts blurred, everything flashed hot and wild; for a moment it felt like every synapse in my body had rewired, unplugged, gone off. Her hand slipped over me fast, my orgasm barreling down my spine and I came with a quiet groan, the heat crawling up my spine and pouring from me into her hand and over her bare stomach.

Just when I needed her to, she stopped moving but didn't let go. I could feel her eyes on where she held me in her hand, and I jerked when she moved down my length again, experimentally.

"No more," I gasped, my voice tight.

"Sorry." She slid the thumb of her free hand over where I'd come on her palm, rubbed it over her hip, eyes wide and fascinated. She was breathing so hard her chest jerked with the movement.

"Holy shit," I exhaled.

"Was it . . . ?" The room seemed full with her unfinished question and the sound of my heavy breathing. I felt a little dizzy, and wanted to pull her down onto the floor with me and pass out.

"That was fucking unreal, Hanna."

She looked up at me, almost triumphant with discovery. "I was right—you made the best noise when you came."

The world dropped into an abyss when she said that, because here I was, growing soft in her hand, and all I wanted was to find out whether doing that to me had made her wet.

I bent forward and asked, "Is it my turn now?" into the soft skin of her neck.

With a trembling breath, she whispered, "Yes, please."

"Do you want my hands?" I asked. "Or do you want something else?"

She let out a little nervous laugh. "I'm not really ready for more, but . . . I don't think hands work on me."

I leaned back enough to give her my most skeptical look, unbuttoning the top button of her jeans and just daring her to stop me.

She didn't.

"I just mean I don't know if I can get off with fingers, like, just inside," she clarified.

"Well, of course you can't get off just with fingers inside. Your *clit* isn't inside." I slid my hand beneath her cotton underwear and froze at the sensation of soft, bare skin. "Uh, Hanna? I did not peg you as a waxer."

She wiggled a little, embarrassed. "Chloe was talking about it. I was curious. . . ."

I slipped a finger between her lips—holy *fuck,* she was drenched. "Jesus Christ," I groaned.

"I like it," she admitted, her mouth pressed against my neck. "I like how it feels."

"Are you fucking kidding? You're so fucking soft; I want to lick up and down every part of this."

"Will . . ."

"I'd have my mouth on you in two seconds if we weren't in some random guy's bedroom."

She shivered under my touch, letting out a quiet moan. "I can't tell you how many times I've imagined that."

Holy hell. I felt myself lengthen between us again, already. "I think you'd melt like sugar on my tongue. What do you think?"

She laughed a little, holding on to my shoulders. "I think I'm melting now."

"I think you are. I think you're going to melt all over my fucking hand and I'll lick it off after. Are you loud, little Plum? When you come are you wild?"

A tiny choking sound escaped before she whispered, "By myself I'm not loud."

Fuck. That's what I wanted to hear. I could build fantasies for a decade just thinking about Hanna, legs spread on her couch or while she was lying in the middle of her bed, touching herself.

"By yourself, what do you do? Just the clit?"

"Yeah."

"With a toy or . . . ?"

"Sometimes."

"I bet I can make you come like this," I said, and slid two fingers carefully inside, feeling her squeeze me. I brushed my nose against hers. "Tell me. Do you like my fingers here? Fucking you?"

"Will . . . you're so *dirty*."

I laughed, nibbling at her jaw. "I think you *like* dirty."

"I think I'd like your dirty mouth between my legs," she said softly.

I groaned, moved my hand faster and harder into her.

"Do *you* think about it?" she asked. "Kissing me there?"

"I have," I admitted. "I think about it and wonder if I'd ever come up for air."

So wet. She was wiggling all over my hand, making these little desperate sounds I wanted to eat. I pulled my fingers out, ignoring her angry little growl, and with them painted a wet line up her chin and across her lips, following almost immediately with my tongue, covering her mouth with mine.

Fuuuck.

She tasted all woman, soft and heady, and her tongue was still sticky sweet from her girly drink. She tasted like plum, ripe and soft and small in my mouth, and I felt like a fucking king when she begged me to touch her *more, again, please Will I was close.*

Returning to her, I shoved her pants and underwear all the way down her legs, waiting as she stepped out of them. She was completely naked and my arms were shaking with the need to slide inside her perfect, warm heat.

She reached for my wrist, pulling my hand back between her legs.

"Greedy girl."

Her eyes went wide, embarrassed. "I just—"

"Shh." I quieted her with my mouth on hers, sucking on her lip and licking her sweet tongue. Pulling back, I whispered, "I like it. I want to make you explode."

"I will." She jerked in my hand when I slid my fingers between her legs and over her clit. "I've never felt this."

"So wet."

Her mouth opened in a sharp gasp when I slid my fingers back inside her. She stared at my lips, my eyes, my every reaction. I loved that she was so curious she couldn't even look away.

"Do me a favor," I asked. She nodded. "When you're close, tell me. I'll know, but give me the words."

"I will," she gasped. "I will, I will, just . . . please."

"Please what, Plum?"

She weaved slightly against me. "Please don't stop."

I slid my fingers deeper, faster, pressing my thumb up against her clit and working it right there in tighter, smaller circles. *Yes. Holy shit, she's so close.*

I was hard again, rubbing over her bare hip where I'd already come on her only minutes ago, and close again myself.

"Grab my dick, okay? Just hold on. You're so fucking wet and your sounds . . . holy fuck, I . . ."

And then she was there, holding on to me tight enough to fuck her fist, and every thought became about how smooth she was around my fingers and the fruit plumpness of her lips and tongue.

She started to dissolve, her body completely losing it. She was quietly gasping the same thing over and over—*Oh my God*—which I was thinking, too.

"Say it."

"I'm going . . ." She hiccupped, tightened her hold on my length as I fucked her fist.

"Fucking *say it.*"

"Will. My God." Her thighs started to shake and I wrapped my free arm around her waist to keep her from falling. "I'm coming."

And with a wild jerk of her hips she did, shaking and wet. Her orgasm rippled along the lengths of my fingers as she cried out, digging her nails into my shoulders. It was exactly what I needed—*how did she fucking know?* With a low groan, I felt my second orgasm surge forward, hot and liquid into her hand.

Fuck. My legs shook and I leaned into her, pinning her to the wall.

We'd been loud. Too loud? We were far down the hall, separated from the raging party by a number of rooms, but I still had no sense what the outside world had done while mine had melted in Hanna's arms.

Her breath came out warm and sweet on my neck and I carefully pulled out my fingers, rubbing along her sex to relish in her warm, sensitive skin.

"Good?" I murmured into her ear.

"Yeah," she whispered, wrapping her arms around my shoulders and pressing her face into the crook of my neck. "*God,* so good."

I left my hand where it was, my mind reeling as I gently ran my fingers up her clit, down back to her entrance and along the soft crease of her pussy. It was quite possibly the best first time I'd ever had with a girl.

And it had only been our hands.

"We should probably get back out to the party," she said, her voice muffled by my skin.

Reluctantly, I pulled my hand away, and immediately winced as she turned on the light switch behind her back. As I pulled up my pants, I stared at her, completely naked in the bright room.

Well, fuck. She was smooth and toned, with lush breasts and gently curved hips. Her skin was still flushed from her orgasm, and I relished the sight of the blush that spread up her neck and across her cheeks as I studied the moisture on her stomach from my orgasm.

"You're staring," she said, bending to reach for a box of tissues on the dresser. She looked down, cleaning herself up and then tossing the tissue into a trash can.

I buckled my belt and then sat at the edge of the bed, watching her put her clothes back on. She was unbelievably sexy, and she had no fucking idea.

The room smelled like sex, and I knew she could feel my attention on her but she didn't rush. In fact, she seemed perfectly content to let me look at every angle, every curve as she slid on her panties, shimmied into her pants, put her bra on, slowly buttoned her shirt.

Looking over at me, she licked her lips and my heart tripped as I registered she could taste herself from my fingers. I wondered if I'd be remembering her taste until the end of time.

"What now?" I asked, standing.

"Now"—she reached for my arm, tracing the double helix from my elbow to my wrist—"we go back out there and have another drink."

My blood cooled a bit, hearing her voice return to steady. No longer breathy and excited, no longer tentative and hopeful. She was back to her regular bubbly self, the same Hanna everyone else saw. No longer mine.

"Works for me."

She looked at my face for several long moments, at

my eyes and cheeks, chin and lips. "Thanks for not being weird."

"Are you kidding?" I bent down and kissed her cheek. "What's there to be weird about?"

"We just touched each other's private parts," she whispered.

I laughed, fixing the collar of her shirt. "I noticed that."

"I think I could totally do the friends-with-benefits thing. It feels so easy, so relaxed. We're just going to head back out there," she said, grinning widely up at me. With a little wink, she added, "And we're the only ones who know you just came all over my stomach and I just came all over your hand."

She turned the knob, opened the door, and let in the roar of the party. No way would anyone have heard us. We could pretend it didn't even happen.

I'd done this before, scores of times. Hooked up with a woman and then returned to the throes of a party, blending into the room and losing myself in another form of fun. But despite the genuinely nice crowd of people, I couldn't ever lose track of where Hanna was and what she was doing. In the living room, talking to the tall Asian guy I remembered as Dylan. Heading down the hall, waving to me before ducking into the restroom. Filling her plastic cup with water in the kitchen. Looking over to me across the room.

Dylan found Hanna again, smiling as he bent and said something to her. He had a wide smile, clothes that suggested he got out enough to be on the cutting edge of grad student chic, and seemed genuinely fond of her. I watched her smile grow, and then turn a little unsure. She hugged him, and watched him head into the kitchen. I had no idea what was happening; I loved seeing her have a good time. But the itch for something else started to spread across my skin, and after two hours of partying post–hand job, I realized I wanted to take her home where we could feel each other for real for the remainder of the night.

I slid my phone from my pocket, typing a text to her. `Let's get out of here. Come to my place tonight and stay with me.`

I moved my thumb to the SEND button before I noticed that she was also typing in our iMessage window. I paused, waiting.

`Dylan just asked me out,` she said.

I stared at my phone before looking up to meet her anxious eyes across the room.

Deleting what I'd written, I typed instead, `What did you tell him?`

She looked down when her phone buzzed in her hand, and then replied, `I told him we could figure it out on Monday.`

She was looking for guidance, maybe even looking for permission. Only a month ago I was regularly having sex with two to three different women every week. I had no idea where my head was concerning Hanna; my own thoughts were too jumbled and complex to help her translate hers right now.

My phone buzzed again and I glanced down. Is this really weird after what we just did?? I don't know what to do, Will.

This is what she needs, I told myself. *Friends, dates, a life outside of school. You can't be the only thing in it.*

For once I was looking for complicated, and she was trying on simple.

Not at all, I typed back. This is called dating.

Chapter Seven

If I'd ever wondered what a cat in heat sounded like, now I knew. The noises—the meows, the whining, the howls—had started about an hour ago and had only gotten worse until the sexually frustrated animal was practically screeching outside my bedroom window.

I knew exactly how it felt. Thanks, Life, for giving me the living, breathing metaphor for how I was feeling.

With a groan, I rolled to my stomach, reaching blindly for a pillow to drown out the sound. Or to use to smother myself. I hadn't decided. I'd been home from my date with Dylan for three hours and hadn't gotten even a few minutes of sleep.

I was a mess, having tossed and turned since I'd climbed into bed, staring up at the ceiling as if the secret to all my problems lay hidden in the mottled plaster overhead. Why did everything feel so complicated? Wasn't this what I'd wanted? Dates? A social life? To have an orgasm in the company of another person?

So what was the problem?

The way Dylan tripped my *only-a-friend* vibe was the problem. The fact that we'd gone to one of my favorite restaurants and I'd been completely zoned out, thinking about Will when I should have been swooning over Dylan, was an even bigger one. I wasn't thinking about Dylan's smile as he'd picked me up, the way he'd opened my door and the adoring way he'd looked at me all through dinner. Instead, I was obsessing over Will's teasing smile, the look on his face as he'd watched me touch his cock, his flushed cheeks, how he'd told me exactly what to do, the way he'd sounded when he came, and how it had looked on my skin.

Annoyed, I flopped onto my back and kicked off the blankets. It was March, light snow had been falling all day, and I was *sweating*. It was two o'clock in the morning and I was wide awake and frustrated. Really, *really* frustrated.

The hardest part to wrap my head around was how sweet Will had been at the party, how gentle and caring, and how I knew without a doubt how easily all of that would translate into sex. He'd been encouraging, saying everything I'd needed to hear, but never pushing, never asking for more than I'd been willing to give. And holy shit he was hot . . . those hands. That mouth. The way he sucked on my skin, kissing me as if he had years of pent-up need and it was finally unleashed. I wanted him to fuck me, probably more than I ever wanted anything, and it was the most logical next step in the world: we were both there, it was dark, he was worked up and God knows I'd been ready to explode, there'd been a bed . . . but, it hadn't felt right. I hadn't felt ready.

And he hadn't pushed. In fact, when I expected it to be weird, it wasn't. When he'd been the only person I wanted to talk to about Dylan, he'd encouraged me. On the taxi ride home he'd told me I needed to go out, have fun. He told me he wasn't going anywhere, and what we'd done was perfect. He told me to explore, and be happy. *God*, it just made me want him even more.

Deciding this was a losing battle and I would never get to sleep now, I sat up and went into the kitchen. I stared into the fridge, closing my eyes as the cool air floated along my heated skin. I was slick between my legs and even though it had been six days since Will had touched me there, I *ached*. I'd seen him every day for our run, and we'd had breakfast afterward on three of those days. It had been easy; with Will, it was *always* easy. But each time he was near, I wanted to ask if he could touch me again, if I could touch him. I could still feel the echo of every stroke of his fingers, but I didn't trust my memory. It couldn't possibly have been so good as all that.

I walked into the living room and looked out the window. The sky was dark but silver-gray, the rooftops glittering with frost. I counted the streetlights and calculated how many of them there were between his apartment building and mine. I wondered if there was even a chance he was awake, too, feeling even a fraction of the want I felt now.

My fingers found the pulse in my neck and I closed my eyes, feeling the steady thrum beneath my skin. I told myself to go back to bed. Maybe this was a good opportunity to sample the brandy Dad always kept in the living room. I told myself that calling Will was a bad idea and that there was absolutely no way that anything good could come from this. I was smart and logical and thought everything through.

I was so tired of thinking.

Ignoring the warning inside my head, I grabbed my things, stepped outside, and started walking. The lingering snow had been stomped down during the day and formed a thick crust along the sidewalk. My boots crunched with every step and the closer I got to Will's apartment, the more the chaos in my thoughts settled into a steady hum in the background.

When I looked up, I was standing in front of his building. My hands shook as I pulled out my phone and found his picture, typing the only thing that came to mind: Are you awake?

I almost dropped the phone in surprise when an answer came only a few seconds later. Unfortunately.

Let me in? I asked, and honestly, did I want him to say yes? Or send me home? At this point I didn't even know.

Where are you?

I hesitated. In front of your building.

WHAT. Down in a sec.

I'd barely had time to consider what I was doing, turning to look back in the direction I'd come, when the front door flew open and Will stepped outside.

"Holy shit, it's freezing!" he yelled, and then looked behind me to the empty curb. "For fuck's sake, Hanna, did you at least take a cab here?"

Wincing, I admitted, "I walked."

"*At three a.m.?* Are you out of your goddamn mind?"

"I know, I know. I just . . ."

He shook his head and pulled me inside. "Get in here. You're crazy, you know that? I want to strangle you right now. You don't just walk around Manhattan alone at three in the morning, Hanna."

My stomach twisted with warmth when he said my name, and I knew I'd stand out in the cold all night if it meant he'd say it again. But he shot me a warning look, and I nodded as he led me to the elevator. The doors closed and he watched me from the opposite wall.

"So did you just get home from your date?" he asked, looking far too sleep-rumpled and sexy for my current state of mind. "The last you texted, you were getting in the cab to meet Dylan at the restaurant."

I shook my head and blinked down to the carpet, trying to understand what exactly I'd been thinking when deciding to come here. I hadn't been thinking, that was the problem. "I got home around nine."

"*Nine?*" he asked, looking completely unimpressed.

"Yes," I challenged.

"And?" His tone was even, his face impassive, but the

speed of his questions told me he was worked up about something.

I shifted from foot to foot, not sure exactly what to say. The date hadn't been a complete disaster. Dylan was sweet and interesting, but I'd been totally checked out.

I was saved from answering when we reached Will's floor. I followed him out of the elevator and down the long hallway, watching his back and shoulders flex with every step. He wore blue pajama bottoms and the outlines of some of his darker tattoos were visible through his thin white T-shirt. I had to push down the urge to reach out and trace them with my fingertip, to take off his shirt and see them all. There were obviously more than there had been all those years ago, but what were they? What stories hid beneath the ink on his skin?

"So are you going to tell me?" he asked.

He'd stopped in front of his door and my eyes shot up to his. "What?" I asked, confused.

"Date, Hanna."

"Oh," I murmured, blinking away and trying to make some order of the chaos inside my head. "It was dinner and blah blah blah, I took a cab home. You're sure I didn't wake you?"

He sighed long and deep, gesturing for me to lead us inside. "Unfortunately, no." He tossed me a blanket from the back of the couch. "I haven't been able to fall asleep yet."

I wanted to pay attention, but I was suddenly surrounded by so many pieces of Will's life. His apartment was one of the newer buildings in the area, and it was modern, but modest. He flipped a switch to a small fireplace against one wall, and the flames bit to life with a soft whoosh, washing the honey-colored walls in flickering light.

"Warm up while I get you something to drink," he said, motioning to the rug in front of the hearth. "And tell me more about this date that ended at *nine*."

The kitchen was visible from the living room and I watched as he opened and closed cupboards, filling an ancient-looking kettle before setting it to heat on the stove. His place was smaller than I'd have imagined, with wood floors and bookcases packed to the brim with dog-eared novels, thick genetics texts, and an entire wall dedicated to what looked like a rather impressive collection of comic books. Two leather couches dominated the living room and simple framed art lined the walls. There were magazines in a basket on the floor, a stack of mail tucked into the mantel, a glass full of bottle caps resting on a shelf.

I tried to focus on what he was asking, but every object in his apartment was a fascinating puzzle piece to the story of Will. "There's really not much to tell," I said distractedly.

"Hanna."

I groaned, taking off my jacket and folding it over the back of a chair. "My head just wasn't in the game, you know?" I said, and stopped at the expression on his face. His eyes were wide, his mouth open as his gaze moved slowly down my body. "What?"

"What are you . . ." He coughed. "You came all the way over here in *that?*"

I looked down and if possible, became even more mortified than I'd been before. I'd gone to bed in shorts and a tank top, only taking time to throw on a pair of pajama pants, my fuzzy boots, and Jensen's giant old coat. My shirt left nothing to the imagination and my nipples were hard, completely visible beneath the thin material.

"Oh. Oops." I crossed my arms over my chest, trying to hide the fact that it was obviously very, *very* cold outside. "I probably should have paid more attention but I . . . I wanted to see you. Is that weird? It's weird isn't it? I'm probably breaking about twelve of your rules right now."

He blinked. "I, uh . . . I think there's a clause in there to make an exception for any rule-breaking while wearing an outfit like that," he said, managing to pull his eyes from my chest long enough to finish up in the kitchen. There was an unfamiliar sense of power in being able to fluster him, and I tried not to look too smug as he walked out, carrying two steaming mugs.

"So why was this date so uneventful?" he asked.

I sat on the floor in front of the fire, legs stretched out in front of me. "Just had other things on my mind."

"Like?"

"Liiiiiike . . ." I said, dragging the word out long enough to decide if I really wanted to go there. I did. "Like the party?"

A moment of long, heavy silence stretched between us. "I see."

"Yeah."

"Well, in case you hadn't noticed," he said, glancing over at me, "I wasn't exactly sound asleep here."

I nodded and turned back to the fire, not sure how to proceed. "I've always been able to control where my mind went, you know? If it's time for school I think about school. If it's work, I think about work. But lately," I said, shaking my head, "my concentration is crap."

He laughed softly next to me. "I know exactly how you feel."

"I can't focus."

"Yeah." He scratched the back of his neck, looking up at me through dark lashes.

"I'm not sleeping very well."

"Same."

"I'm so fucking wound up I can hardly sit still," I admitted.

I heard the sound of his exhale, a long, measured breath, and only then did I realize how close we'd gotten. I looked up to see him watching me.

His eyes searched every inch of my face. "I don't know . . . if I've ever been this distracted by someone," he said.

I was *so close,* close enough to see each of his eyelashes in the firelight, close enough to make out the tiny scattering of freckles along the bridge of his nose. Without thinking I leaned in, brushing my lips over his. His eyes widened and I felt him stiffen, frozen for only a moment before his shoulders relaxed.

"I shouldn't want this," he said. "I have no idea what we're doing."

We weren't kissing, not really, just teasing, breathing the same air. I could smell his soap, a hint of toothpaste. Could see my own reflection in his pupil.

He tilted his head and closed his eyes, moving in just enough to kiss me once, lips parted. "Tell me to stop, Hanna."

I couldn't. Instead I reached up, cupping the back of his neck to bring him closer. And then it was he who pushed forward, harder, longer, and I had to grip his shirt to keep myself steady. He opened his mouth, sucking on my lower lip, my tongue. Heat pulsed low in my belly and I felt like was dissolving, melting until I was nothing more than a racing heart and limbs that twisted with his, pulling us both to our sides and down to the floor.

"I don't . . ." I started, breath tight. "Tell me what I should do."

I felt the shape of him hard against my hip and I wondered how long he'd been that way, if he'd been thinking about this as much as I had. I wanted to reach down and touch, watch him fall apart like he had at the party, the way he did in my mind every time I closed my eyes.

His lips moved over my jaw, down my throat. "Just relax, I'll make it good. Tell me what you *want* to do."

My hand moved under his shirt and I felt the solid strength of muscle in his back, his arms as he rolled us over to hover above me. I said his name, hating how weak and unfamiliar my voice sounded, but there was something new there, something raw and desperate, and I wanted more.

"I used to imagine what it'd be like to have you on top of me," I admitted, not sure where the words were coming from. He rested his body more fully on mine, his hips settling between my open legs. "When you were lounging in the living room with my brother. When you'd take your shirt off outside to wash the car."

He moaned, moving a hand to my hair, his thumb drawing a path along my face and pressing into the skin along my jaw. "Don't tell me that."

But it was *all* I could think about: how I remembered him from those years, and the reality of him *now*. I couldn't possibly count the number of times I wondered what he would look like without his clothes, the sounds he'd make when he was chasing his release. And here he was, heavy on me, hard between my legs, beneath his clothes. I wanted to catalog every tattoo, every line of muscle, every inch of his carved jaw.

"I used to watch you from my window," I said, gasping as he shifted so that the length of him pressed directly over my clit. "God, when I was sixteen you starred in every one of my dirty dreams."

He pulled back just enough to meet my eyes; he was clearly surprised.

I swallowed. "Should I not have told you that?"

"I . . ." he began and licked his lips. "I don't know?" He looked dazed and conflicted. I couldn't look away from his mouth. "I know I shouldn't think that's hot but

Christ, Hanna. If I come in my pants you have no one to blame but yourself."

I could do that? His words lit a fuse in my chest and I wanted to tell him everything. "I would touch myself, under the covers," I admitted in a whisper. "Sometimes I could hear you talking . . . and I would pretend . . . wonder what it would be like if you were there. I used to make myself come and pretend it was you."

He swore, dipping back down to kiss me again, deeper and wetter, his teeth dragging along my bottom lip. "What would I say?"

"How good I felt and how much you wanted me," I said into his kiss. "I wasn't very creative at the time, and I'm pretty sure your mouth is way filthier in reality."

He laughed, the sound so low and rough it was a physical pressure on my neck where he breathed. "So let's pretend you're sixteen, and I just snuck into your room," he said, moving his mouth just over mine, his voice coming out the slightest bit unsure. "We don't have to take our clothes off if you aren't ready."

And I wasn't sure what to say because *yes*, I wanted to be completely bare under him, to imagine what it would feel like to have him naked and over and inside me. But *actual* sex with Will tonight felt too fast, too soon. Too dangerous.

"Show me?" I asked, "I don't know how to with clothes on." I paused, adding in a whisper, "Or even off, I guess. I mean obviously."

He laughed, kissing over to my ear and growling quietly as he nipped at my earlobe. The way his hands moved over me, the way his lips slid across my skin . . . touching like this seemed as second-nature to Will as breathing.

He exhaled into my neck, groaning quietly. "Move under me. Find what feels good for you, okay?"

I nodded, shifting beneath him and feeling the hard press of his cock between my legs.

"Can you feel that?" he asked, pressing meaningfully against my clit. "Is that where it feels good?"

"Yeah." I moved my hands to his hair and pulled hard, hearing him hiss in a breath as he rocked against me, faster and faster.

"Fuck, Hanna." He pushed my tank top up over my ribs, bunching it above my chest. And then he bent, gripped my breast, plumping it, and sucked a nipple deep into his mouth. The air left my lungs, my hips pressed up from the floor, searching. I scratched at his skin, and was rewarded each time with a mumbled curse or groan.

"That's it," he said. "Don't stop." His mouth followed his hands everywhere and I closed my eyes, feeling the heat of his tongue as it moved over me. He kissed my lips, my throat. The ache between my legs grew and I could feel how wet I was, how empty, how much I wanted his mouth against me, his fingers inside. His cock. We slid along the floor and I felt something wedge beneath my back, but didn't care. All I wanted was to chase down this feeling.

"So close," I gasped, surprised to find him looking down at me, lips parted and hair falling across his forehead.

His eyes widened, blazing with thrill. "Yeah?"

I nodded, the rest of the world blurring as the feeling between my legs grew, becoming hotter and more urgent. I wanted to claw at my skin and beg him to take off my clothes, to fuck me, to make me beg.

"Fuck. Don't stop what you're doing," he said, rocking his hips forward against me, the perfect drag of heat and pressure exactly where I needed. "I'm almost there."

"Oh," I said, my fingers twisting in the thin fabric of his shirt as I felt myself start to fall, closing my eyes as my orgasm moved down my spine to explode between my legs. I cried out, calling his name and feeling him speed up as he moved against me. His fingers pressed tightly into my hips as he pushed once, twice, grunting into my neck as he came.

Feeling seeped back into my body one limb at a time. I felt heavy and limp, suddenly so exhausted I could hardly keep my eyes open. Will collapsed against me, his breath hot on my neck, his skin damp with sweat and warmed by the fire.

He pushed up onto his elbows and looked down at me, his expression drowsy and sweet and a little timid. "Hi," he said, a crooked smile sliding into place. "Sorry for sneaking into your bedroom, teenage-Hanna."

I blew the bangs from my forehead and smiled back. "You're welcome there anytime."

"I . . . uh," he started, and laughed. "I don't mean to rush off but I sort of . . . need to clean up."

The absurdity of the entire situation seemed to bubble up out of nowhere and I started to laugh. We were on his floor, I think I had a shoe or something lodged under my back, and he'd just come in his pants.

"Hey," he said. "Don't laugh. I said it'd be your fault."

I was suddenly so thirsty and licked my lips. "Go," I said, patting his back.

He kissed me softly, twice on the lips before pushing himself to stand and walking into the bathroom. I stayed there for a moment, sweat drying on my skin and heart rate slowly returning to normal. I felt both better and worse. Better because I was actually tired, but worse because the new echo of Will's cock moving between my legs was infinitely more distracting than the memory of his fingers.

I called a taxi, then walked into the kitchen to splash some cool water on my face and get a drink.

He came back into the room wearing different pajamas, and smelling of soap, and toothpaste.

"I called a cab," I assured him, giving him the *don't-worry* look. His face fell—or it seemed to—but it happened so fast that I wasn't sure I believed my eyes.

"Good," he murmured, walking over to me and handing me my sweatshirt. "I actually think I'll be able to sleep now."

"Just needed the orgasm," I said, grinning.

"Actually," he said, voice deep, "I'd tried that a few times already tonight. It hadn't worked so far. . . ."

Holy shitballs. Any drowsiness I'd felt immediately evaporated. I was going to imagine what it would be like to watch Will get himself off for the rest of the night. I wasn't sure if I'd ever be able to sleep again.

He walked me downstairs, kissed my forehead at the door, and stood watching as I walked to the curb, climbed into the cab, and drove off.

My phone lit up with a text from him: Tell me when you get home.

I lived only seven blocks from him; I was home in minutes. I climbed into bed, curling into my pillow before answering, Home safe.

CHAPTER EIGHT

The promise of crowds was always a reality, living near the Columbia campus, but, mysteriously, the Dunkin' Donuts nearest my building always seemed busiest on Thursdays. Even during a slow stretch, though, I probably wouldn't have recognized Dylan in line, just ahead of me.

So, when he turned, eyes widening in recognition, and let out a friendly "Hey! Will, right?" I startled.

I blinked, feeling caught off guard. I'd just been daydreaming about taking things with Hanna in a different direction than I had two nights ago, when she'd come to my apartment in the middle of the night and ended up beneath me, both of us coming with our clothes on. The memory of that night was a current favorite, one I'd pulled out in almost every quiet moment since, to play with, take down a different path, warm my blood. It had been years since I'd dry-humped a girl, but fuck, I'd forgotten how dirty and forbidden it felt.

But the sight of this kid in front of me—the guy Hanna was *dating*—felt like an ice bucket dumped over my head.

Dylan looked like every other Columbia student in the place: dressed down to the point he was toeing the line between pajama-clad and hobo.

"Yeah," I said, extending my hand to shake his. "Hi, Dylan. Good to see you again."

We stepped forward as the line moved ahead, and the awkwardness hit me slowly. I hadn't realized at the party how young he looked: he had that silently vibrating, feet-bouncy thing going on, where he seemed constantly excited about something. He nodded a lot, looked at me as if I was someone to be treated as a superior.

Looking between us, I registered how much more formal I looked in my suit. Since when was I the guy in a suit? Since when did I have little patience for stupid, twenty-something grad students? Probably the same day Hanna jacked me off in the back room of a grad student party and it was the best sex I'd ever had, I reminded myself.

"Did you have fun at Denny's?"

I stared at him for a long moment, trying to remember when I had last been to Denny's. "I . . ."

"The party, not the restaurant," he prompted, laughing. "The apartment belonged to a guy named Denny."

"Oh, right. The party." My mind immediately went to the image of Hanna's face as I slid my fingers beneath her underwear and across her bare skin. I could remember with perfect clarity her expression just before she came, like I'd done something fucking *magical*. She looked like she was discovering sensation for the first time. "Yeah, the party was pretty great."

He fidgeted with his phone, looking up at me, and seemed to be working up to something.

"You know," he said, leaning in a little, "this is the first time I've run into someone who's sort of dating the same girl I'm sort of dating. Is this really weird?"

I bit back a laugh. Well, he certainly had blunt-force honesty in common with Hanna. "What makes you think I'm dating her?"

Dylan immediately looked mortified. "I just assumed . . . because of how it seemed at the party. . . ."

Giving him a sly smile, I chided him, "And yet you asked her out anyway?"

He laughed as if he, too, couldn't believe his own audacity. "I was so drunk! I guess I just went for it."

I wanted to punch him. And I registered that I was the world's biggest hypocrite. I had absolutely no right to feel so indignant about any of this.

"It's fine," I said, calming down. I'd never been on this side of a conversation before, and for a beat wondered if any of my lovers had ever run into each other in places like this. How awkward. I tried to imagine what Kitty or Lara—all sparkles and sunshine—and Natalia or Kristy—who would barely crack a smile even in the best of moods—would do if they were put in this kind of situation.

Shrugging, I told him, "Hanna and I go way back. That's all."

He laughed, nodding as if this answered all of his un-asked questions. "She said she's just dating right now. I get that. She's a really fun girl, I've been wanting to ask her out for ages, so I'll take whatever I can get, you know?"

I stared at the cashier, silently begging her to ring up customers just a little faster. Unfortunately, I knew exactly what he meant. "Yeah."

He nodded again and I was tempted to tell him the rule of silence: *sometimes an awkward silence is actually far less awkward than forced conversation.*

Dylan stepped up to order his coffee and I could return to the safety of distraction via smartphone. I didn't meet his eye again as he paid and walked away, but I felt like my gut was made of lead.

What the fuck was I doing?

With every step to my office, I felt more and more uncom-fortable. In the past near-decade, the lines were drawn with each of my sexual partners before the sex even happened. Sometimes the conversation occurred as we left an event together, other times it came up organically when they asked if I had a girlfriend and I could simply say, "I'm dating, but not seeing one person exclusively right now." In the few cases when the sex turned into something more, I'd always made a point to be clear about where I stood, find out where they stood, and discuss—openly—what we both wanted.

I hadn't registered how blindsided I'd been by the appearance of Dylan—in my world, and, more importantly, in Hanna's. For the first time ever, I'd made the assumption that when she pulled me to that back bedroom, she would want to explore sex with me . . . and *only* me.

Karma was clearly a bitch.

———

That morning, I dove into work, burning through three prospectuses and a stack of bullshit paperwork I'd been putting off for the past week. I followed up on calls, arranged for a business trip to the Bay Area to check out a few new biotechs. I barely stopped to breathe.

But when the afternoon rolled around, and I hadn't eaten anything for hours and my caffeine rush had long since tapered, Hanna pushed her way back into my thoughts.

My office door opened and Max walked over, tossing an enormous sandwich on my desk before sinking into the chair across from me. "What's going on, William? You look like you just found out DNA is a right-handed helix."

"It *is* a right-handed helix," I corrected him. "It just turns to the left."

"Like your dick?"

"Exactly." I pulled my sandwich toward me, unwrapping it. I hadn't realized until it was in front of me, smelling delicious, just how hungry I was. "Just thinking too much."

"Why do you look mental, then? Thinking too much is your fucking superpower, mate."

"Not about this it isn't." I rubbed my face, opting for honesty over jokes. "I'm kind of confused over something."

He took a bite, studied me. After several long moments, he asked, "This is about Tits, isn't it?"

I looked up at him, expression flat. "You *can't* call her that, Max."

"'Course I can't. Not to her face anyway. I mean, I call my Sara 'Tongue' after all, but she doesn't know it."

Despite my angst-ridden mood, I laughed at this. "You do not."

"No, I don't." His smile gave way to a frown of mock contrition. "That would be tacky, wouldn't it?"

"*Very* tacky."

"I can't help but notice that Hanna does have a fantastic pair, though."

Laughing again, I murmured, "Maximus, you have no idea."

He sat up straighter in his chair. "No, I don't," he said. "But it sounds like *you* do. Have you seen them? I wasn't aware things had progressed beyond your dating-mentoring bullshit."

When I looked up at him, I knew he could see it all in my face: I was in deep with Hanna. "I have. Things . . . uh . . . *progressed* the other night. And then again a couple of nights ago." I picked at my sandwich. "We haven't had sex, but . . . Alas, tonight she's going on another date with this one guy."

"Doing the 'dating' thing she was so keen on, eh?"

I nodded. "Seems like it."

"Does she know you're walking around under a lovesick rain cloud?"

I took a bite of my sandwich and threw him a look. "No," I mumbled. "Dick."

"She seems pretty great," he hedged carefully.

I wiped my mouth on my napkin and leaned back in my chair. *Great* didn't seem to cover it with Hanna. I hadn't known a girl like her, maybe ever. "Max, she's the entire package. Funny, sweet, honest, beautiful . . . I just feel so out of my depth on this." As soon as the words were out of my mouth, I could sense how foreign they sounded coming from me. A strange ringing silence filled the room, and I knew the wave of mockery was coming straight at me. It was evident in the little twitch of Max's lips.

Fuck.

He stared at me a beat longer before holding up a finger for me to wait, and pulling his phone out of his jacket pocket.

"What are you doing?" I asked, wary.

He shushed me, hitting speaker so we could both hear the call ringing. Bennett's voice answered on the other end: "Max."

"Ben," Max said, leaning back in his chair with a giant grin. "It's finally happened."

I groaned, resting my head on my hand.

"You got your period?" Bennett asked. "Congratulations."

"No, you twat," Max said, laughing. "I'm talking about Will. He's gone arse over tits for a girl."

A loud slap sounded in the background and I imagined Bennett's desk had just received a very enthusiastic high-five. "Fantastic! Does he look miserable?"

Max pretended to study me for a beat. "As miserable as they come. And—*and!*—she's going on a date with another bloke tonight."

"Oooh, that's rough. What's our boy up to?" Bennett asked.

"Looking like a sad sack of shite, is my guess," Max answered for me, and then raised his eyebrows as if I was allowed to answer now.

"Just hanging at home," I said. "Watching the Knicks. I'm sure Hanna will tell me all about her date. Tomorrow. When we go running."

Bennett hummed on the other end of the line. "I should probably inform the girls."

I groaned. "Don't *inform* the girls."

"They'll want to come over and mother-hen you," Bennett said. "Max and I have a dinner meeting anyway. We can't leave you alone in this pathetic state."

"I'm not pathetic. I'm fine! Jesus," I muttered, "why did I say anything?"

Ignoring me, Bennett said, "Max, I'll take care of this. Thanks for letting me know." And the line went dead.

Chloe pushed past me, into my apartment. Her arms were full of bags of takeout.

"Having some people over at my place tonight?" I asked. She threw me a look over her shoulder and disappeared into my kitchen.

Behind her, Sara lingered in the hall, holding a six-pack and some sparkling water. "I was hungry," she admitted. "I made Chloe order one of everything."

I pushed the door open wider to let her in and followed her into the kitchen, where Chloe was busy unpacking enough food for seventeen people.

"I already ate," I admitted, wincing. "I didn't realize you were bringing dinner."

"How can you think we weren't bringing dinner? Bennett said you were a hot mess. Hot mess means pad thai, chocolate cupcakes, and beer. Besides, I've seen you eat," she said, pointing to the cabinet where I kept my plates. "You can eat more."

Shrugging, I grabbed three plates, some silverware, and a beer. I eased back to the living room and set up our plates on the coffee table. The girls joined me, Chloe sitting on the floor, Sara curling up next to me on the couch, and we all dug in. We sat and ate in front of the television, watching basketball in comfortable, intermittent conversation.

After all of it, I was glad they were here. They didn't bother me with a thousand questions about feelings; they just came, ate with me, kept me company. Kept me from getting too lost in my own head. I was fairly certain it wasn't the first time someone I was dating was out on a date with someone else, but it was the first time it even occurred to me to care.

I was happy Hanna was out, having fun. That was the weirdest part of all of it—I wanted her to have what she wanted. I just wanted her to want only me. I wanted her to come over tonight, admit that she would prefer to just fuck me and quit this dating nonsense, and that would be that. It was ridiculous, and I was the world's biggest asshole for thinking it, especially since in the past I'd made a hundred girls feel just like I did now, but it's what I wanted.

And, fuck, I was restless. As soon as I finished eating, I began obsessively checking my phone, checking the clock. Why hadn't she texted? Didn't she even have one question she needed answered? Didn't she even want to say "hi"?

God I hated myself.

"Have you heard from her?" Chloe asked, correctly reading my fidgeting.

I shook my head. "It's fine. I'm sure she's fine."

"So what did Kitty and Kristy say?" Sara asked, putting her glass of water down on the table.

"To what?" I asked.

Silence filled the space between us and I blinked, confused. "To what?" I asked, again.

"When you *ended* things with them," Sara prompted.

Fuck. Fuuuuuuck.

"Oh," I said, scratching my jaw. "I haven't technically ended things."

"So, you're hung up on Hanna, but you haven't let your other two lovers know that you have sincere feelings for someone else?"

I picked up my beer, stared down into it. It wasn't just the hassle of going through the awkward let's-end-this conversation with Kitty and Kristy. If I was honest with myself, it was also partly about the security of the distraction they could provide if this whole thing with Hanna went downhill. That sounded like a dick move even to me.

"Not yet," I admitted. "It's all so casual. Who knows if a conversation is really needed?"

Chloe leaned forward, setting her bottle down and waiting until I looked her in the eye. "Will, I love you. I really do. You are going to be a part of our wedding; you will be a part of our family. I want the best things in the world to happen to you." She narrowed her eyes at me, and I felt my balls crawl up into my body. "But I still wouldn't tell a girlfriend of mine to take a chance with you. I'd tell her she should let you fuck her brains out, but keep her emotions out of it because you are a clueless little shit."

I winced, kind of chuckled, and shook my head. "That's refreshingly honest."

"I'm being serious. Yes, you're always open with your sex buddies. No, you don't have anything to hide. But what's your thing against relationships?"

Throwing my hands in the air, I said, "I don't have anything against relationships!"

Sara jumped in, saying, "You assume from day one that you won't want anything more than convenient sex," before continuing more gently, "and let me tell you, from a woman's point of view? When you're younger you want the boy who knows how to play the game but when you're older you want the man who knows when it's not a game anymore. *You* don't even know that yet, and you're, what? Thirty-one? Hanna may be young in years, but she's an old soul, and she's going to quickly figure out that your model isn't the right one for her. You're teaching Hanna how to balance multiple lovers but you should be teaching her what it feels like to be *loved*."

I smiled at her, and then rubbed my face with both hands, groaning, "Did you guys come over here to lecture me?"

Sara said, "No," at the same time that Chloe said, "Yes."

Finally, Sara laughed and said, "Yes." She leaned forward to put her hand on my knee. "You're just so clueless, Will. You're like our adorable, derpy mascot."

"That is awful," I said, laughing. "Don't ever repeat that."

We all turned back to the basketball game. It wasn't awkward. I didn't feel defensive. I knew they were right; I just wasn't sure what I could actually do about any of it, seeing as how Hanna was out with fucking *Dylan*. It was fantastic for me to be able to admit that I wanted more with her, and that I didn't want her out with another guy, but it one hundred percent did not matter as long as Hanna and I were on differ-ent pages about it. And the truth was, I wanted her to fuck only me, but I didn't really want things between us to change.

Did I?

I picked up my phone, checking to see if I'd somehow missed a text from her in the past two minutes.

"Jesus, Will. Just fucking *text* her!" Chloe said, throwing a napkin at me.

I stood abruptly, less to comply with Chloe's bossy shit and more to just *move*. What was Hanna doing right now? Where were they? It was almost nine. Shouldn't they be done with dinner by now?

Actually, given his track record, she was probably at home . . . unless they were at his place?

I felt my eyes go wide. Was it possible she was in his bed? Having sex with him? I closed them just as fast, jaw bulging as I remembered how she felt beneath me, her curves, the feeling of her knees pressed to my sides. And to think she might be with that weaselly kid? *Naked?*

Fuck that.

Turning, I walked down the hall toward my bedroom, stopping when my phone buzzed in my palm. I don't think even my knee-jerk reflex was as fast as my reaction to the lit screen. But it was only Max.

Your girl is here at the restaurant with me and Ben. Nicely done on the Project Hanna, Will. She looks bloody hot.

I groaned, leaning against the wall in my hallway as I typed. Is she kissing the kid?

No, Max replied. She keeps checking her phone though. Stop texting her, you little shit. She's "exploring life" right now, remember.

Ignoring his obvious attempt to rile me, I stared at the text, reading it again, and again. I knew I was the only person who regularly texted Hanna, and I hadn't sent her anything all night. Was it possible she was checking her phone as obsessively as I'd been checking mine?

I moved down the hall, slipping into the bathroom under the ruse of actually using it for its intended purpose and instead sitting on the edge of my tub. It *wasn't* a game with her. Sara was wrong there; I *knew* it wasn't a game. It wasn't even fun right now. My time away from Hanna oscillated wildly between exhilaration and obsessive anxiety. Is this what it was about? Taking this kind of risk, opening up and gambling on someone else's ability to tread carefully with your feelings?

My thumbs hovered over the letters for several pounding heartbeats and then I typed a single line, reading it over, and over, checking it for diction, tone, and the overall *no-big-deal-I'm-not-obsessing-about-your-night-or-anything* vibe of it. Finally, I closed my eyes, and hit SEND.

Chapter Nine

I was not going to text Will.

"... and then maybe live abroad someday ..."

I was not going to text Will.

"... maybe Germany. Or, maybe Turkey ..."

I blinked back to the conversation and nodded to Dylan, who sat opposite me and who had basically trekked the entire globe during our conversation. "That sounds really exciting," I said, smile stretched wide across my face.

He looked down to the linen tablecloth, cheeks slightly pink. Okay, so he was pretty cute. Like a puppy. "I used to think I'd want to live in Brazil," he continued. "But I love visiting there so much, I don't want it to ever feel familiar, you know?"

I nodded again, doing my best to pay attention and rein in my thoughts, to focus on my date and not the fact that my phone had been silent all night.

The restaurant Dylan had chosen was nice, not overly romantic but cozy. Soft lighting, wide windows, nothing heavy or too serious. Nothing that screamed *date*. I'd had the halibut; Dylan had ordered a steak. His plate was practically empty; I'd hardly touched mine.

What had he been saying? A summer in Brazil? "How many languages did you say you spoke again?" I asked, hoping I was close enough to the mark.

I must have been because he smiled, obviously pleased I'd remembered this detail. Or at least that such a detail existed.

"Three."

I sat back a little, genuinely impressed. "Wow, that's . . . that's really amazing, Dylan."

And that wasn't even stretching the truth. He *was* amazing. Dylan was good-looking and smart and everything an intelligent girl would be looking for. But when the waiter stopped at our table to refill our drinks, none of those things kept me from glancing quickly down to my phone again, and frowning at the blank screen.

No messages, no missed calls—nothing. Damn.

I swiped a finger over Will's name, and reread a few of his texts from earlier in the day. Random thought: I'd like to see you stoned. Pot amplifies personality traits so you'd probably talk so much your head would explode, though I don't know how you could possibly say even crazier things than you do now.

And another: Just saw you on 81st and Amsterdam. I was in a cab with Max and watched you cross the street in front of us. Were you wearing panties under that skirt? I plan on filing that away in the old spankbank so whatever you do, just say no.

The time stamp on his last message was just after one this afternoon, almost six hours ago. I scrolled through a few more before pressing the box to type, my thumb hovering over the keyboard. What could he possibly be doing? The phrase *or who* crept into my thoughts and I felt my frown deepen.

I started typing out a message and deleted it just as quickly. *I will not text Will*, I reminded myself. *I will not text Will. Ninja. Secret agent. Get the secrets, and get out unharmed.*

"Hanna?"

I looked up again; Dylan was watching me.

"Hmm?"

His brows drew together for a moment before he laughed a small, uncertain sound. "Are you okay tonight? You seem a bit distracted."

"Yeah," I said, horrified to have been caught. I lifted the phone from my lap. "Just waiting for a text from my mom," I lied. Horribly.

"But everything's good?"

"Absolutely."

With a small, relieved sigh, Dylan pushed his plate away and leaned forward, resting his forearms on the table. "So what about you? I feel like I've done nothing but talk. Tell me about the research you're doing." For the first time all night, I felt the grip on my phone lessen.

This I could do. Talk about my work and school and science? Hell yes.

We'd just finished dessert and my explanation of how I was collaborating with another lab in our department to engineer vaccines for *Trypansoma cruzi* when I felt a tap on my shoulder, and turned to see Max standing behind me.

"Hey!" I said, surprised to see him here.

He was about ten feet tall and yet when he bent to kiss my cheek, he didn't look awkward at all. "Hanna, you look absolutely smashing tonight."

Damn. That accent was going to kill me dead. I smiled. "Well, you can pass your compliments to Sara; she's actually the one who picked out this dress."

I wouldn't have thought it possible for him to get even more attractive, but the proud grin that stretched across his face did just that. "I'll do that. And who is this?" he said, turning to Dylan.

"Oh!" I said, turning back to my date. "Sorry, Max, this is Dylan Nakamura. Dylan, this is Max Stella, my friend Will's business partner." The two men shook hands and chatted for a moment, and I had to talk myself out of asking about Will. I was on a date, after all. I shouldn't be thinking of him in the first place.

"Well, I'll just leave you two to it, then," Max said.

"Tell Sara I said hi."

"Absolutely. Enjoy the rest of your evening."

I watched Max walk back to his table, where a group of men were waiting for him. I wondered if he was out for a business dinner, and if so, why hadn't Will gone with him? I realized I didn't know much about his job, but didn't they do this kind of stuff together?

A few minutes later, just as the bill came, my phone vibrated in my lap.

How's your night, Plum?

I closed my eyes, feeling that word vibrate through me like an electrical current. I thought back on the last time he'd called me that and felt my insides liquefy.

Fine. Max is here, did you send him to check on me?

Ha! As if he'd ever do that for me. And he just messaged. Said you look pretty hot tonight.

I'd never known I was much of a blusher before Will, but I felt the heat as it flashed through my cheeks. He looked pretty hot himself.

Not funny, Hanna.

You home? I hit SEND and then held my breath. What would I do if he said no?

Yes.

I was really going to have a talk with myself; knowing Will was home and texting me should not have made me quite so damn happy. Running tomorrow? I asked.

Of course.

Quickly wiping the smile from my face before Dylan noticed, I tucked my phone away. Will was home and I could rest easy and attempt to enjoy the rest of my night.

"So how was your date?" he asked, stretching beside me.

"Good," I said. "Fine."

"Fine?"

"Yeah." I shrugged, unable to get it up for a more enthusiastic response. "Fine," I said again. "Good." I felt decidedly worse about my Will codependency this morning than I did last night. I would need to get my act together and remember: *Secret agent. Like a Ninja. Learn from the best.*

He shook his head. "What a glowing review."

I didn't respond, instead walking to retrieve the water bottle I'd stowed against a nearby tree. It was cold—so cold the water had turned to slush and sloshed around as I tried to force it open. We were at the post-workout stage of our run, where Will would give me a pep talk and say something inappropriate about my boobs, and I would complain about the cold or the lack of easily accessible bathrooms in Manhattan.

And I really wasn't sure I wanted to have this conversation today, or admit that while I actually liked Dylan, I didn't daydream about kissing him or sucking on his neck or watching him come on my hip, like I did a certain someone else. I didn't want to tell him I was constantly distracted on our dates and having a hard time becoming invested. And I also refused to admit that I was failing at this whole dating thing, and might never learn how to keep things casual, enjoy life, be young, and experience things the way Will could.

He ducked to meet my eyes and I registered that he was repeating a question. "What time did you get back?"

"A little after nine, I think?"

"Nine?" he said, laughing. "Again?"

"Maybe a little later. Why is that so funny?"

"Two dates in a row end at nine o'clock? Is he your grandfather? Did he take you out for the early bird special?"

"For your information I had to run into lab early this morning. And what about your wild night, Player? Partake in any orgies? Maybe a rave or two?" I asked, intent on changing the subject.

"Kind of did the Fight Club thing," he said, scratching his jaw. "Except without the guys or the punching." At my confused stare, he clarified, "Basically, I had takeout with Chloe and Sara at my place. Hey, you sore today?"

I immediately remembered the delicious ache his fingers had left me with after Denny's party, and the way my pelvic bone felt almost bruised from grinding against him on the floor of his apartment.

"Sore?" I repeated, blinking quickly back to him.

He smiled knowingly. "Sore from yesterday's *run*. Jesus, Hanna. Get your mind out of the gutter. You were home by nine—what else *could* I possibly have been talking about?"

I took another pull from my water bottle, and winced at the cold on my teeth. "I'm good."

"Another rule, Plum. You can only use the word *good* so many times in a conversation before it becomes disingenuous. Find better adjectives to describe your state of mind post-dates."

I wasn't exactly sure how to handle Will this morning. He seemed a little edgy. I'd thought I had him figured, but my thoughts, too, seemed to be all over the place, a growing problem when we were together. Or judging by last night, when we were apart, too. Did he care at *all* that I'd been out with Dylan?

Did I want him to care?

Ugh. This dating thing was way too complicated, and I wasn't even sure whether Will and I were technically dating. It seemed to be one of the only questions I *couldn't* ask him.

"Well," he said, sliding his gaze to me with a teasing little smile. "Just so you're clear on the meaning of the word 'dating', maybe you should go out with someone else. Just to see how it all works. What about another one of the guys at the party? Aaron? Or Hau?"

"Hau has a girlfriend. Aaron . . ."

He nodded encouragingly. "He seemed pretty fit."

"He's fit," I agreed, hedging. "But, he's sort of . . . SN2?"

Will's brows pulled together in confusion. " 'SN2'?"

"*You* know," I said, waving my hands awkwardly. "Like when the C-X bond is broken, and the nucleophile attacks the carbon at one hundred-eighty degrees to the leaving group?" The words came out in a breathless rush.

"Oh, my God. Did you just use an O-chem reference to tell me Aaron looks better from the back than the front?"

I groaned and looked away. "I think I just broke some sort of nerd record."

"No, that was amazing," he said, sounding genuinely

awed. "I wish I thought of that about ten years ago." His mouth turned down at the corners when he considered this. "But honestly, it's awesome when you say it. If I said it, I would just sound like a giant dick."

I swallowed, most definitely *not* glancing down at his shorts.

Despite the dropping temperatures and early hour, more people than usual had decided to brave the cold. A cute pair of college guys kicked a soccer ball back and forth, dark beanies pulled down over each of their heads and Styrofoam cups of rapidly cooling coffee in the grass nearby. A woman with a giant stroller power-walked by us, and a handful of others ran along the various trails. I looked over just in time to see Will bend in front of me, reaching to tie his shoe.

"I've got to hand it to you. I'm really impressed with how hard you're working," he said to me over his shoulder.

"Yeah," I mumbled, moving to stretch my hamstrings the way he'd taught me, and most definitely not look at his ass. "Hard."

"What was that?"

"Hard work," I repeated. "Really hard."

He straightened and I followed the movement, forcing myself to blink away before he turned.

"Not going to lie to you," he said, stretching his back. "I was surprised you didn't punk out that first week."

I should have glared and been annoyed that he'd assumed I'd give up so quickly, but instead I nodded, attempting to look pretty much everywhere other than that strip of stomach that showed when he stretched his arms over his head or the line of muscle that cut down both sides of his abdomen.

"Might even place in the top fifty at the race if you keep it up."

My eyes darted across that small sliver of skin, and the landscape of muscle beneath it. I swallowed, immediately recalling what it felt like under my fingertips. "Definitely keeping it up," I mumbled, giving up and staring outright at his exposed skin.

Clearing my throat, I turned away from him and began walking back down the trail because honestly, that body was just *obscene.*

"So what time's your date tonight?" he asked, jogging to catch up.

"Tomorrow," I said.

He laughed beside me. "Okay, what time's your date *tomorrow?*"

"Um . . . six?" I scrunched my nose, trying to remember. "No, eight."

"Shouldn't you be sure?"

I slid my eyes to him, giving a guilty smile. "Probably."

"Are you excited?"

I shrugged. "I guess."

Laughing, he wrapped his arm around my shoulder. "What does he do again?"

"Drosophila stuff," I mumbled. He'd given me an opening to talk about science and I couldn't even get it up for that this morning. I was a mess.

"A genetics man!" he said in a playfully booming voice. "Thomas Hunt Morgan gave us the chromosome, and now labs across the country give other labs tiny, escapee fruit flies all over the building." He was trying to be jovial, but his voice was so deep and sexual, even when he geeked out, he only made my bones rattle, my limbs go all liquid. "And Dylan is nice? Funny? Great in bed?"

"Sure."

Will stopped, his look thunderous. *"Sure?"*

I looked up at him. "I mean, of course he is." And then his words sunk in. "Well, except the great in bed part. I haven't sampled the goods."

Will turned to keep walking, staying silent, and I chanced another look over at him. "Speaking of which, can I ask you a question?"

He glanced at me from the corner of his eye, wary. "Yes," he said slowly.

"What exactly is third-date etiquette? I googled it—"

"You *googled* it?"

"*Yes,* and the consensus seems to be that the third date is the sex date."

He stopped and I had to turn to face him. His face had gone red. "Is he pressuring you to have sex?"

"What?" I stared at him, bewildered. Where did he get that idea? "Of course not."

"Then why are you asking about sex?"

"Calm down," I said. "I can wonder what the expectations are without him having to be pushy about it. Good Lord, Will, I just want to be *prepared*."

He exhaled and shook his head. "You drive me insane sometimes."

"Likewise." I stared off into the distance, thinking out loud. "It just seems there's like some sort of progression chart. Dates one and two seemed pretty much the same. But how does one go from that to sex date? A cheat sheet would definitely make this less confusing."

"You don't need a cheat sheet. Jesus." He pulled his beanie from his head, pushed his hair back, I could practically see the wheels turning in his head. "Okay, so . . . the first date is sort of like the interview. He's scanned your resume"—he looked at me meaningfully and lifted his brows, eyes moving directly to my chest—"and now it's time to see if you live up to that. There's the field trip portion, the Q and A, the *could this person be a serial killer?* thought process, and of course, the *do I want to have sex with this person?* elimination decision. And let's be honest, if a man has asked you out he already wants to have sex with you."

"Okay," I said, eyeing him skeptically. I tried to imagine Will in this scenario: meeting a woman, taking her out, deciding if he wants to have sex with her or not. I was ninety-seven percent sure I didn't like it. "And date two?"

"Well, the second date is the callback. You've passed the preliminary screening—so the other party obviously likes what you bring to the table—and now it's time to follow up. To take it to human resources and see if your charming answers and sparkling personality were all just a fluke. And also to see if they still want to have sex with you. Which again . . ." he said, and shrugged as if to say *duh.*

"And the third date?" I asked.

"Well, this is where shit gets real. You've gone out twice and obviously still like the other person; they've met all your requirements so this is where it's all put to the test. You're compatible on some level and usually this is where you get naked, to see if you can 'work well together.' Guys usually up the stakes: flowers, compliments, romantic restaurant."

"So . . . sex."

"Sometimes. But not always," he stressed. "You don't have to do anything you don't want to, Hanna. *Ever.* I will remove the balls of any man who pressures you."

My insides went warm and fluttery. My brothers had said almost the same thing to me on different occasions and I can assure you, it sounded very different coming out of Will Sumner's mouth. "I know that."

"Do you *want* to have sex with him?" he asked, attempting to sound casual but failing miserably. He couldn't even look at me, and instead stared down where he was pulling at a string in the hem of his shirt. I felt a shiver move down my spine at the hint that he wasn't entirely okay with this.

I took a deep breath, thought about it. My first instinct was to rush to an automatic no, but instead, I just shrugged, noncommittal. Dylan was cute and I'd let him kiss me good night at my doorstep, but it was *nothing* compared to what I'd experienced with Will. And that was one hundred percent of my problem. I was pretty sure the reason Will made me feel good was that he was experienced. But that was exactly why he was off-limits.

"Honestly," I admitted. "I'm not even sure. I guess I'll just have to see how I feel when the time comes."

Any doubts I may have had about Will's third-date protocol were quickly put to rest as soon as Dylan and I stepped inside the restaurant I had chosen.

Dylan had wanted to take me somewhere I'd never been before—not hard considering I'd been in New York three years and barely left the lab to eat. He smiled proudly when the cab pulled up and deposited us at Daniel, at Park and Sixty-fifth.

If I'd been asked to draw you a picture of a romantic eatery, it would have looked exactly like this: cream walls, silvery grays and chocolate browns, arches and Grecian columns that skirted the main dining area. Round tables draped in sumptuous linens, vases of greenery everywhere and all of it set beneath giant glass light fixtures. The complete opposite of our second-date place. The stakes had been raised.

I was not prepared.

Dinner started off well enough. We selected appetizers and Dylan ordered a bottle of wine, but it had gone downhill from there. I'd promised myself that I wouldn't text Will but near the end when Dylan excused himself to go to the bathroom, I caved. I think I'm failing third date 101.

He answered almost immediately. What? Impossible. Have you seen your teacher?

He ordered some expensive wine and then seemed insulted when I didn't want any. You never care that I don't drink, I typed.

The icon appeared to show that he'd entered text—quite a bit of it if the amount of time it took was any indication—so I waited and looked around to make sure Dylan wasn't headed back my way.

That's because I'm a genius and can do basic math: I pour you half a glass, you pretend to drink it all night, and so the rest of the bottle's for me. Boom, smartest man alive.

Pretty sure he doesn't see it that way, I typed.

So tell him you're much more fun when you're actually awake and not drooling into your soup. Why are you texting me, btw? Where's Prince Charming?

Bathroom. We're leaving.

A full minute elapsed before he answered, Oh?

Yeah, my place. He's coming back, I'll let you know how it goes.

The ride back to my apartment was awkward. Stupid dating rules and expectations and Google, and stupid Will for getting in my head in the first place.

I didn't understand what was happening. I didn't really *want* Will. Will had a program of lovers and a shady past. Will didn't want attachments or relationships, and I at least wanted to be open to it. Will wasn't an option or part of the plan. I liked sex; I wanted to do it with another person again soon. Wasn't this how it happened? Boy meets girl, girl likes boy, girl decides to let boy in her pants. I was definitely ready to let someone into my pants. So where was the rush, the feeling of heat climbing up my legs and settling in my stomach, the ache I'd felt at the very *idea* of pulling Will into that bedroom? The feeling that had sent me out into the snow at 3 a.m. and the thought that I might explode the moment his hands found my skin?

I most certainly didn't feel that now.

The snow had just started to fall outside by the time we reached my building. Upstairs in my apartment, I switched on the lamp and Dylan hovered near the front door awkwardly for a moment before I invited him in. I was moving on autopilot. My stomach was in knots and the white noise in my head was so loud I wanted to turn on the most obnoxious music I could find just to block it out.

Should I? Shouldn't I? Do I even want to?

I offered him a nightcap—I actually said "nightcap"—to which he said yes. I moved to the kitchen, pulled down some glasses and poured a tiny bit for me, a large drink for him, hoping maybe it would make him sleepy. I turned to hand him his glass and was surprised to find him right there, completely in my space. A strange sense of wrongness seeped into my chest.

Dylan wordlessly took the glass from my hand and set it back on the counter. Soft fingertips brushed along my cheeks, over my nose. He took my face in his hands. His first kiss was tentative, slow and exploring. A small peck before he came back in for another. I closed my eyes tight at the first touch of his tongue, felt the racing of my heart and wished it had something to do with longing and lust, and not this clawing sense of panic that had started to build in my throat.

His lips were too soft and tentative. Pillow lips. His breath tasted like potatoes. I was aware of the ticking clock above the stove, the sound of someone yelling in an apartment nearby. Did I notice anything when I kissed Will? I noticed the way he smelled, the way his skin felt beneath my fingertips and the way it felt like I might explode if he didn't touch me *there* and deeper. But never anything as commonplace as the garbage trucks rumbling outside.

"What's wrong?" Dylan said, taking a step back. I touched my lips; they felt fine, not swollen or abused. Not thoroughly ruined.

"I don't think this is going to work," I said.

He was quiet for a moment, eyes searching mine, obviously confused. "But I thought—"

"I know," I said. "I'm sorry."

He nodded, taking another step back before running his hands through his hair. "I guess . . . If this is about Will, well, tell him congratulations."

⌖

I closed the door behind Dylan and turned, pressing my back to the cool wood. My phone felt heavy and leaden in my pocket and I pulled it out, found the name of He Who Effectively Hijacked My Brain, and started to type.

I started and erased a dozen different messages before finally stopping on one. I typed it and waited just a moment before I pressed SEND.

Where are you

Chapter Ten

Honestly, I had no idea what I was doing. I was walking—
walking like I had somewhere to be. But in reality, I didn't
have to be anywhere, and I *really* didn't need to be headed
directly to Hanna's apartment building.

Yeah, my place. He's coming back, I'll
let you know how it goes.

My hands formed fists at the memory of the text—the
words were burned onto my brain—and the image of her in
there, with Dylan. It made my chest literally ache. And I kind
of wanted to break everything I saw.

It was cold; so cold I could see my breath, and my fingertips were growing numb even shoved deep into my pockets. As soon as I got her text, I'd run out of the house, no
gloves, a too-light jacket, and running shoes, no socks.

For the span of seven city blocks, I was furious with her
for doing this to me. I'd been fine until she came fumbling

into my life with her chatterbox mouth and mischievous eyes. I'd been *fine* before she pushed her way into my easy routine, and I half wanted Dylan to get the fuck out of her apartment so I could go upstairs and tell her what a pain in the ass she was, how pissed I was at her for pulling the very stable, predictable ground out from under me.

But as I approached, and saw lights on in her window, saw the shadows of bodies upright and moving around, I felt only relief that she wasn't already prone on her bed, beneath him.

Pulling my hat farther down over my head, I growled through my teeth, looking along the street for a coffee shop, or something else to do. But there were only more apartment buildings, retail shops that had long since closed, and, in the distance, a little bar. The last thing I needed right now was alcohol. And if I was two blocks away from her apartment, then I might as well be home.

How long would I wait here? Until she texted me again? Until morning, when they emerged together, rumpled and smiling over their shared memories of the night before—of Hanna's perfection and Dylan's lame inexperience?

I groaned, looking up just in time to see a man leaving the apartment building, head bent into the wind, collar up. My heart tripped. It was definitely Dylan, and although my veins filled with the warm hum of relief, the fact that I could so easily recognize him from a distance made me feel like the creepiest asshole of all time. I waited to see if he was going to return, but he kept moving down the block, never slowing his pace.

That's it, I told myself. *You've crossed a line and need to find your way back to the other side.*

But what if she needed me? I should probably stay to make sure she was okay before walking home. I stared at my phone, brows drawn. If I left here, I was going for a run. I didn't care that it was almost eleven at night and freezing out; I was going to run for fucking miles. I was so buzzed with relief, and frustration, and nervous energy that I could barely steady my thumb long enough to click on the icon and open our text thread.

I exhaled when I saw that she was already typing something to me.

It felt like minutes, entire *minutes* during which I gripped my phone, staring intently and waiting for her message to appear. Finally it delivered, and instead of the paragraphs I was expecting, it said only, `Where are you`

I laughed, dragging my hand through my hair, and took a deep breath. `OK, don't kill me,` I typed. `I'm outside your apartment.`

Hanna came out of the building wearing a heavy down jacket over a silky blue dress, bare legs, and Kermit the Frog slippers. She shuffled toward me and I couldn't move, could barely breathe.

"What are you doing here?" she asked, stopping in front of where I sat, perched on a fire hydrant.

"I don't know," I murmured. I reached for her, pulling her closer and spreading my hands over her hips.

She winced a little when I squeezed—*what the fuck is going on with me?*—but instead of stepping away, she leaned closer. "Will."

"Yeah?" I asked, finally looking up at her face. She was fucking *beautiful*. She'd put on the smallest amount of makeup, had let her hair dry in soft, loose curls. Her eyes were heavy with the same look I'd seen when I'd been braced over her on the floor of my living room, or when I'd slid my fingers over the soft rise of her clit. When my attention focused on her mouth, her tongue peeked out, wetting her lips.

"I *really* need to know why you're here."

Shrugging, I leaned forward, resting my forehead against her collarbone. "I wasn't sure you were really into him, and it was bothering me knowing he came back here with you."

She slid her fingers under the collar of my jacket, stroking the back of my neck. "I think Dylan thought we were going to have sex tonight."

Without meaning to, I dug my fingers deeper into the flesh just above her hips. "I'm sure he did," I mumbled.

"But . . . and I don't know how to handle this, because it should be easy, right? It should be easy to enjoy being with people I like. I mean, I find him attractive. I have fun with him! He's nice, and thoughtful. He's funny, and he's good-looking."

I remained silent, trying not to howl.

"But when he kissed me? I didn't feel lost in him the way I get lost in you."

Pulling back, I looked up at her face. She shrugged, looking almost apologetic. "He was nice to me tonight," she whispered.

"Good."

"And he didn't even seem mad when I asked him to go."

"*Good,* Hanna. If he gave you grief I swear to God—"

"*Will.*"

I closed my mouth, calmed by her interruption, and waiting to hear what she needed. I would do anything she wanted, even if she asked me to crawl. If she asked me to leave, I would. If she asked me to help her zip her jacket, I'd do that, too.

"Come upstairs with me?"

My heart climbed into my throat. I watched her for a few seconds more, but she didn't take it back by breaking eye contact, or laughing at herself. She just studied me, waiting for my answer. I stood, and she moved back to give me space, but not too much space, because I was almost pressed against her once I was upright. She ran her hands down my sides, letting them come to rest on my hips.

"If I go up with you . . ." I started.

She was already nodding. "I know."

"I don't know if I can be slow."

Her eyes darkened and she pressed against me. "I *know.*"

———

A light was out on one side of the elevator, casting the space in a strange half shadow. Hanna leaned into the corner, watching me from where she stood at the dark end.

"What are you thinking?" she asked. Always such a little scientist, trying to dissect me.

I was thinking *everything:* wanting everything, and panicking, wondering if I was cutting the last thread of control I had over my emotions. I was thinking about what I was going to do to this woman when we got up to her bed. "A lot of things."

Even in the shadows, I could see her smile. "You want to be more specific?"

"I don't like that that guy came up to your apartment tonight."

She tilted her head, assessing me. "I thought that was part of dating. Sometimes guys will come up to my apartment."

"I get that," I murmured. "But you did ask what I was thinking. I'm telling you."

"He's a nice guy."

"I'm sure he is. He can be a nice guy who doesn't get to kiss you."

She stood up a little straighter. "Are you *jealous*?"

I stared at her, nodded.

"Of *Dylan*?"

"I don't relish the thought of anyone else having you."

"But all this time you're still seeing Kitty and Kristy."

I didn't bother to correct her yet. "What were you thinking when you were with him tonight?"

Her smile faded a little. "I was mostly thinking about you. Wondering if you were with someone."

"I wasn't with anyone tonight."

This seemed to throw her and she fell silent for what felt like forever. We reached her floor, the doors opened, hovered, and then closed with a small ding. The elevator car fell quiet and wouldn't move again until it was called.

"Why?" she asked. "It's Saturday. That's your night with Kristy."

"Why do you even *know* that?" I asked, tamping down the white-hot frustration with whoever told her this information. "And I was with you the last *two* Saturdays."

She looked down at her feet, thinking for a beat, and then back at me. "Tonight, I thought about what I wanted you to do to me," she said, adding, "and what I wanted to do to *you*. And how I didn't want any of those things with Dylan."

I took a step closer into the darkness, ran a hand up her side and over the curve of her breast. "Tell me what you want now. Tell me what you're ready for me to do."

I could feel the rise and fall of her chest as she breathed

faster. I ran the pad of my thumb over the tight peak of her nipple.

"You go down on me," she said, voice shaking a little. "You do it until I come."

"Obviously," I whispered, laughing a little. "When I do it, you'll come more than once."

Her lips parted, and she wrapped her hand around my wrist, pressing my palm more firmly against her breast. "You lean over me on the couch, jerking off, and come on my chest."

I was already so hard and *fuck*, that was a good visual. "What else?"

Shaking her head, she finally shrugged and looked away. "*Everything* else. Sex in all kinds of places on my body. How you like me to bite you, and how good it feels to do it. We're having sex and I'm doing everything you want and it isn't just good for me, it's good for you, too."

I lost my words for a beat, surprised by this. "Does that worry you? That I'm somehow *humoring* you?"

She looked up, met my eyes. "Of *course*, Will."

I stepped even closer so I was pressed against her and she had to tilt her head back to maintain eye contact. Angling my hips, I pushed the rigid shape of my erection into her stomach.

"Hanna. I don't know if I've ever wanted something more than I want you. I really don't think I have," I said. "I think about just kissing you, for fucking *hours*. Do you know that kind of kissing? Where it's enough for so long you don't even think of doing anything else?"

She shook her head, breath coming out against my neck in short, sharp bursts.

"I don't know about that kind of kissing, either, because I've never wanted just that before."

Hanna slid her hands under my jacket and beneath my shirt. Her hands were warm, and the muscles of my abdomen jumped and tensed beneath her fingers.

"I think about having you spread over my face," I said. "And taking you on the floor just inside my apartment because I can't wait long enough to get us anywhere more comfortable. I don't want to be with anyone else lately, and it means I spend an awful lot of time going for runs at random hours, or with my hand on my own dick wishing it was yours instead."

"Let's get out of the elevator," she said, pushing me gently through the opening doors and into the hallway.

She fumbled slightly with the key to her place and my hands shook as I reached for her sides, ran my palms from her waist to her hips. It took every ounce of self-control I had left to not take it from her and shove it into the lock myself.

When she finally got the door open, I pushed her inside, slamming it closed behind us and pressing her into the wall just a few steps in. I bent, sucking her neck, her jaw, running my hands under the skirt of her dress to feel the smooth skin of her thighs.

"You're going to have to tell me to stop if I move too fast."

Her hands shook as she slid them into my hair, dug her nails into my scalp. "I won't."

I kissed up her chin to her mouth, sucking and licking, tasting every millimeter of her soft lips and sweet hungry tongue. I wanted her to lick me, suck marks into my chest and feel the bite of her teeth on my hips, my thighs, my fingers. I felt a little like a criminal unchained, sucking and biting at her, stepping away from her only long enough to pull our jackets off, tug my own shirt over my head, unzip her dress, and push it to the floor. With a flick of my fingers her bra came undone and she shrugged out of it, stepping into my arms. Her breasts pressed against my skin and I just wanted to rub on her, wild and fucking *inside* her already.

She pushed me back, taking my hand and leading me down the hall to her bedroom, throwing me a little smile over her shoulder.

Her room was tidy, sparse. A king bed was positioned against one wall, which, other than Hanna, was basically all I saw. She stood in only her panties, hair loose and soft around her shoulders as she looked from my chest, up my neck, to my face.

The room seemed to tick in the silence.

"I've thought about this so many times," she said, hands running up my stomach and then lightly tickling through the hair on my chest. She traced the patterns of the tattoo on my left shoulder, trailed her fingers down my arm. "God, it feels like I've been thinking about this forever. But actually having you here . . . I'm nervous."

"You have no reason to be nervous."

"It helps me when you tell me what to do," she admitted in a small voice.

I cupped her breast, lifting it and bending my head to suck the tight peak into my mouth. She gasped, hands sliding into my hair. I smiled into a sharp bite at the full curve below her nipple. "You could start by taking off my pants."

She unfastened my belt, tugged the buttons free on my jeans. I'd grown obsessed with the memory of the way her hands shook when she was excited like this, a little nervous, too. I studied her almost-naked body in the dim street light filtering in from outside: her neck and breasts, the dip of her waist, curved hips and long, soft legs. I reached forward, ran two fingers down her navel and between her thighs, gliding over the fabric of her underwear.

Sliding a knuckle beneath the lace and through the heady slickness there, I whispered, "I love your skin, love feeling your wet."

"Step out of your pants," she said, coyly. "You can touch me all night."

I blinked, realizing my jeans were pooled around my ankles and I stood only in my boxers. She hadn't taken those off; whether she was nervous still, or just wanted one more chance to remove something, it was all fine with me. I pulled my feet free and walked her backward to her bed, urging her down. She inched back, pushing toward the headboard as I crawled over her. Hanna's gray eyes were wide and clear— my thrilled, breathless prey.

Her panties were light blue, accentuating the creamy color of her skin, making her look like she was made of blown glass. Only the tiny freckle on her navel hinted that she was even remotely real.

"Did you wear these for him?" I asked before my brain had time to think better of it.

She looked down at the lace, and I moved my eyes up to her full, plump breasts as she said, "I didn't even let him take my shirt off. So, I don't think I wore them for him."

I kissed down her belly to the elastic hem of her under-wear. Hanna had never been timid, or flighty, but this was all new. She was propped on her elbows, watching. Beneath where I was braced over her, she was trembling, her heart beating so fast I could see the trip of her pulse in her neck. This didn't feel like our standard game of How to Play Sex-bomb, didn't have that veneer. This felt too real, and Hanna looked too perfect lying almost naked in front of me. I'd kick my own ass for an eternity if I ever fucked this up. "Well, then I'll pretend that you wore them for me."

"Maybe I did."

I pulled at the elastic with my teeth, releasing it with a sharp snap against her hip. "And I'll pretend that whether you're naked or clothed, you're always thinking about me."

She looked up at me, gray eyes wide and searching. "Lately, I think I am. Does that worry you?"

Looking up the length of her body, I asked, "Why would it worry me?"

"I know what this is about, Will. I don't expect you to be anything you're not."

I had no idea what she meant; in truth I had no idea what this could or couldn't be, and for once I didn't want to define it before it even started. Inching up so my face hovered just over hers, I bent to kiss her, whispering, "I don't know where to start."

I felt wild and a little rough, wanting to eat her and fuck her and feel those lips around me. I had a flash of fear that this was all a fleeting moment, a single night, and I had to find a way to condense everything into a few hours. "I'm not going to let you sleep."

Her eyes widened, and she gave me a tiny smile. "I don't want to sleep." Tilting her head, she said, "And start with the first thing I told you in the elevator."

I kissed my way down her neck, chest, ribs, stomach. Every inch of her was tight and smooth and twitching under my lips, *wanting*. She never closed her eyes, never once. I'd been with women who watched, but it had never felt like this, so fucking intimate and connected.

As I got closer to the space between her legs, I could see her muscles tense, heard her breath hitch. I turned my head, sucked on her inner thigh. "I'm going to lose my fuck-ing *mind* with my mouth on you."

"Will, tell me what to do," she said, her voice tight. "I've never . . ."

"I know. You're perfect," I told her. "You like watching?"

She nodded.

"Why, Plum? Why do you watch everything I do?"

She hesitated, holding back some truth in a little swal-low. "You know how to . . ." She let the words trail away, ending the thought with a one-shouldered shrug.

"You mean you like to watch me because I know how to make you come?"

She nodded again, eyes widening as I pulled at her pant-ies, sliding them down over her hips.

"You can make yourself come with your hand. Do you watch your hand when you touch yourself?"

"No."

I pulled her underwear the rest of the way down her legs, tossing them behind me and onto the floor before returning to the stretch of mattress between her spread legs.

"You have a vibrator?"

She nodded, eyes dazed.

"*That* can make you come. Does looking at your vibrator make you this wet?" I dipped a finger inside, raising myself up and over her again, slipping the same fingertip into her mouth. She moaned, sucking hard and pulling me closer to kiss her instead. Her lips tasted like sex and heat and, *fuck*, I wanted to taste her directly. "Is it because you like watching me do this to you?"

"Will . . ."

"Don't go shy on me now." I kissed her, sucking on her bottom lip. "Are you being a little engineer, watching the mechanics of how a man would lick your pussy? Or is it the image of *my* mouth doing it?"

She ran her hands down my chest and wrapped them around my cock through my boxers, giving me a slow, hard squeeze. "I like watching *you*."

Groaning, I managed to say, "I like when you watch me. I can't think straight when you have those crazy gray eyes on me."

"Please . . ."

"Now let go so you can watch my mouth."

"Will," she said, voice shaking.

"Yeah?"

"After this? Please don't break me."

I paused, searching her expression. She'd sounded scared, but her face was only hunger.

"I won't," I said, kissing down her neck, over her breasts, sucking, nipping. I moved farther down her body, and her thighs shook as I pushed them apart, blowing a soft stream of air across her heated flesh.

She propped herself up on her elbows again, and I gave her one more smile before dipping my head and opening my mouth over her sweet slide of skin. My eyes rolled closed at the heat of her, and I groaned, sucking gently.

With a shaky cry, her head fell back, hips arching from the bed. "Oh *God*."

I smiled into her, licking up one side and down the other before covering her clit with my tongue, circling over and over and over.

"Don't stop," she whispered.

I wouldn't. I *couldn't*. I added my fingers, sliding them lower to where she was wettest and sweetest, and the heavy drag of my touch as I pushed two fingers into her caused her to fall back, reach blindly for the headboard. As I watched, she turned her head, pulled the pillowcase between her teeth, tugging. Tiny sounds of pleading misery and pleasure slipped from her lips and I did everything I could to not let up on the intensity of it for a single fucking second.

She was right there, hovering at the edge. Fucking her with two fingers, I pushed them deep, sucking her so hard my cheeks hollowed, staring up the length of her body at her fucking perfect breasts and long neck. With a twist of my wrist, she arched off the mattress, pushing into my mouth. Hanna let out a cry again and again as she contracted around my fingers.

One.

I was so hard I was practically fucking the mattress, and I could feel the tightening of the tendons in her thighs, relished the way her sounds became strained and higher and her hands reached down, threading into my hair and *fuck,* she started to rock into me, legs wide and hips fast, unself-consciously fucking my face for several long, perfect minutes. Oral sex had never felt so much like *fucking* as it did with this woman, and I gave into it, wild and wide open, roughly devouring her.

With a cry she came again, sweet and hot, her hands pulling so hard on my scalp I thought I might come right along with her. I couldn't close my eyes, couldn't for one second look away from the sight above me on the bed. I sucked and sucked on the silk of her skin, completely fucking lost in the feel of her.

"Please," she gasped, legs shaking and eyes as dark and heavy as I'd ever seen them. She pushed up on one elbow, leaving the other pulling at my hair. "Come up here."

I pushed my boxers down, dragging the weight of my cock against her leg as I slid up her body, tasting, licking the dip of her belly button, the rise of her breasts, the tight pull of her nipples.

I wanted to fuck every part of her: the valley between her breasts and the sweet fullness of her mouth, her round backside, and her soft, capable hands. But right now I wanted only to slide into the warmth of her sex. Her legs spread wider as she reached for her bedside table, for a box of condoms. I stared at the flush blooming across her chest, absently pulling along the length of my cock, until I registered she was extending the box to me.

"Let's just start with one." I chuckled.

Pushing the box into my hand, she nodded, eyes wide and pleading.

"So get one out," I growled.

"I don't know how to put it on," she whined sweetly, fingers fumbling to open the packaging. She opened it messily, cardboard ripping wide open, and a snake of condoms spilled out onto her stomach.

I tore a single packet from the train and handed it to her, pushing the others onto the bed beside her. "It's not complicated. Take it out, roll it down my dick."

Her hands shook, and I hoped it was anticipation rather than nerves but I was quickly relieved when she reached for me, hungrily, and covered the head of my cock with latex.

But I knew immediately it was on the wrong way; it wouldn't unroll.

She realized it after several painful seconds, tossing it away with a little growl and a "damnit!" before grabbing another packet.

I was hard and swollen and so fucking ready I could feel my teeth grinding as she pulled the second condom out, studying it closely, and this time put it on the right way. Her hands were warm and her face was so close to my cock, I could feel her excited breath on my thighs.

I needed to fuck her.

She unrolled it awkwardly, fingers too tentative and light, and the whole process seemed to take an eternity. She slid it over me in tiny increments as if I were made of glass and not about to fuck her so hard the bed would drop into the apartment below us.

When she reached the base of my cock, she exhaled in relief, lying back and pushing her hips to me. But with an evil smile, I pulled the condom off and tossed it away.

Gritting my teeth through my agony, I told her, "Again. Don't be so tentative. Put the condom on my dick so I can *fuck* you."

She stared up at me, silver eyes full of confusion. And finally, they cleared as if she'd been able to hear my thoughts: *I don't want you to have a single second of uncertainty. I am as hard as I have ever been in my life, I just sucked your pussy until you were screaming, and I'm not fucking delicate.*

With her eyes on mine, she lifted the package to her teeth, tore it open, and pulled out the roll of latex. Feeling the shape, she turned it in her hand, rolled it down my length smoothly, quickly, giving me a rough squeeze at the base. She slid her hand down lower, pulled gently on my balls, and then slid her hand to my inner thigh.

"Good?" she whispered, stroking the sensitive skin there, no smile, no frown, simply needing to know.

I nodded, reaching to run my thumb over her cheek. "You're perfect."

With a relieved smile she leaned back and I followed, sliding through the heat of her sex, teasing her, teasing myself, and *fuck,* I was dizzy with how much I wanted her. My hips were tense, ready to arch and thrust, spine already itching with the need to explode inside this woman.

I was unprepared for the feeling of my bare chest fully over hers, her thighs slipping around my hips. It was too much. *Hanna* was too much.

"Put me inside you."

She gasped, slipping her hand between us; I hadn't given her much space. I was lying heavily on her, warm skin to warm skin, but she found me, guided me up until I could feel the dip of her entrance, and then she led me higher, slipping and teasing my cock over the slick rise of her clit, the soft warm folds of her sex.

"I might be rough."

She exhaled a burst of air, breathlessly telling me, "Good. Good."

Pushing onto my hands, I watched as she rubbed me over her skin. Her eyes fell closed and a small moan slipped from her. "It's just . . . it's been a while," she whispered.

I pulled my eyes up to her face, watching her lick her lips, her lashes flutter open so she could look down at the space between us, watch herself play with me.

"How long?" I asked.

She blinked back up at me again, her hand stilling between us. "About three years." Her forehead wrinkled slightly as she said, "I've had sex with five guys but probably only had sex about eight times. I *really* don't know what I'm doing, Will."

I swallowed, bending to kiss her jaw. "Maybe I won't be so rough then," I whispered, but she laughed, shaking her head.

"I don't want you to be gentle, either."

I looked at her breasts, her belly, where she held me between her legs. I wanted to feel her bare skin on my cock. I'd never in my life had sex without a condom and wanted to feel her so much it hardened me further. "I'll make it good," I spoke into the skin of her neck. "Just let me feel you."

Hanna jerked beneath me, pressing me into her opening, her eyes fluttering closed as I shifted forward.

A hot flush crawled up her neck and her lips parted in a sweet sigh. It was overwhelming for me to watch her process what we were about to do, and I could see the moment when it happened, when it *really* hit her that we were about to have sex. She opened her eyes again, and her gaze fell to my lips and went softer, calmed momentarily from the frenzy. She ran her hands up my chest and cupped my neck, whispering, "Hey."

That look, that tenderness in her eyes, made me realize for the first time what was happening to me: I was falling in love.

"Hey," I rasped, bending to kiss her.

It was a relief so enormous it wrung the air from my lungs, and I deepened the kiss, wondering whether she could feel from my touch that I had just put a name to what we were doing—making love—or if she simply tasted her sex on my tongue, and didn't understand that my entire world had just spun free of its programmed orbit.

I pulled my face back but pushed my hips forward, aching to feel the softness of her body fully pressed to mine; I just wanted to get inside her and stay deep.

Fuck.

Good, hot, holy fuuuck.

She looked up at me as I slid deeper, but she no longer seemed to be able to see my face. Her eyes were glazed, overwhelmed, and tiny little inward gasps accompanied her every inhale. A tight twinge of pain passed over her face. I was only a few inches in, and it was tight, but it was so fucking good.

I heard my own voice come out but it sounded faraway: "Open up for me, Plum. Move with me."

Hanna relaxed, lifting her legs higher up her sides so I slid in deeper, and we both let out a taut moan. She gave her hips an experimental roll, pulling me fully inside, and the sensation of her warm thighs pressed to my hips caused me to let out a loud grunt.

"I can't believe we're doing this," she whispered, stilling below me.

"I know." I kissed her jaw, her cheek, the corner of her lips.

She nodded, pushing up, unconsciously telling me with her body that she needed me to move.

I pulled back, starting an easy rhythm, getting lost in the feel of her warmth. I would pick up my pace, sucking savagely on her neck, growing wild and heated and then slow, and eventually stop, kissing her deeply, relishing the way her hands explored my back, my ass, my arms, my face.

"You okay?" I asked, moving—but slowly—again. "Not too sore?"

"I'm good," she whispered, turning into my hand when I swept some damp hair off her forehead.

"You look so fucking perfect under me."

I wanted to build the need in her, make her go off like a bomb when she finally came with me inside her like this. She started to shake when I sped up, but growled in tight frustration when I slowed again. But I knew she trusted me, and I wanted to show her how fucking good it could be if there was no rush, no need to do anything but this for hours, and *hours*.

I kissed her, sucked on her tongue, stole every one of her sounds into my mouth, swallowing them like a greedy fucking bastard. I loved her hoarse noises, how often she said *please*, how much she let me drive what we were doing. The reality of *her*, sweaty and pliable beneath me, ate away at my calm, and I shifted from lazy pushing into quicker, hungrier thrusts. She answered with mirrored movements of her hips, arching into me, and I knew this time she was close and I couldn't stop or slow.

"Feel good?" I ground out, pressing my face to her neck.

She nodded, unable to answer, hands gripping my ass and fingernails digging sharply in my flesh. I pulled her leg up, pushing her knee to her shoulder and let go, fucking her as fast and hard and close to her body as I could.

It was wild, unreal, *explosive* the way her orgasm built beneath her skin first as a flush, and then a tightening of her muscles until she was shaking, and sweaty and begging unintelligible words beneath me, preparing to come.

"That's it," I whispered, struggling to hold back my own release even as it itched low in my belly. "Fuck, Plum, you're right there . . ."

I watched her eyes squeeze closed, her mouth open, and her body bow off the bed as she screamed in climax. I moved through it, giving her every single second of pleasure I could possible wring from her body.

Her arms fell away, leaden, and I propped myself up on my hands, looking down at where I moved in her, feeling her eyes on my face.

"Will," she exhaled, and I heard the languid glee in her voice. "My *God*."

"Fuck, it's so good. You're so wet."

She reached up, slid her finger into my mouth so I could taste her sweetness. I moved one hand between us, rubbing her clit, knowing she was going to be sore soon, but needing to feel her come around me one more time.

After only a few minutes she arched, hips rocking faster with me. "Will . . . I . . ."

"Shh," I whispered, watching my hand move over her, my cock slide in and out. "Give me one more."

I closed my eyes, my mind diving down into pure sensation: her quivering thighs all around me, the rhythmic tightening of her pussy as she came again with a hoarse, surprised cry. I cut the last chain of my self-control, hitting deeper and harder, prolonging her release with my thumb pressed to her clit. Hanna's head was thrown back into the pillow, hands on my ass, pulling me forward while she rocked up into me. Her eyes were squeezed shut, lips parted, and all around her head, her hair was a wild mess on her pillow. I'd never seen anything more beautiful in my life.

She dragged her nails up my back, watching my face, fascinated. The sensation was too much: her rough touch, soft body beneath, and her wide-eyed, fascinated study.

"Tell me it feels good," she whispered, lips swollen and wet, cheeks flushed, hair matted with sweat.

"So good," I hissed in a rush. "I can't . . . I can't fucking think straight."

Her nails pushed down, in a rough pinch and in a flash I knew with the pain of her nails and sweet pleasure of her body wet and squeezing me, I wasn't going to last. Pleasure flooded my veins, hot and frantic.

"Harder," I begged.

She curled into me, biting down my shoulder to my chest. "Come," she gasped, dragging her nails possessively down my back. "I want to *feel* you come."

It was as if I'd been plugged into an outlet, every inch of my skin alive and buzzing with heat. I stared down at her: breasts moving with the force of my thrusts, skin sweaty and perfect, angry red bite marks from my teeth all over her neck, shoulders, and jaw. But when I looked up and met her eyes, I lost it. She was staring at me and it was her— *Hanna,* this girl I saw every morning and fell in love with a little bit more every single time she opened her mouth.

It was so fucking *real.* With a loud shout, I collapsed on her, bucking wildly and flooded with a pleasure so intense I barely registered the warmth of her arms around my shoulders, the press of her kiss to my neck when I stilled on top of her, or the way she whispered, "Stay on top of me like this forever."

"Don't ever stop being so fucking open," I murmured, pulling my gaze to her face. "Don't stop asking for what you want."

"I won't," she whispered. "I got you tonight, didn't I?"

And just that simply, I was claimed.

Chapter Eleven

I woke to the shifting of the mattress, the sound of springs as Will climbed out of bed.

Dim, blue light seeped through the window and I blinked into the darkness, trying to make out the shape of objects nearby—the doorway, my dresser, his silhouette disappearing through the bathroom door.

Without switching on a light, I heard the water start, the shower door opening and closing again. I considered joining him but seemed unable to move: my muscles felt like rubber, my body heavy and sinking into the mattress. There was a deep, unfamiliar ache between my legs and I stretched, squeezing my thighs together to feel it again. To remember. Now my room smelled of sex and Will and I could feel myself grow dizzy from it, from his proximity and the thought of so much of his naked skin just on the other side of the wall. Arms, legs, a stomach like granite. What exactly was the protocol here? Was I lucky enough that he'd come back and we'd do it all over again? Is that how this worked?

My thoughts drifted to Kitty and Kristy and I wondered whether last night was just like all the other nights he'd spent with numerous other women. If he held them the same way, made the same sounds, offered the same promises of how good he'd make them feel. Will didn't spend every night with me, but we did spend a lot of them together. When did he see them? A part of me wanted to ask, so I could know the specifics of how he slotted all of us into his life. But a bigger part of me didn't, not really.

I ran my hand through my tangled hair and thought of last night: of Dylan and our disastrous date, of Will, and how it felt to realize he'd been just outside my apartment. Worrying. Waiting. Wanting. Of the things we'd done and how he'd made me feel. I'd never known sex could be like that: both hard and soft and alternating between the two for what felt like *forever*. It was wild; his hands and teeth left me deliciously bruised, and there were moments I thought I might break into a million pieces if I couldn't get him even deeper into me.

The familiar squeak of the faucet sounded above the pounding spray and I turned my head toward the door. The water slowed before the shower fell silent, and I listened as he stepped out, pulled a towel from the rack on the wall, and dried himself off.

I couldn't pull my eyes away as he walked out, his naked body moving through a slice of moonlight. Sitting up, I crawled to the edge of the bed. He stopped just in front of me, his cock lengthening as I stared.

Will reached up, running his fingers carefully through my tangled hair before drawing a line down the side of my face and, finally, tracing my lips with his fingertip. He didn't duck down to look me in the eye. It was as if he knew I was studying him. As if he *wanted* me just to look.

I swear I could hear my heart hammering in my ears. I wanted to touch him. I wanted, more than that, to *taste* him.

"You look like you want to put your mouth on me," he said, his voice thick and hoarse.

Swallowing heavily, I nodded. "I want to see how you taste."

He slid his hand down his length and he took another step closer, sweeping the head of his cock across my lips, painting me with the bead of moisture there. When my tongue darted out to taste it—and him—he let out a low groan, letting his hand slide up and down the base as I slipped my mouth around the tip, licking a little.

"Yeah," he whispered. "That's so . . . *so* good."

I don't know what I was expecting but it wasn't this, to be so turned on by the actual act, or how empowering it was to be the person who made this gorgeous man unravel. His hands moved to my hair and I closed my eyes. His breaths were ragged as I moved my mouth farther and farther onto him. Finally, I heard him swallow and then gasp with a shaky inhale.

"Stop, stop," he said, and took a step back. He sounded

like he'd been running a marathon. "You have no idea how much I'd love to let you play with me like this, your tongue and fuck, those lips, Hanna." His thumb brushed over my chin. "But I want to be careful with you the first time you take me in your mouth, and right now I feel too wild, and too fucking greedy."

I knew exactly how he felt. My body hummed, my pulse hammered in my neck, and I squeezed my thighs together again, feeling the sweet, impatient ache grow with every second.

He leaned down, kissed me, and whispered, "Roll over, Plum. I want to fuck you facedown."

I could only nod, moving to lie on my stomach, my mind too hazy to even come up with a response. The bed dipped and I felt him behind me, settling between my parted legs. His hand moved along the back of my thighs, over my ass. He gripped my hips, fingerprints burning into my skin as he pulled me to my knees and farther down the bed, closer to where he wanted. I could feel how wet I was, feel it on his fingers as he moved them against me, on my thighs. My heart hammered in my chest and I tried to shut out everything but the heat of his skin, the brush of his lips and hair along my back.

I'd always understood why women wanted Will in the first place. He wasn't beautiful in the same way Bennett was, and he wasn't tender like Max. He was visceral and imperfect, dark and *knowing*. He gave the sense that he looked at a woman and in an instant read every need she had.

But now I knew why women truly lost their mind over him. Because in the end, he *did actually* know every need a woman had, that I had. He'd ruined me for any other man, even before the first touch. And when he leaned in behind me, dragging his lips across the shell of my ear—not a kiss, not exactly—and asked, "You think you'll scream when you come this time, too?"—I was *lost*.

He reached across me, pulling a condom from the pile. I heard the foil tear, the sound of it as he rolled it over himself. I could still remember what it looked like, that thin piece of rubber stretched impossibly tight around the length of him. I wanted him to hurry. Needed him to hurry and fuck me, make this ache go away.

"I can go deeper this way," he said, bending to kiss my back again. "But tell me if I hurt you, okay?"

Nodding frantically, I pushed back into his hands, wanting him to quell the frantic hunger inside me.

His palm was surprisingly cool and I gasped in surprise when he pressed it to my lower back, steadying me. Was I shaking? In the darkness I could see my hand against the stark white of the sheet, see the fabric twisted in my grasp, wound tight just like every part of me. "You just feel," he said as if reading my thoughts, his voice so deep it was more vibration than sound. "I just want to *take* right now, okay?"

I felt the solid muscle of his legs moving between mine, the tip of his cock as he positioned himself. With every slide of our skin across each other, I arched back, lifting my ass to change the angle and hoping that this time, *this time* he might slip inside.

I felt his mouth along my shoulder, down my back and around my ribs. It was still early, still cold in my room, and I shivered as the air landed on skin he'd just kissed, tasted, scraped with his teeth.

And when he whispered against the shell of my ear how amazing I looked from his vantage, how badly he needed me, it seemed like my heart might burst through my ribs. It was so different like this, when he was behind me, out of sight. I couldn't rely on his overwhelmed expressions and the reassurance of his steady gaze on my face. I had to close my eyes and pay attention to his hands, how they shook, how rigid he felt when he slid forward across my clit. I listened to his choppy breathing and tiny grunts, pressed back into him and felt my chest twist in pleasure when the contact between his thighs and my ass made him moan.

He was so thick, so *stiff,* and my breath caught as he shifted back so he could position himself against my tender skin, and—*finally*—slowly inch inside.

"*Oh,*" I said, a sound that felt like it must have been torn from my throat because it was the only word I could think.

Oh I didn't know it would feel like this.

Oh it hurts but in the most delicious way.

Oh please don't ever stop. More, more.

As if I'd said those words aloud, Will nodded against my skin, moving slower, deeper. We'd only just started but it was already too good, too perfect. I felt the drag of him deep inside, so close to that place that brought me to the edge of a tiny explosion.

"Okay?" he asked, and I nodded, overwhelmed. He started to move, small stabs of his hips that pushed me farther up the mattress, pushed me closer to that point where everything inside me threatened to shatter. "Fuck, look at you."

I felt his hand on my shoulder and then in my hair, fingers wrapping in the strands to brace me, keep me just where he wanted. "Spread your legs wider," he grunted. "Drop to your elbows."

Immediately I did what he said, crying out at the depth of the position. Heat settled in my stomach and between my legs at the idea of him using my willing body to get off. I was positive I'd never felt sexier in my entire life.

"Knew it would be like this," he said, and I couldn't even comprehend the words. I felt like I might collapse and I slid my arms down farther, face pressed to the pillow and my ass in the air as he continued to fuck me. The fabric was cool against my cheek and I closed my eyes, tongue darting out to wet my lips as I listened to the sounds of our bodies moving together, his uneven breaths. He was so good, and I straightened my arms over my head, the tips of my fingers brushing along the headboard and my body stretched so fully beneath him that I felt like I'd been hammered too thin. Like I might snap in half when I finally came.

His damp hair tickled along my back and I imagined what he must look like: hovering above me, arms supporting his weight as he leaned over my shaking body, pushing into me again and again, the bed rocking beneath us.

I remembered when I used to hide under my blankets and imagine this very thing, touching myself, tentative and unpracticed until I came. It felt the same—every bit as dirty and forbidden but even better now, better than all the fantasies and all the secret dreams combined.

"Tell me what you want, Plum," he managed to say, his voice so hoarse it was almost inaudible.

"More," I heard myself say. "Go *deeper.*"

"Touch yourself," he rasped. "I'm not going without you."

I slipped my hand between the mattress and my sweaty body and found my clit, smooth and swollen. He was so close to me, close enough that I could feel the heat of each exhale and the slick of his skin. I could feel the tremble of muscle, note the way his breath changed and his sounds grew louder as he shifted the angle of his hips, drove so deep my spine arched sharply, involuntarily.

"Fucking *come* for me, Hanna," he said, hips speeding up.

It took only a moment, a few more circles of my fingers before I was coming, choking on sounds that got stuck in my throat and swallowed by a wave that hit me so hard I swore my bones were vibrating.

White noise filled my ears but I felt the slap of his skin against mine and the way he stiffened behind me, muscles growing tense before he groaned, low and long into my neck.

I was exhausted; limbs loose and joints feeling as if they might come apart at the seams. My skin was prickly with heat and I was so tired I couldn't bring myself to open my eyes. I felt Will reach for the base of the condom, grabbing it securely before pulling out. There was a shuffle before he climbed from the bed and moved to the bathroom, and then the sound of water again.

When the mattress dipped and the heat of him returned, I was barely conscious.

I opened my eyes to the smell of coffee, the sound of the dishwasher opening and the clank of dishes. I blinked up to the ceiling, the final remnants of sleep slipping from my brain as the reality of last night hit me.

He's still here, was my first thought, followed by *What the hell happens now?*

Last night had come easily; I'd shut off my brain and done what felt good, what I'd wanted. What I'd wanted was *him* and somehow, he'd wanted me in return. But now, with the sun pouring through the windows and the world awake and breathing outside, I was filled with uncertainty, unsure what our boundaries were or where we stood.

My body was stiff, sore in the most random places. I felt like I'd done a thousand sit-ups. My thighs and shoulders ached. My back was stiff. And between my legs I was throbbing and tender, as if Will had driven into me for hours and hours in the black of night.

Imagine that.

I eased myself off the bed, tiptoed to the bathroom, and carefully closed the door, hissing at the way the latch seemed to click too loudly.

I didn't want things to be weird between us, or to ruin the easy comfort we'd always had. I didn't know what I'd do if we lost that.

So with my teeth brushed and hair smoothed, I slipped into a pair of boy shorts and a tank and made my way out to the kitchen, intent on letting him know I could do this and that things didn't have to change.

He was standing in front of the stove in nothing but black boxers, his back to me, flipping what looked to be pancakes.

"Morning," I said, crossing the room and making a beeline straight for the coffeepot.

"Morning," he said, grinning down at me. He leaned over and twisted the fabric of my shirt in his hand, using it to pull me toward him for a quick kiss on the lips. I ignored the tiny, girlish flutter in my stomach and reached for a mug, careful to keep a long stretch of counter between us.

My mother had cooked breakfast for us every Sunday we spent on vacation in this kitchen, and had insisted the room be large enough to accommodate her ever-expanding family. The space was twice the size of any other in the building, with gleaming cherry cabinets and warm tile. Wide windows that overlooked 101st Street took up one wall; a large counter with enough stools for all of us filled another. The wide marble expanse of counter had always felt too big for the apartment, and a waste of space now that it was just me using this as a home. But with the memory of last night playing on a loop in my head, and with so much of his perfectly naked skin on display, I felt like I was in a shoe box, like the walls were closing in and pushing me closer and closer in this strange, sexy man's direction. I definitely needed some air.

"How long have you been up?" I asked.

He shrugged, the muscles of his shoulders and back flexing with the movement. I could see the edge of the tattoo that wrapped around his ribs. "A while."

I glanced at the clock. It was early, too early to be awake on a Sunday with no plans, especially after the night we'd had. "Couldn't sleep?"

He flipped another pancake, placed two others on a plate. "Something like that."

I poured my coffee, eyes trained on the dark liquid as it filled the mug, the steam as it twisted through a beam of sunlight. The counter was set, placemats and a plate for each of us, glasses of orange juice off to the side. I had a flash of Will with one of his *not girlfriends* and couldn't help but wonder if this was part of the well-honed routine: making his ladies breakfast before leaving them in their empty apartments with wobbly legs and dopey smiles.

With a small shake of my head I replaced the carafe, and straightened my shoulders. "I'm glad you're still here," I said.

He smiled, and scraped the last bit of batter from the bowl. "Good."

We stood in comfortable silence while I added sugar

and cream, then moved with my coffee to a stool on the other side of the counter. "I mean, I would have felt ridiculous if you'd left. This is easier."

He flipped the last pancake and spoke to me over his shoulder. "Easier?"

"Less awkward," I said with a shrug. I knew I needed to keep this casual, keep it from becoming a *thing* between us. I didn't want him to think I couldn't handle it.

"I'm not sure I'm getting you, Hanna."

"It's just easier to do this part now, the awkward *I've seen you naked* part, rather than later when we're trying to remember how we interact with our clothes on."

I watched him pause, staring down into the empty pan, obviously confused. He hadn't nodded or laughed, hadn't thanked me for saying it before he'd had to. And now I was the one clearly confused.

"You don't think all that highly of me, do you?" he said, finally turning to face me.

"Please. You know I think you practically walk on water. I don't want you freaking out or thinking I expect you to change anything."

"*I'm* not freaking out."

"I'm just saying that I know last night meant different things for each of us."

His brows pulled together. "And what was it to you?"

"Amazing? A reminder that even though I failed miserably with Dylan, I can have fun with a man. I can let go, and enjoy it, I know it probably didn't change who you are, but it feels a little like it changed me. So, thank you."

Will's eyes narrowed. "And who exactly am I, do you think?"

I walked over to him and stretched to kiss his chin. His cell phone buzzed where it sat on the counter, the name *Kitty* lighting up the screen. So that answered *that* question. I took a deep breath, gave myself a moment for all the pieces to line up in my head.

And then I laughed, nodding to where it continued to vibrate across the counter. "A man who's good in bed for a reason."

He frowned, reaching for the phone and shutting it off. "Hanna," he said, pulling me back toward him. He placed a lingering kiss on my temple. "Last night—"

I sighed at how easily we slotted together, at how perfectly my name was shaped by his mouth. "You don't have to explain, Will. I'm sorry I made it weird just now."

"No, I—"

I pressed two fingers to his lips, wincing. "God, you must hate the postsex processing and I don't need it, I swear. I can handle all of this."

His eyes searched my face and I wondered what he was looking for. Did he not believe me? I reached for his jaw and kissed him softly, feeling the tension slip from his body.

His hands came to rest on my hips. "I'm glad you're okay with this," he said finally.

"I am, I promise. No weirdness."

"No weirdness," he repeated.

CHAPTER TWELVE

The only reason I ever skipped a run was if I was deathly ill or on a plane headed somewhere. So Monday morning, I hated myself a little for shutting off my alarm and rolling back over into the pillow. I just had no interest in seeing Hanna.

But as soon as I had the thought, I had to consider its accuracy. I didn't want to see *Ziggy*, bouncing and chatting away as if she hadn't blown me apart two nights ago with her body and words and needs in the guise of *Hanna*. And I knew if Ziggy showed up this morning, acting like Saturday night never happened, it would wreck me a little.

I'd been raised by a single mother, with two older sisters who didn't give me any choice but to understand women, know women, *love* women. In one of the two serious relationships in my life, I'd talked to my girlfriend about the possibility that this comfort with women worked out pretty well for me when I hit puberty and ended up wanting to have sex with every girl I met. I think that girlfriend had been trying to not-so-subtly hint that I manipulated women by pretending to listen. I didn't probe the issue much; we broke up pretty soon after that.

But whatever my comfort with the opposite sex, it didn't seem to help me at all with Hanna. She felt like a separate creature, a separate *species*. She threw all my experience out the window.

Somehow, when I fell back asleep I started dreaming about fucking her on a giant pile of sports equipment. A lacrosse stick dug into my back but I didn't care. I just watched her rock on top of me, eyes clear and locked to mine, her hands moving up and around my chest.

My phone buzzed beneath me, wedged into my spine, and I woke with a start. Glancing at my clock, I realized I'd overslept; it was nearly eight thirty. I answered without looking, assuming it was Max asking me where the fuck I was for our Monday morning meeting.

"Yeah, man. I'll be there in an hour."

"Will?"

Fuck. "Oh, hey." My heart squeezed so tightly beneath my ribs that I groaned, and ran a hand over my mouth to stifle it.

"You're still asleep?" Hanna asked. She sounded out of breath.

"I *was*, yeah."

She paused, and the wind on the other end whipped through the phone line. She was outside *and* out of breath. She'd gone running without me. "Sorry to wake you."

I closed my eyes, pressing a fist to my forehead. "Don't worry about it."

She stayed quiet for a few long, painful seconds and in that time we had several different conversations in my head. One where she told me I was being a dick. One where she apologized for implying that I could be so cavalier about the intense night we had. One where she prattled on about nothing in particular, Ziggy-style. And one where she asked if she could come over.

"I went running," she said. "I thought you'd started and maybe I'd see you on the trail."

"You thought I started without you?" I asked, laughing. "That would be rude."

She didn't answer and I realized too late that what I had done—not shown up, not even bothered to call—was just as bad.

"Shit, Ziggs, I'm sorry."

She sucked in a sharp breath. "So I'm Ziggy today. Interesting."

"Yeah," I mumbled, and then hated myself immediately. "No. *Fuck*, I don't know who you are this morning." I kicked away my sheets, willing my groggy brain to wake the fuck *up* already. "It messes with my head to call you Hanna."

It makes me think you're mine, I didn't add.

Laughing sharply, she started walking again, the wind

whipping even louder through the receiver. "Get over your man-angst, Will. We had sex. You're supposed to do this kind of thing better than anyone. I'm not asking for a key to your apartment." She paused, and my heart dropped into my stomach as I understood how my distance was coming across to her. She assumed I was brushing her off. I opened my mouth to backpedal, but her words came out faster: "I'm not even asking for a repeat, you egomaniacal jerk."

And with that, she hung up.

———

I requested we move our regular group lunch from Tuesday to Monday on the basis that I'd lost my balls and my mind, and no one argued. It seemed that I'd reached a level of moony lovesickness that made giving me shit a lot less fun for my friends.

We met at Le Bernardin, ordered whatever we always ordered, and life seemed to move on as it had for the past nine months. Max kissed Sara until she batted him away. Bennett and Chloe pretended to hate each other over the salad she insisted they split for lunch, in some confusing form of flirty foreplay. The only thing that seemed different was that I drank my alcoholic lunch beverage in less than five minutes and then earned a raised eyebrow from our regular waiter when I ordered another.

"I think I'm the Kitty," I said once the waiter left. When conversation came to a screeching halt, I registered that my friends had been happily babbling on about whatever-thefuck while my brain was practically melting next to them.

"With Hanna?" I clarified, searching each of their faces for any sign of understanding. *"I'm* the Kitty. I'm the one saying I'm fine with just fucking around, but I'm not. I'm the one saying I'll be happy to fuck only on the third Tuesday of odd-numbered months just so I can be with her. She's the one who's like, 'Oh, I don't need to hook up again.'"

I was met with Chloe's flat palm held up in my face. "Hold up, William. You're *fucking* her?"

I sat up straight, eyes wide and defensive. "She's twenty-four, not thirteen, Chloe. What the *hell?*"

"I don't care that you're fucking her—I care that you've fucked her and she didn't call one of us immediately. When did this happen?"

"Saturday. Two days ago; settle down," I mumbled.

She sat back, expression softening somewhat.

Relaxing, I reached for my new drink almost as soon as the waiter put it in front of me. But Max was faster, pulling it out of my reach before I could get it. "We have an afternoon meeting with Albert Samuelson and I need you sharp."

I nodded, bending to rub my eyes. "I hate all of you."

"For being right?" Bennett correctly surmised.

I ignored him.

"Have you actually ended things with Kitty and Kristy?" Sara asked gently.

Fuck. This again.

I shook my head. "Why should I? There's nothing going on with Hanna."

"Except you have *feelings* for her," Sara pressed, eyebrows drawn together. I hated her disapproval. Of any of my friends, Sara only gave me shit when it was fully deserved.

"I just figure why create more drama right now," I reasoned, lamely.

"Has Hanna actually said that she doesn't want anything more with you?" Chloe asked.

"It's pretty obvious from the way she acted Sunday morning."

Already nodding, Max added, "I hate to state the obvious, mate, but why haven't you had the Will Sumner sit-down with her? Aren't you sort of proving the long-suffering point you always throw at us regarding your hookups: that it's better to discuss things up front than leave questions?"

"Because," I explained, "it's easy to have that convo when you know what you want and don't want."

"Well, what *do* you know?" Max asked, shifting to the side so the waiter could place his food down in front of him.

"I know I don't want Hanna fucking anyone else," I growled.

"Well," Bennett began wincing slightly, "what if I told you I saw Kitty clearly hooking up with someone else the other night?"

Relief inundated me. "Did you?"

He shook his head. "No. But your reaction sure is telling.

Fix things with Hanna. Figure your shit out with Kitty." Picking up his fork, he said, "And now shut up so we can eat."

———

I was up at five fifteen the next morning, waiting outside Hanna's apartment building. I knew that now that she had a taste for running she wouldn't miss a day. I had to fix things with her . . . . I just wasn't sure how to do it yet.

She drew up short when she saw me, eyes widening before she put on a calm, unaffected mask. "Oh, hi, Will."

"Good morning."

She started to walk past me, eyes straight ahead. Her shoulder brushed mine as she passed, and I could tell from the way she winced that it had been unintentional.

"Wait," I said, and she stopped but didn't turn around. "Hanna."

She sighed. "And today it's Hanna again."

I walked to where she stood, turning to face her and putting my hands on her shoulders. I didn't miss the way she shivered slightly. Was it anger or the same thrill at contact I felt? "It's *always* been Hanna."

Her eyes darkened. "It wasn't yesterday."

"Yesterday I fucked up, okay? I'm sorry I didn't show for our run, and I'm sorry I came off like a dick."

She watched me, eyes wary. "An *epic* dick."

"I know I'm supposed to be the one who knows what I'm doing here, but I'll admit that Saturday night was different for me." Her eyes softened, shoulders relaxing. I continued, my voice quieter, "It was intense, okay? And I realize that this sounds insane, but I was a little taken aback when you were so casual about it the next day."

I let go of her shoulders, stepping back to give her space.

She looked at me as if I'd sprouted the head of a lizard from my forehead. "How was I *supposed* to be? Weird? Angry? In *love*?" Shaking her head, she said, "I'm not sure what exactly I did wrong. I thought I handled it pretty well. I thought I acted just like *you* would have told me to if it was anyone else I'd had sex with." She blushed, hotly, and I had to push my hands into the pockets of my hoodie to keep them to myself.

I took a deep breath. This was the moment I could tell her, *I have feelings for you I haven't had before. I've been struggling with them since the first second I saw you, weeks ago. I don't know what these feelings mean, but I want to find out.*

But I wasn't ready for that. I looked up at the sky. I was clueless and had no idea what I was doing. For all I knew, this was nothing more than what I'd feel if I were having sex with anyone whose family I'd known forever; a protectiveness, a yearning to take caution with both of our feelings. I needed more time to sort things out.

"I've known your family for so long," I said, turning back to her. "It isn't the same as hooking up with some random person, no matter how much we want it to be casual. You're more to me than just someone I want to be sexual with, and . . ." I ran my hand over my face. "I'm just trying to be careful, okay?"

I wanted to punch myself. I was pussing out. Everything I'd said was true, but it was a flimsy half-truth. It wasn't only just about knowing her for so many years. It was wanting to know her, like this, for so many more.

She closed her eyes for a beat, and when she opened them, she was looking to the side, to some unknown point in the distance. "Okay," she murmured.

"Okay?"

Finally she looked up at me and smiled. "Yeah." Tilting her head in indication that we should get moving, she turned and soon our feet were slapping the pavement in an easy, steady rhythm, but I had no idea what conclusion we'd just reached.

It was gorgeous out, for the first time in months, and even though it was probably still under forty degrees, it felt like spring. The sky was clear, no clouds or gray shadows, just light, and sun and crisp air. Only three blocks from her house, I grew too warm, and I slowed slightly, pulling my long-sleeved thermal up and over my head and then tucked it into the back of my track pants.

I heard the sound of a toe butting into pavement, and before I knew what was happening, Hanna was sprawled out on the sidewalk, the wind knocked from her in a forceful gust.

"Holy crap, are you okay?" I asked, kneeling next to her and helping her sit up.

It was several long seconds before she could inhale and when she did, it was loud and desperate. I hated that sensation more than almost anything, getting all of the air knocked out of my lungs. She'd tripped on a large crack in the sidewalk and landed hard, her arms pressed to her ribs. Her pants were torn at one knee, and she was holding on to her ankle.

"Owwww," she groaned, rocking.

"Shit," I murmured, reaching behind her knees and around her waist, picking her up. "Let's get you home and ice that."

"I'm fine," she managed, struggling to keep me from lifting her.

"*Hanna.*"

Swatting at my hands, she begged, "Don't carry me, Will, you'll break your arms."

I laughed. "Hardly. You're not heavy, and it's three blocks."

She gave in, wrapping her arms around my neck.

"What happened?"

Hanna was quiet, and when I ducked my head to catch her eye, she laughed. "You took off your shirt."

Confused, I murmured, "I had another shirt on, you goof."

"No, I mean, the tattoos." She shrugged. "It's been cold. I've only seen them a couple of other times, but I saw *a lot* of them on Saturday, and it made me think . . . I looked over just now . . ."

"And *fell*?" I asked, laughing despite my better judgment.

Groaning, she whispered, "Yes. Shut up."

"Well, you can stare at them while I carry you," I told her. "And feel free to nibble on my earlobes while we walk," I whispered, smiling. "You know I like your teeth."

She laughed, but not for long, and as soon as I'd caught up with her and realized what I'd said the tension grew into a heavy *thing* between us. I moved down the sidewalk to her building and with every step in silence, the monster tension only grew. It was the unspoken *oh, right,* the way I'd so casually referenced how she knew what I liked in bed, the reality of where we were heading—her apartment, where we'd had sex all night long Saturday.

I dug around inside my head for what to say, but the only words that bubbled right near the surface were words about *us,* or that night, or her, or my own fucked-up brain. I put her down when we reached the elevator and I had to hit the up button. It arrived with a quiet ding, and I helped Hanna limp inside.

The doors closed, I hit the button for the twenty-third floor, and the lift jerked with the initial ascent. Hanna settled into the same corner she'd been in the last time we were in here together.

"You okay?" I asked quietly.

She nodded, and everything we'd said right here two nights ago filled the elevator car like smoke rising from the floor. *You go down on me. You do it until I come.*

"Can you move your ankle?" I asked in a rush, my chest tightening with how much I wanted to step closer, kiss her.

She nodded again, eyes locked to mine. "It's sore, but I think it's okay."

"Still," I whispered. "We should ice it."

"Okay."

The gears of the elevator creaked; something just above us in the elevator shaft slid into place with a loud thunk.

You lean over me on the couch, jerking off, and come on my chest.

I licked my lips, finally letting my eyes move to her mouth, my mind wander to the memory of how it felt to kiss her. The echo of her words was loud enough in my head that it was as good as if she'd said them aloud: *Sex in all kind of places on my body. How you like me to bite you, and how good it feels to do it.*

I stepped closer, wondering if she remembered saying, *We're having sex and I'm doing everything you want and it isn't just good for me, it's good for you, too.* And, if she did, I wondered if she could see in my eyes that it *had* been good, so good for me; it was making me want to kneel at her feet right now.

We arrived at her floor and I relented as she insisted on limping down the hall, needing to break the tension some-how. Inside her apartment, I grabbed a bag of frozen peas from the freezer and guided her to the bathroom, making her sit down on the toilet seat while I dug around under her sink for Bactine or some type of antiseptic. I settled for water and hydrogen peroxide.

Her pants were only ripped on one knee, but the other was scuffed enough to tell me that both knees were probably pretty scraped. I rolled up each pant leg, ignoring the way she swatted my hands away at the sight of the mild stubble on her legs.

"I didn't know you would be touching my legs today," she said, laughing a little.

"Oh, stop."

Dabbing at the cuts with a wet cotton ball, I was relieved to see they weren't too bad. They were bleeding, but there wasn't anything that wouldn't heal in a few days, and without stitches.

Finally, she looked down, straightening one leg as I cleaned up the other. "I look like I was walking around on my knees. I'm a *mess*."

I grabbed a couple of clean cotton balls and dabbed her cuts with hydrogen peroxide, trying—but failing—to tamp down a smile.

She leaned down to get a better look at my face. "You are such a pervert, smiling at my scraped knees."

"*You're* such a pervert, knowing why I'm smiling."

"You like the idea of getting my knees all scraped up?" she asked with a growing smile of her own.

"I'm sorry," I said, shaking my head with absolute insincerity. "I *really* do."

Her smile dissolved slowly and she ran a finger over my chin, studying the little scar there. "How did you get this?"

"Happened in college. A woman was giving me head and freaked out and bit down on my dick. I slammed my face into the headboard."

Her eyes widened in horror: her worst oral sex nightmare realized. "*Really*?"

I burst out laughing, unable to keep up the story any longer. "No, not really. I was hit in the face with a lacrosse stick in the tenth grade."

She closed her eyes, pretending she wasn't amused, but I could see her swallow a laugh. Finally, she looked back down at me. "Will?"

"Mmm?" I put down the last cotton ball and screwed the cap back on the hydrogen peroxide bottle as I blew gently across the cuts. Once I had it all clean, I didn't even think she would need a Band-Aid.

"I heard what you said about wanting to be careful because of our history. And I'm sorry that I came off as too casual."

I smiled at her, absently running my hand slowly down her calf, before realizing how familiar that was.

She sucked on her bottom lip for a beat before whispering, "I've thought about Saturday night almost constantly since."

Outside a horn blared, cars sped down 101st, and people rushed off to work. But in Hanna's apartment it fell completely silent. She and I just stared at each other. Her eyes grew anxious and wide, and I realized she was getting embarrassed the longer I took to reply.

I couldn't push any air past the tangle in my throat. Finally, I managed, "Me, too."

"I never thought it could be like that."

I hesitated, worrying she wouldn't believe me when I said, "Me, either."

Her hand lifted at her side, pausing before reaching out. Sliding her fingers into my hair, she followed forward with her body, eyes wide open as she slid her mouth over mine.

I groaned, and my heart slammed against my sternum, skin growing hot as my cock lengthened; every part of me felt tight and stiff.

"Okay?" she asked, pulling back, eyes anxious.

I wanted her so fiercely I was worried I wouldn't be able to be gentle. "Fuck yes, it's okay. I was worried I wouldn't ever have you again."

She stood on wobbly legs, reaching for the hem of her shirt and pulling it up and over her head. Her skin shone with a thin sheen of sweat, and her hair was a mess, but I wanted nothing else than to bury myself in her and feel her give in to me for hours.

"You're going to be late to work," I whispered, watching as she pulled off her sports bra.

"So are you."

"Don't care."

She shimmied out of her pants. With a little ass wiggle, she turned and hopped on one foot to her bedroom.

I stripped as I walked, pulling off my shirt, kicking off my pants—and leaving it all in piles in the hallway. I found Hanna on her bed, lying on top of the covers.

"Do you need more first aid?" I asked, smiling as I climbed over her, kissing my way up her belly to her breasts. "Does anything else hurt?"

"One guess," she said on an exhale.

Without needing to ask, I stretched, reaching for the drawer where she'd kept her condoms. Wordlessly, I tore one from the pack and handed it to her. Her hand was already extended expectantly.

"Fuck. We should fool around a little first," I said into her neck even as I felt her begin to roll the condom down my length.

"We've been fooling around in my head since Sunday morning," she whispered. "I don't think I need more warm-up."

She was right. When she positioned me and then reached for my hips, pulling me deep in one, slow move, she was wet and ready, quickly pulling on my ass to get me moving fast, and hard.

"I like when you're hungry like this," I murmured into her skin. "I feel like I can't get my fill of you. Just like this, against me, under me."

"Will . . ." She pushed into me, sliding her hands over my shoulders.

I could hear the rustle of the sheets as we moved, the slick sounds of our lovemaking, and nothing else. The rest of the world seemed to have fallen away, been put on mute.

She was quiet, too, staring, fascinated, down at where I moved in and out of her.

I slid a hand between us, played with her body, loving the way her back arched off the bed, her hands reached above her head, seeking anchor on the headboard.

Fuck.

With my free hand, I reached up, pinning her wrists and letting myself dissolve into her, mindless and warm, the rhythm of our bodies working together, rolling and wet with sweat. I sucked and bit at her chest, pressing down on her wrists and feeling the familiar build of my orgasm grip me somewhere between my hips, low in my spine. I jerked over her, going faster and hard, relishing the sounds of my hips slapping her thighs.

"Aw fuck, Plum."

Her eyes opened, burning with understanding and the wild thrill of seeing my pleasure unfolding.

"Almost," she whispered. "I'm right there."

I circled her clit faster, three fingers flat and rubbing, her little hoarse cries growing louder and tighter, the telltale flush spreading up her neck. She struggled, pulling her wrists apart from my grip in abandon, and then she went off with a sharp cry, hips bucking wild and body coiling and sucking all around me.

I held on by a fucking thread, moving hard and fast until she went limp and soft, and then let go, rasping, "Coming . . ."

I pulled out, jerking the condom off and tossing it away before gripping my cock, squeezing as I stroked up my length.

Hanna's eyes flamed with anticipation, and she propped herself on her elbows, staring intently down at where my hand flew over my length between us. Her attention, how much she clearly enjoyed watching . . . it overwhelmed me.

Heat burned up my legs and down my spine and my back arched in a sharp jerk. My orgasm pulsed through me unbelievably strong, tearing a loud groan from my throat as I came. Stuck in my head were images of Hanna, thighs spread under me, skin slick, her eyes open and telling me without words how good it felt. How good I made her feel.

Pulsing, pulsing, *pulsing* heat . . . and my entire body let go.

My hand slowed, and I opened my eyes, dizzy and breathless.

Her eyes burned, dark gray and fascinated as she ran her fingers over her stomach and stared at my orgasm on her skin.

"Will." My name came out of her mouth in a purr. No way were we done here.

I propped one hand on the pillow beside her head, staring down at her. "Did you like that?"

She nodded, her bottom lip trapped viciously between her teeth.

"*Show* me. Touch yourself for me."

She initially looked uncertain, but then it transformed into determination. I watched as she ran her hand down her torso, reaching briefly for my still-erect cock, her fingers first on me and then herself. She slid two fingers down over her clit, arching into her touch.

I ghosted my hand up her side and over her breast, bending to suck at the tight peak, before telling her, "Make yourself come."

"Help me," she said, eyes heavy.

"I'm not there when you do this alone. Show me what you do. Maybe I like to watch, too."

"I want you to watch while you *help*."

She was still so warm from the friction of our sex; flesh soft and so fucking wet. With my fingers inside and hers out, we found a rhythm—she stroked up as I pushed in—and fuck if it wasn't the most amazing thing to see her so unchained and intense, alternating between staring down at where I'd come on her and where I was growing hard again between us.

It didn't take long to get here there, and soon she was pushing into my hand, her legs pulled up tight to her sides and lips parted as she grew tense, and then fucking exploded with a scream.

She was beautiful when she went off, skin flushing and nipples tight; I couldn't help but taste her skin, nibbling the underside of her breast and slowing my hand in her as she came down.

She took stock of our appearance: covered in sweat and, on her stomach, my orgasm.

"I think we need a shower."

I laughed. "I think you may be right."

But we didn't. We started to get up, but then I would kiss her shoulder, or she would bite mine, and each time we would just slide back onto the mattress, until eventually it was nearly eleven in the morning, and we'd both long since given up on the idea of going in to work.

After the kissing escalated again, and I took her while she was bent over the edge of the bed, collapsing over her, she rolled onto her back and stared up at me, playing with my sweaty hair. "Are you hungry?"

"A little."

She started to get up but I pushed her back down, kissing her stomach. "Not hungry enough to get up yet." I spotted a pen on her bedside table and reached for it without thinking, murmuring, "Stay still," as I pulled the cap off with my teeth and pressed the tip to her skin.

She'd left the window near her bed open a crack, and we listened to the sounds of the city outside as I drew on the smooth skin just beside her hip. She didn't ask what I was doing, didn't even really seem to care. Her hands slid through my hair, down over my shoulders, along my jaw. She carefully traced my lips, my eyebrows, down the bridge of my nose. It was the way she might touch me if she were blind, trying to learn how I fit together.

When I finished, I pulled back, admiring my handiwork. I'd written a fragment of my favorite quote in tiny script, from her hipbone to just above her bare publc bone.

All that is rare for the rare.

I loved the dark ink on her. Loved seeing it in my handwriting even more. "I want to tattoo this on your skin."

"Nietzsche," she whispered. "Overall a good quote, actually."

"'Actually'?" I repeated, rubbing my thumb over the unmarked skin below, considering all the things I could put there.

"He was a bit of a misogynist, but came out of it with a few decent aphorisms."

Holy fuck, the brain on this woman.

"Like what?" I asked, blowing across the drying ink.

"'Sensuality often hastens the growth of love so much that the roots remain weak and are easily torn up,'" she quoted.

Well. I looked up in time to catch her teeth release her lip, her eyes shining with amusement. That was interesting. "What else?"

She ran a fingertip across the scar on my chin, and studied my face carefully. "'All that glitters is not gold. A soft sheen characterizes the most precious metal.'"

I felt my smile falter a little.

"'In the end one loves one's desire and not what is desired.'" She tilted her head, running her hand through my hair. "Do you think that one is true?"

I swallowed thickly, feeling trapped. I was too wrapped up in my own tangled thoughts to figure out whether she was selecting meaningful quotes about my past or just quoting some classic philosophy. "I think it's sometimes true."

"But all that is rare for the rare . . ." she said quietly, looking down at her hip. "I like it."

"Good." I bent to even out one letter, darken another, humming.

"You've been singing that same song the entire time you wrote on me," she whispered.

"I have?" I hadn't realized I'd even made a noise. I hummed a few more bars of it, trying to remember what it was I'd been singing: *She Talks to Angels*.

"Mmmm, an oldie but a goodie," I said, blowing a stream of air on her navel to dry the ink.

"I remember hearing your band cover it."

I looked up at her, searching for her meaning. "A recording? I don't even think *I* have that."

"No," she whispered. "Live. I was visiting Jensen in Baltimore the weekend your band covered it. He said you guys always covered a different song at every show so you'd never play it again. I was there for that one." There was something restrained behind her eyes when she said this.

"I didn't even know you were there."

"We said hi before the show. You were onstage, adjusting your amp." She smiled, licking her lips. "I was seventeen, and it was right after you came to work for Dad, over fall break."

"Oh," I said, wondering what seventeen-year-old Hanna had thought of that show. It was one I still thought about, even just over seven years later. We had played tight that night, and the crowd had been amazing. It was probably one of our best shows ever.

"You were playing bass," she said, drawing small circles with her fingers on my shoulders. "But you sang that one. Jensen said you didn't often sing."

"No," I agreed. I wasn't much of a singer, but with that one I didn't care. It was more about emotion anyway.

"I saw you flirting with this Goth girl up front. It was funny, how I felt jealous then when I never had before. I think it was because you'd lived in our house, I felt a little like you belonged to us." She smiled down at me. "God, that night I wanted to be her so bad."

I watched her face as she walked through the memory, waiting to hear how this night ended for her. And me. I couldn't remember seeing Hanna when I lived in Baltimore, but there were a million nights like this, at a bar with the band, some Goth girl or preppy girl or hippie chick up front and, later in the night, under or over me.

She licked her lips. "I asked if we were meeting up with you later, and Jensen just laughed."

I hummed, shaking my head and trailing my hand up her thigh. "I don't remember what happened after that show." Too late, I realized how awful it sounded, but the reality was, if I wanted to be with Hanna, she would eventually know the truth of just how wild I'd been.

"Was that the kind of girl you liked? 'She paints her eyes as black as night now'?"

I sighed, climbing up her body so we were face-to-face. "I liked all kinds of girls. I think you know that."

I'd tried to emphasize the past tense, but realized I'd failed when she whispered, "You're such a player."

She said it with a smile but I hated it. I hated the tight edge to her voice and knowing that was exactly how she saw me: fucking anything that moved, and now *her*, in this conglomeration of limbs and lips and pleasure.

In the end one loves one's desire and not what is desired.

And I had no defense; it had been mostly true for so long.

Rolling closer, she wrapped her hand around my semi-erect cock, stroking up, squeezing. "What's your type now?"

She was giving me an out. She didn't want it to be true anymore, either. I leaned in, kissed her jaw. "My type is more along the lines of a Scandinavian sex bomb named Plum."

"Why did it bother you when I called you a player?"

I groaned, rolling away from her touch.

"I'm serious."

I threw my arm over my eyes, trying to collect my thoughts. Finally, I said, "What if I'm not that guy anymore? What if it's been twelve years since I was that guy? I'm open with my lovers about what I want. I don't *play* anyone."

She pulled back a little and looked at me, wearing an amused smile. "That doesn't make you receptive and deep, Will. No one says a player has to be an asshole."

I rubbed my face. "I just think the word 'player' has a connotation that doesn't fit me. I feel like I try harder than that to be good to the women I'm with, to talk about what we're doing together."

"Well," she said. "you haven't talked to *me* about what you want."

I hesitated, my heart exploding in a wild gallop. I hadn't, and it was because it felt so different with her from every other time I'd been with a woman. Being with Hanna wasn't just about intense physical pleasure; it also made me feel calm, and thrilled, and *known*. I hadn't wanted to discuss this because I hadn't wanted either of us to have the chance to limit it.

Taking a deep breath, I murmured, "That's because with you, I'm not really sure if what I want is *sex*."

She pulled away, sat up slowly. The sheets slid off her body and she reached for a shirt at the end of the bed.

"Okay. This is . . . awkward."

Oh, shit. That hadn't come out right. "No, no," I said,

sitting up behind her and kissing her shoulder. I pulled her shirt from her hands, dropping it on the floor. I licked down her spine, slipping my hand around her waist and sliding up, resting my palm over her heart.

"I'm trying to find a way to say I want it to be *more* than sex. I have feelings for you that go way past sexual."

She stilled, growing completely frozen. "You don't."

"I don't?" I stared at her rigid back, my pulse picking up from anger rather than anxiety. "What do you mean I *don't*?"

She stood, wrapping the sheet around her body. Ice slid into my veins, cooling every part of me. I sat up, watching her. "Are you—what are you doing?"

"I'm sorry. I just—I have some stuff to do." She walked over to the dresser, began pulling things from a drawer. "I need to get to work."

"Now?"

"Yes," she said.

"So I tell you I have feelings and you're kicking me out?"

She spun around to face me. "I need to go right now, okay?"

"I can see that," I said, and she limped into the bathroom.

I was humiliated and furious. And I was terrified this was it. Who would have thought I'd fuck it up with a girl by falling for her? I wanted to get the hell out of there, and I wanted to climb out of the bed, pull her back. Maybe we both needed to think about a few things.

Chapter Thirteen

I closed the door behind me and took a few deep breaths. I needed some space. I needed a minute to wrap my head around what the hell was going on. This morning I thought I'd been discarded like one of Will's many conquests, and now he was saying he wanted more?

What the fuck?

Why was he complicating this? One of things I loved about Will was that people always knew where they stood with him. Good or bad, you always knew the score. Nothing about him had ever been complicated: sex, no complications. End of story. It was easier when I didn't have the option to consider more.

He'd been the bad boy, the hot guy my sister fooled around with in a shed in the backyard. He'd been the object of my earliest fantasies. And it wasn't that I'd spent my youth pining over him—the opposite, in fact—because knowing I could lust for him, but never *actually* stood a chance, made it easier somehow.

But now? Being able to touch him and have him touch me, hearing him say that he wanted more when there was no way he could actually mean it . . . complicated things.

Will Sumner didn't know the meaning of *more*. Hadn't he admitted to never having even a single long-term monogamous relationship? Having never found anyone who kept him interested long enough? Didn't he get a text from one of his nongirlfriends the *morning after we first had sex?* No thanks.

Because as much as I loved spending time with him, and as fun as it was to pretend I could learn from him, I knew that I would never be a player. If I let him into more than my pants—if I let him into my heart and fell for him—I would *submerge*.

Deciding I actually did need to get to work, I started the shower, watching as steam filled the bathroom. I moaned as I stepped under the spray, letting my chin drop to my chest and the sound of water drown out the chaos in my thoughts. I opened my eyes and looked down at my body, at the smeared black ink on my skin.

All that is rare for the rare.

The words he'd drawn so carefully across my hip were now bleeding into each other. There were marks where the ink had rubbed off onto his hands, and touches that alternated between pressing bruises and feather-light caresses had left a necklace of smudged fingerprints between my breasts, over my ribs, lower.

For a moment I let myself admire the gentle curve of his handwriting, remembering the determined expression on his face while he'd worked. His brows had knitted together, his hair fell forward to cover one eye. I was surprised when he didn't reach up to push it back—a habit I'd come to find increasingly endearing—but he was so focused, so intent on what he'd been doing he'd ignored it and continued meticulously inking the words across my skin. And then he'd ruined it by losing his mind. And I'd freaked out.

I reached for the loofah and covered it in way too much body wash. I began scrubbing at the marks, half of them gone already from the heat and pressure of the spray, the rest dissolving into a sudsy mess that slipped down my body and into the drain.

With the last traces of Will and his ink washed from my skin and the water growing cold, I stepped out, dressing quickly and shivering in the cool air.

I opened the door to find him pacing the length of the room, running clothes back in place and a beanie on his head. He looked like he'd been debating leaving.

He whipped off his hat and spun to face me. "Fucking finally," he muttered.

"Excuse me?" I said, temper flaring again.

"You're not the one who gets to be mad here," he said. My jaw dropped. "I . . . you . . . *what*?"

"You left," he spit out.

"To the next room," I clarified.

"It was still fucked-up, Hanna."

"I needed space, *Will*," I said, and, as if to further illustrate my point, walked out of the bedroom and down the hall. He followed.

"You're doing it again," he said. "Important rule: don't freak out and walk away from someone *in your own house*. Do you know how hard that was for me?"

I stopped in the kitchen. "*You?* Do you have any idea what kind of a bomb that was to drop? I needed to think!"

"You couldn't think there?"

"You were naked."

He shook his head. "What?"

"I can't think when you're naked!" I shouted. "There was too much." I motioned to his body but quickly decided that was a bad idea. "It was just . . . I freaked, okay?"

"And how do you think I felt?" He glared at me, the muscles of his jaw flexing. When I didn't answer, he shook his head and looked down, shoving his hands into his pockets. That was a bad idea. The waist of his track pants slipped lower, the hem of his shirt moved up. And *oh*. That little slice of toned stomach and hipbone was most definitely not helping.

I forced myself back into the conversation. "You just told me you don't know what you want. And then you said you had feelings that went past sexual. I have to be honest, it doesn't seem like you have a very good grasp on anything that's going on here. The first time we had sex you basically brushed me off, only to now tell me you want *more*?"

"Hello!" he yelled. "I didn't brush you off. I told you, it was jarring to have you be so cavalier—"

"Will," I said, voice firm. "For twelve years I've lived with the stories of you and my brother. I saw the aftermath of you hooking up with Liv—she was hung up on you for *months* and I bet you had no idea. I've seen you sneak off with bridesmaids or disappear at family gatherings and *nothing's* changed. You've spent the majority of your adult life acting like a nineteen-year-old guy, and now you think you want more? You don't even know what that means!"

"And *you* do? Suddenly you know everything? Why would you assume that I knew this thing with Liv was so monumental? Not everyone discusses their feelings and sexuality and whatever comes to mind as openly as you do. I've never known a woman like you before."

"Well, statistically speaking, that's really saying something."

I didn't even know where all this was coming from, and the minute the words left my mouth I knew I'd gone too far.

All at once the fight seemed to leave him and I watched his shoulders fall, the air leave his lungs. He stared at me for a long beat, eyes losing their heat until they were just . . . flat.

And then, he left.

⚯

I paced the old rug in the dining room so many times I wondered if I was wearing a track in it. My head was a mess, my heart wouldn't stop pounding. I had no idea what had just happened, but all along my skin and into my muscles I felt tight and tense, afraid that I had just chased off my best friend, and the best sex of my entire life.

I needed something familiar. I needed my family.

The phone rang four times before Liv picked up.

"Ziggy!" my sister said. "How's the lab rat?"

I closed my eyes, leaning into the doorway between the dining room and kitchen. "Good, good. How's the baby maker?" I asked, quickly adding, "And I was most definitely not talking about your vagina."

Her laugh burst through the line. "So the verbal filter hasn't grown in yet. You're going to confuse the hell out of some man one day, you know that?"

She didn't know the half of it. "How're you feeling?" I asked, steering the conversation to safer waters. Liv was married now and very pregnant with the first, oft-heralded Bergstrom grandchild. I was surprised my mother ever left her alone for more than ten minutes at a time.

Liv sighed, and I could imagine her sitting at the dining room table in her yellow kitchen, her giant black Labrador moving to lie down at her feet. "I'm good," she said. "Tired as hell, but good."

"Kiddo treating you okay?"

"Always," she answered, and I could hear the smile in her voice. "This baby's going to be perfect. Just wait."

"Of course it is," I said. "I mean, look at its aunt."

She laughed. "My thoughts exactly."

"You guys picked a name yet?" Liv was thoroughly set on not knowing the sex of their incoming package until it was born. It made spoiling my new niece or nephew a lot more difficult.

"We may have narrowed it down."

"And?" I asked, intrigued. The list of gender-neutral names my sister and her husband had come up with was bordering on comical.

"Nope, not telling you."

"What? Why?" I whined.

"Because you always find something wrong with them."

"That's ridiculous," I gasped. Though . . . she was right. So far her name choices were terrible. Somehow she and her husband Rob had decided that tree names and types of birds were gender-neutral and fair game.

"Now what's new with you?" she asked. "How has your life improved since your epic showdown with the boss man last month?"

I laughed, knowing of course she meant Jensen, and not Dad, or even Liemacki.

"I've been running, and getting out more. I mean, we came to sort of a . . . compromise?"

Liv didn't miss a beat. "A compromise. With Jensen?"

I'd spoken to Liv a few times in the past weeks, but had steered clear of my growing friendship, relationship, *whatever*ship with Will. For obvious reasons. But now I needed my sister's thoughts on all of it, and my stomach clenched into a giant ball of dread.

"Well, you know Jens suggested I go out more." I paused, running my finger around a swirling pattern carved into the antique hutch in the dining room. I closed my eyes, wincing as I said, "He suggested I call Will."

"Will?" she asked, and a beat of silence passed in which I wondered if she was remembering the same tall, gorgeous college-aged lad that I was. "Wait—Will *Sumner*?"

"That's the one," I said. Even talking about him made my stomach twist.

"Wow. Was not expecting that."

"Neither was I," I mumbled.

"So did you?"

"Did I *what*?" I asked, instantly regretting the way it came out.

"*Call* him," she said, laughing.

"Yeah. Which is sort of why I'm calling you today."

"That sounds *deliciously* ominous," she said.

I had no idea how to do this, so I started with the simplest, most innocuous detail there was. "Well, he lives here in New York."

"I thought I remembered that. And? I haven't seen him in ages, sort of dying to know what he's been doing. How's he look?"

"Oh, he looks . . . good," I said, trying to sound as neutral as possible. "We've been hanging out."

There was a pause on the line, a moment where I could almost see the way Liv's forehead would furrow, her eyes narrowing as she tried to find the hidden meaning in what I'd said.

"'Hanging out'?" she repeated.

I groaned, rubbing my face.

"Oh my God, Ziggy! Are you banging *Will*?"

I groaned, and laughter filled the line. Pulling back, I looked at the phone in my hand. "This isn't funny, Liv."

I heard her exhale. "Yes, it totally is."

"He was your . . . boyfriend."

"Oh, no, he wasn't. Not even a little. I think we made out for like ten minutes."

"But—girl code!"

"Yes, but there's some sort of time limit. Or base limit. Like, I think we barely shanked it down the first base line. Though, at the time, I was completely prepared to let him enter the batter's box, if you know what I'm saying."

"I thought you were devastated after that holiday."

She started cracking up. "Take it down a notch there. First of all, we were never together. It was a horny fumble behind Mom's gardening tools. Jesus, I barely remember."

"But you were so upset, you didn't even come home the summer he worked with Dad."

"I didn't come home because I'd fucked around all year and needed to catch up on credits over the summer," she said. "And I didn't tell you because Mom and Dad would have found out and killed me."

I pressed my hand to my face. "I am so confused."

"Don't be," she said, her tone changing to concerned. "Just tell me, what's actually going on with you guys?"

"We've been hanging out a lot. I really like him, Liv. I mean he's probably my best friend here. We hooked up and then he was weird the next day. Then he started talking about feelings, and it just seemed like he was using me as a test subject in some sort of weird emotional-expression experiment. He didn't exactly have the best track record with Bergstrom girls."

"So you ripped him a new one because in your twelve-year-old memories he was the man of my dreams and left me, brokenhearted and alone."

I sighed. "That was part of it."

"What was the rest of it?"

"That he's a whore? That he doesn't remember a fraction of the women he's been with and less than twenty-four hours after brushing me off, he's telling me he wants more than just sex?"

"Okay," she said, considering. "Does he? Do *you*?"

I sighed. "I don't know, Liv. But even if he did—if *I* did—how could I trust him?"

"I don't want you to be an idiot, so I'm going to do a little overshare here. Ready?"

"Not even a little bit," I said.

She went on anyway: "Before I met Rob he was a *giant* slut. I swear to God his penis had been everywhere. But now? Different man. Worships the ground I walk on."

"Yes, but he wanted to get married," I said. "You weren't just banging him."

"When we first got together it was definitely just banging. Look, Ziggy, a lot of stuff happens to a person between the ages of nineteen and thirty-one. A lot changes."

"I'll believe *that*," I mumbled, imagining Will's even-deeper voice, his expertly wicked fingers, his broad, solid chest.

"I'm not just talking about the developing male body, you know." She paused, adding, "Though that, too. And now that I think of it, you should totally send me a picture of Will Sumner at thirty-one."

"Liv!"

"I'm kidding!" she laugh-yelled through the phone and then paused. "No, I'm serious, actually. Send me a picture. But I really would hate for you to pass up a chance to spend time with him just because you expect him to always act like a nineteen-year-old man-whore. The truth is, don't you feel like you've changed a lot since you were nineteen?"

I didn't say anything, just chewed on my lip and continued to trace the carving on my mother's antique hutch.

"And that was only five years ago for you. So think how he feels. He's thirty-one. There's a lot of wisdom to be gained in twelve years, Ziggs."

"Blerg," I said. "I hate when you're right."

She laughed. "I assume your logical brain has been using all this as some sort of a force field against the Sumner charm?"

"Not very well, apparently." I closed my eyes and leaned back against the wall.

"Oh God, this is amazing. I'm so fucking happy you called today. I'm giant and pregnant and nothing about me is interesting right now. This is awesome."

"Isn't this weird to you at all?"

251

She hummed, considering. "I guess it could be, but honestly? Will and I . . . he was the first boy I fell in lust with, but that's pretty much it. I got over that two seconds after Brandon Henley got his tongue pierced."

I pressed my hand over my eyes. "Oh *gross.*"

"Yeah, I didn't tell you about that one because I didn't want to ruin you, and I didn't want you to ruin it for *me* by researching how the piercing affected the contractility of the muscle or whatever."

"Well, this has been a scarring conversation," I said. "Can I go now?"

"Oh stop."

"I really made a mess of things," I groaned, rubbing my face. "Liv, I was a total dick to him."

"Looks like you have some ass to kiss. Is he into that sort of thing now?"

"Oh my God!" I said. "Hanging up!"

"Okay, okay. Look, Zig. Don't see the world from the eyes of a twelve-year-old. Hear him out. Try and remember that Will has a penis and this makes him an idiot. But a sweet idiot. Even you can't deny that."

"Stop making sense."

"Impossible. Now go put on your big-girl panties and fix things."

⸻

I spent the entire walk to Will's apartment trying to dissect every memory I had of that Christmas, trying to reconcile them with what Liv had told me.

I'd been twelve and fascinated by him, fascinated by the idea of him and my sister together. But now that I'd heard Liv's version of events of that week and what had come after, I wondered how much of it had been real, and how much my overdramatic brain had manufactured. And she had a point. Those memories had made it so much easier to shove Will into a man-whore-shaped box, and almost impossible to imagine him out of it. Did he want more? Was he capable of it? Did I?

I groaned. I had a lot of apologizing to do.

He didn't answer the door when I knocked; he didn't answer any of the messages I sent standing there.

So I did the only thing I could think, and resorted to texting him bad dirty jokes.

What's the difference between a penis and a paycheck? I'd typed. When there was no reply, I continued. A woman will always blow your paycheck.

Nothing.

What did one boob say to the other? And when no answer came: You're my breast friend. Jesus these were bad.

I decided to try one more. What comes after sixty-nine?

I'd used his favorite number, and hoped this might be enough to lure him out.

I almost dropped my phone when the word What popped up on my screen.

Mouthwash.

Oh for fucks sake, Hanna. That was ter-

rible. Get up here before you embarrass us
both.

———

I practically sprinted to the elevator.

His door was unlocked, and when I walked in, I saw
he'd been in the middle of cooking dinner, pots boiling
on the stove, the counter colored in produce. He was
wearing an old Primus T-shirt and faded, ripped jeans—
looking good enough to eat. He didn't glance up when
I entered, but kept his head down, his eyes on the knife
and the cutting board in front of him.

Unsure feet took me across the room and I stood at his
back, pressed my chin into his shoulder. "I don't know
why you put up with me," I said.

Breathing in deeply, I wanted to memorize the smell
of him. Because what if I'd really done it—what if he'd
had enough of silly Ziggy and her idiotic questions and
fumbling sexual encounters and jumping to conclusions?
I would have kicked me to the curb ages ago.

But he surprised me by putting down his knife, and
turning to face me. He looked miserable, and guilt
twisted my stomach.

"You might have had the details wrong about Liv," he
said, "but that doesn't mean there weren't others. Some I
don't even remember." His voice was earnest, apologetic,
even. "I've done some things I'm not proud of. It's all
sort of catching up with me."

"I think that's why the idea of you wanting more terrified me," I said. "That there have been so many women in your past and I can tell you have *no* idea how many hearts you've broken. Maybe no idea how to *not* break them. I like to think I'm too smart to join those ranks."

"I know," he said. "And I'm sure that's part of your charm. You're not here to change me. You're just here to be my friend. You make me think more about the decisions I've made than I ever have before, and that's a good thing." He hesitated. "And I'll admit I got a little wrapped up in our post-coital moment . . . I just got carried away."

"It's okay." I stretched to kiss his jaw.

"Just friends is good for me," he said. "Friends who have sex is even better." He pulled me back to meet my eyes. "But I think that's a good place to stay for now, okay?"

I tried to read his expression, understand why he seemed to be so carefully considering every word he spoke.

"I'm sorry about what I said," I told him. "I panicked and said something hurtful. I feel like an idiot."

He reached out, hooked a finger into my belt loop, and pulled me to him. I went willingly, feeling the press of his chest against mine.

"We're both idiots," he said, and his eyes dropped to my mouth. "And just so you know, I'm about to kiss you."

I nodded, pushing up onto my toes to bring my mouth to his. It wasn't really a kiss, but I wasn't sure what else to call it. His lips brushed against mine, each time with just a bit more pressure than the time before.

His tongue licked out softly, barely touching before he pulled me closer, deeper. I felt him tuck his fingers beneath the fabric of my shirt and stay there, resting on my waist.

My mind was suddenly spinning with ideas of what I wanted to do to him, how much closer I needed to be. I wanted to taste him, all of him. I wanted to memorize every line and muscle.

"I want to go down on you," I said, and he pulled back, just enough to gauge my expression. "For real this time. Like, making you orgasm and everything."

"Yeah?"

I nodded, brushing my fingertips over the line of his jaw. "Show me how to be awesome at it?"

Laughing, he said, "*Christ*, Hanna," quietly into another kiss.

I could feel him already hard against my hip and I slid my hand down his body to palm him. "Okay?" I asked.

Eyes wide and trusting, he took my hand, leading me to the couch. He hesitated for a moment before sitting. "I might pass out if you keep looking at me like that."

"Isn't that the point?" I didn't wait for an invitation and kneeled on the floor between his legs. "Tell me how you want me to do it."

His eyes grew heavy, staring down at me. He helped me with his belt, helped push his pants down his hips, and watched as I bent and kissed the tip.

He paused for a moment when I sat back up, and gauged my expression. And then he gripped his cock at the base. "Lick from base to tip. Start slow. Tease me a little."

I bent, drawing my tongue up the underside of his length, along the thick vein, and slowly over the tightness of the crown. He leaked a little at the top and it surprised me with its sweetness. I kissed the tip, sucking for more.

He groaned. "Again. Start at the bottom. And suck it a little at the top again."

I kissed his cock, whispering, "So specific," with a smile.

But he seemed unable to smile back; his blue eyes turned stormy with intensity. "*You* asked," he growled. "I'm telling you step by step what I've imagined a hundred times."

I started again, loving it, loving to see him like this. He looked a little dangerous, and at his side, his free hand had formed a fist. I wanted him to unleash himself, digging hands into my hair, and start pushing hard into my mouth.

"Now suck."

He nodded as I surrounded him with my lips, then my mouth, using my tongue to stroke a little.

"*Suck* more. Hard."

I did what he asked, closing my eyes for a beat and trying not to panic at the thought of choking on him and losing control. Apparently, I did it right.

"Oh fuck yes, like that," he groaned when I sealed my lips around him. "Be sloppy . . . use a little teeth on the shaft." I looked up at him for confirmation, before letting my teeth graze his skin. He grunted, hips jerking so he hit the back of my throat. "That's it. Jesus. Everything you do feels so *fucking* good."

It was just the compliment I needed to take over, suck him harder and let go, unleash *myself.*

"Yes, oh . . ." His hips moved harder, rougher. His eyes were fixed on my face, his hands pushed into my hair just the way I'd wanted. "Show me how much you like it."

I closed my eyes, humming around him, sucking in earnest now. I could feel small noises escaping my throat and all I could think was *yes,* and *more,* and *fall apart.*

His deep grunts and choppy breaths were like a drug to me, and I felt my own ache build as his pleasure grew and grew. We fell into a rhythm, my mouth and fist working him in tandem with the movements of his hips, and I could tell he was holding back, making it last.

"*Teeth,*" he reminded me in a hiss, and then groaned in relief when I complied.

With one hand, he used his fingertip to trace my lips around him, and the other hand remained threaded in my hair, guiding me and, eventually holding me in place while he carefully thrust up. Against my tongue, he swelled and his hand in my hair formed a tight fist.

"Coming, Hanna. Coming." I could feel the muscles of his stomach jump and tighten, his thighs tensing. I gave his cock one last long suck before I pulled off, taking him in my hands and, sliding up fast and rough, gripping him the way he liked, squeezing.

"Oh fuck," he warned, hissing in a breath as he came, warm on my hands. I worked him through it, continuing to pull in slow drags until it was too much and he batted me away, smiling as he pulled me up to him.

"Fuck, you're a fast learner," he said, kissing my forehead, my cheeks, the corners of my mouth.

"Because I have an excellent teacher."

He laughed, pressing his smile to mine. "I can assure you I didn't learn *that* from experience." He pulled away, eyes traveling over every inch of my face. "Stay and have dinner with me?"

I curled into his side and nodded. There wasn't anywhere I'd rather be.

CHAPTER FOURTEEN

It had been so long since I'd cuddled on my couch with a woman, I forgot how awesome it was. But with Hanna, it was borderline blissful to simultaneously enjoy a beer, a basketball game, some nerdy science talk and nice lady with curves at the ready. I finished my drink with a long swallow and then looked over at Hanna, her eyes glazed as if she was on the cusp of a nap.

I was disappointed that I'd backpedaled after seeing her reaction this morning. But as I was quickly learning, I'd do anything for her. If she wanted to keep things casual, then that's what we'd do. If she wanted us to be friends with benefits, I could pretend. I could be patient, I could give her time. I only wanted to be with her. And as pathetic as it sounded, I'd take what I could get.

For now, I was okay being the Kitty.

"You good?" I murmured, kissing the top of her head. She nodded, humming, and wrapping her hand more firmly around the beer bottle in her lap. Hers was still mostly full and, at this point, probably pretty warm, but I liked that she had one anyway.

"Don't like the beer?" I asked.

"This one tastes like pinecones."

Laughing, I pulled my arm out from behind her neck and leaned forward to put my empty down. "That's the hops."

"Is that like what they make marijuana clothes from?"

I bent over farther, laughing harder. "That's hemp, Hanna. Holy shit you're amazing."

When I looked over at her, she was smiling and I realized, of course, she'd been fucking with me.

She patted my head patronizingly and I shrugged away from her hand, saying, "I like how I forgot for a minute there that you've probably memorized the name of every plant, ever."

Hanna stretched, her arms shaking slightly over her head as she hummed in pleasure. Naturally I took the opportunity to check out her chest. She also happened to be wearing a totally badass Doctor Who shirt, I hadn't even noticed earlier.

"Are you looking at the goods?" she said, opening one eye and catching me, slowly lowering her arms.

I shook my head. "Yes."

"Are you always such a boob man?" she asked.

In what was clearly becoming a pattern, I ignored the implied question about other women, deciding I wasn't going to address anything about that entire taboo conversation again . . . for now. Beside me, she grew still and I knew she felt the same unspoken question settle back between us: *is this conversation over?*

We were saved by the bell, or in this case the buzzing of my phone on the coffee table. A text from Max lit up my screen.

Headed to Maddie's for some pints. Coming?

I showed the phone to Hanna, in part wanting her to see that it wasn't a woman texting me on a Tuesday night, and in part to see if she'd be up for coming along. I raised my eyebrows in silent question.

"Who's Maddie?"

"Maddie is a friend of Max's, who owns and runs *Maddie's,* a bar in Harlem. It's usually pretty empty, and it has great beer. Max likes it for the horrible British pub food."

"Who's going?"

Shrugging, I said, "Max. Probably Sara." I stopped, considering. It was Tuesday, so Sara and Chloe would probably be testing to see if I was with Kitty. It was all probably a quasi-causal ruse to check up on me. "I'm betting Chloe and Bennett are coming, too."

Hanna tilted her head, studying me. "Do you guys go out to bars on weekdays a lot? Seems strange for all of these serious business career people."

I sighed, standing and pulling her up with me. "I think they're trying to track my sex life, to be honest." If she knew

Saturdays had been my nights with Kristy, then she may also know Tuesdays were usually reserved for Kitty. May as well be up front with her about how meddling my friends could be.

Her expression remained unreadable, and I couldn't tell if she was irritated, jealous, nervous, or maybe even just listening neutrally. I wanted so much to know what was going on in her head, but I couldn't possibly start the talk again and have her freak out. I was a man; a man perfectly capable of accepting sex from a woman even under the murkiest of emotional circumstances. Especially when that woman was Hanna.

I bent to pick up both beer bottles.

"Will it be weird if I'm there? Do they know about us?"

"Yes, they know. No, it won't be weird."

She looked skeptical, and I put my hands on her shoulder. "Here's a rule: things are only weird if you let them be."

——————

As the bar was roughly fifteen blocks from my apartment building, we decided to walk. Late March in New York was either gray and cold, or blue and cold, and luckily the snow had finally disappeared and we were having a pretty decent spring.

Only a block from my apartment, Hanna reached for my hand.

I threaded my fingers with hers, and pressed our palms together. I'd somehow always expected love to be primarily a mental state, so I still felt unaccustomed to the physical manifestation of my feelings for her: the way my stomach would grow tight, my skin would start to feel hungry for her touch, the way my chest would press in, my heart pounding blood hard and fast through my arteries.

She squeezed my hand, asking, "Do you actually like doing sixty-nine? I mean, really."

I blinked over to her, laughing and *fuck*, falling even harder for her. "Yeah. I love it."

"But, and I know you're going to hate what I'm about to say—"

"You're going to ruin it for me, aren't you?"

She looked up at me, tripping slightly on a crack in the sidewalk. "Is that even possible?"

I considered this. "Probably not."

Opening her mouth, she started to speak and then closed it again. Finally, she blurted, "Your face is basically in someone's *ass*."

"No, it isn't. Your face is on someone's cock or someone's pussy."

She was already shaking her head. "No. Let's say I'm on top of you, and—"

"I like this hypothetical." I kept waiting for her to take charge and ride me. In fact, I wanted it so much that as soon as I pictured it, I had to take a moment to discreetly adjust myself in my jeans with my free hand.

Ignoring my hint, she continued, "So that means you're

under me. My legs are spread over your face, so my ass is . . . it's like *eyeball* level."

"Fine with me."

"It's my *ass*. By your *eyes*."

I let go of her hand and reached up to tuck a stray hair behind her ear. "This won't surprise you, but I have zero aversion to asses. I think we should try it."

"It's not awkward?"

Pulling up short, I turned her to face me. "Have we done anything yet that feels awkward?"

Her cheeks went pink, and she blinked down the street, mumbling, "No."

"And you believe me when I say I'll make *everything* good for you."

She looked back up at me, eyes soft and trusting. "Yeah."

I took her hand in mine again, and we continued walking. "It's settled then. There will be some sixty nine in your future."

We walked in silence for several blocks, listening to the birds, the wind, the sound of traffic in bursts organized by the streetlights.

"You think I'll ever teach *you* something?" she asked just before we reached the bar.

I smiled down at her, growling, "Without a doubt." And then I opened the door to Maddie's for Hanna, gesturing that she lead us inside.

My friends, seated at a table just to the side of the little dance floor, saw us as soon as we walked in. Chloe, facing the door, noticed us first, her mouth forming a tiny, surprised O that she almost immediately tucked away. Bennett and Sara turned in their seats, each of them deftly hiding any reaction. But fucking Max had an enormous shit-eating grin spreading from ear to ear.

"Well, well," he said, standing to walk around the table and give Hanna a hug in greeting. "Look who's here."

Hanna smiled, greeting everyone alternately with little hugs and waves, and then pulled up a chair to the end of the table. I made Max move down so I could sit next to her, and didn't miss his amused laugh, and under his breath, a guffawed "Smitten."

Maddie herself approached our table, tossing down a couple more coasters in front of us and asking what we wanted to drink. She listed the beers on tap, and because I knew she wouldn't like any of them, I leaned close to tell Hanna, "They also have regular bar drinks, or sodas."

"Soda is expressly forbidden," Max chided. "If you don't like beer, there is whiskey."

Hanna laughed, making a face. "Would you drink a vodka and 7-Up?" she asked, anticipating our usual routine where she ordered the drink and I was the one who actually drank it.

I shook my head and made a face, leaning into her, our foreheads practically touching. "Probably not."

Humming, she thought about it some more. "Jack and Coke?"

"I'd drink that." I looked up at Maddie and said, "Jack and Coke for the lady, and I'll have a Green Flash."

"Ooh, what's that?" Hanna asked.

"It's a really hoppy beer," I told her, kissing the corner of her mouth. "You wouldn't like it."

Once Maddie left us, I pulled away from Hanna and glanced around the table, finding four very interested faces looking back at us.

"You two look rather cozy," Max said.

With a little wave of her hand, Hanna explained, "It's our system: I'll only have a few sips of my drink and then he'll finish it. I'm still learning what he orders. "

Sara squeaked out a tiny, thrilled noise and Chloe smiled at us as if we had turned into a photograph of two cuddling baby sloths. I shot them a warning look. When Hanna asked where the restrooms were, then headed in that direction, I leaned in toward the group, meeting each of their eyes.

"This is not going to be the Will and Hanna show, you guys. We're in a weird place. Just act normal."

"Fine," Sara said, but then narrowed her eyes. "But for the record, you two look really cute together and since we all know you guys have been hooking up, she's really brave for coming out with the entire group tonight."

"I know," I mumbled, lifting my beer when Maddie had delivered it and taking a sip. The sharp bite of the hops mellowed almost immediately into a warm, malty finish. I closed my eyes, moaning a little while the others began chatting.

"Will?" Sara said, quieter now, so only I could hear her. She turned, looking behind her before turning back to me. "Please only do this with Hanna if you know it's what you want."

"I really appreciate the meddling, Sara, but stop meddling."

Her face straightened and I registered my mistake. Hanna was a bit older than Sara had been when she started dating the douchebag congressman in Chicago, but I was exactly the same age he had been: thirty-one. Sara probably felt it was her duty to look out for other women who could fall into the same situation she was in for so long.

"Shit, Sare," I said. "I get the meddling. Just . . . it's different. You know that, right?"

"It's always *different* at first," she said. "It's called infatuation, and it will make you promise anything."

It wasn't as if I hadn't been infatuated with a woman before; I had. But I'd always kept my head about me, knowing how to let myself take as much as I could physically, while taking the emotional side more slowly, or pushing it aside entirely. What was it about Hanna that made me want to shed that model and dive straight to the bottom, where things were the most tender and terrifying?

Hanna returned, smiling at me before sitting down and taking a sip of her drink. She coughed and looked up at me, eyes wide and watery as if her throat were on fire.

"Right," I said, laughing. "Maddie makes the drinks on the strong side. I should have warned you."

"Keep drinking," Bennett advised. "It gets easier once your throat is numb."

"That's what he said," Chloe quipped.

Max's laugh boomed across the table, and I rolled my eyes, hoping Hanna stayed oblivious to their banter.

She seemed to be, taking another sip and coming out of it with a more normal reaction. "It's fine. I'm fine. Holy crap, you guys must feel like you're watching someone have her first drink. I promise you I drink sometimes, just—"

"Just not very capably," I finished, laughing.

Below the table, Hanna's palm covered my knee and slid up to my thigh. She found my hand there and curled her fingers around it.

"I remember the first drink I ever had," Sara said, shaking her head. "I was fourteen, and I went up to the bar at my cousin's wedding. I ordered a Coke, and the woman next to me ordered a Coke but with some kind of booze in it. I accidentally took hers and went back to my table. I had no idea what was wrong with my drink and why it tasted so funny, but let me tell you it was the first time this white girl ever tried to bust out some break-dancing moves."

We all laughed, particularly of the image of sweet, reserved Sara doing the robot or some spin drunk. Once our humor died down, it seemed as though our thoughts all drifted to the same topic, because we all turned to Chloe almost in unison.

"How's the wedding planning going?" I asked.

"You know, Will," she said, wearing a sly smile. "I think that's the first time you've ever asked about the wedding."

"I spent four days in Vegas with these sad bastards." I nodded to Bennett and Max. "It's not like I don't know it's happening. Do you want me to tie ribbons on the flower arrangements or some shit?"

"No," she said, laughing. "And the planning is going . . . fine."

"Mostly," Bennett muttered.

"Mostly," Chloe agreed. They shared a knowing look and she started laughing again, leaning into his shoulder.

"What does that mean?" Sara asked. "Is this about the caterer again?"

"No," Bennett said, before taking a sip of his beer. "The caterer is settled."

"Thank God," Chloe interjected.

Bennett continued, "It's just unbelievable the things that families do around weddings. All kinds of drama comes out of the woodwork. Swear to God, if we manage to pull this off without a quadruple homicide we will both deserve a fucking medal."

Reflexively, I gripped Hanna's hand tighter.

After a small pause, she squeezed back, turning to look at me. Her eyes searched mine, and then lightened into a little smile.

I was thinking about her, and me. I was thinking about her family, and how, over the past twelve years, they'd become my surrogate east coast family, and how in this tiny desperate breath I could even see this future—falling in love, getting married, deciding to start a family—for myself down the road.

I released her hand rubbing my palm on my thigh and feeling my pulse explode in my neck. *Holy fuck, what happened to my life?* In only a couple of months, almost everything had changed.

Well, not everything. My friends were still the same, my finances were fine. I still ran (almost) daily, still caught basketball on TV whenever I could. But . . .

I'd fallen in love. How often does anyone see that coming?

"You okay?" she asked.

"Yeah, I'm good," I whispered. "Just . . ." I couldn't say anything. We'd agreed on just-friends. I'd told her it was what I wanted, too. "It's just crazy to see friends going through this," I said, gesturing to Chloe and Bennett, covering myself up that way. "I totally can't relate."

And with that, everyone was looking back to us, eyes soft and fucking *invested* in every single look or touch that passed between me and Hanna. I glared at each of them quickly and then stood. My chair squeaked across the floor, making my awkwardness even more evident. I was okay with being the center of attention within this group, whether I was teasing one of them or the other way around. But this felt different. I could laugh off the jokes about my scheduled hookups or colorful past with women, but right now I felt fucking *vulnerable* in this new place with Hanna, and wasn't used to being on this side of the knowing looks.

I wiped my sweaty palms on the thighs of my jeans. "Let's . . . I don't know." I looked around the bar helplessly. We should have just stayed on my couch, maybe fucked again out there in my living room. We should have stayed put until things were slightly less up in the air between us.

Hanna looked up at me, amused expression in place. "Let's . . . ?"

"Let's dance."

I jerked her out of her chair and out to the empty dance floor, realizing when we got there that it would be even worse than what I was escaping. I'd taken us from the pack-safety of the table and onto what was essentially a *stage*. She stepped close to me, pulling my arms around her waist and running her hands up my chest and into my hair.

"Breathe, Will."

I closed my eyes, taking a deep breath. I'd never felt more awkward in my life. Come to think of it, I'd never really felt awkward at all before.

"You're a mess," she said, laughing into my ear when I pulled her close. "I've never seen you so discombobulated. I have to admit, it's really kind of cute."

"It's been a really fucking weird day."

Maddie was playing some mellow indie shit, and this particular song was only instrumental. It was sweet, almost a little melancholy, but just the right speed for the kind of dancing I wanted to do with Hanna: slow, pressing. The kind of dancing where I could pretend to dance but really just stand and hug her for a few minutes away from the table.

On a slow spin, I turned and could see that my friends weren't even looking at us anymore; they had returned to their conversation. Chloe was speaking animatedly about something, arms flapping above her head and I was almost positive she was reenacting some wedding-related fiasco. Now that the weird Will Inspection moment had cleared, I was torn between staying put, here with Hanna, and heading back to the table so I could be kept up to date on the increasing number of shenanigans Bennett and Chloe were dealing with. I could only imagine they were pretty epic.

"I like being with you," Hanna said, breaking back into my thoughts. Maybe it was the lights in the bar, or maybe it was her mood, but her eyes had more blue in them today than they normally did. It made me think of spring being released full bore into New York City. I wanted winter gone. I think I needed everything around me to transition so it didn't feel like I was the only one going through something.

She paused, and her eyes focused on my lips. "I'm sorry about earlier."

Laughing, I whispered, "You said that already. You apologized with words. And then with your mouth on my dick."

She laughed, tucking her head into my neck, and I could pretend we were alone, just dancing in my living room, or bedroom. Only, if we were there, we wouldn't be dancing.

I clenched my jaw, trying to keep my body from reacting to this fresh reminder that she was pressed against me, had given me the blow job of my life earlier, and that it might be possible to convince her to come back to my place again later. Even if she just wanted to curl up and sleep, I'd be completely down for that. After all the drama of the day, I didn't really want her to go home after this.

"I guess I don't really know what to do," she admitted. "I know we talked earlier but things still feel kind of weird."

I sighed. "Why is it complicated, though?" The lights from the dance floor ran shadows across her face, and she looked so fucking beautiful, I felt like I was losing my mind. The question filled my throat like smoke until I felt too full. "Isn't *this* good?" I smiled so she might think I knew it was; maybe she would believe for a second that I didn't actually need the reassurance.

"It's actually amazing how good it is," she whispered. "I feel like I didn't know you at all before, even though I *thought* I did. You're this brilliant scientist, with these really amazing, meaningful tattoos. You run triathlons and have this close, sweet relationship with your sisters and your mom." Her nails scratched lightly down my neck. "I know you've always been sexual, *really* sexual. From the first time I met you when you were nineteen, to now, twelve years later. I really like spending time with you for that reason, too, because you're teaching me things I didn't know about my body, and what I like. I think what we have right now is actually really perfect."

I was a second away from kissing her, running a hand up her side to feel the shape of her ribs and her spine. I wanted to pull her down onto the floor and feel her under me. But we were at a bar. *Fucking idiot, Will.* I looked away, and inadvertently over at my group of friends behind her. All four of them were back to watching us. Bennett and Sara had actually turned their chairs so they could see us without having to crane their necks, but as soon as they noticed I had noticed them, they snapped their attention elsewhere: Max to the bar, Sara up at the ceiling, Bennett down at the watch on his wrist. Only Chloe continued to stare, a big smile on her face.

"This was a bad idea, coming here," I said.

Hanna shrugged. "I don't think so. I think it was good to get out of the house and talk a little."

"Is that what we did?" I asked, smiling. "Talked about how we don't need to talk about it?"

Her tongue peeked out to wet her lips. "Sure. But I think I just want to go back to your place and *do* things while we talk."

———

I pulled my keys from my pocket, sifting through them to locate the right one. "You're not coming up here to grab a cup of tea and then head home."

She nodded. "I know. But I do need to go to lab tomorrow. I don't think I've ever just not shown up like I did today."

I unlocked my front door, pushing it open and letting her lead us inside. She headed straight for the kitchen.

"Wrong way."

"I won't leave after tea," she said over her shoulder. "But I do want some. That drink made me sleepy."

"You had *two sips*." We'd left her mostly full Jack and Coke on the table while Bennett and the rest did their best to convince us to stay and not only finish the one, but have another.

"I think there was the equivalent of seven shots in those two sips."

Stepping up to the stove, I grabbed the kettle and then turned to fill it with water. "Then you're a pretty boring drunk. If I had seven shots I would have been stripping on the table."

She laughed, opening my fridge, rooting around, and finally pulling out a carrot. She walked over to my counter and hopped up on it, swinging her legs. Even though this was so new, it seemed like she'd been coming over here for years.

Her hair had started to come undone and a few pieces fell in small curls next to her face and down the back of her neck. The warmth of the bar, or maybe the two sips of her drink, had left her cheeks flushed, her eyes bright. She blinked slowly as she looked over at me and I smiled.

"You look pretty," I said, leaning against the counter beside her.

She snapped into the carrot. "Thanks."

"Think I might fuck you senseless in a few minutes."

Shrugging and pretending to look nonchalant, she murmured, "Okay."

But then she reached out with her legs and pulled me closer, between her thighs. "Despite that whole 'work' thing I mentioned, I think you could probably keep me up all night again, if you really wanted."

I reached forward with one hand and slipped the top button of her shirt free. "What do you want me to do to you tonight?"

"Anything."

I lifted an eyebrow. "Anything?"

She reconsidered, whispering, "Everything."

"I love this," I said, stepping closer and running my nose up the column of her neck. "This kind of sex where I get to learn everything you like. I discover all of your sounds."

"I don't know . . ." She trailed off, waving her carrot in a vague circle next to my head. "Isn't sex with someone you've been with forever the best kind, though? Like she's in bed, falls asleep, he comes in, and she just instinctively rolls to him, you know? And it's like, her face in his warm neck and his hands all up and down her back, then her pants come off and he's pushing inside her before her shirt is even off. He knows what's under there. Maybe he can't wait to be inside her first. He doesn't have to take things off in order anymore."

I pulled back and stared at her as she snapped another bite of her carrot. She had quite the vivid image of such a moment. I personally would never have said familiar sex is

the best kind. A good kind, sure. But the way she said it—
the way her voice dropped and her eyes kind of closed—
fuck, yes, it sounded like the *best* kind. I could see that life
with Hanna, where we shared a bed, and a kitchen, and
finances and fights. I could see her getting angry with me,
and me coming to find her later and making it up to her
in whatever sneak-attack ways I had learned over time because she was mine and, being Hanna, she couldn't help
but let every thought and desire slip out of her mouth.

Damn. She wasn't sexy in any of the ordinary ways. She
was sexy because she didn't care if I was watching her chow
down on a carrot, or that her hair was in this half-assed ponytail she hadn't bothered to fix since we were lounging on
the couch earlier. She was so comfortable in her skin, so
comfortable being *watched*—I'd never known a woman like
her. She would never assume I was staring and judging. She
assumed I was staring because I was listening. And I was.
I would listen to her ramble about familiar sex and anal sex
and porn films forever.

"You're looking at me like I'm food." She held out her
carrot, grinned wickedly. "Want some?"

I shook my head. "I want you."

She moved her hands up, unbuttoning her shirt now, and
slid it off her shoulders.

"Tell me what you like," I said, stepping even closer and
kissing the hollow of her throat.

"I like when you come on me."

I let out a quiet laugh into her neck. "I know *that*. What else?"

"When you watch where you're moving in me."

Shaking my head, I said, "Tell me what you like that I do *to* you."

Hanna shrugged a little, running her fingertips down my chest before reaching for the hem of my shirt and pulling it up and over my head. "I like when you throw me around a little, have your way with me. I like when you act like my body is yours."

The teakettle whistled, screeching in the quiet kitchen, and I moved away just long enough to grab her mug and pour some hot water over a tea bag. "When I'm touching you," I told her, putting the kettle down, "your body *is* mine. Mine to kiss, and fuck, and taste."

She lifted her eyebrow and smiled at me. "Well, when *I'm* touching *you*, your body is mine, too, you know."

My mind went completely, directly into the gutter when she leaned across the counter, reached for the honey, and drizzled some into the mug.

Taking the honey wand from her, I swiped some excess on the lip of the jar then ran the stickiness across the top swell of her breast. She watched me, her tea apparently forgotten.

"So take control," I told her, kissing her jaw. "Tell me what to do next."

She hesitated for only a beat. "Suck it off."

I groaned at the quiet command, licking across the honey

before sucking her skin into my mouth with such force I left a small, red mark. "What else?"

Her hands slipped behind her, unlatching her bra just as I ran my tongue over her skin. I moved to her nipple, blowing lightly across the peak before sucking her into my mouth. Gasping, she whispered, "Make it wet."

I leaned forward, doing exactly what she asked, licking her breasts, sucking them deeply, laving her skin with my tongue until it glistened. "These will be fucked soon."

"Teeth," she whispered. "Bite me."

With a groan, I closed my eyes, biting small circles into the swell of her breasts, finding small traces of honey remaining on her skin. My hands slid lower, to her jeans, and I worked them and her underwear down her hips so she could kick them to the floor.

Her hands ran over my shoulders, legs spread open. "Will?"

"Mmmm?" I teased down her ribs, lifting both breasts in my hands. I knew her tone; knew what she was about to beg me to do.

"Please."

"Please what?" I asked, pressing my teeth carefully into her nipple. "Please hand you your tea?"

"Touch me."

"I *am* touching you."

She let out an angry little growl. "Touch me between my legs."

I dipped my finger into the small bowl of honey, and pressed it against her clit, rubbing it across her skin as I pressed my teeth into the delicate flesh of her breast. She moaned, head falling back, and pulled her feet up onto the counter, legs spread wide.

Crouching, I ran my tongue over her, not teasing, not even able to. The honey was warm from her skin, and tasted fucking amazing. "Holy fuck," I whispered, sucking gently on her small fold of nerves.

Her hand ran into my hair, pulling, but not for pleasure. She raised me up to her face, leaning forward to kiss me. She'd put honey on her tongue, too, and I knew in a hot pulsing heartbeat that I would now associate this flavor with Hanna forever.

Her quiet little moans filled the space between our lips and our tongues, echoing mildly, growing tighter when I reached between us, slid my fingers over her skin, playing where she was slippery and hot. The counter was a little higher than my hips, but I could make it work if she wanted to fuck in the kitchen.

"Let me get a condom."

"Okay," she said, pulling her fingers from my hair.

I turned, padding in bare feet down the hall, unbuttoning my jeans. I pulled a packet out of the box in my drawer and moved to return to the kitchen, but Hanna was standing just inside my bedroom.

She was completely naked, and without saying anything, walked over to my bed and climbed to the middle. Resting back on her heels, she sat with one hand on her knee. Waiting for me.

"I want to be in here."

"Okay," I said, pushing my jeans down my hips.

"On your bed."

I got it, I thought. *It's pretty obvious you want to have sex on my bed, what with the nakedness and condom in my hand.* But then I realized she was actually asking me something. She was wondering whether my bed was off-limits, whether I was that kind of playboy, who never brought girls home and took them into the inner sanctum of the bedroom.

Would it always be like this? Her unspoken questions, uncertainty about what I was giving her that was new and special? Wasn't it enough that I was secretly giving her the chance to break my heart?

I joined her on the bed, beginning to tear the condom packet open with my teeth before she reached up and took it from me.

"Fuck," I mumbled, watching her duck down to run a tentative tongue across the tip of my dick. "Holy hell. I just love your fucking mouth."

She kissed the tip, running her tongue up and over me. Drawing me into her mouth.

"I like watching you," I babbled. I was so fucking tight and the vision of her doing this . . . I wasn't sure I could hold out. "I feel like I'm going to come."

"I'm barely touching you," she said, clearly proud of herself.

"I know. I'm just . . . it's a lot."

She took the condom and rolled it over me, laid back on the bed. "Ready?"

I hovered over her, looking down the length of our bodies before I positioned myself to slide into her. She was so warm, so slippery, and I wanted to last, draw this moment out just a tiny bit longer. I pulled my hips back slightly, tapping my cock gently against her clit.

"Will," she whined, hips arching up.

"Do you realize how wet you are?"

With a shaky hand, she reached between us, touching herself. "Oh God."

"Is that because of me? Plum, I don't know if I've ever been this hard." I felt my pulse reverberating down my length, pounding.

She gripped me then, and inhaled sharply, whispering, "Please."

"Please what?"

Her eyes opened and she whispered, "Please . . . inside."

I smiled, enjoying her sweet, urgent agony. "Does your pussy ache a little?"

"*Will.*" Beneath me, she moved, searching with her hands and hips. I brought her fingers to my mouth, sucked each into my mouth to taste her sweetness.

Then I reached between us, circling a finger around her slick opening. "I asked you, does it ache right here?"

"Yes . . ." She tried to push up, to get even my finger

inside but I slid it up and over her clit, making her moan loudly. I dragged my finger back down, dipping into the unbelievable wetness. "Does it ache in your thighs? Are these sweet little petals right here—" I bent, sucking her nipple into my mouth and playing a little with my tongue. "Are they tight and aching, too?" *Fuck,* her breasts. So fucking soft and warm. "God, Plum," I whispered, feeling desperate. "I'm going to make it so good tonight. I'm going to make you feel so *fucking* good."

She arched off the bed, hands in my hair, down my neck, scratching along my back.

Drawing my finger down across her pussy and lower, I pressed it against her backside. "I bet I could make you do anything right now. I could fuck you right here."

"Anything," she agreed. "Just . . . please."

"Are you . . . begging me?"

She nodded urgently and then blinked up to my face, eyes wide and wild. Her pulse thrummed in her throat. "Will. Yes."

"So those girls in the porn movies you so love," I whispered, smiling as I rocked my hips. We both groaned when the crown of my cock slid over the taut rise of her clit. "The ones who beg. Say they *need* it . . ." I tilted my head, jaw tight as I resisted the urge to sink into her, pound her into the bed. "Would you say right now *you* need it?"

She groaned, fingernails digging into my chest just below my collarbones and dragging down so roughly she left a trail of fire-red marks from my sternum to my navel. "I'll do whatever you want tonight, just make me come first."

Unable to tease any longer, I rasped, "Put me inside."

Her hands flew to my cock, wrapping around me and rubbing over herself before sliding me inside, pushing her hips off the bed to take me deeper. My skin flushed warm, and with a grunt, I met her movements, sinking in deep and pushing her legs to her sides so I could press all the way in, so I could rub her right where she needed it.

I closed my fists around the sheets on either side of her shoulders, struggling to control myself. She was so wet. She was so *fucking* warm. I squeezed my eyes closed, blood thundering in my veins as I pulled back and pushed in again, and again, hard and deep.

Her noises—sweet moans and growls that it was good, *so good*—made me want to dive deeper, press harder, make her come over and over until she could never imagine feeling anyone else inside her like this. She knew now I would go all night, and it wasn't just that first night we shared. I would *always* keep her up for hours. With Hanna, I would rarely let it to be over quickly.

She was perfect, and gorgeous, and wild—hands on my face, thumb in my mouth, begging me with little noises and her wide, pleading eyes.

But when those eyes rolled closed I stopped, groaning loudly and rasped, "Watch me. I'm not going to be gentle tonight."

She looked up at my face—not down at my cock—so I let her see every single sensation as it passed over me: the way it wasn't enough even with my punishing thrusts and savage hands rasping over every inch of her skin; the way I relished how she began to jut up into me, and it started to be just right, *just fucking right,* and I laughed through a growl, watching her chest flush and her first orgasm sneak up on her, tearing from her screaming and frenzied; the way I wanted to slow down, enjoy the long drag of my cock in her, the warm, perfect hum in my blood, run my finger between her breasts and feel her sweat, slow down enough to make her beg again.

She pulled at my shoulders, begging for *faster.*

"So demanding," I whispered, pulling out and flipping her over to lick down her back, bite her ass, her thighs. I left a pattern of red marks across her skin.

I pulled her down to the edge of the bed, bending her over the mattress, and sank back into her, so goddamn deep it made us both cry out. I closed my eyes, needing that sense of distance. Before, with every woman, I had watched everything. I'd needed that layer of visual stimulation when I was ready to come. But with Hanna, it was too much. *She* was too much. I couldn't watch her when I was close like this, the way her spine arched, or how she'd look at me over her shoulder, eyes full of question and hope and that sweet adoration that spiked me right between my ribs.

I felt her begin to tighten around me, and lost myself in

the way she got even wetter when I gripped her hair, roughly gripped her breasts in my hungry hands, and smacked her ass to hear a sharp crack, which was followed by her eager moan. Her sounds morphed from sharp cries to tiny gasps of breath as I bit her shoulder and told her to *fucking come, Plum*. And when she started to, I tried to hold on, tried to block out the image of us together, the way we must look. My hand tightened on her hip, the other on her shoulder as I pulled her forcibly onto me with every thrust until I was so close, could feel it barreling down my spine.

She said my name, pushed back into me and suddenly it felt like I was falling, spinning into darkness. My eyes flew open, both my hands gripping her tightly for support as I came, filling the condom with a groan. I continued to thrust into her, fucking her through her orgasm as my head swam, my legs on fire. I felt like I was made of rubber and could barely hold myself up.

I pulled out and discarded the condom, watched as she slid down onto the mattress. She looked so fucking perfect in my bed, her hair a mess, her skin bite-marked and flushed and sweaty, a glint here and there from the honey that still clung to her. I climbed on the bed, collapsing behind her and wrapping my arms around her waist. There was something so familiar about this. It was the first time she'd slept in my bed and yet it felt like she'd always been there.

Chapter Fifteen

I woke the next morning to the feel of unfamiliar sheets and the smell of Will still clinging to my skin. The bed was a disaster. The sheets were dislocated from the mattress and twisted around my body; the pillows had been shoved to the floor. My skin was covered in bite marks and fingertip bruises, and I had no idea where my clothes were.

A glance at the clock told me it was just after five, and I rolled over, pushing the tangled hair from my face and blinking into the dim light. The other side of the bed was empty and bore only the telltale indentation of Will's body. I looked up at the sound of footsteps to see him walking toward me, smiling and shirtless, carrying a steaming mug in each hand.

"Morning, sleepyhead," he said, setting the drinks on the bedside table. The mattress dipped as he sat next to me. "You feel okay? Not too sore?" His expression was tender, a smile curving the corners of his mouth, and I wondered if I'd ever get used to the reality of him looking at me so intimately. "I wasn't particularly easy on you last night."

I took the mental inventory: in addition to the marks he'd left all over my body, my legs were weak, my abdomen felt like I'd done a hundred sit-ups, and, between my legs, I could still feel the echo of his hips pounding into me. "Sore in all the right places."

He scratched his jaw, letting his eyes move over my face before dropping to my chest. Predictably. "That is now my favorite thing you've ever said. Maybe you could text that to me later tonight. If you're feeling generous, you could include a picture of your tits."

I laughed, and he reached for a mug, handing it to me. "Someone forgot their tea last night."

"Hmmm. Someone was distracted." I shook my head, motioning for him to put it back down. I wanted both hands free. Will was predatory and seductive every minute of the day; but in the morning, he should be *illegal.*

He grinned in understanding, slowly brushing his hands through the ends of my hair, smoothing it down my spine. I shivered at the emotion in his eyes, how his fingers set off sparks that settled warm and heavy between my thighs. I wished I knew what exactly it was I saw there: friendship, fondness, something more? I bit back the question that continued to rise up in the back of my throat, not sure either of us was ready to have an honest conversation so soon after the last, disastrous one.

The sky that peeked through the window was still purple and hazy, making each inked line across his skin seem sharper, each tattoo stark against his skin. The blue-bird looked almost black; the words that wrapped around his ribs seemed as if they'd been carved there in delicate script. I reached to touch them, to press my thumb into the groove formed by his obliques, the flat planes of his stomach and lower. He hissed in a breath when I slipped a finger just under the waistband of his boxers.

"I want to draw on you," I said, and blinked quickly back to his face to gauge his reaction. He looked surprised, but more than that, he looked *hungry*, his blue eyes heavy and hidden in shadow.

He must have agreed, because he leaned over to search the small table next to the bed, and returned with a black marker. He climbed over me and lay down on his back, stretching out long and sculpted in the middle of his bed.

I sat up, feeling the sheet slip down my body, the cool air reminding me just how completely naked I was. I gave myself no time to think about what I was doing or how I looked as I crawled over and straddled him, my thighs bracketing his hips.

The air in the room seemed to condense, and Will swallowed, eyes wide as I took the marker from him and removed the cap. I could feel the length of him starting to harden against my backside. I bit back a moan at the way he flexed his thighs and rocked his hips upward the tiniest bit in an attempt to rub against me.

I looked down, not even sure where to start. "I love your collarbones," I said, brushing my fingers along them to the little hollow below his throat.

"Collarbones, huh?" he asked, voice warm and still raspy.

I ran my fingers down his chest, biting back a triumphant smile over the way his breathing spiked, jagged and excited, under my touch.

"I *love* your chest."

He laughed, murmuring, "Likewise."

His was perfect, though. Defined, but not bulky. His chest was broad, with smooth skin leading from his muscular shoulders to his pectorals. I traced a line with my index finger. He didn't shave or wax his chest like the men in magazines or on my rare night zoning out in front of mindless television. Will was a *man,* with a smattering of dark hair on his chest, smooth bare stomach, and the soft trail leading from his navel to his . . .

I bent down, dragging my tongue down his happy trail.

"Good," he grunted, shifting impatiently beneath me. "Oh, God yes."

"And I love this spot right here," I said, veering my mouth away from where he wanted me and over to his hip. Pulling his boxers down just an inch, I drew an *H* just inside his hipbone, a *B* below. I sat back to examine it, smiling wide. "I like that."

He lifted his head to see where I'd written my initials on his skin and blinked up to me. "Likewise."

I remembered the smudged words and drawings I'd scrubbed from my body the other day, and brought the marker to my thumb, scribbling across the pad until it was wet with ink. I pressed it to his skin, right below where his hipbone jutted out, pushing hard enough that he sucked in a breath, and then pulled my hand away, leaving my thumbprint.

I sat back and admired it.

"Fuck," he hissed, eyes fixed on that black mark. "That's probably the hottest thing anyone's ever done to me, Hanna."

His words plucked at something raw inside my chest, a resurfacing of the knowledge that there were others: others who had done *hot* things, others who made him feel good.

I blinked away from his pressing gaze, not wanting him to see the thoughts that simmered steadily in the back of my mind—the nongirlfriend thoughts. Will had been good for me. I felt sexy and fun; I felt *wanted*. I wouldn't bog it down with worries of what happened before me, or inevitably, what would happen after. Hell, what probably happened on those days we weren't together. He'd never said anything about ending things with the other women. I saw him most nights of the week, but not *every* night. If I knew anything about Will, it was that he valued variety, and was pragmatic enough to always have a backup plan.

Distance, I reminded myself. *Secret agent. In and out, unharmed*.

Will sat up beneath me, sucking on my neck before moving his mouth to the shell of my ear. "I need to fuck you."

I let my head fall back. "Didn't you do that last night?"

"That was *hours* ago."

Goose bumps exploded across my body, and my tea was forgotten again.

———

The air was still cool but it was starting to feel like spring. There were leaves and blossoms, birds chattering in trees, and the blue-skied promise of better weather to come. Central Park in the spring always rocked me; it was amazing how a city of such size and industry could hide a jewel of color, water, and wildlife in its very heart.

I wanted to think about what I had to do that day, or the upcoming Easter weekend, but I was sore, and tired, and having Will running beside me was proving only more distracting with time.

The rhythm of his feet on the pavement, the cadence of his breath . . . all I could think about was sex. I could remember the hard bunch of muscle beneath my hands, the quiet teasing way he asked me to bite him, as if he was doing it for me, knowing I needed to tear something loose in him, too, and that maybe I'd find it buried beneath his skin. I could remember how he breathed near my ear in the middle of the night, in a rhythm, holding himself back for what felt like hours as he made me come, and then again, and again.

He lifted his shirt and wiped his forehead as he continued to run, and my mind flashed hot and sharp back to the way his sweat felt on my stomach, his come on my hip at the party.

He dropped his shirt, but I couldn't seem to tear my eyes from where he'd just exposed his stomach. "Hanna."

"Hmm?" Finally, I managed to snap my eyes to the trail in front of us.

"What's up? You have this sort of glazed look on your face."

I took a gulping breath and squeezed my eyes shut for only a beat. "Nothing."

His feet stopped, and the cadence of sex and his hips thrusting over and into me halted abruptly. But the tenderness between my legs didn't go away at all when he bent to meet my gaze. "Don't do that."

I filled my lungs, the words escaping with my exhale, "Fine, I was thinking about you."

Blue eyes scanned my face before taking stock of the rest of me: nipples pebbled beneath his too-big T-shirt I wore, stomach in tangles, legs on the verge of collapsing and, between them, muscles coiled so tight, I clenched harder just to relieve the ache.

A tiny smile skittered across his face. "Thinking of me how?"

This time, when I closed my eyes, I kept them closed. He said my strength was in my honesty, but it was really in how he made me feel when I told him everything. "I've never been distracted by someone like this before." I'd always only been *drive*. Right now, I was *lust, want, desire, insatiable student.*

He was quiet for too long and when I looked again, I found him watching me, considering. I needed him to joke or tease, to say something filthy and bring us back to the baseline of Hanna and Will. "Tell me more," he whispered, finally.

I opened my eyes, looked up at him. "I've never had a hard time focusing before, staying on task. But . . . I think about you—" I stopped abruptly. "*Sex* with you all the time."

Never before had my heart felt like such a thick organ, beating with heavy, squeezing pulses. I loved these reminders he gave me that my heart was a muscle and my body was made, in part, for being raw and animalistic, fucking. But not emotions. Definitely not those.

"And?" he pressed.

Fine.

"And it's scary."

His lip twitched in a suppressed grin. "Why?"

"Because you're my friend . . . you've become my *best* friend."

His expression softened. "Is that bad?"

"I don't have a lot of friends and I don't want to screw things up with you. It's important."

He smiled, brushing a strand of hair away from where it clung to my sweaty cheek. "It is."

"I'm scared that this whole friends-who-bang thing will, as Max says, 'go tits up.'"

He laughed, but didn't say anything in response to this.

"Aren't you?" I asked, eyes searching his.

"Not for the same reasons you are, I don't think."

What did that even mean? I loved Will's ability to remain contained, but right now I wanted to throttle him.

"But is it weird that even though you're my best friend, I can't stop thinking about you naked? Me naked. *Us* naked together and the way you make me feel when we're naked? The way I hope *I* make you feel when we're naked? I think about that a lot."

He took a step closer, resting one hand on my hip and the other on my jaw. "It's not weird. And Hanna?"

When he swept his thumb down over the pulse in my neck, I knew he was trying to tell me that he knew how much this scared me. I swallowed, whispering, "Yeah?"

"You know it's important for me to be up front about things."

I nodded.

"But . . . do you want to talk about this now? We can if you want but," he said, squeezing my hip in reassurance, "we don't have to."

A tiny spike of panic went through me. We'd had this conversation before and it hadn't gone well. I'd panicked and he'd taken it back. Would it be different this time? And how would I respond if he said he wanted me, but he didn't want *only* me? I knew what I would say. I would tell him it wasn't working for me anymore. That eventually . . . I'd walk away from this.

Smiling, I shook my head. "Not yet."

He tilted his head, his lips moving to the shell of my ear. "Fine. But in that case I should tell you: *nobody* makes me feel like you do." He said each word carefully, as if each one were placed on his tongue and he had to inspect them before he could let them go. "And I think about sex with you, too. A *lot*."

It wasn't exactly that it surprised me he thought about sex with me; that was fairly clear, given his ongoing commentary. But I suspected he wanted to be with me in some clarified, almost contract-oriented way as he did with all of his women, where it was discussed, and laid out in some sterile mutual agreement. I simply wasn't sure whether for Will that meant committed fucking, or . . . less-committed fucking. After all, if nobody made him feel the way I did, then obviously someone else was out there trying, right?

"I realize you may have . . . *plans* for this weekend," I started and his brows pulled together in frustration or confusion, I couldn't tell, but I barreled on: "But if you do but you don't want to have plans, or if you don't have plans but would *like* to have plans, then you should come home with me for Easter."

He pulled back just enough to see my face. "What?"

"I want you to come home with me. Mom always does an amazing Easter brunch. We can head up Saturday and head home Sunday afternoon. *Do* you have plans?"

"Uh—no," he said, shaking his head. "No plans. You're serious?"

"Would it be weird for you?" I asked.

"Not weird. It would be great to see Jensen, and your folks." Mischief lit up his eyes. "I realize we probably

297

won't be telling the family about our recent sexcapades, but do I get to see your boobs while I'm there?"

"In private?" I asked. "Maybe."

He tapped his chin, pretending to consider this. "Hmm . . . This is going to make me sound totally creepy, but . . . in your room?"

"My *childhood* room? You *are* a pervert," I said, shaking my head. "But perhaps."

"Then I'm in."

"That's all it took? Boobs? You're *that* easy?"

He leaned in, pressed a kiss to my mouth, and said, "If you have to ask, then you still don't know me very well."

Will showed up at my apartment Saturday morning, having parked an ancient green Subaru Outback at the fire hydrant gap. I lifted my brows as I looked from the car to him, at the way he proudly spun the keys around his finger.

"Very nice," I said, stepping back through the door long enough to grab my bag.

He took it and kissed my cheek, smiling widely at my approval. "Isn't it? I keep it in storage. I miss this car."

"When's the last time you drove it?" I asked.

He shrugged. "A while."

I followed him down the stairs, trying not to think about where we were going. Inviting Will had seemed like a great idea at the time, but now, barely a week later, I wondered how everyone was going to react—if I could keep my stupid grin to myself or my hands out of his pants. As I forced my eyes from his ass I realized the odds weren't looking good.

He looked unbelievable in his favorite jeans, a worn-to-perfection Star Wars T-shirt, and green sneakers. He appeared to be as relaxed as I was nervous.

We hadn't really talked about what would happen once we arrived. My family knew we'd been hanging out—it had been their idea, after all—but this, what was happening between us now, had most certainly *not* been part of the plan. I trusted Liv to keep our secret, because if Jensen knew the things Will had done to his little sister's body, there was a good chance there would be fisticuffs, or, at the very least, some horrifically awkward conversations. It was easy to keep that particular reality in check when we were here, in the city. But heading home meant being faced with the reality that Will was Jensen's best friend. I couldn't act the way I did here, as if . . . as if he belonged to *me*.

Will placed my bag in the trunk and moved to open my door, making sure to press me against the side of the car and leaning in for a long, slow kiss. "Ready?"

"Yeah," I said, recovering from my small epiphany. I *liked* feeling like Will belonged to me. He stared down at me and smiled until we both seemed to realize we had but a few hours in the car to enjoy being so unself-conscious about this comfortable intimacy.

He kissed me one more time, humming against my lips and sweeping his tongue gently across mine before stepping back so I could get in the car.

Walking around to the other side, he jumped in the driver's seat and immediately said, "You know we could take a few minutes, hop in the back? I could put the seat down to make it work for you. I know you like your legs spread wide."

I rolled my eyes, grinning. With a little shrug, Will turned the key in the ignition. The car started with a roar and Will put it in gear, winking at me before pressing the gas. We lurched forward, jerking to a stop only a few feet from the curb.

He frowned but restarted the engine and managed to pull out smoothly into traffic the second go-round. I snatched his phone from the cup holder and began scrolling through his music. He gave me a disapproving look but didn't comment, instead turning his eyes on the road.

"Britney Spears?" I asked, laughing, and he reached out blindly, attempting to take it from me.

"My sister," he mumbled.

"Suuuure."

We reached a light at Broadway and the car stalled again. Will coughed but started it, swearing when it stalled just a few minutes later.

"You sure you know how to handle this thing?" I asked, smirking. "Been a New Yorker so long you've forgotten how to drive?"

He glared at me. "This would be a lot easier if we'd had sex in the back first. Help me clear my head."

I looked out the windshield and then back to him, smiling, as I ducked beneath his arm and went to work on his zipper. "Who needs the backseat?"

Chapter Sixteen

I turned off the car and the engine ticked in the answering silence. Beside me, Hanna was asleep, her head resting away from me and against the passenger window. We were parked in front of the Bergstrom family home on the outskirts of Boston, which featured a wide, white porch wrapping around clean brick. The front windows were framed by navy shutters and inside could be seen the hint of heavy cream curtains. The house was large, and beautiful, and held so many of my own memories I couldn't even imagine what it was like for Hanna to come back here.

I hadn't been here in a couple of years, not since I'd visited with Jensen for a random summer weekend to catch up with his folks. None of the other kids had been there. It was quiet and relaxing, and we'd spent most of the weekend on the back veranda, sipping gin-and-tonics and reading. But now I was parked in front of the house, sitting next to my friend's sister, who had given me two rounds of stellar car head, the last one ending less than an hour ago with my hands white-knuckling the steering wheel and my cock so deep in her throat I could feel her swallowing when I came. She really was a natural with the oral skills. She thought she needed further instruction, and I was happy to keep up the ruse long enough for her to practice on me a few more times.

In the city, enmeshed in our day-to-day lives, it was easy to forget the Jensen connection, the *family* connection. The *they'd-all-kill-me-if-they-knew-what-we-were-doing* connection. I'd been blindsided when she'd brought up Liv because it had felt like such ancient history. But I would be faced with all of that this weekend: my brief history as Liv's former flame, as Jensen's best friend, as Johan's intern. And I would have to face all of that while trying to hide my infatuation with Hanna.

I put my hand on her shoulder, shaking gently. "Hanna."

She startled a little, but the first thing she saw when she opened her eyes was me. She was groggy and not quite conscious but she smiled as if looking at her favorite thing in the world, and murmured, "Mmmm, hey, you."

And, with that reaction, my heart exploded. "Hey, Plum."

She smiled shyly, turning her head to look out her window as she stretched. When she saw where we'd parked, she startled a little, sitting up straighter, looking around. "Oh! We're here."

"We're here."

When she turned back to me, her eyes looked mildly panicked. "It's going to be weird, isn't it? I'm going to be staring at your button fly and Jensen will see me staring at your button fly and then you'll check out my chest and someone will see that, too! What if I touch you? Or"—her eyes went wide—"what if I *kiss* you?"

Her impending little freak-out calmed me immeasurably. Only one of us was allowed to feel weird at a time.

I shook my head, telling her, "It's going to be fine. We're here as friends. We're visiting your family as *friends*. There will be no public dick appreciation, and no public breast admiration. I didn't even pack another pair of button flies. Deal?"

"Deal," she repeated woodenly. "Just friends."

"Because that's what we *are*," I reminded her, ignoring the organ inside my chest that twisted as I said this.

Straightening, she nodded and reached for her door handle, chirping, "Friends! Friends visiting my house for Easter! We're going to see your old friend, my big brother! Thanks for driving me up here from New York, friend Will my friend!"

She laughed as she got out of the car and walked around to get her bag from the trunk.

"Hanna, calm down," I whispered, placing a soothing hand on her lower back. I felt my eyes move down her neck and settle on her breasts. "Don't be a lunatic."

"Eyes up here, William. Best start now."

Laughing, I whispered, "I'll try."

303

"Me, too." With a little wink, she whispered, "And remember to call me Ziggy."

Helena Bergstrom was such a good hugger she could have been from the Pacific Northwest. Only her softly lilting accent and dramatically European features gave her away as Norwegian-born. She welcomed me in, pulling me just past the front door and then into her familiar embrace. Like Hanna, she was on the tall side, and she had aged beautifully. I kissed her cheek, handing her the flowers we'd bought for her when we stopped to refuel.

"You're always so thoughtful," she said, taking them and waving us in. "Johan is still at work. Eric can't make it. Liv and Rob are here, but Jensen and Niels are still on the road." She looked past me, eyebrows drawn together. "It is going to rain, so I hope they all get here for dinner."

She rattled off her children's names as easily as she breathed. What had her life been like, I wondered, herding so many kids? And as each of them got married and had little ones of their own, this house would only grow more full.

I felt an unfamiliar ache to be part of it somehow and then blinked, looking away. This weekend had the potential to be strange enough without my new emotions thrown into the mix.

Inside, the house felt the same as it had years ago, even though they'd redecorated. It was still comfortable, but instead of the blue and gray décor I remembered from before, it was done in deep browns and reds with plush furniture and bright, cream walls. In the entryway and along the hallway leading deeper into the house, I could see that, redecoration or no, Helena still embraced her American life with a healthy smattering of life-affirming quotes masquerading as art on the walls. I knew what I would see farther into the house:

In the hallway, *Live, Laugh, Love!*

In the kitchen, *A balanced diet is a cookie in each hand!*

In the family room, *Our children: We give them roots so they can take flight!*

Catching me reading the one closest to the front door—*All roads lead home*—Hanna winked, wearing a knowing smile.

As feet tapped down the wooden stairs just to the side of the entryway, I looked up and met Liv's bright green eyes. My stomach dropped a little.

There was no reason for me to let things be weird with Liv; I'd seen her a handful of times since we'd hooked up, most recently at Jensen's wedding a few years ago, where we'd had a nice conversation about her job at a small commercial firm in Hanover. Her fiancé—now husband—had seemed nice. I'd walked away from the evening not thinking twice about where things stood with Liv of all people.

But that was because I hadn't considered that our brief

fling had meant anything to her, I hadn't known she'd been heartsick when I returned to Yale after the Christmas holiday so many years ago. It was as if a huge chunk of my history with the Bergstrom family had been rewritten—with me as the flaky lothario—and now that I was here, I realized I hadn't done anything to mentally prepare for it.

As I stood stiff as a statue, she walked up and hugged me. "Hey, Will." I felt the press of her very pregnant belly against my stomach and she laughed, whispering, "*Hug* me, silly."

I relaxed, wrapping my arms around her. "Hey yourself. I think it's safe to say congratulations are in order?"

She stepped back, rubbing her stomach and smiling. "Thanks." Amusement twinkled in her eyes and I remembered that Hanna had called her after our fight, and that Liv probably knew *exactly* what was going on with me and her little sister.

My stomach twisted back into a knot, but I pushed past it, forcing the weekend to not be peculiar on every level. "Are we expecting a boy or a girl?"

"It's going to be a surprise," she said. "Rob wants to know, but I don't. And so that means, of course, that I win." Laughing, she moved to the side to let her husband shake my hand.

We shared a few more pleasantries in the foyer; Hanna updated her mother and Liv on the latest news from graduate school, Rob and I spoke idly about the Knicks before

Helena gestured to the kitchen. "I'm going to get back in there. Come on down for a cocktail after you've settled in a little."

I grabbed our bags and followed Hanna up the stairs.

"Put Will in the yellow room," Helena called.

"Was that my room before?" I asked, checking out Hanna's perfect ass. She had always been slender, but the running was doing really great things for her curves.

"No, you were in the white guest room, the other one," she said, and then turned to smile at me over her shoulder. "Not that I remember *every* detail of that summer or anything."

I laughed and stepped past her into the bedroom that was meant to be mine for the night. "Where is your room?" The question came out before I'd really considered whether it was a good thing to ask, and certainly whether I'd checked to make sure no one else had followed us up here.

She looked back over her shoulder and then stepped inside, closing the door. "Two doors down."

The space seemed to shrink, and we stood, staring at each other.

"Hey," she whispered.

It was the first time since we left New York that I considered this might be a horrible idea. I was in love with Hanna. How would I be able to keep that from showing every time I looked at her?

"Hey," I managed.

Tilting her head, she whispered, "You okay?"

"Yeah." I scratched my neck. "Just . . . want to kiss you."

She took a few steps closer until she could run her hands under my shirt and up my chest. I bent, pressing a single, chaste kiss to her mouth.

"But I shouldn't," I said against her lips when she came back for another.

"Probably not." Her mouth moved over my chin, down my jaw, sucking, nibbling. Beneath my shirt, she scratched my chest with her fingernails, lightly sliding over my nipples. In only seconds I was rigid, ready, felt the fever slide over my skin and dig down into my muscles.

"I won't want to stop at just kissing," I said, half-warning for her to stop, half-plea for her to keep going.

"We have a little time before everyone else gets here," she said. She stepped back far enough to unbutton my jeans. "We could—"

I stilled her hands, the cautious side winning out. "Hanna. No way."

"I'll be quiet."

"That isn't the only issue I have with *fucking* you in your *parents' house*—during daylight, no less. Didn't we just have this conversation outside?"

"I know, I know. But what if this is the only time we'll be alone together?" she asked with a smile. "Don't you want to fool around with me here?"

She had lost her mind. "Hanna," I hissed, closing my eyes and stifling a groan as she pushed my jeans and boxers down my hips and wrapped a warm, tight hand around my shaft. "We really shouldn't."

She stopped, holding me gently. "We can be quick. For once."

I opened my eyes, looking at her. I didn't like to be quick ever, but especially not with Hanna. I liked to take my time. But if she was offering herself to me and we only had five minutes, I could handle five minutes. The rest of the family hadn't arrived yet; maybe it would be okay. And then I remembered: "Fuck. I don't have any condoms. I didn't pack any. For *obvious reasons*."

She cursed, wincing. "Me, either."

The question hung between us when she looked at me, eyes wide and pleading.

"*No*," I said without her having to say a word.

"But I've been on the pill for years."

I closed my eyes, jaw tight. *Fuck*. Pregnancy was the only thing I'd really been worried about. Even in my wildest days, I'd never had sex without a condom. In the past several years I was tested for anything every few months anyway. "*Hanna*."

"No, you're right," she said, thumb sweeping over the head of my cock, spreading the moisture there. "It's not just about getting pregnant. It's about being safe . . ."

"I've never had sex without a condom," I blurted. Who knew I had a death wish?

309

She stilled. "Ever?"

"Never even rubbed around on the outside. I'm too paranoid."

Her eyes widened. "What about 'just the tip'? I thought every guy did just the tip as a point of habit."

"I'm paranoid and careful. I know it only takes one time." I smiled at her, knowing she'd understand the reference: I was an "oops" baby.

Her eyes darkened, moved to stare at my mouth. "Will? This would be your first time like this?"

Fuck. When she looked at me like that, when her voice got all husky and quiet, I was lost. It wasn't just a physical attraction between us. Of course I'd been attracted to women before. But there was something more with Hanna, some chemistry in our blood, something between us that snapped and crackled, that made me always want just a little more than I should take. She offered her friendship, I wanted her body. She offered her body, I wanted to hijack her thoughts. She offered her thoughts, I wanted her heart.

And here she was, wanting to feel me inside her—just me, just her—and it was nearly impossible to say no. But I tried.

"I really don't think it's a good idea. We should be a little more thoughtful about that decision."

Particularly if there will be other guys in your "experiment," I didn't say.

"I just want to feel it. I haven't had sex without a condom, either." She smiled, stretching to kiss me. "Just inside. Just for a second."

Laughing, I whispered, "Just the tip?"

She stepped backward and leaned against the edge of the mattress, pushing her skirt up her hips and shimmying her panties down her legs. She faced me, spread her thighs and leaned back on her elbows, her hips hovering at the edge of the mattress. All I had to do was step closer and I could push inside. Bare.

"I know it's crazy and I know it's stupid. But God, that's how you make me feel." Her tongue slipped out, pressed to her bottom lip. "I promise to be quiet."

I closed my eyes, knowing as soon as she said that, I'd decided. The more important question was whether *I* could be quiet. I shoved my pants farther down and stepped between her legs, holding my cock and leaning over her. "Fuck. What are we even doing?"

"Just feeling."

My heart hammered in my throat, in my chest, in every inch of my skin. This felt like the final sex frontier; how weird that I'd done almost everything except this? It seemed so simple, almost innocent. But I'd never wanted to feel anything as much as I wanted to feel her, skin to skin. It was like a fever, taking over my mind and my reason, telling me how good it would feel to sink into her for just a second, just to feel and that would be enough. She could go back down to her room, unpack, freshen up, and I'd jerk off harder and faster than I'd ever jerked off in my life.

It was settled.

"Come here," she whispered, reaching for my face. I lowered my chest, opening my mouth to taste her lips, sucking on her tongue, swallowing her sounds. I could feel the slick skin of her pussy against the underside of my cock but that wasn't where I wanted to feel her. I wanted to feel her all around me.

"You good?" I asked, reaching between us to rub her clit. "Can I make you come first? I don't think we should finish like this."

"Can you pull out?"

"Hanna," I whispered, sucking on her jaw. "What happened to 'just the tip'?"

"You don't want to feel what it's like?" she countered, hands sliding over my ass, hips rocking. "You don't want to feel *me*?"

I growled, nipping at her neck. "You are a fucking devious girl."

She reached down and moved my fingers away from her clit, and took hold of me, rubbing my length over and around her sweet, drenched skin. I groaned into her neck.

And then she guided me there, holding, waiting for me to move my hips. I shifted forward, and back again, feeling the subtle give of her body when the head of my cock slid just inside. I moved deeper, the tiniest bit into her, just until I felt her stretch around my shaft and I stopped, groaning.

"Fast," I said. "Quiet."

"I promise," she whispered.

I'd expected warmth, but I was unprepared for *how* warm, how soft, how fucking *wet* it would feel. I was unprepared to feel dizzy from the feel of her, the sensation of her pulse beating all around me, muscles fluttering, of her tight hungry sounds in my ear telling me how different it was for her, too.

"Fuck," I grunted, unable to stop from moving all the way into her. "I don't . . . I can't fuck like this yet. It's too good. I'll come fast."

She held her breath, hands gripping my arms so tight it hurt. "It's okay," she managed, and then let out her breath in a gust. "You always hold out so long. I want it to feel so good you can't last."

"You're so evil," I hissed and she laughed, turning her head to capture my mouth in a kiss.

We were propped at the edge of the bed, our shirts still on, my jeans around my ankles and her skirt bunched at her hips. We'd just came upstairs to put our things away, freshen up, get situated. It was so *bad* that we were doing this here, but somehow we were hardly making any sound, and I convinced myself that if I could keep my wits about me, maybe I could fuck her slow enough to keep the bed from squeaking. But then I realized that I was *inside* her, completely *bare,* in her *parents'* house. I almost came just looking down at where I was buried inside her.

I slid almost all the way out—reveling in how wet I was

from her—and inched back in, and then again, and again. And *fuck,* I was ruined. Ruined for sex with anyone else, ruined for using a condom with this girl.

"Executive decision," she whispered, voice hoarse, breaths coming out in sharp spikes. "Forget the running. We need to do this five times a day." Her voice was so faint I pressed my ear to her lips to hear what else she might say. But all I could make out in my haze of sensation were whispered broken sentences with words like *hard,* and *skin* and *stay inside me after you come.*

It was that last idea that did me in, that made me think about coming inside her, kissing her until she grew fevered and urgent again and then growing hard with her tensing all around me. I could fuck her, stay there, and fuck her again before falling asleep inside her.

I moved harder, holding on to her hip, finding that perfect rhythm that didn't jolt the bed frame, didn't bounce the aluminum headboard into the wall. The pace where she could still stay quiet, where I could try to hold on until I got her there . . . but it was a losing battle, and it had barely been a few minutes.

"Oh shit, Plum," I groaned. "I'm sorry. I'm sorry." I threw my head back, feeling my orgasm barreling up my legs, down my spine, coming too soon. I pulled out, jerking my cock hard in my fist as she reached between her legs, pressing her fingers to her clit.

Footsteps sounded just outside in the hall, and my eyes

flew to Hanna's to see if she heard it, too, just a split second before someone pounded on the door.

My vision blurred and I felt myself starting to come.

Fuck. Fuuuuuck.

Jensen yelled, "Will! Hey, I'm here! You in the bathroom?"

Hanna sat up abruptly, eyes wide and wild with apology but it was already too late. I closed my eyes, coming in my hand, on the bare skin of her thigh.

"Just a second," I wheezed, staring down at where I still pulsed in my grip. I bent over the bed, leaning one hand on the mattress for support. When I looked up at Hanna, she couldn't seem to tear her eyes away from where my release landed on her skin, and—*fuck*—all over her skirt.

"I'm just changing. I'll be right out," I managed, my heart feeling like it was about to pound out of my body with the sudden flush of adrenaline that pumped through my blood.

"Cool. I'll meet you downstairs," he said, his footsteps retreating.

"Shit, your skirt . . ." I stepped back, scrambling to get dressed quickly, but Hanna hadn't moved.

"Will," she whispered, and I saw the familiar hunger darken her eyes.

"Fuck." That was too fucking close. The door wasn't even locked. "I don't . . ."

But she leaned back, pulling me over her. She was so completely unconcerned about her brother walking in, seeing us. And he *had* left, hadn't he?

This girl made me insane.

My heart still racing, I bent down, pressing two fingers inside her and sliding my tongue over her pussy as she let her eyes fall closed. Her hands went in my hair, her hips rocked up to my mouth, and within only seconds, she started to come, lips parted in a silent cry. Beneath my touch, she shook, hips rising from the bed, fingers pulling my hair tight.

As her orgasm subsided, I continued slowly moving my fingers inside her, but kissed a gentle path from her clit, to her inner thigh, to her hip. Finally, I rested my forehead against her navel, still struggling to catch my breath.

"Oh God," she whispered once her hands had eased their grip on my hair, and she slid them up and over her breasts. "You make me feel *crazy*."

I pulled my fingers from her and reached to kiss the back of her hand, inhaling the scent of her skin. "I know."

Hanna remained still on the bed for a quiet minute and then opened her eyes, gazing up at me as if she'd just come back to her senses. "Whoa. That was close."

Laughing, I agreed, "*Very* close. We should probably get changed and head downstairs." I nodded to her skirt. "Sorry about that."

"I'll just wipe it off."

"Hanna," I said, stifling a frustrated laugh. "You can't go downstairs with a giant jizz stain on your *skirt*."

She considered this and gave me a goofy smile. "You're right. I just . . . I kind of like it there."

"Such a twisted girl."

She sat up straight as I pulled my pants up, and she kissed my stomach through my shirt. I wrapped my arms around her shoulders, holding her to me, and just reveling in the feel of her.

I was so lost in love with this girl.

After a few seconds, the sun passed behind a cloud outside, dimming everything a little, beautifully, and her voice rose out of the quiet: "Have you ever been in love?"

I stilled, wondering if I'd said it out loud. But when I looked down at her, she was only glancing up in open curiosity, eyes calm. If any other woman had said this to me after we just had a quickie, I would have felt the hot flush of panic and the itching need to extract myself from the situation immediately.

But with Hanna, the question seemed somehow appropriate for the moment, especially given how reckless we'd just been. In the past several years I'd grown, if anything, overly cautious about when and where I had sex, and—Jensen's wedding aside—rarely put myself in situations that would ever require a quick exit or explaining. But lately, being with Hanna made me feel slightly panicked, as if there were a limited number of times I would be able to feel her like this. The thought of having to give her up made me nauseous.

There were only two other lovers in my life for whom I'd ever felt something deeper than fondness, but I'd never told a woman I loved her before. It was weird, and at thirty-one

I knew this omission made *me* weird, but I'd never felt the weight of that strangeness until just this moment.

I grew hyperaware of every blasé comment I'd made to Max and Bennett about love, and commitment. It wasn't that I didn't believe in them; I just had never been able to relate, exactly. Love was always something I'd find at some vague point in the future, when I was somehow more settled or less adventurous. The image of me as a player was very much like the deposit of minerals on glass over time; I hadn't bothered to care it was forming until it was hard to see past it.

"I'm guessing not," she whispered, smiling.

I shook my head. "I've never said 'I love you' before, if that's what you mean."

Though Hanna would have no way of knowing I said it to her, silently, nearly every time we touched.

"But have you ever *felt* it?"

I smiled. "Have you?"

She shrugged, and then nodded to the door to the Jack-and-Jill bathroom that I was pretty sure adjoined Eric's bedroom. "I'm going to go clean up."

I nodded, closing my eyes, and slumping down after she left. I thanked every lucky power in the universe that Jensen hadn't just walked in. That would have been a disaster. Unless we wanted her family to know what was happening— and I was pretty sure that since Hanna still wanted this to remain friends-with-benefits—we would have to be *way* more careful.

———

I checked my work email, sent a couple texts, and then pulled myself together in the bathroom, with some soap, water, and vigorous scrubbing. Hanna met me in the living room, wearing a bashful smile.

"I am so sorry," she said softly. "I don't know what got into me." She blinked, putting a hand to my mouth just as I started to crack the obvious joke. "Don't say it."

Laughing, I looked behind her into the kitchen, making sure no one was close enough to hear. "That was awesome. But holy shit it could have gone *very* wrong."

She looked embarrassed, and I smiled at her, making a goofy face. Out of the corner of my eye I caught sight of a little ceramic Jesus statue on an end table. I picked it up, holding it between Hanna's breasts. "Hey! Look! I found Jesus in your cleavage after all!"

She looked down, cracking up and started to shimmy a little, as if letting Jesus enjoy this most perfect of locations. "Jesus in my cleavage! Jesus in my cleavage!"

"Hey, guys."

When I heard Jensen's voice for the second time today, my arm flailed, hand flying away from the vicinity of Hanna's tits. Feeling as if I were watching it happen in slow motion and somewhere outside my own body, I flung the Jesus statue as quickly as I could, only realizing what I'd done when it landed on the hardwood floor several feet away from me, bouncing and exploding into a million little ceramic pieces.

"Oh, shiiiiiit," I groaned, running over to the massacre. I kneeled down, trying to pick up the biggest shards. It was a worthless effort. Some of the pieces were so small they could be characterized as dust.

Hanna bent over, wheezing in laughter. "Will! You broke Jesus!"

"What were you *doing*?" Jensen asked, kneeling to help me.

Hanna left the room to get a broom, leaving me alone with the person who had witnessed much of my early-twenties bad behavior. I shrugged at Jensen, trying to not look like I'd just been playing with his little sister's breasts. "I was just looking at it. I mean, at the statue, and seeing what it was. And looking at the shape—of *Jesus*, I mean."

I ran a hand over my face and realized I was sweating a little. "I don't even know, Jens. You just startled me."

"Why are you so jumpy?" He laughed.

"Maybe the drive? It's been a while since I was behind the wheel." I shrugged, still unable to look at him for very long.

With a pat to my back, Jensen said, "I think you need a beer."

Hanna returned, and shooed us away so she could sweep the shards into a dustpan, but not before giving me a conspiratorial *holy shit* look. "I told Mom you broke this and she couldn't even remember which of her aunts gave it to her. I think you're fine."

I groaned, following her into the kitchen and apologizing

to Helena with a kiss on her cheek. She handed me a beer and told me to relax.

At some point when I'd been upstairs fucking Hanna, or maybe when I'd been madly washing her scent off my dick and my fingers and my *face*, her father had arrived home. *Jesus Christ.* With some clarity away from naked Hanna and a closed bedroom door, I realized how insane we had been. What the fuck were we *thinking*?

Looking up from where he'd been digging in the fridge for a beer, Johan came over to greet me with his own brand of warmth and awkwardness. He was good at eye contact, bad with words. It usually meant that he ended up staring at people while they scrambled to come up with things to say.

"Hi," I said, returning his handshake and letting him pull me into a hug. "Sorry about Jesus."

He stepped back, smiled, and said, "Nah," and then paused, seemed to reconsider something. "Unless you've suddenly become religious?"

"Johan," Helena called, breaking our moment. I could have kissed her. "Honey, can you check the roast? The beans and bread are done."

Johan walked to the oven, pulling a meat thermometer out of the drawer. I felt Hanna step beside me, heard her clink her water glass to my beer bottle.

"Cheers," she said with an easy smile. "Hungry?"

"Famished," I admitted.

"Don't just stick the tip in, Johan," Helena called out to him. "Shove it all the way in there."

I coughed, feeling the burn of beer as it almost came out my nose. Cupping my hand over my mouth, I urged my throat to open, to allow me to swallow. Jensen stepped behind me, slapping my back and wearing a knowing grin. Liv and Rob were already sitting at the kitchen table, bent over in silent laughter.

"Holy shit, this is going to be a long night," Hanna mumbled.

———

Conversation looped around the table at dinner, breaking into smaller groups and then returning to include everyone. Partway through the meal, Niels arrived. Whereas Jensen was outgoing and one of my oldest friends, and Eric—only two years older than Hanna—was the wild child in the family, Niels was the middle child, the quiet brother, and the one I never really knew. At twenty-eight, he was an engineer with a prominent energy firm, and almost a carbon copy of his father, minus the eye contact and smiles.

But tonight, he surprised me: he bent to kiss Hanna before he sat down, and whispered, "You look amazing, Ziggs."

"You really do," Jensen said, pointing a fork at her. "What's different?"

I studied her from across the table, trying to see what

they saw and feeling mysteriously irked at the suggestion. To me, she looked as she always had: comfortable in her skin, easy. Not fussy with clothes, or hair or makeup. But didn't *need* to be. She was beautiful when she woke up in the morning. She was radiant after a run. She was perfect when she was beneath me, sweaty and postcoital.

"Um," she said, shrugging and spearing a green bean with her fork. "I don't know."

"You look thinner," Liv suggested, head tilted.

Helena finished a bite and then said, "No, it's her hair."

"Maybe Hanna's just *happy*," I offered, looking down at my plate as I cut a bite of roast. The table went completely still and I looked up, nervous when I saw the collection of wide eyes staring back at me. "What?"

Only then did I realize I'd called her by her given name, not Ziggy.

She covered smoothly, saying, "I'm running every day, so yes, I'm a little thinner. I did get my hair cut. But it's more. I'm enjoying my job. I have friends. Will's right—I *am* happy." She looked over at Jensen and gave him a cheeky little grin. "Turns out, you were right. Can we stop examining me now?"

Jensen beamed at her and the rest of the family all mumbled some variation of "Good," and returned to their food, quieter now. I could feel Liv's smile aimed at my face, and when I looked up from my plate, she winked.

Fuck.

"Dinner is delicious," I told Helena.

"Thanks, Will."

The silence grew, and I felt silently *inspected*. I'd been caught. It didn't help that Jesus' tiny decapitated porcelain head was watching me from the sideboard, judging. He knew. Ziggy was a nickname as ingrained in this family as their father's crazy work hours, or Jensen's tendency to be over-protective. I hadn't even known Hanna's given name when I'd gone running with her nearly two months ago. But fuck it. The only thing I could do was embrace it. I had to say it again.

"Did you know that Hanna has a paper coming out in *Cell*?" I hadn't been particularly smooth; her name came out louder than any other word but I went with it, smiling around the table.

Johan looked up, eyes widening. Turning to Hanna, he asked, "Really, *sötnos*?"

Hanna nodded. "It's on the epitope mapping project I was telling you about. It was just this random thing we did but it turned into something cool."

This seemed to steer the conversation into less awkward territory, and I let go of the little extra breath I'd been holding in. It was possible that the only thing more stressful than *meeting the parents* was *hiding everything from the family*. I caught Jensen watching me with a little smile, but simply returned it, and looked back down at my plate.

Nothing to see here. Keep moving along.

But during a break in the chatter, I found Hanna's eyes lingering on me, and they were surprised and thoughtful. "You," she mouthed.

"What?" I mouthed back.

She shook her head slowly, finally breaking eye contact to look down at her plate. I wanted to reach under the table with my leg, slide my foot over hers to get her to look back at me, but it was like a minefield of non-Hanna legs under there, and the conversation had already moved on.

———

After dinner, she and I volunteered to wash the dishes while the others retired to the family room with a cocktail. She snapped me with her dish towel and I flung soap suds at her. I was on the verge of leaning close and sucking on her neck when Niels came in to get another beer and looked at us both as if we had traded clothes.

"What are you doing?" he asked, suspicion heavy in his voice.

"Nothing," we answered in unison, and—making it worse—Hanna repeated, "Nothing. Just dishes."

He hesitated for a second before tossing his bottle cap in the trash and heading back to the others.

"That's twice today we've almost been busted," she whispered.

"Thrice," I corrected her.

"Nerd." She shook her head at me, amusement lighting

up her eyes. "I probably shouldn't risk sneaking into your room tonight."

I started to protest but stopped when I caught the sly grin curving her lips.

"You're the devil, do you know that?" I murmured, reaching out to glide my thumb across her nipple. "No wonder Jesus didn't want to be in your cleavage."

With a sharp gasp, she smacked my hand and looked over her shoulder.

We were all alone in the kitchen, could hear the others' voices trailing in through from the other room, and all I wanted to do was pull her into a kiss.

"Don't." Her eyes grew serious and the next words came out shaking, as if she couldn't catch her breath: "I won't be able to stop."

After staying up for a few hours to catch up with Jensen, I finally headed to bed. I stared at the wall for an hour or so before giving up on waiting for the quiet padding of Hanna's feet from down the hall or the creak of the door as she snuck into my room.

So I drifted off and missed it when she actually did slip in, get undressed, and climb naked under the blankets with me. I woke only to the feel of her smooth, bare body curling around mine.

Her hands ran up my chest, mouth sucking at my neck,

my jaw, my bottom lip. I was hard and ready to go before I was entirely conscious, and when I groaned, Hanna pressed a hand over my lips, reminding me, "Shh."

"What time is it?" I murmured, inhaling the sweet smell of her hair.

"A little after two."

"Are you sure no one heard you?" I asked.

"The only people who could hear me at this end of the hall are Jensen and Liv. Jensen's fan is on, so I know he's asleep. He can barely stay awake for ten seconds once that thing starts."

I laughed because she was right. I'd been his roommate for years, and I hated that fucking fan.

"And Rob is snoring," she murmured, kissing my jaw. "Liv has to fall asleep before him or else his snoring will keep her awake."

Satisfied that she'd been sufficiently stealthy—and that no one would be likely to knock on the door again while we were making love—I rolled to my side, pulling her close.

She snuck in for sex, clearly, but it didn't feel like all she wanted was a quick fuck. There was something else there, something brewing beneath the surface. I saw it in the way she kept her eyes open in the darkness, the way she kissed me so earnestly, each touch offered tentatively, as if she were asking a question. I saw it in the way she pulled my hand where she wanted it: over her neck, down across her breasts, coming to rest over her heart. It was *pounding*. Her bedroom was only a few doors down the hall; she wasn't winded from the effort. She was worked up over something, her mouth opening and closing a few times in the moonlight, as if she wanted to speak but couldn't find air.

"What's wrong?" I whispered, lips pressed to her ear.

"Are there still others?" she asked.

I pulled back and stared at her, confused. *Other women?* I'd wanted to have this conversation again a hundred times, but her subtle evasion had finally worn down my need for clarity. *She* wanted to date around, didn't trust me, and didn't think we should try to be exclusive. Or had I misunderstood? For *me*, there was no one else.

"I thought that's what you wanted?" I replied.

She stretched to kiss me; her mouth felt so familiar already, molding to mine in the easy rhythm of soft kisses that grew heated, and I wondered for a fevered beat how she could ever imagine sharing herself with anyone else.

She pulled me over her, reaching between us to slide me across her skin. "Is there a rule about having unprotected sex twice in a day?"

I sucked on the skin below her ear, and whispered, "I think the rule should be that there *aren't* any other lovers."

"So we break that rule then?" she asked, lifting her hips.

Fuck that. Fuck that noise.

I opened my mouth to protest, to put my foot down and tell her I'd had enough of this circular nondiscussion, but then she made a quiet, hungry sound and arched into me so that I slipped all the way inside her and I bit my lip to stifle a groan. It was unreal; I'd had sex thousands of times and it had never, *ever* been like this.

I tasted blood on my lip and fire beneath my skin wherever she touched me. But then she began to circle her hips, finding her pleasure beneath me, and I felt the words dissolve from my mind.

I'm only one man, for Christ's sake. I'm not a god. I can't resist taking Hanna now and figuring out everything afterward.

It felt like cheating; she wouldn't give me her heart but she'd give me her body, and maybe if I took enough of her pleasure, stored it up, I could pretend it was more.

It didn't matter at the time how much I might regret it later.

Chapter Seventeen

It had never been like this, ever. Slow. Almost so slow that I wasn't sure either of us could get there, or that I even cared. Our lips were only millimeters apart, sharing breaths and noises and the whispered pleas to *Feel that? Do you feel that?*

I *did* feel it. I felt every one of his stuttering heartbeats under my palm, and the way his shoulders shook above me. I felt the unformed words on his lips, how he seemed to be trying to say something . . . maybe the same something I'd been skirting around since I snuck into his dark room. Even before that.

He didn't seem to understand what I was asking.

I'd never expected it to be so hard to put myself on the line. We'd made love—what felt like the true meaning of the phrase earlier; his skin, my skin, nothing else between us. He called me Hanna at the dinner table. . . . I don't think anyone had ever said that name out loud in this house before that. And even though Jensen—Will's best friend—was in the other room, Will had stayed with me to do dishes. He'd given me a meaningful look before I headed to bed, and texted me good night, saying, In case there's any question, my bedroom door shall remain unlocked.

It seemed like he was mine when we were in a room full of people. But here, alone behind his closed door, it was suddenly so unclear.

Are there others?. . .

I thought that's what you wanted.

The rule should be that there aren't other lovers . . .

So we break this rule then?

. . . Silence.

But what was I expecting? I closed my eyes, wrapping my arms tighter around him as he pulled almost all the way out and then slid slowly back inside, inch by perfect inch, and groaned quietly in my ear.

"So good, Plum." His hips rolled over me, one hand sliding down my ribs and back up to cup my breast and simply hold it, his thumb sweeping over the tight peak.

I loved the deep, molten sounds of his pleasure, and it helped distract me from the truth that he hadn't given me the words I'd wanted tonight. I'd wanted him to say, *There are no other women anymore.* I'd wanted him to say, *Now that we're doing this without protection, we don't break that rule, ever.*

But he'd been the one to open this conversation before, only to have me shut it closed. Was it true that he really wasn't interested in being more than friends-who-fuck? Or was he unwilling to be the one to start the conversation again? And why was I being so *passive?* It was as if my fear of messing things up with him had stolen all of my words.

He arched his neck back, groaning quietly as he slid in and out of me, achingly slow. I closed my eyes, pressing my teeth into his neck, biting down, giving him every bit of pleasure I could think. I wanted him to want me so much that it didn't matter that I was inexperienced or unsure. I wanted to find a way to erase the memory of every woman who came before me. I wanted to feel—to *know*—that he belonged to me.

I wondered for a sharp, painful beat how many other women had thought the exact same thing.

I want to feel like you're mine. I pushed on his chest so he had to roll off me and I could climb over him. I'd never been on top with Will, not for sex, and looked down at him, feeling unsure, guiding his hands to my hips. "I've never done this."

He gripped his base with one hand and guided me over him, grunting as I sunk down. "Just find what feels good," he murmured, watching me. "This is where you get to drive."

I closed my eyes, trying different things and struggling to not feel foolish in my inexperience. I was so hyperaware of this earnest feeling pulling my ribs tight, I wondered if I moved differently, more clunky, less carefree and sexy. I had no idea if it felt good to him.

"Show me," I whispered. "I feel like I'm doing it wrong."

"You're perfect, are you fucking kidding?" he mumbled into my neck. "I want to last all night."

I grew sweaty, not from exertion but from being so wound up I thought I might burst from my skin. The bed was old and squeaky; we couldn't move the way we were used to—roughly for hours and using the entire mattress and frame and pillows. Before I realized what was happening, Will lifted me off him, carried me to the floor, and sat up beneath me so I could lower myself back onto him. He went so much deeper this way; he was so hard I could feel the press of him in some unknown, tender place. His open mouth moved across my chest and he ducked his head to suck and blow on my nipple.

"Just *fuck* me," he growled. "Down here you won't have to worry about the noise."

He thought I was worried about the creaky bed frame. I closed my eyes, rocking self-consciously, and just when I thought I would stop, tell him this position wasn't working for me, tell him I was choking on words and unanswered questions, he kissed my jaw, my cheek, my lips and whispered, "Where are you right now? Come back to me."

I stilled over him and rested my forehead on his shoulder. "I'm thinking too much."

"What about?"

"I'm nervous all of a sudden, and I just feel like you're mine only for these little bits of time. I guess I don't like that as much as I thought I would."

He slid his finger under my chin and tilted my face up so I had to look at him. His mouth pressed against mine, once, before he told me, "I'll be yours every second if that's what you want. You just have to tell me, Plum."

"Don't break me, okay?"

Even in the darkness I could see his brows pull together. "You said that before. Why do you think I would break you? Do you think I even *could*?" His voice sounded so pained, it plucked at something raw and taut in me, too.

"I think you *could*. Even if you didn't want to, I think you could now."

He sighed, pressing his face into my neck. "Why won't you give me what I want?"

"What *do* you want?" I asked, shifting so that my knees were more comfortable, but in the process, I slid up his cock and back down. He stilled me with forceful hands on my hips.

"I can't think when you're doing that." Taking several deep breaths, he whispered, "I just want *you*."

"So . . ." I whispered, running my hands into the hair at the nape of his neck. "Are there going to be others?"

"I think *you* need to tell *me* that, Hanna."

I closed my eyes, wondering if that would be good enough. I could tell him I wouldn't date anyone else, and I imagined he would agree to the same. But I didn't *want* it to be up to me. If Will was going to do this, to be with one person, it had to be something that wasn't negotiable for him—it had to be him wanting to call it off with the others because of how he felt for *me*. It couldn't be some loose decision, a maybe-maybe-not, a whatever-you-decide.

His mouth found mine then, and he gave me the sweetest, most gentle kiss I'd ever felt from him. "I told you I wanted to try," he whispered. "You were the one who said you thought it wouldn't work. You know who I am; you *know* I want to be different for you."

"I want it, too."

"Okay then." He kissed me and our pace started again, small thrusts from him beneath me, tiny circles from me on top. His exhales were my inhales; his teeth slid deliciously over my lips.

I'd never felt so close to another human in my life. His hands were everywhere: my breasts, my face, my thighs, my hips, between my legs. His voice rumbled low and encouraging in my ear, telling me how good I felt, how close he was, how he needed this so much he felt like he worked every day just to get back to me. He told me being with me felt like being home.

And when I fell, I didn't care whether I was awkward or jagged, whether I was inexperienced or naïve. I cared only that his lips were pressed firmly to my neck and his arms were wrapped around me so tight the only way I could move was closer to him.

⌒⌒⌒

"You ready?" Will asked Sunday afternoon, slipping into my bedroom and pressing a quick kiss to my cheek. The majority of the morning had played out this way: a covert kiss in an empty hallway, a rushed grope session in the kitchen.

"Almost. Just packing a few things Mom is sending home with me." I felt his arms fold solid around my waist and I leaned back, melting into him. I'd never noticed how much Will touched me until he couldn't do it freely. He'd always been tactile—small brushes of his fingers, a hand lingering at my hip, his shoulder bumping against mine—but I'd grown so used to it, so comfortable, I hardly noticed anymore. This weekend I'd felt the loss of every one of those small moments, and now I couldn't get enough. I was already debating how many miles we'd need to put between the car and this place before I could tell him to pull over and make good on his offer to take me in the backseat.

He pushed my ponytail out of the way as his lips moved along my neck, stopping just below my ear. I heard the tinkling of his keys in his hand, felt the cool metal against my stomach where my shirt had ridden up the tiniest bit.

"I shouldn't be doing this," he said. "I think Jensen's been trying to corner me since brunch and I don't really have a death wish."

His words cooled my blood and I stepped away, reaching for a shirt on the opposite side of the bed. "Sounds like pretty standard Jensen," I murmured with a shrug. I knew it would be weird for my oldest brother—hell, it would be weird for Will and me, too, when the family knew about us—but all morning long I'd been replaying the previous night in the guest room. I wanted to ask him in the light of day: *did you really mean it when you said you wanted only me?* Because I was finally ready to take the leap.

I zipped my bag, started to lug it off the bed.

He reached around my body, grabbing the handle. "Can I take that?"

I felt the heat of him, the scent of his shampoo. When he straightened he didn't step away, didn't move to put distance between us. I closed my eyes, felt myself grow dizzy with how his proximity seemed to suck all the air out of the room. He tilted my chin and pressed his lips to mine, just a slow, lingering touch and I moved toward him, chasing the kiss.

He smiled. "Let me get this stuff in the car and we'll get out of here, okay?"

"Okay."

He brushed his thumb over my lower lip. "We'll be home soon," he whispered. "And I'm not going to my apartment."

"Okay," I said again, legs shaking.

He grinned, lifted the bag, and I watched, barely able to stand, as he left the room.

Going downstairs, I found my sister in the kitchen.

"Leaving?" Liv asked, rounding the counter to hug me.

I leaned into her, nodding. "Is Will already outside?" I glanced out the kitchen window but didn't see him. I was anxious to get on the road, to say everything in the light of day where it couldn't be ignored.

"Think he went out back to say goodbye to Jens," she said, walking back to the bowl of berries she'd been rinsing. "You two sure are cute together."

"What? No." Cookies cooled on the counter and I reached for a handful, tucking them away in brown paper sack. "I told you, it's not like that, Liv."

"Say what you want, Hanna. That boy is smitten. Frankly, I'd be surprised if I'm the only one who's noticed."

Beginning to feel warm, I shook my head. Pulling two Styrofoam cups from the cupboard, I filled them with coffee from a huge stainless steel carafe, adding sugar and cream to mine and cream only to Will's. "I think pregnancy's mottled your brain. That's not what this is about." My sister wasn't an idiot; I'm sure she heard the lie in my voice as plainly as I had.

"Maybe not for you," she said with a skeptical shake of her head. "Though I don't really buy that one, either."

I stared blankly out the back window. I knew where Will and I stood . . . at least I thought I did. Things had shifted over the past few days and now I was eager to define this relationship. I'd been so afraid to give it limits because I thought I wanted more room to breathe. I thought it would upset me to hear how he slotted me into his schedule as conveniently as he did other women. Lately, my desire to avoid the conversation felt more about keeping my own heart caged than about how free he was with his. But it was a useless exercise. I knew we needed to have the full conversation now—the one he'd tried to have before. The one we'd touched on last night.

I would need to put myself out there, take a risk. It was time.

A door shut loudly somewhere and I jumped, blinking back to the coffee I was still stirring. Liv touched my shoulder. "I have to be big sister for just one minute, though. Be careful, okay?" she said. "This is the infamous Will Sumner we're talking about."

And that, right there, was reason number one I was terrified I was making a mistake.

With coffee and snacks for the road in hand, I made the rounds and said my goodbyes. My family was scattered all over the house, but the only two I couldn't seem to find were my brother and my ride.

I headed out front to check the car, the gravel path crunching beneath my feet. I neared the garage and stopped as voices filtered out through the cool morning air, above the birds and the creaking of the trees overhead.

"I'm just wondering what's going on between you two," I heard my brother say.

"Nothing," Will said. "We're just hanging out. Per your request, I might add."

I frowned, remembering that old saying about not eavesdropping because you probably won't like what you hear.

"Is 'hanging out' code for something?" Jensen asked. "You seem awfully familiar with her."

Will started to speak but paused, and I stepped back a bit to make sure my long shadow wouldn't be visible to anyone standing in the garage.

"I am seeing a few people," Will started, and I could just picture him scratching his jaw. "But no, Ziggy isn't one of them. She's just a good friend."

I felt like I'd been dropped in ice water, goose bumps spreading along my skin and despite knowing he was just following the rules we'd agreed on, my stomach dropped.

Will went on: "Actually, I am . . . interested in exploring something more with one of the women I'm seeing." My heart started to hammer, and I was tempted to step forward, and keep him from saying too much. But then he added, "So I feel like I should end it with the other women I'm seeing. I think for the first time I might want more . . . but this girl has been cagey, and it's been hard to take that extra step and just cut off the old routine, you know?"

My arms felt like limp noodles and I leaned against the gate, steadying myself. My brother said something in reply, but I wasn't really listening anymore.

<hr>

To say the atmosphere in the car was merely tense was laughable. We'd been on the road for almost an hour and I'd barely strung together more than two words at a time.

Are you hungry?

No.

Temperature okay? Too warm? Too cold?
It's fine.
Could you put this into the GPS?
Sure.
Mind if we stop for a bathroom break?
Okay.

The worst part was that I was pretty sure I was being bratty and unfair. With what Will said to Jensen, he was only following the rules that I'd put out there. I'd never really expected him to be exclusive before last night.

Open your mouth, Hanna. Tell him what you want.

"You okay over there?" he asked, ducking briefly to catch my eyes. "You're being awfully monosyllabic."

I turned and watched his profile as he drove: his stubbly jaw, his lips curled up in a smile just knowing I was staring at him. He let his eyes dart my way a couple of times, reaching for my hand and squeezing it. It was so much more than sex. He was my best friend. He was the one I wanted to call *boyfriend*.

The idea of him being with other women this whole time made me faintly nauseous. I was pretty sure that, after this weekend, he wouldn't be with them again since—*Jesus*—we'd had sex without a condom. If that didn't warrant a serious discussion, I didn't know what did.

I felt so close to him; I really felt like we had become something much more than friends.

I pressed my hands to my eyes, feeling jealous and nervous and . . . *God*, just so impatient for us to figure it out *now*. Why was it easy to talk to Will about every feeling I had but the ones we needed to declare between us?

When we stopped at a gas station to refuel, I distracted myself by going through the music on his phone, building the proper sequence of words in my head. Finding a song I was pretty sure he hated, I smiled, watching him hang up the pump, walk back to his side of the car.

He climbed back in, his hand hovering with the key perched in the ignition. "Garth *Brooks*?"

"If you don't like it, then why is it on your phone?" I teased. This was good, this was a start, I thought. Actual words were a step in the right direction. Ease into the conversation; prepare a soft landing and then jump.

He gave me a playful sour look, as if he'd tasted something gross, and started the engine to pull away. The words cycled through my head: *I want to be yours. I want you to be mine. Please tell me you haven't been with anyone else in the past couple of weeks, when things seemed so good with us. Please tell me that hadn't all been in my mind.*

I opened his iTunes and started scrolling through his music again, looking for something better, something that made my mood lighter and more sure of myself, when a text message flashed across his screen.

`Sorry I missed this yesterday! Yes! I'm free Tuesday night and I can't wait to see you. My place? xoxox`

Kitty.

I don't think I took a breath for an entire minute.

Turning off the screen, I sank lower into my seat, feeling like someone had reached down my throat and pulled my stomach inside out. My veins flushed hot with adrenaline, with embarrassment, with anger. Sometime between fucking me without a condom at my parents' house yesterday afternoon and kissing my neck this morning, Will had messaged Kitty about getting together on Tuesday.

I looked out the window as we pulled away from the gas station and got back on the road, dropping the phone gently into his lap.

A few minutes later he glanced at his phone before wordlessly putting it back down.

He had clearly seen Kitty's message, and he didn't say anything. He didn't even look *surprised*.

I wanted to climb into a hole.

We arrived at my apartment but he made no attempt to come upstairs. I carried my bag to the door and we stood there awkwardly.

He pulled a stray hair from my cheek and then quickly dropped his hand when I winced. "You sure you're okay?"

I nodded. "Just tired."

"I guess I'll see you tomorrow?" he asked. "The race is Saturday so we should probably do a couple of longer runs early in the week and then rest."

"That sounds good."

"So I'll see you in the morning?"

I was suddenly desperate to hold on, to give him one last chance, a way to come clean and maybe clear up a huge misunderstanding.

"Yeah, and . . . I was wondering if you wanted to come over Tuesday night," I said, reaching out to place my hand on his forearm. "I feel like we should talk, you know? About everything that happened this weekend?"

He looked down at my hand, moved so his fingers could twist with mine. "You can't talk to me now?" he asked, brow furrowed and clearly confused. It was, after all, only seven at night on a Sunday. "Hanna, what's going on? I feel like I'm missing something."

"It was just a long drive and I'm tired. Tomorrow I have a late night in the lab, but Tuesday is open. Can you make it?" I wondered if my eyes were pleading as much as the voice inside my head was. *Please say yes. Please say yes.*

He licked his lips, glanced at his feet and up to where his hand was holding mine. It felt like I could see the actual seconds tick by and the air felt thick, almost solid, and so heavy I could hardly breathe.

"Actually," he said, and paused as if he was still considering, "I have a late . . . thing, for work. I have a late meeting on Tuesday," he babbled. *He lied.* "But I could make it during the day or—"

"No, it's fine. I'll just see you tomorrow morning."

"You sure?" he asked.

My heart felt like it had frozen over. "Yeah."

"Okay well, I'll just"—he motioned to the door over his shoulder—"go now. You sure everything's fine?"

When I didn't answer, and just stared at his shoes, he kissed my cheek before leaving and I locked up, heading straight for my room. I wouldn't think of another thing until morning.

I slept like the dead, not waking until my alarm went off at five forty-five. I reached over to hit the snooze button and lay there, staring at the illuminated blue dial. Will had lied to me.

I tried to rationalize it, tried to pretend it didn't matter because maybe things weren't official with us, maybe we weren't *together* yet . . . but somehow, that didn't feel true, either. Because as much as I'd tried to convince myself that Will was a player and couldn't be trusted, deep down . . . I must have believed that Saturday night changed everything. I wouldn't feel like this otherwise. Still, apparently he was fine hooking up with other women until we sat down and made it *officially* official. I could never be that cavalier about separating emotion from sex. The simple realization that I wanted to be only with Will was enough to make me faithful.

We were entirely different creatures.

The numbers in front of me blurred and I blinked back the sting of tears as the snooze alarm broke through the silence. It was time to get up and run. Will would be waiting for me.

I didn't care.

I sat up long enough to unplug the clock from the wall and then rolled over. I was going back to sleep.

———

I spent the majority of Monday at work with my phone off, not heading home until long after the sun had gone down.

Tuesday I was up before my alarm and down at the local gym, running on the treadmill. It wasn't the same as the trails at the park with Will, but at this point, I didn't care. The exercise helped me breathe. It helped me think and clear my head, and gave me a brief moment of peace from thoughts of Will and whatever—*whoever*—he was doing tonight. I think I ran harder than I ever had. And later, in the lab, when I had barely came up for air all day, I had to leave early, around five, because I hadn't eaten anything other than a yogurt and felt like I was going to fall flat on my face.

When I got home, Will was waiting at my door.

"Hi," I said, slowing as I neared him. He turned around, shoved his hands in his pockets, and spent a long time just looking at me.

"Is there something wrong with your phone, Hanna?" he asked finally.

I felt a brief pang of guilt before I straightened, meeting his eyes. "No."

I moved to unlock the door, keeping some distance between us.

"What the fuck is going on?" he asked, following me inside.

Okay, so we were doing this now. I looked at his clothes. He'd obviously just come from work and I had to wonder if he'd stopped by here before going to meet . . . *her*. You know, to make the rounds and settle things down before stepping out with someone else. I wasn't sure I would ever understand how he could be so wild about me, while fucking other women.

"I thought you had a late meeting," I murmured, turning to drop my keys on the counter.

He hesitated, blinking several times before saying, "I do. It's at six."

Laughing, I murmured, "Right."

"Hanna, what the hell is going on? What did I do?"

I turned to face him . . . but chickened out, staring at the tie loosened at his neck instead, his striped shirt. "You didn't do anything," I started, breaking my own heart. "I should have been honest about my feelings. Or . . . lack of feelings."

His eyes went wide. "*Excuse* me?"

"Things at my parents' house were weird. And being so close, almost getting caught? I think that was the real thrill for me. Maybe I got carried away with everything we said on Saturday night." I turned away, fidgeted with a stack of mail on a table and felt the crackling, dried layers of my heart peel away and leave nothing but a hollow shell. I forced a smile on my face and gave him a casual shrug. "I'm twenty-four, Will. I just want to have fun."

He stood there and blinked, swaying slightly as if I'd hurled something at him heavier than words. "I don't understand."

"I'm sorry. I should have called or . . ." I shook my head, trying to shake the sound of static in my ears. My skin felt hot; my chest ached like my ribs were caving in. "I thought I could do this but I can't. This weekend just solidified that for me. I'm sorry."

He took a step back and glanced around like he'd just woken up and realized where he was. "I see." I watched him swallow, run a hand through his hair. As if he'd remembered something, he looked up. "Does this mean you won't run on Saturday? You've trained really hard and—"

"I'll be there."

He nodded once before turning, walking out the door, and disappearing, probably forever.

CHAPTER EIGHTEEN

There was a hill near my mom's house, just before the turn down the driveway. It was an uphill followed by a blind downhill curve, and we'd learned to honk whenever we went over it, but when people drove it for the first time, they were never aware of how tricky it was at first and would later always tell us how crazy that turn was.

I supposed my mom or I could have put up a curved mirror at some point, but we never did. Mom said she liked using only her horn, she liked that moment of faith, where she knew my schedule and she knew the curve so well she didn't need to see what was ahead in order to know it was clear. The thing was, I was never sure whether I loved or hated that feeling myself. I hated having to hope the coast was clear, hated not knowing what was coming, but I loved the moment of exhilaration when the car would coast downhill, clear and free.

Hanna made me feel this way. She was my blind curve, my mysterious hill, and I'd never been able to shake the lingering suspicion that she'd send something the other way that would crash blindly into me. But when I was with her, close enough to touch and kiss and hear all of her crazy theories on virginity and love, I'd never felt such a euphoric combination of calm, elation, and hunger. In those moments, I stopped caring that we might crash.

I wanted to think her brush off tonight as a glitch, a scary curve that would soon straighten out, and that my relationship with her wasn't over before it even started. Maybe it was her youth; I tried to remember myself at twenty-four and could really only see a young idiot, working crazy hours in the lab and then spending night after night with different women in all manners of wildness. In some ways, Hanna was such an older twenty-four than I'd ever been; it was like we weren't even the same species. She was right so long ago when she said she always knew how to be a grown-up and needed to learn how to be a kid. She'd just accomplished her first immature blow-off with a complete lack of clear communication.

Well done, Plum.

I'd put Kitty in a cab and returned to work around eight, intent on diving into some reading, and trying to get out of my own head for a few hours. But as I passed Max's office on the way to mine, I saw that his light was still on, and he was sitting inside.

"What are you still doing here?" I asked, stepping just inside the room and leaning against the doorway.

Max looked up from where he'd been resting his head in his hands when I walked into his office. "Sara's out with Chloe. Just decided to work a bit late." He studied me, mouth turning down at the corners. "And I thought you left a few hours ago. Why are you back? It's Tuesday . . ."

We stared at each other for a beat, the implied question hanging between us. It had been so long since I'd spent a Tuesday night with Kitty, I don't think even Max knew exactly what he was asking.

"I saw Kitty tonight," I admitted. "Earlier, just for a bit."

His brows pulled together in irritation, but I held up a hand, explaining: "I asked her to meet me for a drink after work—"

"Seriously, Will, you're a right toss—"

"To *end* it, you ass," I growled, frustrated. "Even though things with her were always meant to be casual, I wanted her to know they were done. I haven't seen her in forever but she still checks in every Monday to ask. The fact that she even thinks it's a possibility made me feel like I've been cheating on Hanna."

Just saying that name out loud made my stomach twist. The way we had left things tonight had been a mess. I'd never seen her look so distant, so closed off. I clenched my jaw, looking over at the wall.

I knew she'd been lying; I just didn't know *why*.

Max's chair creaked as he leaned back. "So what are you doing here? Where is your Hanna?"

I blinked back over to him, finally taking in his appearance. He looked tired, and shaken, and . . . not at all like Max, even at the end of a long workday.

"What's with you?" I asked instead of answering. "You look like you've been through the wringer."

Finally he laughed, shaking his head. "Mate, you have no idea. Let's collect Ben and go grab a pint."

We got to the bar before Bennett did, but not by much. Just as we sat at a table in the back, near the dartboards and the broken karaoke machine, Bennett strode in still wearing his crisp dark suit and a look of such utter exhaustion I wondered how long the three of us would manage to remain conscious.

"You sure are making me drink a lot on weeknights lately, Will," Bennett mumbled, taking a seat.

"So order a soda," I said.

We both looked at Max, expecting his usual semi-serious and barely intelligible rant about the blasphemy of ordering a Diet Coke in a British pub, but he just remained uncharacteristically quiet, staring at the menu and then ordering what he always ordered: a pint of Guinness, a cheeseburger, and chips.

Maddie took the rest of our orders and disappeared. We were back on yet another Tuesday night and, just as before, the bar was almost empty. A strange quietness seemed to ring our table. It was as if none of us could get it up tonight to bother shit-talking.

"Really, though. What's up with you?" I asked Max again.

He smiled at me—a genuine Max smile—but then shook his head. "Ask me again after I've had two pints." Grinning up at Maddie as she put our drinks on the table, he gave her a little wink. "Thanks, love."

"The text from Max said we are convening at Maddie's for a girls' night out," Bennett said, and then took a sip of his beer. "So which of Will's women are we discussing tonight?"

"There's only the one woman, now," I murmured. "And Hanna ended it earlier tonight, so I guess technically there are *no* women." Both men looked up at me, eyes concerned. "She said, essentially she didn't want this."

"Fuck," Max murmured, rubbing his face in his hands.

"The thing is," I said, "I *think* she's full of shit."

"Will . . ." Bennett cautioned.

"No," I said, waving him off, and feeling a surge of re-lief, of realization as I thought more about it. Yes, she'd been pissed tonight at her place—and I still had no idea why—but I remembered how it felt making love on the floor this weekend, in the middle of the night, and the hunger in her eyes like she didn't just want me, she was starting to *need* me.

"I *know* she feels this, too. Something happened be-tween us this weekend," I told them. "The sex has always been fucking amazing, but it was so intense at her parents' place."

Christina Lauren

Bennett coughed. "Sorry. You had sex at her *parents'* place?"

I chose to believe his ambiguous tone meant *impressed*, so I continued: "It was like she was finally going to admit there was more between us than just sex and friendship." I lifted my water glass to my lips, took a sip. "But the next morning, she snapped closed. She's talking herself out of it."

Both men hummed thoughtfully, considering this. Finally, Bennett asked, "Did you two ever decide to be exclusive? I'm sorry if I'm not following the map of this relationship very clearly. You leave a very treacherous path of women behind you."

"She knew that I wanted to be exclusive, but then I agreed to keep it open—because that's what she wanted. For me, she's *it*," I said, not caring whether they gave me a mountain of shit for being so whipped. I deserved it, and the funniest part was I *relished* being claimed. "You guys called it, and I have no problem admitting you're right. She's funny, and beautiful. She's sexy and she's fucking brilliant. I mean, she is *completely* it for me. I have to think today was just a bump in the road or else I will probably go on punching walls repeatedly until my hand is broken."

Bennett laughed, lifting his glass to clink it against mine. "Then here's to hoping she comes around."

Max lifted his glass, too, knowing there wasn't really anything he could say. He winced a little, apologetically, as if this was all somehow his fault simply because he'd wished lovesick misery on me only a couple months back.

After my little speech, the silence returned, and the weird mood with it. I struggled to not be pulled under. Of course I was worried I wouldn't be able to win Hanna back. From the first moment she slid her fingers beneath my shirt in the bedroom at the party, I'd been ruined for anyone else.

Hell, even before then. I think I'd been lost in her the second I pulled the wool cap over her adorably rumpled bed head on our first run.

But despite my certainty that she had lied about her feelings, and that she did feel something for me, doubt crept back in. *Why* had she lied? What happened between our obvious *lovemaking* and when we got into the car the next morning?

Bennett interrupted my downward spiral with his own misery: "Well, since we're letting out all of our feelings, I guess it's my turn to share. The wedding is driving us both mad. Everyone in our family is traveling to San Diego for the ceremony—I mean *everyone*—step-great-aunts and second-cousins-twice-removed and people I haven't seen since I was five. The same thing on Chlo's side."

"That's great," I said, and then reconsidered when Bennett slid his cool gaze to me. "Isn't it good when people accept your invitation?"

"I suppose it is, but many of these people weren't invited. Her family is mostly in North Dakota, and mine is all

over Canada, and Michigan, and Illinois. They're all looking for a reason to have a vacation on the coast." Shaking
his head, he continued: "So last night Chloe decided she
wanted to elope. To cancel all of it, and she's so hell-bent
on it that I'm afraid she is going to call the hotel and cancel
and we'll be thoroughly fucked then."

"She wouldn't do that, mate," Max murmured, roused
from his uncharacteristically quiet mood. "Would she?"

Bennett's hands slid into his hair and curled into fists,
his elbows planted on the table. "Honestly, I don't know.
This thing is getting *huge,* and even I feel like it's spiral-
ing out of control. Everyone in our family is inviting whoever
they want—as if it's just a big free party and why not? It's
not even about cost at this point, it's about space, about
having what *we* wanted. We were imagining a wedding of
about a hundred and fifty. Now it's close to three hundred."
He sighed. "It's just one day. It's a *day.* Chloe is trying to
stay sane but it's hard on her because there's only so much
I . . ." He laughed, shaking his head, and then sat up to look
at us. "There are only so many details I give a shit about.
For once in my life, I don't need to control everything. I don't
care what our colors are, or what wedding favors we choose.
I don't care about the flowers. Everything that comes after
is what I care about. I care that I get to fuck her for a week
in Fiji and then we'll be married forever. *That's* what matters. Maybe I should just let her cancel it all and marry her
this weekend so we can get to the fucking."

I opened my mouth to protest, to tell Bennett that I was sure every couple went through this kind of crisis, but the truth was, I had no idea. Even at Jensen's wedding—where I'd been the best man—the only thing keeping me going during the ceremony was the thought of taking the two bridesmaids to the coat closet to bang. I hadn't paid particularly close attention to the more sentimental emotions of the day.

So, I closed my mouth, rubbing a palm across it and feeling a dose of self-loathing sweep over me. *Fuck.* I already missed Hanna, and being with my two closest friends who were so . . . *situated* made it hard. It wasn't that I felt I needed to catch up to some milestone of theirs; I simply wanted that comfort of knowing I could go out with my friends for an evening and still come home to *her.* I missed the comfort of her company, the way she listened so carefully, the way I knew she said whatever came to mind when she was around me, a thing I noticed she didn't do with anyone else. I *loved* her for being so wildly her own self—so fierce and confident and curious and smart. And I missed feeling her body, taking pleasure from her, and, *fuck,* giving *her* pleasure unending.

I wanted to lie in bed with her at night, and bemoan the ordeal of planning a wedding. I wanted it all.

"Don't elope," I said, finally. "I realize that I know shit about any of this, and I'm sure my opinion means nothing, but I'm pretty sure *every* wedding feels like a complete clusterfuck at one point or another."

"It just feels like so much work for a single day," Bennett

mumbled. "Life goes on so much longer beyond this one slip of time."

Max chuckled, lifting his glass, and then reconsidered, putting it back down on the table, before he started laughing again, and harder. We both turned to look at him.

"You *were* acting like zombie Max," I noted, "but now you're creepy clown Max. We're all sharing here—I've had my heart stomped on by Hanna, Bennett is wrestling with the age-old crisis of wedding planning madness. Your turn."

He shook his head, smiling down at his empty pint. "Fine." He waved to Maddie for another Guinness. "But Ben, you're here tonight only as my mate. Not as Sara's boss. Understood?"

Bennett nodded, brows pulled together. "Of course."

Offering a one-shouldered shrug, Max murmured, "Well, lads, it turns out I'm going to be a dad."

The relative quiet we had been enjoying seemed like roaring chaos in comparison to the vacuum that now existed. Bennett and I froze, and then exchanged a brief look.

"Max?" Bennett asked, with an uncharacteristic delicacy. "Sara's pregnant?"

"Yeah, mate." Max looked up, cheeks pink and eyes wide. "She's having my baby."

Bennett continued to watch him, probably assessing every reaction on Max's face.

"This is good," I said carefully. "Right? This is a good thing?"

Max nodded, blinking over to me. "It's bloody *amazing*. I just . . . I'm terrified, to be honest."

"How far along is she?" Bennett asked.

"A little over three months." We both started to respond in surprise but he held up his hand, nodding. "She's been stressed, and she thought . . ." Shaking his head, he continued: "She took a test this weekend, but didn't know until today how far she was. But today, when I was out at meetings . . . we had an ultrasound to measure the baby." He pressed the heels of his hands to his eyes. "Bloody hell, *the baby*. I just found out Sare's pregnant, and today I could see there's a fucking *kid* in there. Sara's far enough along that the ultrasound technician guessed it's a girl but we won't know for sure for a couple months. It's just . . . unreal."

"Max, why the fuck are you out with *us*?" I asked, laughing. "Shouldn't you be at home drinking sparkling cider and picking out names?"

He smiled. "She wanted some time away from me, I think. I've been fucking unbearable the last few days, wanting to remodel the bloody apartment and talk about when we're getting married and all that shite. I think she wanted to tell Chloe. Besides, we've got a date planned for tomorrow." He stilled, his brows pulling together in concern when he said that. "But now that this day is over, I'm just *beat*."

"You're not worried about this, are you?" Bennett asked, studying Max. "I mean, this is unbelievable. You and Sara are going to have a *baby*."

"No, it's just the same worries I'm sure everyone feels I imagine," Max said, wiping a hand across his mouth. "Will I be a good dad? Sara's not much of a drinker, but did we do anything in the past three months that could hurt the baby? And, with my giant spawn growing in there, will little Sara be okay?"

I could barely hold back. I stood, pulling Max out of his chair and into a hug.

He was so in love with Sara he could barely think straight when she was around. And although most of the time I gave him endless shit about it, it was a pretty amazing thing to behold. I knew without him ever having to say it that he was ready for this, ready to settle down and be the devoted husband and dad. "You'll be amazing, Max. Seriously, congratulations."

Stepping back, I watched as Bennett stood, shaking Max's hand and then pulling him into a brief hug.

Holy shit.

The enormity of this started to sink in and I all but collapsed back into my chair. This, here, was life. This was life beginning for us: weddings and families and deciding to step up and be a man for someone. It wasn't about the fucking jobs we had or the random thrills we sought or any of that. Life was built from the bricks of these connections and milestones and moments where you tell your two best friends that you're about to have a child.

I pulled out my phone, sending Hanna a single note.

You're all I can think about anymore.

Chapter Nineteen

When I was little, I'd drive my entire family insane by not sleeping for days before any holiday or big event. Nobody understood why. My exhausted mother would sit up with me night after night, begging me to just go to bed.

"Ziggy," she would say. "Honey, if you go to bed, Christmas will get here sooner. Time goes faster when you're asleep."

But it never seemed to work that way for me. "I can't sleep," I'd insist. "There's too much in my head. My thoughts won't slow down."

I'd spend the countdown to birthdays and vacations wide awake and anxious, pacing the halls of our big house while I should have been asleep upstairs. It was a habit I'd never outgrown.

Saturday wasn't Christmas or the first day of summer vacation, but I was counting every day, every minute as if it were. Because as pathetic as it sounded, and as much as I hated that I was looking forward to it, I knew I'd see

Will. That thought alone was enough to find me up every night, wide awake at the window, recounting the street-lights to his building.

———

I'd always heard the first week after a breakup was the hardest. I hoped that was true. Because getting Will's message on Tuesday night—*You're all I can think about anymore*—was torture.

Could he have texted the wrong number by mistake? Or did he say that because he ended up alone, or because he was with another woman, but thinking of me? I couldn't exactly be angry, and my initial self-righteousness over the prospect of him texting me while he was with Kitty faded quickly; I, too, had texted him when I was on my dates with Dylan.

The worst part was that I had no one to talk to about it, really. Well, I did, but I only wanted Will.

The sun had dipped low in the sky on Friday night as I walked the last few blocks to meet Chloe and Sara for drinks.

I'd tried to put on a brave front all week but I was miserable, and it was starting to show. I looked tired. I looked sad. I looked exactly how I felt. I missed him so much that I felt it with every breath, felt each second pass since I'd last seen him.

The Bathtub Gin was a small speakeasy in Chelsea. Visitors were greeted with an everyday storefront, the words STONE STREET COFFEE stenciled across the top. If you weren't sure what you were looking for, or happened to pass by during the week when there wasn't a crowd of people lined up outside, you might miss it. But if you knew it was there, illuminated by a single, glowing red bulb, you'd find the right door. One that opened up to a Prohibition-era club, complete with dim lighting, a steady hum of jazz, and even a large copper bathtub at the center.

I found Chloe and Sara sitting at the bar, drinks already in front of them and a gorgeous dark-haired man at their side.

"Hey, guys," I said, sliding onto the stool next to them. "Sorry I'm late."

The three of them turned, looked me up and down before the man said, "Oh honey, tell me all about the man who did this to you."

I blinked between them, confused. "I . . . hi, I'm Hanna?"

"Ignore him," Chloe said, sliding the menu across the bar to me. "We all do. And order a drink before you talk. You look like you could use it."

The mystery man looked appropriately offended and the three of them argued among themselves while I scanned the various cocktails and wines, picking the first thing that seemed to fit my mood.

"I'll have a Tomahawk," I told the bartender, noticing in my peripheral vision the way Sara and Chloe looked to each other in surprise.

"So it's like that, I see." Chloe motioned for another drink and then took my hand, leading us all to a table.

In all reality, I'd probably just hold my cocktail for most of the night and absorb the comfort afforded by the *option* to get completely hammered. But I knew I wanted to race tomorrow, and no way was I going to run hungover.

"By the way, Hanna," Chloe said, gesturing to the man currently watching me with curious, amused eyes. "This is George Mercer, Sara's assistant. George, this is the adorable and soon-to-be-drunk and/or facedown-on-the-table Hanna Bergstrom."

"Ah, a lightweight," George said, and nodded to Chloe. "What in the world are you doing with this old boozehound? She should come with a warning label for girls like you."

"George, how would you like my heel up your ass?" Chloe asked.

George barely blinked. "The whole heel?"

"Gross," Chloe groaned.

Laughing, George drawled, "Liar."

Sara leaned forward, elbows on the table. "Ignore them. It's like watching Bennett and Chloe, but though they'd both rather screw Bennett than each other."

"I see," I murmured. A waitress placed our drinks on the table and I took a tentative pull from my straw. "Holy *crap*," I coughed, my throat on fire.

I downed almost an entire glass of water while Sara watched me, appraising. "So what's happening?" she asked.

"This drink is so *spicy*."

"Not what she meant," Chloe said bluntly.

I looked down at my glass, tried to focus on the tiny specks of paprika floating along the surface and not the hollow feeling in my gut. "Have you guys talked to Will lately?"

They each shook their head but George perked up.

"Will Sumner?" he clarified. "You're banging *Sumner*? Jesus hell." He motioned to the waitress again. "We're gonna need another glass, lovely. Just bring the whole bottle."

"Actually, I haven't talked to him since Monday," Sara said.

"Tuesday afternoon," Chloe volunteered, pointing to her chest. "But I know he's had a crazy week."

"Uh-oh," Sara said. "Didn't he go home with you for the holiday?"

George sucked in a breath. "Yikes."

And now I was *that* girl, the one with the breakup story I didn't even want in my head, let alone as something to share over drinks. How did I explain that things had been perfect that weekend? That I had believed everything he said? That I had fallen in—I stopped, the words hardening like concrete in my thoughts.

"Hanna, honey?" Sara reached forward to set her hand on my forearm.

"I just feel like an idiot."

"Sweetie," Chloe said, her eyes full of nothing but concern. "You know you don't have to talk about it if you don't want to."

"The hell she doesn't," George snapped. "How are

we all supposed to make his life appropriately horrible if we don't know every sordid detail? We should probably start at the beginning and work our way to the horror, though. First question: is his cock as epic as I've heard? And the fingers . . . are they truly quote-unquote magical?" He leaned closer, whispering, "And rumor has it the man could win a watermelon-eating contest, if you know what I'm saying."

"George," Sara groaned, and Chloe glared at him but I cracked a smile.

"I'm sure I have no idea what you mean," I whispered back.

"Look it up on YouTube," he said to me. "You'll get the visual."

"But back to the part where Hanna is *upset,*" Sara said, eyes playfully stern and fixed on George.

"I just . . ." I took a deep breath, hunting for words. "What can you tell me about Kitty?"

"Oh," Chloe said, sitting back in her chair. She glanced at Sara. *"Oh."*

I leaned forward, brows drawn together. "What does 'oh' mean?"

"Is this the . . . I mean, is Kitty *one* of his . . ." George trailed off, waving his hand meaningfully.

"Yeah," Sara said. "Kitty is one of Will's lovers."

I rolled my eyes. "Do you know if he's still been seeing her?"

Chloe seemed to be considering her answer carefully. "Well—I don't *officially* know of him ending things with her," she said, wincing a little. "But Hanna, he adores you. Anyone can—"

"But he's still seeing her," I interrupted.

She sighed reluctantly. "I honestly don't know. I know we all gave him a hard time about not ending things, but I can't . . . for a fact, I mean, say that he ever stopped seeing her."

"Sara?" I asked.

Shaking her head, Sara murmured, "I'm sorry, honey. I honestly don't know, either."

I wondered if it was possible for a heart to break by fractions. I'd been sure I'd heard it crack when I'd read the text from Kitty. Felt another piece break with his lie about Tuesday night. And all week, I'd felt bruised, felt every tiny shard as it fell away until I wondered what could possibly still be beating in my chest.

"I'd overheard him talking to my brother about wanting to be serious with someone but being afraid to end things with the others. But I figured, maybe he just meant *officially* end them? Things seemed really good with us. But then Kitty sent him this text," I said. "I was playing with his phone and she replied to a message he'd obviously sent her about getting together Tuesday night."

"Why didn't you confront him?" Chloe asked.

"I wanted him to tell me himself. Will has always been all about honesty and communication, so I figured if I invited him over for dinner Tuesday he'd tell me he was going to be with Kitty."

"And?" Sara asked.

I sighed. "He said he had a *thing*. A meeting that night."

"Ouch," George said.

"Yeah," I mumbled. "So I ended it right there. But I did it really badly because I had no idea what to say. I told him that it was getting too heavy, that I was only twenty-four and didn't want anything serious. That I didn't want this anymore."

"Damn, girl," George sang quietly. "When you want to end things, you dig a hole and drop a bomb in it."

I groaned, pressing the heels of my hands against my eyes.

"There has to be an explanation," Sara said. "Will doesn't say he has a meeting when he's going to be with a woman. He just says he's going to be with a woman. Hanna, I've never seen him like this before. *Max* has never seen him like this before. It's clear he adores you."

"But does it matter?" I asked, my drink long forgotten. "He lied about the meeting, but I'm the one who said we should keep it open. It's just that open for me meant the *possibility* of someone else. Open for him was more of the reality already in hand. And all along he was the one pushing for more between us."

"Talk to him, Hanna," Chloe said. "Trust me on this one. You need to give him a chance to explain."

"Explain what?" I asked. "That he was still seeing her, per the rules I'd initially set? Then what?"

Chloe took my hand and squeezed it. "Then you hold your head high and tell him to fuck off in person."

I dressed as soon as the first hint of light appeared outside the window and walked the ten blocks to the race in a nervous haze. It was held in Central Park and the entire circuit went for just over thirteen miles, snaking through trails and paths in the park. Several local streets were cordoned off to support the sponsor trucks, tents, and herds of people, both racers and spectators.

This was real now. Will would be there and I would decide to talk to him or just leave things the way they were. I didn't know if I could handle either choice.

The sky had just started to brighten and a chill hung in the morning air. But my face felt warm, my blood hot as it raced through arteries and veins, through my heart that beat too fast. I had to focus on pulling every breath into my lungs, pushing it out again.

I didn't know where I was going, or what I was doing, but the event seemed well organized, and as soon as I neared the location, signs directed me to where I was meant to check in.

"Hanna?"

I looked up to see my former training partner, my former lover, standing at the registration table, watching me with an expression I couldn't quite make out. I'd hoped my memory had exaggerated how striking he was, how overwhelming it was to just be near him. It hadn't. Will held my gaze, and I wondered if I would start laughing uncontrollably, cry, or maybe just run away if he got any closer.

"Hi," he said finally.

Abruptly, I held out my hand as if he should . . . what? Greet me with a handshake? *Jesus Christ, Hanna!* But I was committed now, and my trembling hand remained suspended between us as he looked down at it.

"Oh . . . we're . . . going to be like this," he mumbled, wiping his palm on his pants before gripping my hand in his. "Okay, hey. How are you?"

I swallowed, jerking my hand away as soon as I possibly could. "Hey. Good. I'm good."

This was comically bad, and it was the kind of bad I wanted to dissect with Will and only Will. I suddenly had a million questions about awkward post-breakup protocol, and whether handshakes were always a bad idea or just now.

Bending robotically, I signed my name on some line and took a packet of information from a woman seated behind the table. She was giving me instructions I barely comprehended; I felt like I was suspended underwater.

When I finished, Will was still standing there, wearing the same nervous, hopeful expression. "Do you need help?" he whispered.

I shook my head. "I think I'm good." It was a lie; I had no idea what I was doing.

"You just need to go to the tent over there," he said gently, reading me perfectly as always and putting a hand on my arm.

I pulled back and smiled stiffly. "I got it. Thanks, Will."

As the silence stretched on, a woman I hadn't even noticed at his side spoke up. "Hi," she said, and I blinked over to see her smiling with her hand outstretched. "I don't think we've been formally introduced. I'm Kitty."

It took a moment for the pieces to come together, and when they did, I couldn't even contain my shock. I felt my mouth fall open, my eyes go wide. How could he possibly think this was even remotely okay? I looked from her to Will, who, I quickly realized, seemed as surprised as I was to find her standing there. Hadn't he seen her approach?

Will's face could have been at the dictionary entry for *uncomfortable*. "Oh God." He looked back and forth between us for a flash before murmuring, "Oh, shit, um . . . hey, Kitty, this is . . ." He looked to me, his eyes softening. "This is my Hanna."

I blinked to him. *What had he said?*

"Nice to meet you, Hanna. Will has told me all about you."

I knew they were speaking but the words didn't seem to penetrate the echo of that sentence repeating over and over again in my head. *This is my Hanna. This is my Hanna.*

It was a mistake. He was just uncomfortable. I pointed over my shoulder. "I've got to go." Turning, I stumbled away from the table and toward the women's tent.

"Hanna!" he called after me, but I didn't turn back.

I was still a bit foggy when I handed over my information, got my race number, and walked over to an empty spot to stretch and lace up my shoes. At the sound of footsteps, I looked up, already dreading what I would find. Seeing Kitty standing there, it was worse than I thought.

"He's really something," she said, pinning her number to the front of her shirt.

I lowered my eyes, ignored the fire that flared low in my belly. "Yeah, sure is."

She sat on a bench a few feet away and began peeling the label from a bottle of water. "You know, I never thought this would happen." She shook her head, laughing. "All this time and he's always used the *It's not you. I just don't want more with anybody* excuse. And now? Now that he finally ends things, it's because he *does* want more. Just with someone else."

I sat up, met her eyes. "He ended things with you?"

"Yeah. Well," she said, considering. "This week was the *official* end but we hadn't really seen each other since . . ." She looked up at the ceiling of the tent, considering. "Since February? And he'd been canceling on me ever since."

I didn't know what to say.

"At least I know why now." I must have looked completely dumbstruck because she smiled, leaned in a little bit. "Because he's in love with you. And if you're as amazing as he seems to think you are, you won't blow this."

─────

I don't remember crossing the park to where the other runners were gathered. My thoughts were hazy and jumbled.

February?

We had only been running then . . .

. . . March—that's when Will and I actually started sleeping together. . . .

Tuesday night . . . so he could end *things, face-to-face.*

Like a decent human being, like a good man. I closed my eyes when the full force of the realization hit me: he told her all of this even *after* I broke up with him.

"You ready for this?"

I jumped, surprised to see Will standing next to me. He put a hand on my arm, offering a tentative smile. "You okay?"

I looked around, as if I could escape somewhere and just . . . *think*. I wasn't ready for him to stand this close or talk like we were friends again, to be *nice*. I had such an enormous apology to make, and I still had an angry earful to give him for lying. . . . I didn't even know where to start. I met his eyes, looked for any sign there telling me that we could fix this. "I think so."

"Hey," he said, taking the smallest step closer. "Hanna . . ."

"Yeah?"

"You're . . . you're going to do great." His eyes searched mine, heavy with anxiety, and it made my stomach twist with guilt. "I know things are weird with us. Just put everything else out of your head. You need to be here, head in the race. You trained so impressively for it and you can do it."

I exhaled, felt the first flare of pre-race, non-Will anxiety.

Kneading my shoulders, he murmured, "Nervous?"

"A little."

I saw the moment he switched into trainer mode and I took some small level of comfort in it, grabbed on to this splinter of platonic familiarity.

"Remember to pace yourself. Don't start off too fast. The second half is the worst and you'll want to keep enough in the tank to finish, okay?"

I nodded.

"Remember, this is your first race and it's about crossing the finish line, not where you place."

Licking my lips, I answered, "Okay."

"You've done ten miles before; you can do thirteen. I'll be right there so . . . we'll do this together."

I blinked up at him, surprised. "You can *place*, Will. This is nothing for you—you should be in the front."

He shook his head. "That's not what this one is about. My race is in two weeks. This one is yours. I told you that."

I nodded again, numb, and couldn't look away from his face: at the mouth that had kissed me so many times, and wanted to kiss *only* me; at the eyes that watched me intently every time I said a word, every time I'd touched him; and at the hands that were now braced on my shoulders and were the same hands that had touched every inch of my skin. He'd told Kitty he wanted to be with me, only me. It's not like he hadn't said those exact words to me, too. But I'd never believed them.

Maybe the player really was gone.

With one last, searching look, Will dropped his hands

from my shoulders, and pressed his palm to my back, leading me to the starting line.

⟡────────⟡

The race started at the southwest corner of the park near Columbus Circle. Will motioned for me to follow and I went through the routine: calf stretch, quad stretch, hamstring. He nodded wordlessly, watched my form and kept in constant, reassuring contact.

"Hold it a little longer," he said, hovering over me. "Breathe through it."

They announced it was time to begin and we got into place. The crack of the starter pistol burst through the air and birds scattered in the trees overhead. The sudden rush of hundreds of bodies pushing off from the line melded into a collective burst of sound.

The marathon route began at the circle and followed the outer loop of Central Park, arching around Seventy-second Street and back to the start.

The first mile was always the hardest. By the second, the world grew fuzzy at the edges and only the muffled sound of feet on the trail and blood pumping in my ears filtered through the haze. We hardly spoke, but I could hear every one of Will's footsteps beside me, feel the occasional brush of his arm against mine.

"You're doing great," he told me, three miles in.

At mile seven, he reminded me, "Halfway done, Hanna, and you're just hitting your stride."

I felt every inch of the last mile. My body ached; my

muscles went from stiff, to loose, to on fire and cramping. I could feel my pulse pounding in my chest. The heavy beat mirrored every one of my steps, and my lungs screamed for me to stop.

But inside my head it was calm. It was as though I was underwater, with muffled voices blending together until they were a single, constant hum. But one voice was clear, "Last mile, this is it. You're *doing it*. You're amazing, Plum."

I'd almost tripped when he called me that. His voice had gone soft and needy, but when I looked over at him, his jaw was set tight, eyes straight ahead. "I'm sorry," he rasped, immediately contrite. "I shouldn't have—I'm sorry."

I shook my head, licked my lips, and looked forward again, too tired to reach out and even touch him. I was struck by the realization that this moment was probably harder than all the tests I'd ever taken in school, every long night in the lab. Science had always come easy for me—I'd studied hard, of course, I'd done the work—but I'd never had to dig this deep and push on when I'd have liked nothing more than to collapse onto the grass and stay there. The Hanna that met Will that day on the icy trail would have never made it thirteen miles. She would have given it a half-assed try, gotten tired and finally, after having rationalized that this wasn't her strength, gone back to the lab and her books and her empty apartment with prepackaged, single-serving meals.

But not *this* Hanna, not now. And *he* helped get me here.

"Almost there," Will said, still encouraging. "I know it hurts, I know it's hard, but look," he pointed to grouping of trees just off in the distance, "you're almost there."

I shook the hair from my face and kept going, breathing in and out, wanting him to keep talking but also wanting him to shut the hell up. Blood pumped through my veins, every part of me felt like I'd been plugged into a live wire, shocked with a thousand volts that had slowly seeped out of me and into the pavement with every step.

I'd never been more tired in my life, I'd never been in more pain, but I'd also never felt more alive. It was crazy, but even through limbs that felt like they were on fire, and every breath that seemed harder than the last—I couldn't wait to do it again. The pain had been worth the fear that I'd fail or be hurt. I'd wanted something, taken the chance, and jumped with both feet.

And with that last thought in mind, I took Will's hand when we crossed through the finish line together.

CHAPTER TWENTY

Several yards off to the side of the finish line, Hanna walked in small circles, then bent down and cupped her hands over her knees.

"Holy shit," she gasped, facing the ground. "I feel amazing. That was *amazing.*"

Volunteers brought us Luna bars and bottles of Gatorade and we gulped them down. I was so fucking proud of her, and I couldn't hold back from pulling her into a sweaty, breathless hug, kissing the top of her head.

"*You* were amazing." I closed my eyes, pressing my face to her hair. "Hanna, I am so proud of you."

She froze in my arms and then slid her hands to my side, simply bracing there, her face in my neck. I could feel her inhaling and exhaling, could feel her hands shaking against me. For some reason, I didn't think it was only the adrenaline from the race.

Finally, she whispered, "I think we should go get our things."

I'd oscillated so wildly between confident and wrecked all week, and now that I was with her, I didn't particularly want to let her out of my sight. We turned to head back toward the tents; with the race snaking through Central Park, the finish line ended up only a few blocks from where we'd started. I listened to her breathing, watched her feet as she walked. I could tell she was exhausted.

"I'm guessing you've heard about Sara," she said, looking down and fidgeting with her race number. She pulled out the pins, took it off, and looked at it.

"Yeah," I said, smiling. "Pretty amazing."

"I saw her last night," she said. "She's so excited."

"I saw Max on Tuesday." I swallowed, feeling so fucking nervous all of a sudden. Beside me, Hanna faltered a little. "I went out with the guys that night. He has the expected look of terror and glee."

She laughed, and it was genuine, and soft and—*fuck*—I'd missed it.

"What are you up to after this?" I asked, ducking so she'd look up at me.

And when she did, it was there, the *something* I knew I hadn't imagined from the weekend before. I could still feel her sliding over me in the dark guest room, could still hear her quiet whisper-beg, *Don't break me.*

It had been the second time she'd said it, and here I'd been the one left broken.

She shrugged and looked away, navigating through the

dense crowd as we drew nearer to the starting line tents. Panic started to well in my chest; I wasn't ready for goodbye yet.

"I was probably going to head home and shower. Get some lunch." She frowned. "Or stop for lunch on the way home. I'm not sure I have anything edible at my place, actually."

"Old shopping habits die hard," I noted dryly.

She gave a guilty wince. "Yeah. I've been sort of burying myself in the lab all week. Just . . . good distraction."

The words came out rushed, pressed together with how out of breath I felt: "I'd really love to hang out, and I have stuff for sandwiches, or salads. You could come over, or . . ." I trailed off when she stopped walking and turned to face me, looking bewildered and then . . . *adoring*.

Blinking away, I felt my chest squeeze. I tried to tamp down the impossible hope clawing up my throat. "What?" I asked, sounding more annoyed than I meant. "Why are you looking at me like that?"

Smiling, she said, "You're probably the only man I know who keeps his fridge so well stocked."

I felt my brows pull together in confusion. This had caused her to stop walking and stare at me? Cupping the back of my neck, I mumbled, "I try to keep healthy stuff at home so I don't go out and eat junk."

She stepped closer—close enough to feel a loose strand of her hair when the wind blew it across my neck. Close enough to smell the light scent of her sweat, to remember how fucking amazing it felt to *make* her sweat. I dropped my gaze to her lips, wanting to kiss her so much it made my skin ache.

"I think you're amazing, Will," she said, licking her lips under the pressure of my attention. "And stop smoldering at me. There's only so much I can take from you today."

Before I could process any of this, she turned and moved toward the women's tent to retrieve her things. Numbly, I went the opposite way, to get my house keys, my extra socks, and the paperwork I'd bundled in my running jacket. When I emerged, she was waiting for me, holding a small duffel bag.

"So," I started, struggling to keep my distance. "You're coming over?"

"I really should shower . . ." she said, looking past me and down the street that led, eventually, to her building.

"You can shower at my place . . ." I didn't care how I sounded. I wasn't letting her go. I'd missed her. Nights had been almost unbearable, but strangely, mornings had been the worst. I missed her breathless conversation and how it would eventually fall away into the synchronized rhythm of our feet on pavement.

"And borrow some clean clothes?" she asked, wearing a teasing grin.

I nodded without hesitation. "Yes."

Her smile faded when she saw I was serious.

"Come over, Hanna. Just for lunch, I promise."

Lifting her hand to her forehead to block out the sun, she studied my face for a beat longer. "You sure?"

Instead of answering, I tilted my head, turning to walk. She fell into step beside me, and every time our fingers accidentally brushed, I wanted to pull her hand into mine and then pull her to me, pressing her against the nearest tree.

She'd been her old, playful self for those short, euphoric moments, but quiet Hanna reappeared as we walked the dozen or so blocks back to my building. I held the door for her as we stepped inside, slipped past her to push the up button for the elevator, and then stood close enough to feel the press of her arm along mine as we waited. At least three times I could hear her suck in a breath, start to speak, but then she would look at her shoes, at her fingernails, at the doors to the elevator. Anywhere but at my face.

Upstairs, my wide-open kitchen seemed to shrink under the tension between us, caused by the residue from the horrible conversation on Tuesday night, the hundreds of unspoken things from today, the simmering force that was always there. I handed her a blue Powerade because it was her favorite, and poured myself a glass of water, turning to watch her lips, her throat, her hand around the bottle as she took a deep drink.

You're so fucking beautiful, I didn't say.

I love you so much, I didn't say.

When she put the bottle down on the counter, her expression was full of all the things she wasn't saying, either.

I could tell they were there, but had no idea what those things might be.

As we rehydrated in silence, I couldn't help but try to covertly check her out. But the secrecy was wasted. I could see her lips curl into a knowing smile when my attention moved over her face, to her chin, and down to the still-glistening skin of her chest, the hint of her breasts visible beneath her skimpy-ass sports bra—*fuck*. I'd so far managed to avoid looking directly at her chest, and now it pulled a familiar ache through me. Her chest was my happy place, and I wanted to sit down and press my face there.

I groaned, rubbing my eyes. It had been a terrible idea inviting her up here. I wanted to undress her, still sweaty, and feel the slide of her on top of me.

Just as I was pointing over my shoulder to the bathroom and asked, "Do you want the first shower?" Hanna tilted her head and grinned, asking, "Were you just looking at my chest?"

And because of the ease, the comfort, the fucking *intimacy* of the question, anger flared in my blood. "Hanna, *don't*," I bit out. "Don't be the girl who plays head games. Barely a week ago you basically told me to get lost." I didn't expect it to come out like that, and in the quiet kitchen, my angry tone bounced around and surrounded us.

She blanched, looking devastated. "I'm sorry," she whispered.

"Fuck," I groaned, squeezing my eyes closed. "Don't be

sorry just don't . . ." I opened my eyes to look at her. "Don't play games with me."

"I'm not trying to," she said, quiet urgency making her voice thin and hoarse. "I'm sorry I disappeared last week. I'm sorry I acted so horribly. I thought . . ."

I pulled out a kitchen stool, sinking down onto it. Running a half marathon didn't exhaust me as much as all of this did. My love for her was a heavy, pulsing, living *thing*, and it made me feel crazy, and anxious, and famished. I hated seeing her stressed and scared. I hated seeing her upset at my anger, but even worse was the knowledge that she had the power to break my heart and had very little experience being careful about it. I was completely at her fumbling, inexperienced mercy.

"I miss you," she said.

My chest tightened. "I miss you so much, Hanna. You have no idea. But I heard what you said on Tuesday. If you don't want this, then we have to find a way to be friends again. Asking me if I'm checking out your chest doesn't help us move past all of this."

"I'm sorry," she said, again. "Will . . ." she started and then the words fell away and she blinked down to her shoes.

I needed to understand what had happened, why everything had crumbled so abruptly after we'd made wildly intimate love only one week ago.

"That night," I started, and then reconsidered. "No,

Hanna, *every* night—it was always intense like that with us—but that night last weekend . . . I thought it all kind of changed. *We* changed. Then the next day? And the drive back? Fuck, I don't even know what happened."

She moved closer, close enough for me to pull her by her hips to stand between my legs, but I didn't, and her hands fumbled at her sides before falling still.

"What happened was I heard what you said to Jensen," she said. "I knew there were other women in your life, but I kind of thought that you had ended things with them. I know I'd avoided talking about it, and that it wasn't fair of me to want that, but I thought you had."

"I hadn't 'officially' ended things, Hanna, but no one has been in my bed since you pulled me down that damn hall and asked to touch me. Fuck, not even before then."

"But how was I supposed to know that?" She dropped her head, stared at the floor. "And hearing what you said to Jensen might have been okay—I knew we needed to talk— but then I saw the text in the car. It popped up when I was picking out music." She stepped closer, pressing her thighs to my knees. "We'd had unprotected sex the night before, but then I saw her message, and it seemed like . . . like you were trying to hook up with her right after. I realized that Kitty still expected to be able to be with you, and I'd been trying—"

"I did *not* have sex with her on Tuesday, Hanna," I interrupted, my blood racing with panic. "Yes, I texted her asking if we could meet, but it was so I could let her know things were over between us. It wasn't like—"

"I know," she said, quietly cutting me off. "She told me today that you haven't been with her in a long time."

I let this sink in for a minute and then sighed. I wasn't sure I wanted to know what Kitty had told Hanna, but in the end, it didn't matter. I didn't have anything to hide. Yes, as someone who values being up front with people, I should have ended things cleanly with Kitty as soon as I told Hanna I wanted more, but I'd never lied to either of them, not once. I hadn't lied when I told Kitty so many months ago that I didn't want to dive into anything deeper. And I hadn't lied to Hanna only a month ago when I told her I wanted more, and only from her.

"I was just trying to stick to *your* rules. I wasn't going to bring up the relationship thing again because you'd determined I was incapable of it in the first place."

"I know," she said quickly. "I know."

But that was it; her eyes searched mine, waiting for me to say . . . what? What could I say that I hadn't said already? Hadn't I laid it all out enough times?

With a tired sigh, I stood. "Do you want the first shower?" I asked. Things were so weird between us, and even when we were still virtual strangers, running together that first, freezing morning, it hadn't ever been this way.

She had to step back to let me move past her. "No, it's okay. Go ahead."

I turned the water as hot as I could bear. I wasn't sore yet from the run—probably wouldn't get too sore anyway—but with the stress of wanting to make love to Hanna and wanting to throttle her at the same time, the hot water and the steam felt amazing.

It was possible she wanted things to be how they'd been before: sex, as friends. Comfortable without expectations. And I wanted her so intensely I knew how easy it would be to fall back into that, to enjoy her body and her friendship in equal measure, to never need or expect it to grow deeper.

But it wasn't what I wanted anymore. Not from anyone, and especially not from her. I soaped up, closing my eyes and inhaling the steam, washing away the race and the sweat. Wishing I could wash away the twisted mess inside.

I heard the faint click of the shower door only a split second before cold air bit across my skin. Adrenaline slid into my veins, pumping through my heart, filling my head with a wildness that made me dizzy. I pressed my hand to the wall, afraid to turn and face her, and feel all my resolve melt. There was only a fraction of me I knew would be able to hold back. The rest would give her anything she asked for.

She whispered my name, closing the door and stepping close enough for me to feel the press of her naked breasts against my back. Her skin was cool. She ran her hands up my sides, over my ribs.

"Will," she said again, moving her hands to my chest, and down over my stomach. "Look at me."

I reached down, gripping her wrists to keep her hands from moving any lower, low enough to feel how hard I was with just this small bit of contact. I was like a racehorse, held back by a single, flimsy gate. The muscles in my arms tensed and jumped; holding her at her wrists was to restrain myself as much as it was to keep her hands from my skin.

Leaning my forehead into the wall, I remained still until I was sure I could face her and not immediately take her in my arms. Finally, I turned, adjusting my grip on her wrists.

"I don't think I can do this," I whispered, looking down at her face.

Her hair was loose, and the wet strands clung to her cheeks, her neck, her shoulders. Her brows were pulled together in confusion and I knew she didn't understand my meaning. But then she seemed to hear me, and a bloom of humiliation spread across her cheeks and she squeezed her eyes shut. "I'm sor—"

"No," I said, interrupting her. "I mean can't do what we did before. I won't share. I don't want this if you still want to date other men."

Hanna opened her eyes, and they softened, her breath picking up.

"I can't fault you for wanting to experiment," I told her, my fists curling tighter around her wrists at the thought, "but I won't be able to keep my feelings for you from deepening, and I won't want to pretend we're just friends. Not even with Jensen. I know I'd take whatever you'll give me because I want you that much, but I would be miserable if it was only sex for you."

"I don't think it was ever just sex for me," she said.

I let her wrists go, studying her face and trying to understand what she was offering.

"When you called me *your* Hanna earlier," she began and then paused, pressing her hand to my chest, "I wanted it to be true. I want to be yours."

My breath formed a brick in my throat. Beneath the delicate skin of her neck, I could see her pulse thrumming.

"I mean, I *am* yours. Already." She stretched, eyes wide open as she carefully took my bottom lip between hers, sucking gently. She lifted my hand, pressed it around her breast and arched into my palm.

If what I felt now was even a small taste of the fear she'd felt all this time that I'd hurt her, then I suddenly understood why she'd been so skittish for so long. Being in love like this was terrifying.

"Please," she begged, kissing me again, reaching for my other hand and trying to pull it around her. "I want to be with you so much it's making it hard to breathe."

"Hanna," I choked, bending involuntarily, giving her better access to my lips, my neck. I curled my hand around her, rubbing my thumb over her nipple.

"I love you," she whispered, kissing down my chin, to my neck, and I squeezed my eyes closed, heart pounding.

When she said this, my resolve shattered and I opened my mouth, groaning when I felt her slide her tongue inside and go over mine. She moaned, clawing at my shoulders, my neck, pressing her stomach into the hard line of my cock.

She gasped at the shock of the cold tile on her back when I turned her, pressing her into the wall, and then gasped again when I ducked and lifted her breast to my mouth, sucking hungrily. It wasn't that my fear was gone; if anything, hearing her say she loved me was infinitely more terrifying because it brought hope along with it: hope that I could do this, that *she* could, that both of us could somehow navigate blindly through this elusive *first*.

I returned to her mouth, feeling wild now, lost in the fever of her kisses and knowing without having to ask that some of the water on her cheeks wasn't from the shower. I felt it, too, the dissolving relief, followed immediately with a fiery need to be inside her, to be moving in her, feeling her.

Reaching down, I cupped the back of her thighs, lifting her so she could wrap her legs around my waist. I felt the slick warmth of her sex, and rocked there, pressing just inside and out again, falling in love all over again at her raspy, impatient sounds.

"Never done this before," I murmured into the skin of her neck. "I have no fucking idea what I'm doing."

She laughed, biting at my neck and gripping my shoulders tightly. Slowly, I pressed into her, stilling when our hips met and knowing in an instant that this would be over fast. Her head fell back against the tile, landing with a quiet thud, and her chest rose and fell with sharp, jagged breaths.

"Oh my God, Will."

Pulling out, I whispered, "Do you feel it, too?"

Hanna hiccupped, begging me to move, pressing into me as much as she could, trapped between the wall and my body.

"That isn't just sex," I told her, sucking along her collarbone. "This feeling that it's so good it almost hurts? It's been like this every single time I've been inside you, Plum. That's what it feels like when you do this with someone you're fucking *insane* for."

"Someone you love?" she asked, her lips pressed to my ear.

"Yeah." I pushed in and pulled out again faster, knowing I was so close I would need to take her to my bed, suck on her pussy, and then fuck her again until we both collapsed. It was too intense, and as soon as I started moving I knew I wouldn't ever get used to the feel of being inside her without anything between us.

I jerked against her, relishing her sounds and whispering my apology into her neck over and over. "It's too intense . . ." All of it was overwhelming: the feeling of her around me, her words, and the understanding that she was really mine now. "I'm too close, Plum, I can't . . ."

She shook her head, nails biting into the skin of my shoulder, and pressed her lips to my ear. "I like when you can't hold back. It's how I always felt with you."

With a groan I let go, feeling myself spiral down

down

down

pressing deeper and harder until I could hear the gentle slap of my thighs on hers and her back on the wall, and felt my body flush warm and wet, coming inside her so hard my shout echoed sharply off the tile all around us.

I don't think I'd ever come that fast in my entire life and I felt both euphoric and mildly horrified.

Hanna pulled my hair, silently begging for my mouth on hers but after only a small kiss I slipped from her with a groan, and fell to my knees. Leaning forward, I spread her with my hands and sealed my mouth around the soft rise of her clit, sucking. I closed my eyes and groaned at the sound of her sweet moan, the feel of her sex against my tongue. Her legs shook—exhausted from the run, probably also exhausted from the rough treatment I'd just given her against a wall—and I slid my arms between her thighs, spreading her legs and lifting her so her thighs rested on my shoulders and my palms gripped her ass.

Above me, she cried out, her arms grappling wildly for something to hold on to, and finally she settled for clutching my head with her thighs and reaching down, bracing her hands on the top my head while she watched me with wide, fascinated eyes.

"I'm so close." Her voice wavered, hands shaking where she gripped my hair.

I hummed, smiling into her and moving my head slowly side to side as I sucked. I'd never done this before and felt so much like I was *loving* someone, making love in every way I possibly could. My chest warmed intensely when it occurred to me: this was our beginning. Right here, partially hidden by the steam of the shower, was where we clarified everything.

I could see the moment she started to come, the hot flush bloomed on her chest and spread upward, reaching her face just as her lips parted in a gasp.

I'd never get tired of this. I'd never tire of *her*. With the most possessive pleasure I'd ever felt, I watched as her orgasm rocked through her, pulling a scream from her throat.

Stopping when her thighs went lax, I carefully slid my arms from her, easing her down on shaking legs. I stood, staring down at her for a beat before she slid her arms around my neck and stretched to hold me.

She was soft and warm from the heat of the water and seemed to melt in my arms.

And it was so fucking different. It had never felt like this—like I was completely connected to her—even when we were in our most intimate moments as "just friends."

Here, she felt like mine.

"I love you," I whispered into her hair, before reaching to the side for my soap. Carefully, I washed every inch of her skin, her hair, and the delicate skin between her legs. I washed my orgasm away from her body, and kissed her jaw, her eyelids, her lips.

We stepped out and I wrapped her in a towel before pulling one around my own waist. I led her into the bedroom, sat her on the edge of the bed, and dried her, before urging her back onto the mattress.

"I'll bring you something to eat."

"I'll come with you." She struggled against my roaming hands, tried to sit up, but I shook my head, bending to suck her nipple into my mouth. "Just stay here and relax," I whispered against her skin. "I want to keep you here in bed all night long, so you're going to need to eat first."

Water from my hair dripped onto her naked skin and she gasped, eyes wide, pupils spreading inky black in the soft gray of her irises. She slid her hands to my shoulders, trying to pull me down and, *fuck*, I was ready to go again . . . but we needed food. I was already starting to feel woozy.

"I'll just throw something together."

———

We ate sandwiches, sitting naked on the bedspread, and talked for hours about the race, about the weekend with her family, and finally, about how it had felt when we thought things had ended between us.

We made love until the sunlight faded outside, and then slept, waking in the middle of the night starving for more. And then it was wild, and loud, and exactly how it had always been when things were best with us: honest.

For the moment, I was sated, and reached for my bedside table to find a pen. Curling around her, I put her tattoo back on her hip—*All that is rare for the rare*—hoping that I could be that rare thing, a recovered wildness, a reformed player, that Hanna deserved.

Epilogue

The flight attendant walked past, snapping the overhead bins shut with decisive clicks before bending to ask, "Orange juice or coffee?"

Will asked for coffee. I shook my head with a smile.

He patted my knee, palm up. "Give me your phone."

I handed it over, but complained anyway: "Why do I need wireless? I'm going to be asleep the entire flight." Never again would I let him book 6 a.m. flights from New York to the West Coast.

Will ignored me, entering some code into a tiny box on my phone's Web browser.

"If you haven't noticed, I'm sleepy. It's *someone's* fault that I was kept up all night," I whispered, leaning into him.

He stopped what he was doing, turning to smolder at me. "Is that how it happened?"

A thrill ran from my chest, down my belly, and between my legs. "Yes."

"You didn't come over after lab, a little . . . worked up?"

"No," I lied.

His eyebrow rose, a smile curling half of his mouth. "And you didn't interrupt my preparation of the very romantic dinner I was planning for you?"

"Me? No."

"And pull me down onto the couch asking me to 'do that thing with my mouth'?"

I held my hand to my chest. "I would *never.*"

"It wasn't you who then ignored the delicious smells coming from the stove and pulled me to the bedroom and asked for some very, *very* dirty things?"

I closed my eyes as he leaned close, grazing his teeth over my jaw and murmuring, "I love you so fucking much, my naughty, sweet Plum."

Images from the night before pulled me deeper into the hungry, achy place I practically lived in anytime I was near Will. I remembered his rough hands, his commanding voice telling me exactly what he wanted me to do. I remembered those hands tugging my hair, his body moving over mine for hours, his voice finally low and begging for my teeth, my nails. I remembered the weight of him collapsing on me, sweaty and exhausted and falling asleep almost as soon as he found his release.

"Maybe that was me," I admitted. "It was a long day working in the safety hood, what can I say? I had a lot of time to think about your magical mouth."

He kissed me and then returned to my phone, smiling

as he finished what he was doing and handing it back to me. "You're all set."

"I'm still going to sleep."

"Well, at least if Chloe needs you, your phone is working."

I slid my eyes to him, confused. "Why would she need me? I'm not in the wedding."

"Have you met Chloe? She's a fearsome general that could conscript you at a moment's notice," he said, gripping the back of his neck in the way he did when he was uncomfortable. "Whatever. Just sleep then."

"I have a feeling about this trip," I murmured, leaning into his shoulder. "Like a premonition."

"How uncharacteristically spiritual of you."

"I'm serious. I think it's going to be amazing, but I also feel like we're in a giant steel tube headed toward a week of insanity."

"Technically airplanes are made of aluminum alloy." Will looked over at me, bent to kiss my nose, and whispered, "But you knew that."

"Do *you* ever have a feeling about something?"

He hummed, kissed me again. "Once or twice."

I stared up at him—at the familiar dark lashes and deep blue eyes, at his five o'clock shadow at six in the morning, and at the goofy smile he'd been wearing since I woke him up—*again*—four hours ago with my mouth on his cock.

"Are you feeling sentimental, Dr. Sumner?"

He shrugged and blinked, clearing a bit of the

lovestruck gleam in his eyes. "Just excited to go on vacation with you. Excited for the wedding. Excited that our little gang is having a baby soon."

"I have a question about a rule," I whispered.

He leaned in conspiratorially, whispering back, "I'm not your dating coach anymore. There are no rules, besides that no other guy touches you."

"Still. You know about these things."

With a smile he murmured, "Fine. Hit me."

"We've only been together two months, and—"

"Four," he corrected, always insisting I was his from that very first run.

"Fine. Have it your way, four. Is it bad form after only four months to tell you I think you're my forever?"

His smile straightened, his eyes moving over my face in that way that felt like a caress. He kissed me once, and then again.

"I would say that's incredibly *good* form." He pulled back to look at me for a long, heavy beat. "Sleep, Plum."

―――

My phone buzzed on my lap, startling me awake. I straightened from where I'd been asleep on Will's shoulder and blinked, looking down at my phone, where a text from him lit up my screen. Beside me, I could almost feel his smile.

I read the text: What are you wearing?

I squinted sleepily at my phone as I typed, A skirt

and no panties. But don't get any ideas, I'm a little sore from what my boyfriend did last night.

He made a sympathetic clucking noise beside me. That brute.

Why are you texting me?

He shook his head next to me, sighing with exaggerated weariness. Because I can. Because modern technology is amazing. Because we are 30,000 feet in the air and civilization has progressed to the point I can beam a filthy proposition to you from a satellite in space to a flying "steel tube."

I turned to look at him, eyebrows raised. "You woke me up to ask me what I'm wearing?"

He shook his head, and kept typing. In my lap, my phone buzzed.

I love you.

"I love you, too," I said. "I'm right here, you nerd. I'm not texting a reply."

He smiled, but kept typing. You're my forever, too.

I stared down at my phone, my chest suddenly so tight it was hard to breathe. I reached over my head, adjusting the airflow of the nozzle aimed at my seat.

And I might propose to you soon.

I stared at my phone, reading this line again, and again.

"Okay," I whispered.

So give me a heads-up if you won't say yes, because I'm mildly terrified.

I leaned back on his shoulder and he dropped his phone into his lap, wrapping his shaking hand around mine.

"Don't be," I whispered. "We've totally got this."

Acknowledgments

By the time we started working on this book, we'd only known our editor, Adam Wilson, for eight months, but together we had already released two books (*Bastard* and *Stranger*), with four more scheduled in the same year. This type of publishing schedule for a new author-editor combination is a bit like summer camp: everything is wild and goes by in a blur, and relationships don't have the luxury of the normal slow easing-in, getting-to-know-you time. As with anything else in life, sometimes those intense experiences work, and sometimes they don't, but with Adam we've been so profoundly lucky. When we finally met in July, we just knew: he is *our people* and is absolutely our brand of crazy (or very convincingly pretends to be because we send him both metaphorical and real cupcakes). Working with him has been one of the best experiences either of us has had, ever, and we can't wait to see what we get to do together next.

When we were first going through the query process, we read probably a hundred blog posts that emphasized the importance of finding an agent that clicks for you.

It's not about finding an agent, everyone said, it's about finding the right one. In truth, Holly Root is not only the right agent for us, she's also one of the best people we've ever known. Without her, these books would never have found the perfect home with Gallery, or with Adam. She still says she knew from the very first time she spoke to him about the project that he would be a perfect fit for us. It's these types of relationships that make us feel eternally grateful.

But it's also the involvement of our beta readers—Erin, Martha, Tonya, Gretchen, Myra, Anne, Kellie, Katy, and Monica—that makes us realize that the process of writing is so much more than putting words to paper; it's also finding your community of people who will help you battle the crazy on the bad days, and help you celebrate the awesome on the good ones. If you've ever sent your work to someone to read, you know what a vulnerable experience that can be, and to every one of our readers who has helped with the *Beautiful* books, thank you for so perfectly balancing support with criticism. Sorry that we've killed some of your brain cells. Anne, thanks for the Nietzsche and the kick-ass line about him. Jen, thank you a million times over for the promo and cheerleading. Lauren, thank you forever for running the *Beautiful* social media, and being excited for every cover, excerpt, and email. We love you all.

We're erecting (hee! we said erecting!) a billboard in honor of our fabulous S&S/Gallery Books home. THANK YOU, Carolyn Reidy, Louise Burke, Jen Bergstrom, Liz Psaltis, the wonderful art department, Kristin Dwyer (we are kidnapping you soon), Mary McCue (SDCC next year, no choice), Jean Anne Rose, Ellen Chan, Natalie Ebel, Lauren McKenna, Stephanie DeLuca, and, of course, Ed Schlesinger for laughing at Hanna's jokes. You've all made us feel like we're family. We get a pullout couch in the offices, right?

Writing isn't a nine-to-five job, or a Monday-to-Friday job. It's a job you do whenever you have a slice of time, and it's also the job that is a slave to inspiration, so if you lack even a tiny slice of time (typical), but you have a flurry of ideas, you drop everything to get those thoughts down before the fickle bastards disappear. Sometimes that means running away to the computer while dinner is boiling on the stove, and sometimes it means that the husband takes the kids to a movie or the zoo or on a hike so that Mommy can get something done. But regardless, writing is a process that requires a lot of patience and support by everyone in the writer's life, and for that, we make loving heart eyes at the loves of our lives, Keith and Ryan. And our children: Bear, Cutest, and Ninja, we hope you someday realize how patient you've been, and how that patience means we now get to spend a lot more time with you. Thanks to our family and friends for putting up with the crazy: Erin, Jenn, Tawna, Jess, Joie, Veena, Ian, and Jamie.

And last but certainly not least, writing these stories would mean nothing without the amazing people who read them. We're still blown away when you tell us you stayed up all night reading, or pretended to have the stomach flu to steal a few hours locked in a bathroom because you couldn't put down our book. Your support and encouragement means more to us than we could ever hope to convey. Thank you. Thank you for continuing to buy our books, for loving our characters as much as we do, for sharing our sense of humor and dirty minds, and for every tweet, email, post, comment, review, and hug. We hope we get to hug each and every one of you one day.

Bennett would like to see you all in his office.

Lo, you are so much more than a co-author, you're my best friend, the moon of my life, the chocolate to my . . . you see where I'm going here. I love you more than all the boy bands and glitter and lip gloss combined.

PQ, you look so pretty today! I love you even though you make me pee myself laughing. In fact, I love you more than I love Excel, GraphPad, and SPSS combined. Is your collar tingling?

ONE BEAUTIFUL BASTARD OF A GROOM.
THE MOST BEAUTIFUL BITCH OF A BRIDE.
A PANTY-RIPPING OFFICE HOOKUP TURNED
TRUE LOVE EVERLASTING.

*You are cordially invited to the wedding
of Bennett Ryan and Chloe Mills*

Take a sneak peek here at the opening of
Beautiful Beginning . . .

"I'm about to cut a bitch," I hissed, pushing my share of the work away from me. Bennett failed to even look up, so I added, "And by that, I mean *paper*-cut a bitch."

At least this got a tiny flicker of a smile. But I could tell, even after doing this for the past hour, he was still in Wedding Preparation Zone, and would keep robotically working until the entire, unending pile of cardstock in front of him was gone. Our normally immaculate dining room table was littered with Tiffany-blue wedding programs. Across from me, Bennett methodically folded each one in half before moving it to the Completed stack.

It was a simple process:

Fold, move.

Fold, move.

Fold, move.

Fold, move.

But I was losing my damn mind. Our flight left at six the following morning for San Diego, and our bags were all packed but for the five hundred wedding programs we had to fold. I groaned as I remembered we *also* had to tie five hundred blue ribbons around five hundred tiny satin bags full of candy.

"You know what would make this night so much better?" I asked.

His hazel eyes flickered to me before returning to the task at hand.

Fold, move.

"A gag?" he suggested.

"Amusing, but no," I said, giving him the finger. "What would make this night better would be getting on a plane and flying to *Vegas,* getting married, and then fucking all night in a giant hotel bed."

He didn't bother to reply to this, not even a whiff of a smile. It was probably fair to say he'd heard this exact sentiment from me approximately seven thousand times in the past few months.

"Fine," I replied to his silence. "But I'm serious. It's not too late to drop all of this and fly to Vegas."

He took a moment to scratch his jaw before reaching for another program to fold. "Of course it isn't, Chlo."

I'd been playing around—*mostly*—up to this point, but with his words genuine irritation swept through me. I slapped my hand on the dining room table, earning a quick blink from him before he resumed his folding. "Don't patronize me, Ryan."

"Yeah. Okay."

I pointed a finger at him. "Like *that.*"

My fiancé gave me a dry look, and then winked.

Damn that man and his goddamn sexy wink. My anger dissipated somewhat and in its place came a flare of desire. He was ignoring me, being a patronizing ass. I was being a bitch.

It was the perfect setup for me to have many, many orgasms.

I looked him over and sucked the edge of my lower lip into my mouth. He was wearing a deep blue T-shirt that was so old and worn, the collar was frayed and—even though I couldn't see it—I knew there was a tiny hole right above the hem that was just big enough for me to slide my finger through and touch the warm skin of his stomach. Last weekend he'd been wearing that T-shirt and I'd asked him to keep it on while he fucked me against the bathroom counter, just so I could wrap it up in my fists.

I rocked a little in my chair to relieve the ache between my legs. "Bed or floor. Your choice." I watched him as he remained impassive, and added in a whisper, "Or I could just climb under the table and suck on you first?"

Smirking down at his work, Bennett said, "You can't get out of wedding preparation with sex."

I pulled back to study him. "What kind of man says that? You're broken."

Finally, he gave me a dark, hungry look. "I promise you, I'm *not* broken. I'm getting this done so I can focus on wearing you out later."

"Wear me out *now*," I whined, standing and walking

over to him. I slid my fingers into his hair and tugged. Adrenaline dripped hot and electric into my veins when his eyes fluttered closed and he suppressed a groan. "Where's all this money you have? Why haven't we hired someone to do this?"

Laughing, Bennett wrapped his hand around my wrist and pulled my fingers from his hair. After kissing my knuckles, he very deliberately set my hand back at my side. "You want to hire someone to *fold programs* the night before we leave for San Diego?"

"Yes! Because sex!"

"But isn't it nicer like *this*? Enjoying each other's company and," he said, lifting his wineglass to take a dramatic sip, "conversing like the happily affianced lovers we are?"

I glared at him, shaking my head at his attempted guilt trip. "I offered sex. I offered hot, sweaty *floor* sex—and then I offered to give you a blow job. You want to fold *paper*. Who is the buzzkill here?"

He picked up a program and studied it, ignoring me. "Frederick Mills," he read aloud, and I began pulling my shirt up and over my head, "together with Elliott and Susan Ryan welcome you to the wedding of their children, Chloe Caroline Mills and Bennett James Ryan."

"Yes, yes, it's so romantic," I whispered. "Come here and touch me."

"Officiant," he continued, "the Honorable James Marsters."

"If only," I sighed, and dropped my shirt on the floor before working my pants down my hips. "I'm going to pretend it's Spike performing our wedding ceremony instead of that hilarious gentleman with early dementia we met back in November."

"Judge Marsters performed my *parents'* wedding ceremony almost thirty-five years ago," Bennett chastened me gently. "It's sentimental, Chlo. The fact that he forgot to zip up his pants is a mistake anyone could have made."

"Three times?"

"Chloe."

"Fine." I did feel a little guilty for making the joke, but I stood quietly for a minute, letting my memory of the old, frazzled man take shape. He'd met us at the wedding site when we went out to see it last fall, and got lost on each of three trips to the men's room in under an hour, returning with his fly open each time. "But do you think he'll remember our na—"

Bennett cut me off with a stern look before he realized I was only wearing my bra and underwear, and then his expression went a completely different kind of dark.

"I'm just saying," I started, reaching behind me to unfasten my bra, "it would be at least a *little* amusing if he forgot what he was doing halfway through the ceremony."

He managed to turn his attention back to folding the program before my breasts were exposed; he made a crisp seam as he slid his thumb along the edge. "You're being a pain in the ass."

"I know. I also don't care."

He quirked an eyebrow as he looked up at me. "We're almost done."

I bit back my response, which was to point out that folding the programs was the least of our worries; the next week with our two families together had the potential to be a disaster of Griswold-family holiday proportions, and wouldn't sex right now be a lot better than thinking about that? My father and his two boozy divorcée sisters alone could make us crazy, but add in Bennett's side of the family, Max, and Will, and we'd be lucky to get out of there without a felony under our communal belt.

Instead I whispered, "Just really quick? Can't we take a little break?"

He leaned forward, inhaling the skin between my breasts before moving to the side and kissing a path to my left nipple. "Once I start, I don't relish stopping."

"You don't like interruptions, I don't like delayed gratification. Which of us do you think will get her way?"

Bennett ran his tongue over my nipple, and then sucked it deeply into his mouth as his hands circled my waist, slid to my hips, and then worked together to pull my panties off with a satisfying rip.

Amusement lit up his eyes as he looked up at me from where he sucked at my other breast, and his fingers teased at the juncture of my hip and thigh. "I suspect, my impossible wife-to-be, that you're going to get your way and then I'll finish folding these later while you sleep."

Sliding my hands back into his hair, I whispered,

"Don't forget about tying the ribbons on the candy bags."

He chuckled a little. "I won't, baby."

And it hit me all over again, like a warm gust of wind: I *loved* him, madly. I loved every inch of him, every emotion that passed through his eyes, and every thought I knew he had right now but wasn't voicing:

One, that I'd been the one to insist we do as much of this ourselves as we could.

Two, that I was the one to assure him it was fine that every distant relative of ours on the planet had somehow squeezed their way into this wedding event.

Three, that I would never, ever back out of the opportunity to wear my wedding dress on the Coronado coastline.

But instead of pointing out the obvious—that he was the one being a good sport here, not me, and that despite all of my bitching I would never be satisfied with a quick Vegas wedding—he stood, turning to walk to our bedroom. "Okay, then. But this is the last night I'm fucking you before we're married."

I was so buzzed by the "fucking" part that it wasn't until he'd disappeared down the hallway to our bedroom that the rest of his words fully sank in.

See how Chloe and Bennett got together in the book that started it all...

More Than 2 Million Reads Online—FIRST TIME IN PRINT!

PICK UP OR DOWNLOAD YOUR COPY TODAY!

"The perfect blend of sex, sass, and heart!"
—S. C. Stephens, bestselling author of *Thoughtless*

Beautiful
BASTARD

A Novel

CHRISTINA LAUREN

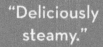